ERRATIC

REVIVAL

REBEL GALLO

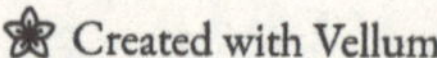 Created with Vellum

PLAYLIST

Amnesia - 5 Seconds of Summer
Control - Halsey
Numb - Linkin Park
Misguided Ghosts - Paramore
Rainbow Veins - Owl City
Papercut - Linkin Park
Kingdom Come - Demi Lovato
Oh My God - Alec Benjamin
In The End - Linkin Park
Thief - Alice Chater

*To the ones who pushed me to follow my dreams and put my
stories out in the world*

Erratic Revival is a new adult, science fiction, contemporary romance. This story contains sexually explicit scenes, as well as mature and graphic content that is not suitable for all readers.

Reader's discretion is advised

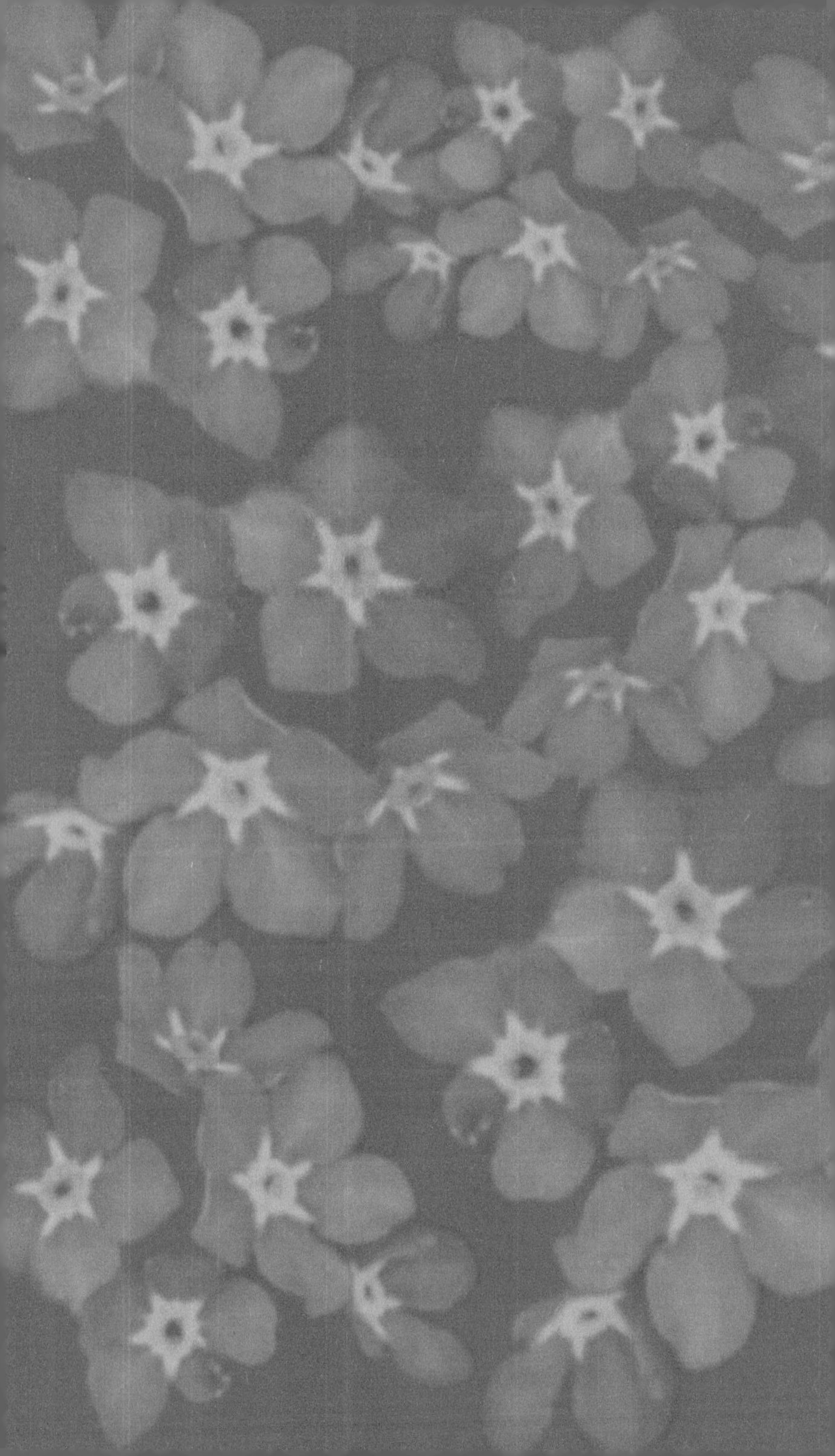

PROLOGUE

A SHAKE of my head pushes out the heavy sigh I was trying to hold in. I fling my head back onto my pillow.

I hate homework.

I don't understand the reason for it at all. Why can't we do in-class assignments and be done with it? The extra work we have to do at home is overkill, honestly.

My mom and dad are out on a once-every-two-weeks date, which they've been doing to "keep the romance alive" or something like that. So I'm left fulfilling my big-sister duties by babysitting my little sister, Sidney. I push my earbuds in and turn my music up enough that it's the only sound I can hear.

How I'm already behind on my schoolwork when the semester just started, I have no idea. I slide to the floor and prop my elbow on my knee, then rest my chin on my fist. I let out another sigh of frustration and shake my head, unsure if I'll ever see the solution. That's when I smell it . . .

It's the smell that comes with someone grilling but stronger. As I sit up, my brows pinch together.

Where is it coming from?

I turn my head to the door. It's right there, coming from under the door. Eyes wide, I throw my headphones to the side and sprint for the knob.

Smoke.

"Sidney!" I yell, running down the hall to her room. "Sidney, can you hear me?" But I can't hear anything.

I slam my body into her bedroom door, bursting through, seeing it. Flames are overtaking half the room, along the once-pink drapes and across the bed, and on the other side, I see the tent—the tent that's base when we play tag, the tent that's a castle when we're royalty, the tent that's safe when nowhere else is, fully intact but only moments from being engulfed like everything else.

"Sidney! I'm comin'! Hold on!" Running across the room, I peer into the tent to see a frightened little girl in the fetal position, crying. "Sidney . . ." She looks up at me and jumps into my arms. "It's time to go—now!"

I pull her off the ground and push her toward the door. I stop her right as we reach the hall and grab her arm. "Go out the front door and across the street to the neighbors' house. Tell them to call 911 because there's a fire and stay there until I come to get you, okay?"

The only response I get is her stricken face staring at me like I'm crazy.

"Okay?"

She jumps with wide eyes at my tone before nodding her head and mumbling, "Okay," then runs down the hall.

Okay, what the hell am I supposed to do now?

Turning on my heels, I head to the living room and straight for the receiver just in case, in her state of shock, Sidney forgets about calling for help, but the phone isn't there. It's missing. I push the call button and listen for the ring that will lead me to the house phone. I run back down the hall, following the faint sound, and find myself in front of the door at the end of the hall with flames on the other side threatening to destroy my home.

I can hear the faint beeping, but I can't see it. Curses fall out of my lips at my parents for not buying me a cell phone. I step into the room, trying to follow the sound, and then I see the phone on the floor on the far side under the bed. I get down on my hands and knees and crawl as fast I can, and as I reach it, a loud crack sounds above me.

I gasp for what little air the flames haven't taken away. The flames have eaten away at the bed frame, and it collapses on top of me. I try to scream in pain, but nothing comes out. Overwhelmed by the pain, the flames, and lack of air, I have trouble concentrating as black spots dot my vision.

I remember the phone in my hand and dial 911. As I hit the call button, everything around me becomes unclear and blurry. The entire room sways.

"Nine-one-one, what's your emergency?" I barely hear the woman's voice. I'm drifting into unconsciousness too quickly to keep up.

"Fire . . . at my house . . ." I struggle to take a breath to continue. "I'm trapped in the back room." My vision starts to go in and out, and I know I'm running out of time. "Nine ninety-three Elk Street . . ."

I hear a woman's voice on the other end of the phone, but it slips from my fingers, and the entire room goes black—but not before I see someone's dark eyes looming over me, looking down at me, saying something, but I can't hear anymore.

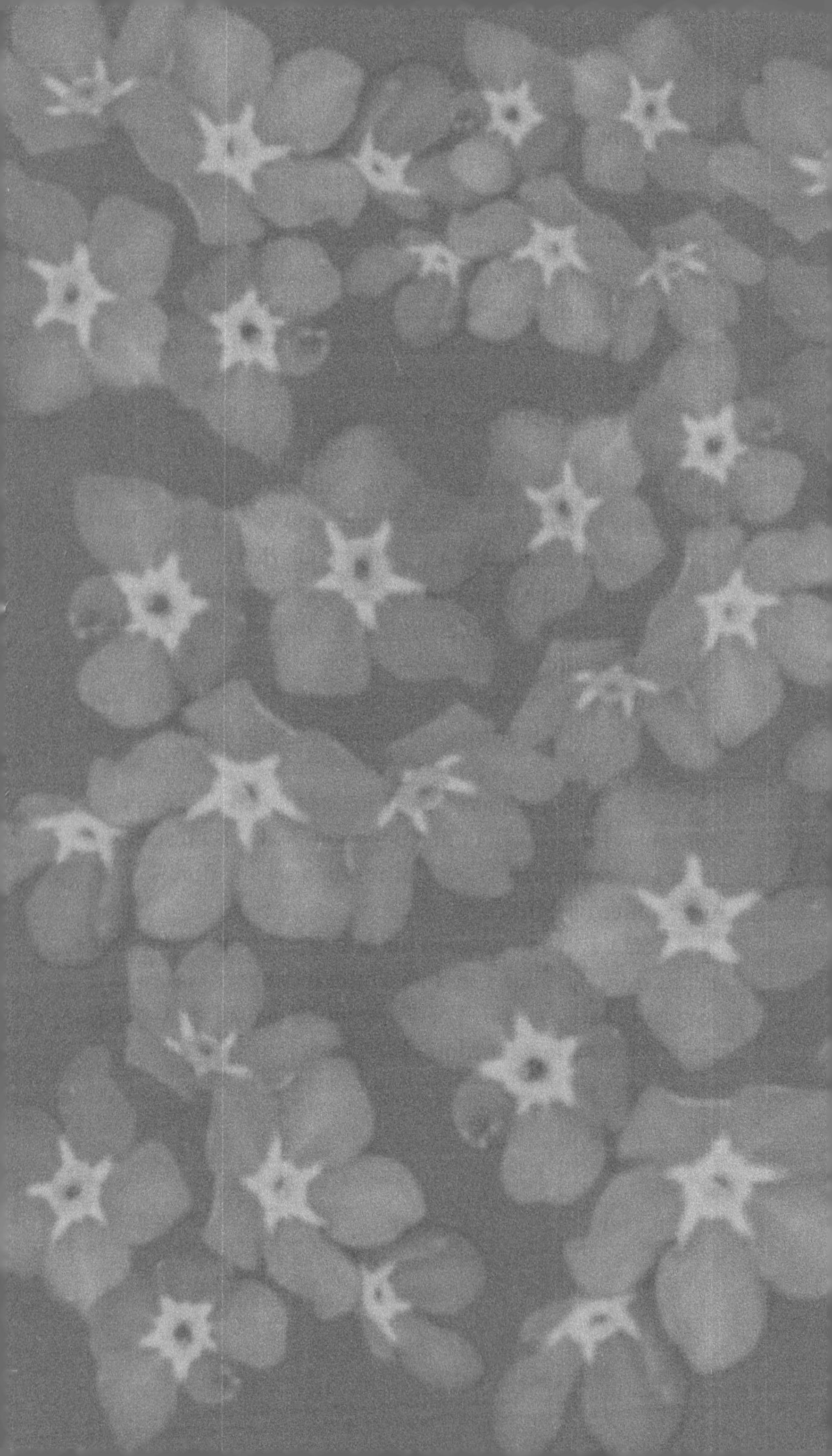

ONE

LIFE HASN'T BEEN the same since the accident.

I look over at Sidney, who sleeps as we drive for an insane amount of hours. Car rides with Dad are unbearable if you don't have some kind of entertainment. He drives in complete silence with the cold air blowing as hard as possible; it takes only seconds before you're ready for the heat again. He says that he's "warm-blooded," and that's his excuse for the constant freezing temperatures. Sidney and I don't have that luxury. After throwing a blanket over Sid when she starts to shiver, I pull my hoodie over my head. I stick my headphones in my ears and turn it up until my eardrums threaten to bust, place my shades over my eyes, and try to ignore the distractions I know I can't escape, no matter how hard I try.

During this long drive, I try not to think of what happened, but that's always a waste of effort. I manage to keep it from my mind, but not Sidney's. She looks so peaceful, but her mind is a raging storm.

Why isn't Momma with us?

Why's Kai actin' so funny?

Why do we have to leave?

Even though she's only six, I can never fool her like I do my parents.

The last few years have been hard on all of us, but I can't help but feel as though I got the short end of the stick. I'm the one that changed without any control of the aftermath. When I woke up in the hospital, I knew immediately that everything had changed. As if being told I'd been in a coma for most of the year—plus the amnesia—wasn't enough, the overwhelming noise taking over my mind almost drove me insane. It took months for my memories to start coming back and to get used to the fact that I can now hear others' thoughts in my head. I was too afraid to tell anyone about it then, and I still am now.

That was a couple of years ago now. The strain took its toll on everyone, especially my parents' marriage, which eventually crumbled.

I can still hear the thoughts of everyone around me, but for the most part, I try to block it all out. I never wanted this. I just want to be normal.

My eyes shift over to Sidney, and though she is asleep, her dreams are full of distress. I look back out the window at the trees passing by in a green blur, but I can't help but watch her dream turn into a nightmare. I turn my music up as loud as I dare and drift off to sleep to the image of pretentious students, ruthless teachers, and lonely lunches as her fears shift to my soon-to-be reality.

Finally made it!

I startle awake at the voice in my mind that's far too baritone to be my own, still not familiar enough with Dad's voice in my mind to stay asleep. Taking in my surroundings outside the window, I have to admit that it's a nice little house—taller than our last. This one is light blue with a black trimming and four windows that I can see from the front, two upstairs and two down. It's the front door that catches my eye though. It seems out of place-a little too dark and Gothic-seeming for the Victorian style home. It's clear someone tried to hide the clash of styles by masking the door with bright red paint, but they failed. Dad grabs our bags as I go around the truck to wake Sleeping Beauty.

"Hey," I whisper in her ear and get a grumble in response. "We're here. Time to pick our rooms, Sis!" I say this with fake enthusiasm to catch her attention.

It works.

We go into the house, and as soon as I step inside the front door, it's a straight shot to the stairs. Unlike the colorful, patriotic paint on the exterior, the inside is plain white. No color added to anything at all.

A blank canvas.

To the left of the entry, there's a medium-sized kitchen with cabinets, a tiny pantry, and ancient appliances, and to the right is the living room, which for now is just an empty room. The house is eerie and too silent. I tell myself it's because there isn't any furniture yet.

Sidney and I go straight up the stairs that split the house right down the middle, walking hand in hand. She goes to the right. I follow her to the door of her room and then turn and go to the left of the staircase: my side.

My new room is bigger than my last one, with two windows—one on the far wall and the other above a nook—and a walk-in closet. The room feels empty because the movers won't be coming for another week.

When I turn around to go get my bags, I'm surprised to see that they're waiting for me at the top of the stairs. Dad must have dropped them there for us. The rest of the night consists of us eating pizza and unpacking the things of our past we brought with us, which actually isn't that much.

"So," Dad says, not looking up from his plate. "Whatcha think of the house, girls?" Now looking up expectantly, his eyes only pause on me for a moment before he focuses his gaze on Sidney.

"It's great, Dad," I say and go back to picking at my pepperoni.

Based on his thoughts, he doesn't believe me-not that he really cares all that much.

"It's . . ." Sidney starts.

Dad and I both look up at her and wait.

"Creepy," she finally says.

I can't help but laugh a little. That is exactly what I was thinking. Maybe I'm not alone in this after all, although I hope I am. I can't imagine Sidney being able to handle all of the stress I'm under these days. Whatever it is that made me the way I am now, hearing the thoughts of those around me, I'm glad I'm bearing the burden and not her.

Dad's eyes cut to me with a disapproving look before moving back at Sid. "Well, that's just 'cause it's new to you, sweetie. Don't worry. It'll feel like home in no time." He shifts his eyes back to his food and fidgets with his fingers before popping his knuckles, then goes back to eating his food.

Later, I eventually go to sleep to mentally prepare for my first day of classes at Lake Region State College.

I turn to the mirror and stare at the girl with practically clear skin and grayish-blue eyes, and watch her brush out the few tangles she has. I've always liked the way my hair has a wave pattern to it. It's easy to manage and rarely gives me any trouble.

I get all the necessities ready to go and head for the kitchen, where I find the refrigerator and cabinets devoid of food.

"Dad, we should really go to the store."

He looks up to me. *We don't have any food?*

I stare at him while he gathers his thoughts.

"Oh, I'll do that today." He takes another sip of his coffee. "So, are you leavin' now?"

"Yeah, I'm gonna go ahead and head out."

"All right. I'll drop Sidney off at school."

We share an awkward smile before I wave goodbye and make my way out the door. I can't sit there and take anymore awkward small talk.

I drive a gray 1986 Ford F-150. It's tall and sturdy and the complete opposite of anything I would have driven before. That's why I love it. I want as few reminders of home as possible.

Thinking of my life in Texas is too painful now. I can't keep reminding myself of all I've lost or thinking back to when I had friends to lean on, when we were a real family, before everyone else's thoughts occupied my mind along with my own. I have to move forward and try to move on.

I take my time driving to town and take in the scenery, passing a lot of open spaces with patches of thick trees. The fact that we live so far out of town gives me plenty of time to take it all in.

Once I make it to the Devils Lake, North Dakota, city limit, I stumble on a donut shop right on cue; my stomach growls viciously.

I don't know what this town is possibly named after, but with a name like that, I'm not sure I want to know, and I have a feeling I won't be going anywhere near the lake either. Better safe than sorry.

When I finally find the campus, it doesn't surprise me that

it's as far away from my new home as it can possibly get. My amazing luck just continues on.

I head for the double doors labeled *ADMINISTRATION*. When I walk into the office, the young woman at the reception desk doesn't look up as she speaks.

"Hi, how may I help you?" she asks, her voice monotone and uncaring.

I hear her thoughts revolving in a sad circle—how she should've continued her education and got a real job, then she could've found a decent man to settle down with and wouldn't be stuck working here.

"Uh, yeah. I'm Kairi Rush. I just moved here."

She finally looks up and stares at me for a minute, deciding what she should do.

"I printed off my schedule. I really just need a map and ID card," I add.

The way she's staring would have made me nervous if I didn't know what she was thinking, which is that I'll stick out and something about my accent. I didn't know what she means about "sticking out," but before I can read any more of an explanation from her thoughts, she spins back to her computer. After a few minutes of typing away, I hear the printer going off.

"Stand over here so I can take your student ID picture, and then you can be on your way." She gestures to her left where a camera is set up like you would see at the DMV.

I shuffle over without a word and stand on the marked spot on the floor before looking up with the most convincing smile I can manage.

"Here's your ID and a map of the campus. You'll need to use your ID to get into some of the buildings. Have a nice day." With that, she hands me everything I need and goes back to her computer screen.

"Thank you," I say, then make my way back outside.

When I get back to my truck, more people are starting to show up. I pull into the line and follow them, which is way better than driving around in circles until someone comes to rescue me and point me in the direction of the student parking.

That's when it hits me.

From the look of all of these shiny cars, it seems like a safe bet to assume all of their parents make a good deal of money. And while I don't know much about fancy cars, I can pick out a BMW, Cadillac, Mercedes, and I think that's a Lexus. I can tell the difference between my class and theirs, and as far as I can tell, I'm the only one in the bottom half. Now I know what the secretary meant.

I drive a jacked-up pickup truck that towers over their little luxury cars. Well, I can always just run them over. The thought makes me smile, even though I'm kidding . . . mostly.

And then my smile vanishes.

Who's driving that monster truck?

What a freak.

Well, great. I haven't even parked, and I've been labeled.

"Perfect," I whisper to myself.

I'm starting to see that tomorrow, I'll need to make sure I remember my headphones to drown out all this sound. I can already feel a headache surfacing. I can't believe I forgot to put them in my bag this morning.

I look over my schedule and map one more time because I don't want to get lost on my way to my first class. I wait till the song playing on the radio is over to walk into this new hell and over the invisible line that, when crossed, ends my old life.

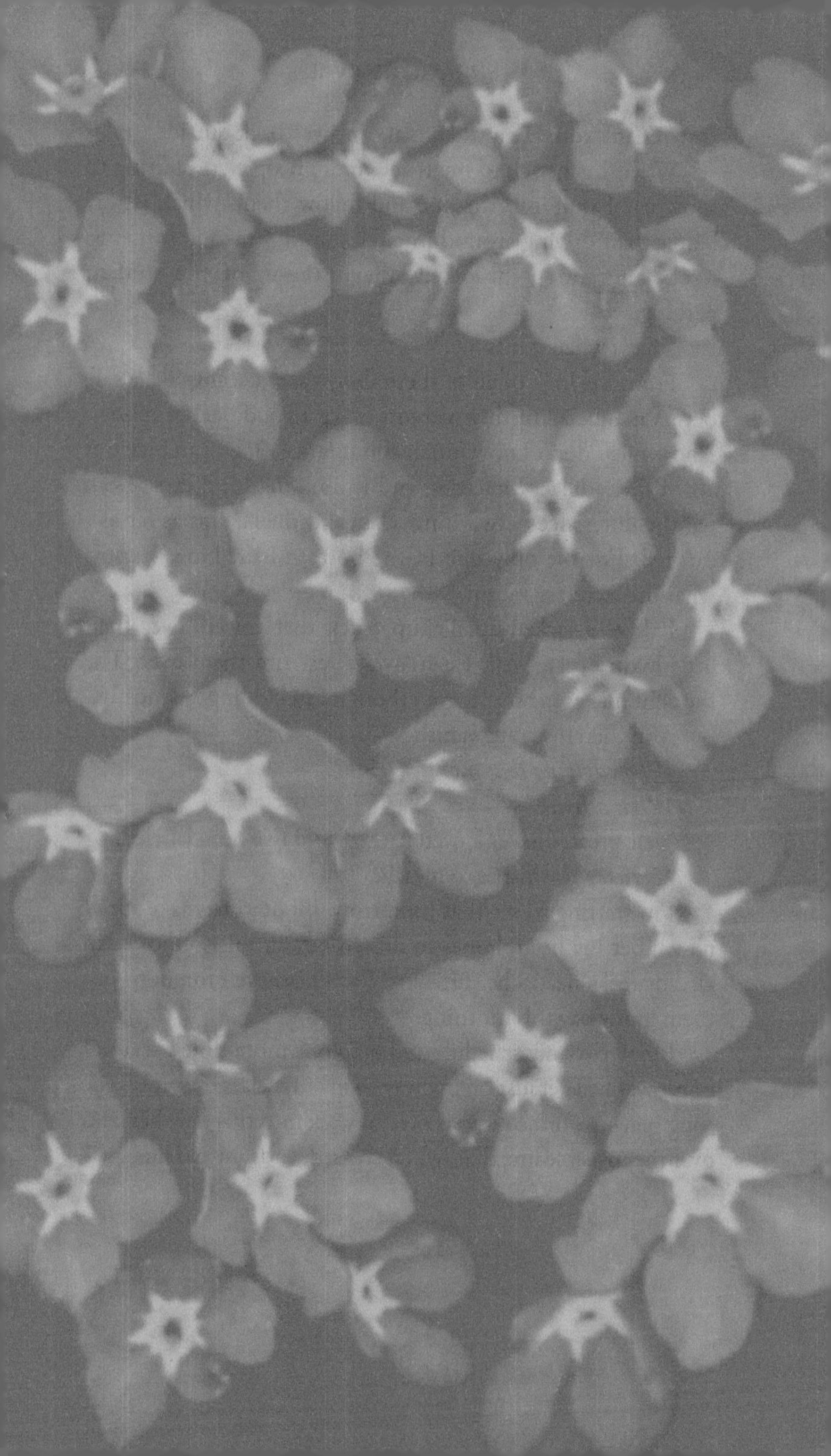

TWO

IT'S EASIER to find my first class than I expected. First is English III. That should be easy enough. I've always liked English and prefer the more creative classes that don't rely heavily on structure. I let out a sigh of relief, taking a seat in the back. I jump right into whatever lesson they're currently on, since I'm joining a little behind the start date.

I finish my work long before the class is scheduled to be dismissed. I sit back in my chair and look around to the other students focusing on their work. I stare at the ceiling. I don't have any music, any books, and all the rest of my things are coming in a few weeks. I'll have my headphones tomorrow, so for now, I decide to try something I haven't done in a while.

I pull out a blank sheet of paper and start writing whatever line pops into my head. Poetry is like therapy to me, and I've missed it. I've never been good at showing my emotions, so I feel better when I write them down. The lines that come out of my imagination aren't the happiest. I write what feels right, and if I like it, that's what counts. It's not like I plan to show anyone anyway.

I'm turning the page in my story,
been forced to start over.
Please, don't forget me now.
Hold all of our memories close to your heart.

I'm so completely absorbed in words that I jump when a folded sheet of paper flies onto my desk.

The teacher didn't introduce you. What's your name? Oh, look to your right.

The smell of Sharpie overwhelms my desk. When I turn to look, sure enough, there's a girl smiling at me. She has long dark brown hair that makes her pale green eyes stand out. I try to smile back but can't feel if it comes out right and turn back to the note.

I'm Kairi.

Instead of tossing it back though, I hold it up for her to see. The smile stays on her face, and she pulls out another sheet of paper. As I wait, I turn back to my poem.

I look up as she finishes her note, which asks me where I'm from.

I'm from a town near the Gulf.

We don't talk much more for the rest of class. She's the victim of being called on more than once by the professor. I honestly don't even know what's going on.

I throw all my stuff in my bag when the professor ends the class, but I fold my poem and put it in my back pocket. When I turn to the door, I jump, not expecting to see that same girl waiting.

"Hi, I'm Chelsea." She smiles like before, and when she realizes all I'm going to do is smile back, she continues: "Do you need help finding your next class?"

I shake my head.

"What classes do you have?"

She seems nice enough, but I just don't feel like talking. A weird pressure starts to form in my head, and I rub my temples for a moment before dropping my hands. A headache is the last thing I need.

The fact that she's being a little more than pushy rubs me the wrong way, but I shove the thought back. I'm sure she's just trying to be friendly, but I still run my tongue over my teeth in irritation.

She doesn't seem bothered by my silence. I hand her my schedule without a word. She studies it for a moment. "Cool, we have biology together too." She points at my schedule. "So you can sit with me at lunch if you want."

"Sure, that sounds . . . great." Chelsea's smile grows—if that's possible—and walks with me out of class.

As we walk side by side, my steps falter for a second as I realize I can't hear any of Chelsea's thoughts pounding in my head. I cut my eyes to her, and for the first time, I try to push my way into her mind but hit nothing but a wall blocking her mind from mine.

Weird . . .

"I can see what you mean now about being from the South."

I smirk, pushing away my curiosity for her mental block and thicken my accent as much as I can. "Ya know, for some reason, I knew I was gonna be stickin' out."

Chelsea giggles. I turn and give her a quick look before we go our separate ways without another word. While I appreciate her trying to befriend me, that isn't what I'm here for. I don't need friends, especially pushy ones that appear to have no thoughts. Something tells me she isn't going to be going away anytime soon though.

I sit at a table by myself at the little café inside the school library but feel claustrophobic. I'm surrounded with the thoughts of people around me, and it feels like they're shouting right in my ears. I rest my head on the table, closing my eyes, trying to imagine my own mental wall going up to block it all out, but my headache is getting worse, and I can't concentrate. I practically run to the biology building when I see it's nearly time for my class.

The entire period, I sit by Chelsea as she babbles on, asking me whatever questions pop in her head. I answer them all without thinking. I sit with my cheek resting in my palm and continue my poem.

> *My life has been torn apart.*
> *Just don't feel sorry for me, please.*
> *My thoughts can't even start to form.*
> *Now everything feels so overwhelming to me.*

"So, what do you like to do?" Chelsea asks.

"Nothin' much really."

"Well, I can see that you like to write or something."

I subtly try to put my poem away but fail. Her eyes are glued to the little piece of paper until it's out of sight. Then she meets my eyes again.

"I just like to put my thoughts down on paper," is all I say. Partly true, but it feels false coming out of my mouth. The pressure in my head is getting worse. Maybe I should keep some pain reliever in my bag from now on too.

"What else do you like to do?" She turns back to her work.

"I don't do much of anythin' anymore, really."

"Okay, well, what did you used to do, then?" Chelsea is pushing and pushing for information, and it's starting to feel less like a friendly conversation and more like an interrogation.

"Not much to be honest."

I turn my attention away from Chelsea. I stare off into space and remember all the good times and friends I had. For some reason, I can only remember them faintly. I guess when I was trying to forget my old life, I actually did. Deep in thought, I didn't notice Chelsea's clenched jaw at first.

"What?" I stare at her now, confused. I rub my temple as the throbbing headache gets more intense. Thinking too hard, I guess.

"Nothing," she says as a bright smile comes to her face again.

Is this chick bipolar or what?

After a while, she goes back to her work, and I watch the professor walk everyone through the slides for the day. I catch a boy's gaze from across the room before he averts his eyes with a shy smile.

"Finally," I breathe out , hoping Chelsea doesn't hear me.

I follow her from class to the cafeteria and into the line but only grab an apple. Lunch goes by quickly. Chelsea introduces me to a group of her friends, whose names I forget as soon as she introduces them to me. I smile though and try to look as friendly as possible.

"Hey, I'm Travis."

I turn to the smiling boy from earlier and give him a small smile in return. "Hi."

"So, how do you like the campus so far?"

"It's loud," I say and want to slap myself.

Travis gives me a quizzical look, but his smile stays on his face. I turn from him to check the time before I send the group a small wave goodbye before making my way home.

As soon as I walk in the house, I see Sidney.

"What're you doing here?" I ask her.

"Dad dropped me off, then went back to work," she says without losing her concentration on the television—one of the only things that came with this house. I get her some popcorn and white grape juice—her favorite.

"How was your first day of school?"

She looks up from the TV, and I get a *Don't even go there* look.

"Oh, c'mon. It couldn't've been that bad."

"I feel so weird here." She shakes her head.

I sigh, pull her into my lap, and wrap my arms around her, trying to make my arms a wall to block out all the bad. "Sid, it's just the first day. It'll get better soon, I promise."

"I miss Mommy," she whispers.

I don't know what to tell her or how to respond. Our parents aren't getting back together, and I don't know if she could even live with Mom if she wanted. So instead of responding, I just pull her into my side and comfort her as best I can.

She doesn't say anything else.

We sit there for a while and watch TV.

When I feel like she's okay, I walk up the stairs and give her as much privacy in her own mind as I can, but sometimes, it's difficult. She's like me in that she likes solitude when she's upset, and I'm going to respect that.

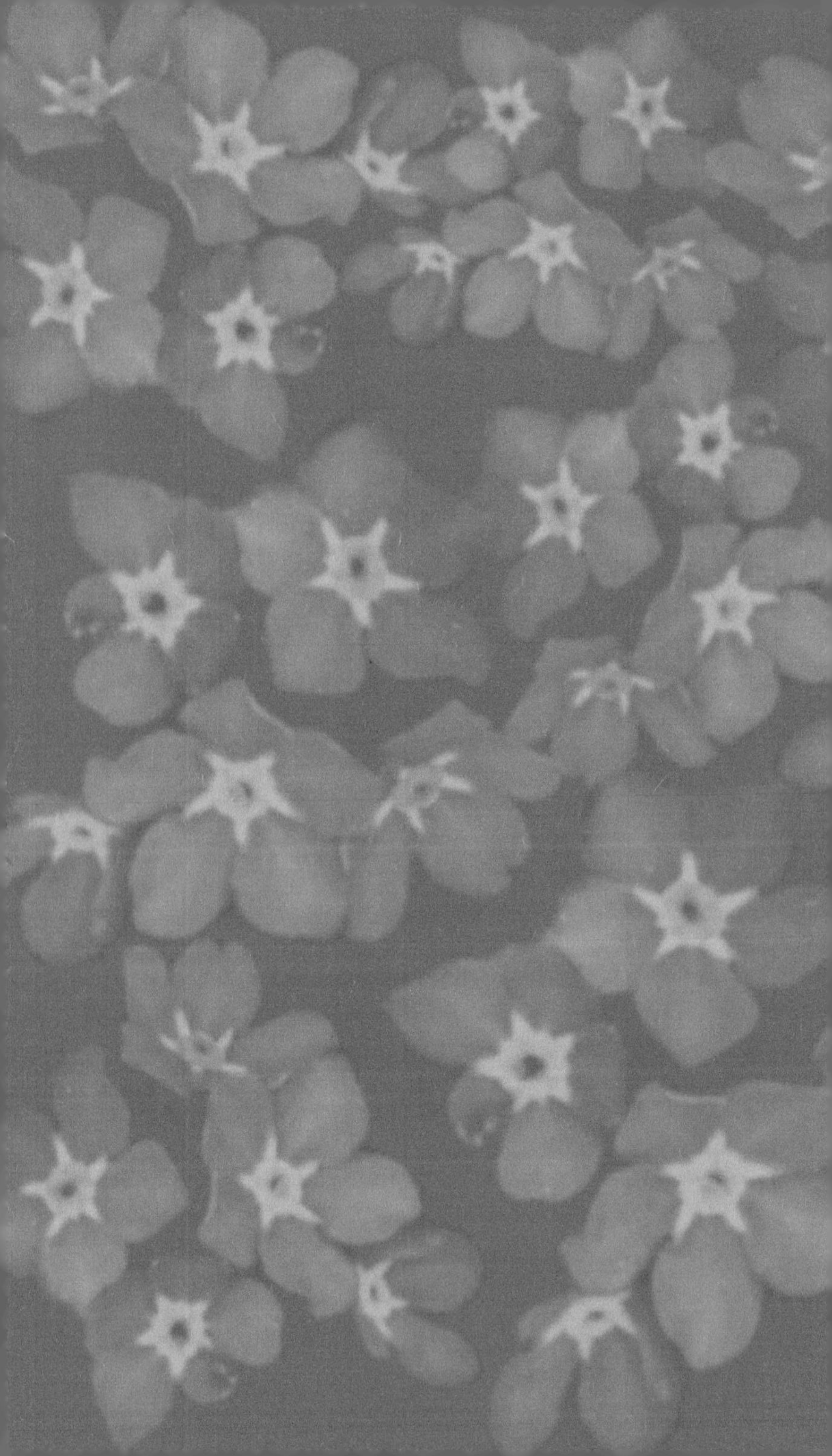

THREE

THE BOY from yesterday's class catches me in the parking lot and walks with me to American Government, which Chelsea conveniently informed me we both have first today. I wish I can remember his name, because he seems genuinely nice, whether I want the company or not. As we walk, he doesn't say much of anything, and I appreciate the silence.

I sit in the first empty seat in the classroom I see and continue my lines from the day before:

All I know is consumed by the flames.
Now nothing I ever knew will be the same.

A girl's thoughts blast through my mind from across the room, knocking my own off track.

I can't believe Travis walked the new bitch to class.

She doesn't try to hide her tone—but I wasn't supposed to hear it either.

My train of thought is lost when someone taps my shoulder. I twist around in my seat to see a guy with dark brown-almost-black hair that waves just past his ears. I let my eyes roam his tall lean body. He's in a fitted gray T-shirt and dark jeans that hang loosely at his waist with what look like motorcycle boots. He has to be around six feet, but it's hard to tell from my seat as he stands over me. I meet his amused gaze and get momentarily lost in the deepest brown eyes I've ever seen, like two black holes drawing me in.

He's tall, dark, and sexy. Classic.

He flashes a full toothy smile. "Excuse me, but you're in my seat."

I furrow my brows, confused by all the silence. I can't hear anything. Not a single word, phrase, or even a hum from his mind.

"I-I'm sorry," I say, finally realizing I'm staring at him like an idiot. "I didn't know there were assigned seats." I gather my things and stand.

Yeah, he's definitely six feet tall at least; my eyes don't even reach his shoulders.

"I'll let you sit here just this once." He winks and takes the open seat next to me.

His voice is so deep and smooth, unlike anything I've ever heard. I take a deep breath before I try to speak, which only makes me want to slap myself for such a silly reaction.

"Oh, okay." I sit back down, keeping my eyes off him. I shift my things back out of my bag without looking up.

"Here, I think this is yours." He hands me a folded sheet of paper. *My poem.* I smile and nod. "Oh, and I'm Jaxon Benievere." He has this crooked smile that gives me butterflies. "But you can call me Jax," he adds with a wink.

"I'm Kairi." I look back to the paper in front of me, searching for the words to continue my unfinished lines and distract myself from this alluring man.

An unexplainable pull draws me to Jaxon in a way I don't remember ever feeling before. It's almost like an invisible string or magnet. In the front of my mind, I know I'm acting like a silly schoolgirl with a crush, but there is still this little voice in the back of my mind urging me to talk to him, get closer to him, see more of him. I've never wanted to be close to anyone outside my family for as long as I can remember, and even then, it's really only Sidney I'm close to.

> *Although this is definitely an end,*
> *I can still rise from the ashes again.*

"Well, Kairi, what are you writing there?" I can't tell from his tone if he's genuinely curious or just asking to make polite conversation.

"It's nothin'." I shake my head.

"Looks like something."

I look at him now. His eyebrow raises with a teasing smile.

My eyes narrow. "It's somethin' to me. I don't see a reason to go into somethin' that has nothin' to do with you," I say very lowly so only he can hear.

I may be snapping at him a little more than I need to. He's trying to be nice, but he's acting more like he deserves to know, which rubs me the wrong way.

He lets out a soft laugh. "Maybe you're right, but I'm still curious."

I take a deep breath and keep my eyes down. "It's a poem."

Why am I tellin' him this?

I can envision his eyebrows rising to match his tone of surprise without even looking at him. "Really?"

Before I can stop myself, the explanation forces itself out: "I used to write a lot before, but I've felt so out of sorts for the last few months that I haven't—until today."

I just told myself I didn't want to overshare with a stranger, but here I am. Sure, he's very easy to talk to, but I need to reel it back in.

"Before what?" Jaxon asks. His curious tone never fades, but all the humor in it disappears.

I wince at the memory flashing behind my eyes.

Panic, smoke, pinned down, unable to breathe, but mainly, just *fire*.

"You don't have to tell me," Jaxon says quickly. "I'm just trying to . . . understand you."

"And why's that?" I open my eyes to look at Jaxon now.

"You've sparked my interest." He shrugs, letting a cheeky smile creep back onto his face.

"Because that makes sense." I let out a shaky laugh as I push the rest of the memories to the deepest part of my mind. Something about him makes me uneasy and nervous and warm and crazy all at the same time.

I feel insane.

"It doesn't have to make sense. Everyone needs someone to talk to, and you're new, so I thought I'd be perfect for the job." He gives me a fox smile. He lures me in with his own brand of charm, but I can tell he's trying to make light of what he said before.

I smile and give serious thought to telling him. Something inside me says that I need to tell someone. While I try to word it in my head, the same girl from earlier interrupts my train of thought.

OMG! Benievere is talking to her! But he never talks to anyone!

He seems very *talkative if you ask me*, I think. I can tell she's been denied more than once by Jaxon, and for whatever reason, it feels good to know I'm getting some kind of special treatment.

"Well, it isn't a memory I like to recall, but I can't seem to forget it either." I pause, and he waits. I take a deep breath and study my paper again, losing my nerve.

He sighs, but he doesn't push the issue. When I look at

him again, he has an expression on his face that I've never seen. It makes me smile. Usually, when someone looks at me this intensely, it's either annoying, unnerving, or plain creepy, but with Jaxon, it just makes me feel warm and wanted.

"Now if I could just get everyone to stop starin' at me like I'm some sorta freak show." I bounce my leg under my desk.

"You do kind of stand out." Jaxon smiles in a way that unleashes a flock of butterflies in my stomach . . . again. "For different reasons than what you might think."

"You mean other than the way I look and my accent?"

His smile grows. "Well, those are just the obvious things. Hey, do you want me to lie?"

I realize I'm scowling at my paper and look back to him with a dark expression.

"I wasn't even going to bring your cute country accent into it, but now that you have . . ." He leans in toward me.

I lean to the far end of my chair away from Jaxon and let out a shaky breath while shaking my head. "Ya know, if I could get rid of it, I would."

"I like it though." Jaxon pouts to keep his smile hidden.

"And that means I have to keep it just for you?" It's my turn to raise a brow at him now.

"Well, why else?"

I search his eyes, because even though his face is light and almost taunting, his eyes are deep and serious. Something about him is luring me in. Maybe it's his smile or maybe his cocky attitude egging me on.

I smirk, and as I'm about to respond, the professor dismisses class for the day. I didn't even notice them come in, much less start class. I look around, and the professor isn't in sight anymore. Jaxon would've noticed if the teacher had started the lesson, right?

I rush to get my things together.

"Where are you off to?"

"Break time for now." I shove my stuff in my bag.

"I'm sure we'll see each other sometime soon." He watches me for an instant, then leaves without another word, and I can't help but stare after him. He walks with such confidence and grace . . .

"Ready?"

I jump and turn to see Travis standing next to me. I nod, and we leave the room.

"That class was brutal." Travis throws his hands in the air and huffs dramatically.

I just hum in response, thinking back to Jaxon. It was weird the way he left with that cryptic goodbye.

"I hate that class, and the sound of his voice is so monotone, it makes me want to sleep."

"Yeah . . ." I try to think of something else to talk about since I didn't even listen during class. "Ya know," I say, "you scared the crap out of me. It was like you appeared out of nowhere." I laugh a little, but when he doesn't, I turn to look at him.

He catches my eye and chuckles. "I guess I'm just light on my feet."

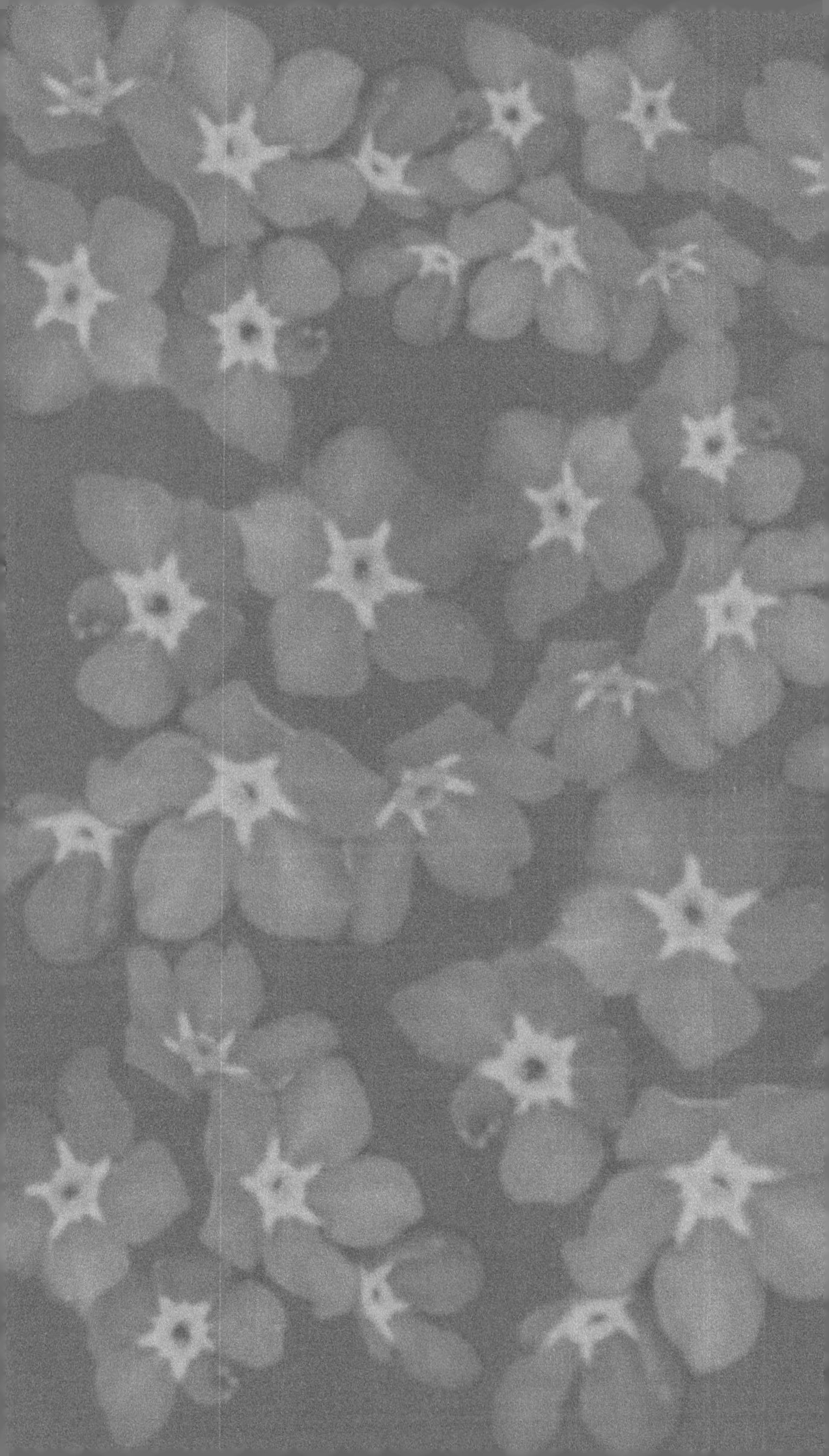

FOUR

TRAVIS and I go our separate ways after a short walk out of the business building. I make my way back to the same little cafe I found myself in yesterday. Today, I remembered my headphones. Plugging them into my ears and turning my current playlist on shuffle, I take a look around me.

Everyone is either drinking their preferred drinks while chatting idly, doing some sort of schoolwork, or taking a moment to relax as I am. So far, this school's atmosphere is pretty mellow.

I close my eyes for a moment, letting the music take me away. Music, much like writing, pulls me out of reality and lets my mind relieve the stress that seems to always weigh me down.

A creeping feeling that I'm being watched comes over me, but when I open my eyes and look around, I don't see anyone particularly standing out to me. Taking one last look around, I try to shake the feeling away and reach for my notebook.

A sharp pain shoots through my temple, making me wince. It soon dulls to a slight headache, and I wish I had remembered to bring some pain reliever with me.

I'll have to remember to pack some tomorrow.

Looking down to check the time, I decide to make my way to the cafeteria to get some food. On the walk over, I'm grateful to have this time to myself. Yesterday, Chelsea was stuck to me like glue, and today, Travis keeps popping up out of nowhere, so this peace and quiet is appreciated. Something about the two of them constantly being around is comforting in that I'm not always alone, but it's also more than irritating. It's hard to know someone's true intentions when you're practically strangers, and the fact that they're so persistent makes me wonder what they're doing this for.

I still can't shake the feeling that someone has their eyes on me. I'm sure it's just the fact that I'm new and this is a small-town college, but the uneasy feeling won't leave. I find myself getting a small meal as quickly as possible and moving to a more secluded area, hoping that will ease the knots in my stomach.

On the ground, under an oak tree, I eat my chicken Caesar wrap and pull out my notebook again. I stare down at my messy string of words but can't think of a way to continue it right now, so I lean back and let the music take me away until it's time for my next and last class of the day.

I walk myself to English lit, and it gives me time to catch a breath and regain my thoughts. No matter how hard I try to resist, now that the headache has finally passed on, my mind keeps steering back to Jaxon.

I'm not sure what it was about our conversation or what he did that made any sort of impact on me, but it's definitely there. Jaxon Benievere is intriguing to say the least.

The professor is at her desk with her nose in a book, so I sit down toward the back without a word.

I can't go back and change the things I've done.
I had so many plans that are now only dreams.

"Well, well, well. Who the hell are you, and why are you in my seat?"

I raise both of my brows and shake my head but don't look up.

"I'm Allison Hastings." Her manicured hand settles over my paper so I can't write. She wants to make me look up at her, but I won't. "Just a friendly reminder, trailer trash . . ." Now I look up at her. "Don't mess around with those clearly at a different level than you." She gives me a sweet smile that makes me laugh, which washes her smile away.

"Yeah, there aren't assigned seats, so . . ."

"I don't care. This is my spot," she grinds out and pushes my things off the desk.

Who does she think she is, and who does she think she's talking to?

I wanna go off on her, but she doesn't seem like she's worth the trouble. I still have to take three deep breaths and look away, or I'll never be sane and calm again. A sudden pulse of energy flows through my body. My mind expands, and I can see images that are not my own flash through it.

One . . .

I can now see that Allison's family has money and her parents are never around, which leaves her alone—all the time. Her parents have more interest in drugs and alcohol than her. I can sense her emotions like they're my own as the flashes of her memories continue.

Two . . .

She was a mistake that they never wanted and wished they never had. She makes everyone feel worse to ease the blow from their frequent reminders of their disappointment in her. These are things I didn't have to see to know. There are so many girls like Allison out there, and it's all the same old story. Actually, I might've been one.

Three . . .

"Allison?"

She spins around, and I take the time to get my stuff while she's distracted. My thoughts are all over the place as I try to make sense of what just happened. I've never been able to look into someone's mind that way before. I have never tried either; I'm too busy trying to drown out everyone else's thoughts that crowd my head.

Miss Queen Bee smiles and says something unintelligent and flirty, then moves out of his way.

"Thank you."

So damn sexy.

I roll my eyes at her thoughts.

"Hey, Kairi."

I don't have to look up to know who it is.

"Hi," I say, pretending I don't feel his penetrating gaze locked on me, but I can't control the knots that are starting to form in my stomach at the sound of his voice.

"I told you I'd see you again." Jaxon smiles when I look up.

You have got to be kidding me! Jaxon Benievere and that bitch? What a joke!

I look around the class, avoiding Jaxon's stare, and find that multiple girls are blatantly looking our way. Their jealous eyes and sneering faces make me uncomfortable. I never realized how much attention Jaxon attracts, and I don't like the negative effects that come from having a simple conversation with him.

"What were you and Allison talking about?" He follows Allison back to her seat with his eyes, and I try to shake the uneasy feeling building in my stomach.

"She just thought she was puttin' me in my place, but the joke's on her, 'cause I'm already there."

"Oh? And what place is that?" He takes a quick glance at Allison, then pulls his notebook from his bag.

"The obvious." I gesture to myself. Seeing that he doesn't

understand, I drop it, not in the mood to get into it. It's not like it matters anyway.

I see his confused expression out of the corner of my eye, but I don't know why he cares. The fact that I can't see into his thoughts is still unnerving and frustrating. He's friendly for someone I've only known for a few hours. Maybe a little too friendly . . .

His voice is a little more agitated than earlier when he leans over and whispers, "She doesn't know what she's talking about."

I ignore him because I don't know how to respond.

"Kairi."

"I heard you."

It doesn't matter what he thinks of me. It doesn't change how everyone else sees me or the way I see myself. I don't know why he's acting like this anyway. He's so . . . intense? His constant efforts to have a conversation or get to know me don't irritate me the way that Chelsea and Travis do, but it doesn't sit well with me either. Something about it all feels wrong and uneasy.

I just keep writing line after line, steadily distracting myself now that the words are coming to mind.

I used to live like I was just a ghost,
going through life with ease and sorrow.

We don't talk much more for the rest of the class, mainly because I make it my personal mission to ignore him. It isn't easy when I can feel the way he keeps looking over to me; it's so magnetic. It's as if he's saying my name or tapping me on the shoulder. His gaze has a physical effect on me. Now I have no idea what this class is even about.

I finally turn to look at him, searching his eyes for whatever he's trying to tell me or wants me to say. I get an urge to please him. Jaxon opens his mouth to say something, but the professor dismisses the class. I pack up my things, then head for the parking lot.

I have to hold myself back so I don't break into a jog to get to my truck.

"Why do you care about what she said?"

Jumping in surprise, I turn to see that Jaxon is walking next to me. He always appears out of nowhere too. I can never hear him coming, out loud or in his mind.

"I don't care," I say.

He deadpans, "Sure . . ."

"I really don't. One person's opinion doesn't define me."

"You seemed upset."

"Maybe I was already upset."

"For some reason, I don't think that's true."

"Good thing you don't really know me then, isn't it?"

Jaxon goes quiet at that but still matches my pace.

When I look over at him, he has a sad smile on his face. "Which is yours?" He dodges my eyes and looks into the sea of cars.

"Take a wild guess." I laugh. "It's the only one that looks like it don't belong," I say, feeling the same about myself.

As soon as we got here, Dad gave me some money to take a bus to the only car lot in the city to purchase something to drive. He doesn't have the time, nor does he want to drive me anywhere, and I had to leave my old ride in Texas. I searched around forever until I found this old Ford.

"Ah, I see it now. It towers over all the others." Jaxon's smile isn't surprising, but it is more genuine now as he walks with me. It confuses me, to be honest.

Why is this sexy man following me around? I know very well my league and his would never collide. I mean, I'm sure I would've gone after him without hesitation before, but things are different now. *I'm different.* I shouldn't even be thinking that he's interested in me that way. He's just being nice or whatever.

I open the door and bring my beast to life with a loud roar that makes everyone in the lot turn my way and laugh. I sigh and manually roll down my window before closing my door. Jaxon has a thoughtful look on his face.

I groan. "What now?"

"The song," he says simply.

I frown and follow his eyes to my stereo, remembering that my mix CD is in. "What about it?" I reach for the dial and turn the volume down to where it's only background noise, starting to feel self-conscious.

"Nothing," he says.

I'm not convinced but let it go.

"What type of music do you listen to?"

"I listen to everything," I say.

"What's your favorite?"

"I don't pick favorites, typically."

He gives me an unknown look I can't put a name to. I raise an eyebrow at *him* for once.

He smiles, and it warms my entire body. "Will I see you tomorrow?"

"If I'm at school, I'm sure it's a possibility."

"If . . .?" Jaxon repeats.

"Well, I can't say I haven't thought about skippin'."

His warm expression drops slightly.

"But I'm not doin' things the same as I used to, so . . . I guess I'll be here." I try to give him a reassuring smile.

"Don't change on my account," he says with a smirk.

"I don't plan on changin' for anyone." I return his smirk, then laugh.

"Until then," Jaxon says, and without another word, he turns to walk away.

"Jaxon!" I call out to him before he can get too far away.

He turns and raises a brow at me expectantly. When I don't say anything right away, he smiles and takes a few steps back over to me.

"Why're you so . . . friendly?" I ask, not sure if that's exactly what I mean.

"Maybe I'm hoping to charm my way into your heart." He gives me a cheeky smirk.

"I wouldn't bet on it."

"That seems like a good bet to me."

"Doesn't surprise me you'd think so, for some reason."

"To answer your question, I'm not particularly friendly to anyone, but you're special, Darlin'." He mocks my accent but it causes a shudder to run down my spine, then leans in, takes my hand gently in his, and gives my knuckles a kiss. "And just Jax is fine." He winks, then walks away again, leaving me sitting here staring after him, still confused and with tingling fingers.

I can hear my heart pulsing in my ears. I pull out and drive home, my thoughts wrapped around *Jax*.

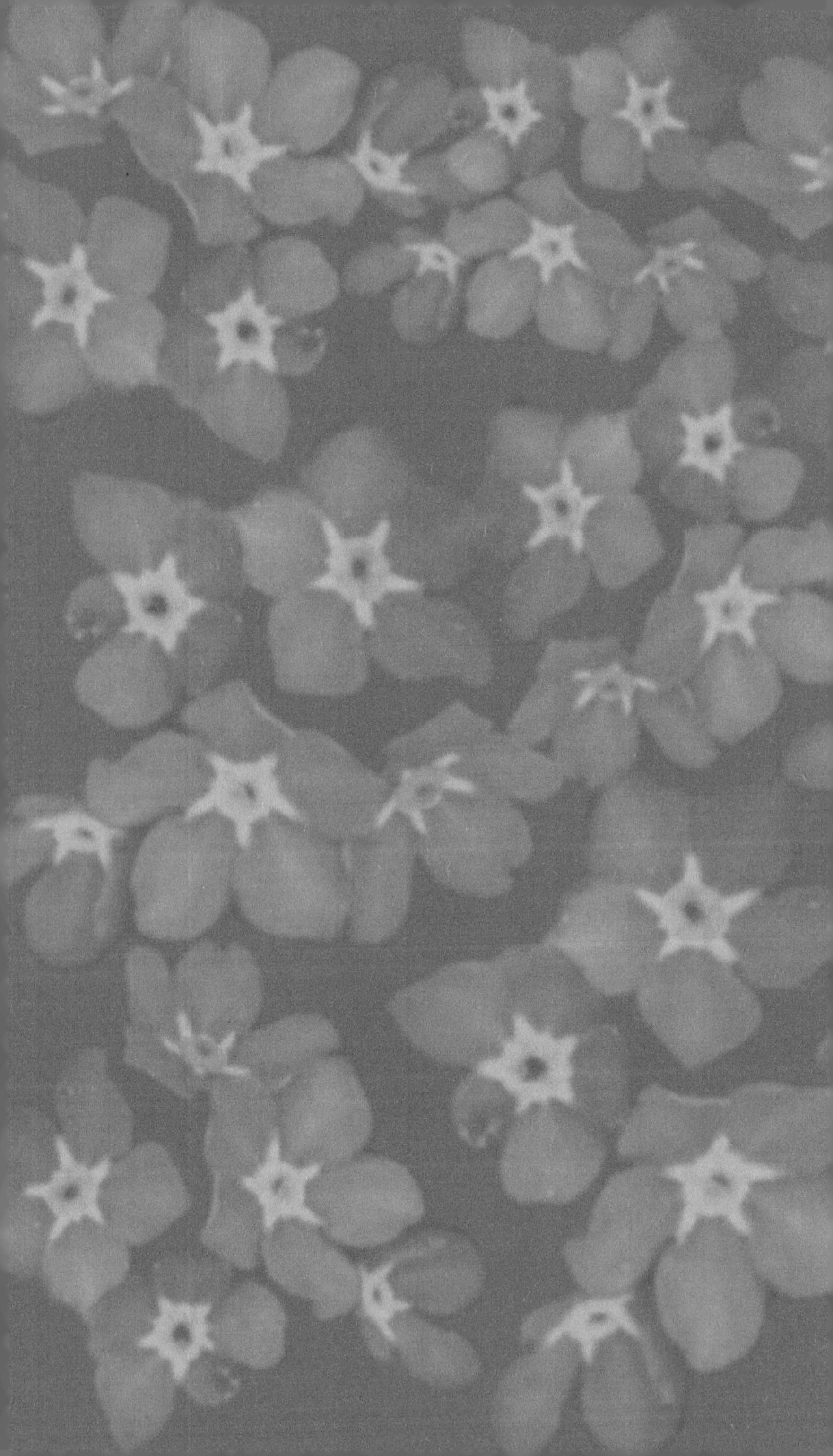

FIVE

TODAY WAS SO WEIRD.

I lie back on my pillows and try to understand it, and by *it*, I mean Jaxon.

He is so confusing and mysterious and arrogant and sweet and . . . I don't even know. I do know that I shouldn't be thinking about him, but he's something else. It's like I've met him before. That's the only way I'd be so comfortable around him, but I'd know if I had. No one can meet a guy like Jaxon Benievere and forget. That's for sure.

He's physically everything any girl would kill for—hard jaw, captivating eyes, muscular, and the most handsome man I've ever seen. All of these girls have crushes on him and think about him when he's around.

It's just a crush that will pass, I tell myself.

There's something that draws me to him like a magnet, as if I don't have a choice but to be near him.

It might not even be that I have a crush on him. He gives me an uneasy feeling and then pisses me off right after. He flips between that sweet smile of his to that cocky ass grin. He acts like he knows all about me, humoring me with all the small talk and questions, and that rubs me the wrong way. It makes me want to slap that dumb grin off his face every time it pops up.

He doesn't know me. He can't know me; I just moved here. I need to be careful around him.

The thought of Jaxon being a serial killer stalker pops into my mind. That'd explain the uneasy feeling I get around him and the way he acts like he knows me, but for some reason, I can't believe that. I have a bad habit of seeing the good in everyone. In all honesty, I feel like I know him too, especially those eyes . . .

The second I think of his deep brown eyes, I can see him staring back at me from behind my eyelids—those eyes searching mine for something I can't see. It's those eyes that seem so familiar, but from where?

I can't place it, but I can feel it in my gut that his eyes have looked into mine before today. I try to convince myself that a lot of people's eyes look similar, but I shake my head, not buying it. I've never seen eyes like his deep pools of darkness before.

I have to stop thinking of Jaxon. The more I think of him, the less likely it will be that I'll ever stop.

I laugh and shake my head.

I haven't worked on my poem since class, so I pull it out. When I grab, it seems much thicker than I remember. I open itup, and there's a second sheet of paper attached to mine.

A sketch.

The girl is beautiful, hair slightly covering her eyes, a thoughtful look on her face, and the drawing itself is incredible. I gasp when I realize who it is. It's a drawing of me, and there is a note at the bottom.

You don't realize how amazing you truly are.

It isn't signed, but I'm pretty sure I know who it's from.

I'm surprised when I hear the front door open around six o'clock. Dad made it seem like he'd be working nonstop once we moved here, so him being home for dinner is unexpected.

Sidney and I run down the stairs at the same time when we smell the pizza.

"Hey, baby girl. Are you hungry?"

Sidney yells, "Yes!"

I laugh and reach for a slice. "I thought you were gonna be workin'," I say right before I shove a slice of pepperoni pizza in my mouth.

"I wanted to be home to ask about my girls day at school." He looks directly at Sidney, and the fact that he's really only talking about her isn't missed on my part. Sidney and I both deflate a tiny bit when he says that but for completely different reasons.

The sadness floods from Sidney's mind to mine in waves. She felt like an outsider and spent most of her day alone. I send her a sad smile, knowing that with her cheerful attitude, the other kids will flock to her sooner or later. I take a deep breath and try not to look dejected at the fact that, though Dad said he wanted to know how both of our days went, we all know he couldn't care less about anything to do with me. He only wants to hear from Sidney.

We stare at our pizza, trying to keep our mouths full so we can delay that subject for a little while longer.

"Aw, c'mon, Sidney! Tell me about your first day."

Sidney looks at me with pleading eyes.

"School is school, Dad," I finally say quietly.

"Kairi." He looks at me with hardened eyes. I'm not sure if his scolding tone is because he wasn't talking to me, doesn't actually care about my day, or if he doesn't appreciate my snippy response.

"I don't know what you want me to say. I went to my classes, a few other kids talked to me, and then I got in my truck and came home when the day was done," I say, pushing through the churning feeling in my stomach at his infamous glare, pretending he wanted a longer, more detailed response from me instead of just sitting here with my mouth shut.

He stares at me blankly for a moment, then I let out a heavy breath as he moves his eyes back to Sid. "Did you make any friends today?"

"I guess so." Sidney keeps her eyes on her plate as she responds to him.

"Well, tell me about them."

I keep quiet for a while and eat my pizza in peace, letting them chat and ignore my presence. Dad's been like this for as long as I can remember now. He's always pushing me to the background of his life, and I've gotten used to the solitude.

"So how do you like it here?" he asks.

"We haven't been here long. Kinda too soon to tell," I say.

"Yeah, I guess you're right."

That's the end of that conversation. Luckily for Sidney, he doesn't seem interested in talking about this anymore.

After I finish my pizza, I run upstairs to escape the awkward silence.

Like most nights, my thoughts go back to night I thought I was going to die. The night I was trapped by flames. The fear I felt as I lost consciousness. The night that I somehow survived with the price of hearing the thoughts of everyone around me. Sometimes it feels more like a curse on my shoulders than a blessing that I'm still alive.

The more I play that night over in my head, I can't see Sid playing with fire that turned into the blaze that changed our family forever. It's not who she is. She's sensitive and innocent. Most of the time, it's annoying, because she never gets in trouble. I can't see her doing something so reckless. The memories come back to me fuzzy now, and there are details missing. It leaves me at a loss—a dead end—and as I lie down, I have yet another headache.

I wake up, but it doesn't feel right. My head feels so light that I can barely control my movements, and it sways from side to side. I go to lay my head back down until I can fully wake up, but I feel carpet on my cheek. I open my eyes but have to shut them immediately.

There's smoke everywhere.

As soon as the realization dawns on me, the coughing starts. I try to pull my arm up to cover my nose and mouth, but they're stuck. I turn my head to the side to see what's pinning me down. I'm underneath something long and heavy, and I can't push it off me.

A bed.

I panic. I struggle to free my arms so I can attempt to block some of the smoke from my face because I can feel my lungs starting to ache from the strain.

The more I struggle, the harder it becomes to breathe. My body isn't responding to the commands I'm trying to give it to get us out of this. My heart beats fast from the lack of oxygen and the claustrophobia setting in. I can't even scream for help because I'm choking on the smoke that has now completely filled the room. I can't see the fire, but I can feel the heat on my skin.

The room spins, and my vision begins to go in and out. I don't know if it's the smoke and heat that's burning my eyes, the lack of air in my lungs that's making my vision blotchy, or the fact that any attempt to escape is useless that's causing tears to stream down my face. It could be all of it.

This is it.

This is the end.

This is where my life ends. Suddenly, my tears stop when I come to the truth within myself—the truth that I'm not going to make it out of this room alive. I close my eyes and hold my breath until I pass out.

The world sways, and cool air brushes across on my face. Strong arms are wrapped around my back and under my legs. I'm being carried. I think I hear something, but I can't make out what it is.

A voice.

I try opening my eyes, but they won't. We come to a stop, and I feel something cool underneath me.

"Kairi."

Someone says my name, but I don't recognize the voice. It's a deep and smooth masculine voice. I try to force words out of my mouth, but all that comes out is as a heavy cough—the last of the smoke in my lungs forcing its way out.

A hand touches my face and strokes my cheek tenderly. I open my eyes and see a field of the greenest grass I've ever seen. Glancing around for a moment, I take in the scenery. The smell of burnt wood and smoke is still in the air, so I know we can't be too far from the house. We're in a small open area with wildflowers scattered around the ground and tall trees that make the place feel open but still hidden from view. It's beautiful. Finally, I bring my eyes to the man whose arms I'm still cradled in.

All I see are deep dark concerned eyes looking back at me. Pools of darkness.

Gasping, I shoot up, looking around frantically, out of breath with sweat coating my skin. I push the hair that's stuck to my forehead away from my face with one hand, clenching my shirt where my heart is trying to beat out of my chest with the other. My fingers move to touch my cheek that is still tingling with the sensation from a dream that felt too much like a memory.

Those eyes . . . They looked just like . . .

Nope.

Not even going to go there.

Pushing the thought out of my mind, I try to force myself back to sleep. I lie in my bed staring at nothing in particular, trying to control my breathing and thoughts. I can't shake the image of those eyes or the fact that they instantly made me think of Jaxon.

Even though I know it was only a dream, it felt so real. I was dreaming that Jaxon saved me from the fire. The dream had a more satisfying ending than the memory I have of what really happened—a firefighter rushing me to the ambulance on a gurney, then being rushed to the hospital. I don't understand why when Jaxon saved me in my dream, it felt more real than the truth. Of course, when anything involves Jaxon, I'm left unsure and second-guessing myself.

Since the second I set my eyes on Jaxon Benievere, I've been at war with myself—in more ways than I care to admit even to myself alone in the dark safety of my bedroom. If I keep letting my thoughts revolve around Jaxon, I'll be up all night trying to control my heart rate among other things. I pop my headphones in my ears and let the music take me to another place, and slowly but surely, I drift off to sleep.

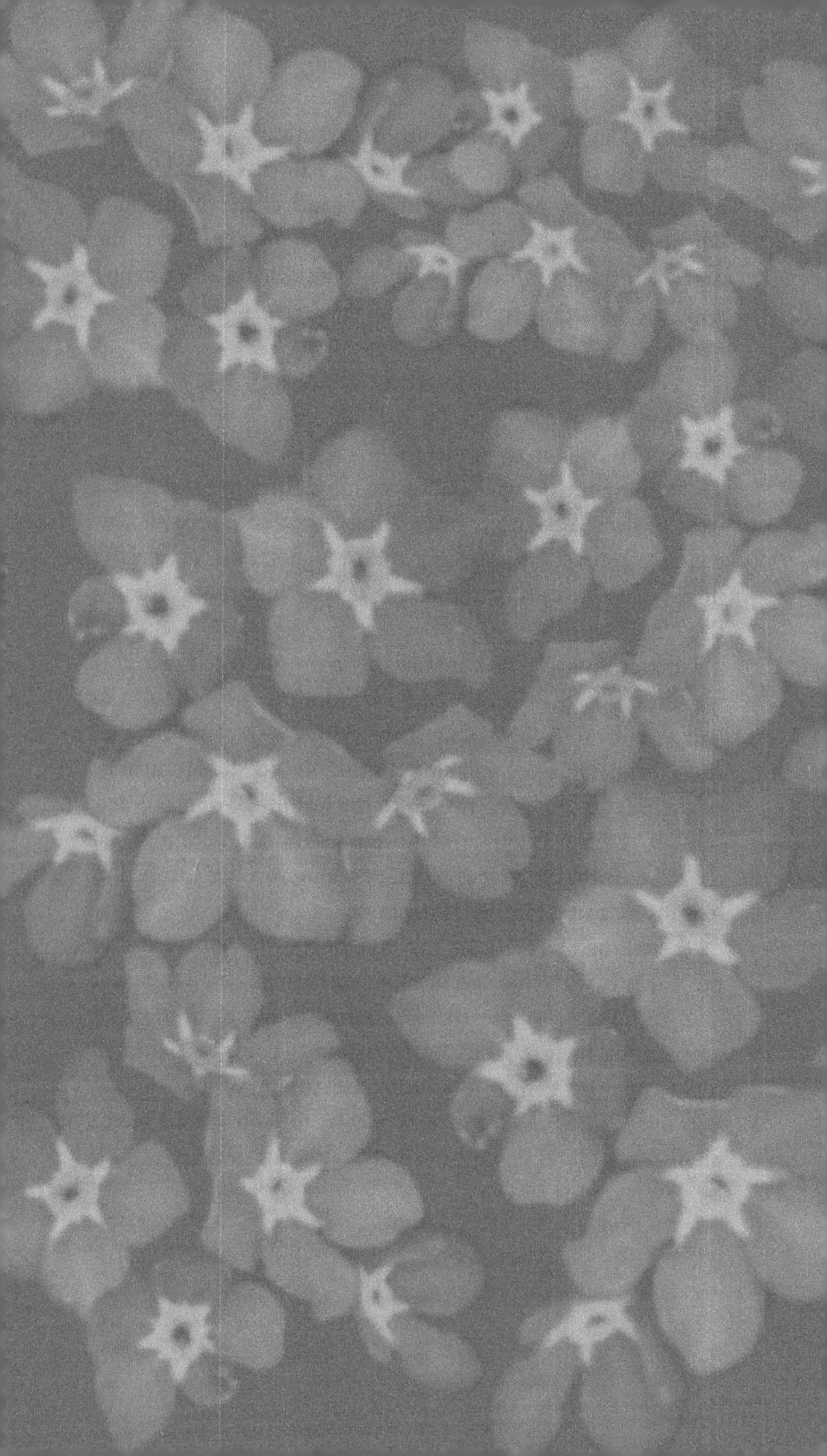

SIX

THE REST of the week is . . . strange. Chelsea and Travis's little group of friends treats me like I've always been here. Chelsea is still as pushy as ever, and Travis follows me around like a shadow, popping up out of nowhere. I'm not sure how I feel about it all just yet. I think I've been thinking too hard, because I've had more headaches this week than I ever remember having in my life. I guess it could be worse than people wanting to be around me, but I still can't shake the uncomfortable feeling I get from them.

Jaxon is a completely different story. His eyes always hold more meaning than I could ever dream to understand. It's times like that when I wish his mind wasn't behind a locked door.

Jaxon is a subject I try to keep from my mind entirely. He makes me feel so many conflicting emotions at once. He gives me butterflies when he looks at me with those haunting eyes. My skin surges like there's electricity in my veins when his fingers barely brush my skin. He always seems to be searching for something inside of me. It makes me feel like I'm under a microscope. The way he talks to me is like an interrogation, which puts me on edge and makes me suspicious. But it feels so familiar to talk to him and be near him, almost to the point to where I feel like we've met. He pulls me in every direction possible, and I always feel like I'm facing the wrong way.

Chelsea and Travis also never leave my side and always seem to be fishing for information by asking questions about my life. I understand they want to get to know me, but this is on another level.

"Where exactly did you say you lived?" Chelsea asks, then takes a bite of her salad.

"I didn't—just that I'm from the coast."

"What's that by?"

"It's right on the Gulf of Mexico."

"So you spent a lot of time on the beach?" Travis chimes in.

"Almost every day if it wasn't rainin', yeah." Thinking of the beach makes me homesick.

"That's why you're so tan, I'd bet," Chelsea says.

Always the perceptive one.

"That'd be a safe bet," is all I say, smiling when I think of Jaxon using a similar statement. Then I try not to grimace as pressure starts to build in my head.

"What's it like living on the coast?" Travis asks.

"Well, it's hot and humid."

"Sounds miserable," Chelsea says more to herself than me.

"Not really," I whisper.

"It sounds like a cool place." Travis rests his hand on my shoulder, giving it a slight squeeze, which I'm sure he means to be comforting.

"It was."

Travis is trying to be sympathetic, but I'm torn between wanting to cry from his support and cringing away from his attempt at intimacy.

"Wait! Don't hurricanes come through that area?" Chelsea asks, making my head pound harder.

"Sometimes." I try to act nonchalant and attempt to relieve some of the pressure by massaging my temples.

"You alright?" Travis frowns with concern before shifting his eyes to Chelsea.

I look between them for a moment before forcing what I hope is a reassuring smile onto my face. "I'm fine. Nothing I can't handle."

I hear a snort, but I'm already collecting my things to head to my next class.

Since Chelsea and Travis have been around, I've barely gotten a chance to talk to Jaxon. We have had occasional small talk here or there, but it's never enough. I'm not sure if I'm more disappointed or relieved.

I tune everything out around me because I'm ready for the weekend. When I get to Government, Jaxon isn't there first like he has been every other day. My face drops before I recover my indifference. I hate to admit it, but I look forward to seeing Jaxon every day.

I sit down and doodle on a blank sheet of paper. I wonder why he has such an effect on me.

Being so deep in my own thoughts, I jump when I hear, "Wow, what's this?"

Jaxon gestures toward my elaborate sketch of randomness.

I shake my head, because I honestly don't know. Actually, it kind of looks like a pair of searching eyes—if you tilt your head to the side and close one eye while squinting the other.

Jaxon chuckles, but his eyes grow serious. "Will you ever be able to talk to me?"

"Maybe if I talked to you more." I keep my eyes glued to my page out of embarrassment. Mostly.

"Well, sometimes it's hard to tear you away from your friends."

So he had noticed that they're smothering me too.

"Speaking of . . ."

"Hey, Kairi," Travis says as he perches himself on the corner of the table I share with Jaxon.

"Oh, hi, Travis."

Travis has a huge smile on his face, seemingly because his presence doesn't appear to sit well with Jaxon.

I go back to sketching those two intense eyes while Travis hovers over my seat and rambles on about what his plans are for the weekend. I only hum every now and then in response, but it doesn't deter him from carrying on anyway.

When the class is dismissed and I finally escape Travis, Jaxon is already gone.

At the end of the day, I make it to my truck to find a note on my window held down by my windshield wiper.

Kairi,
This week didn't nearly give us enough time to talk, but I have a good feeling next week will be different.
–Jax

My heartbeat and breath turn erratic. This weekend is going to be filled with unneeded anxiety now as I wait for Monday.

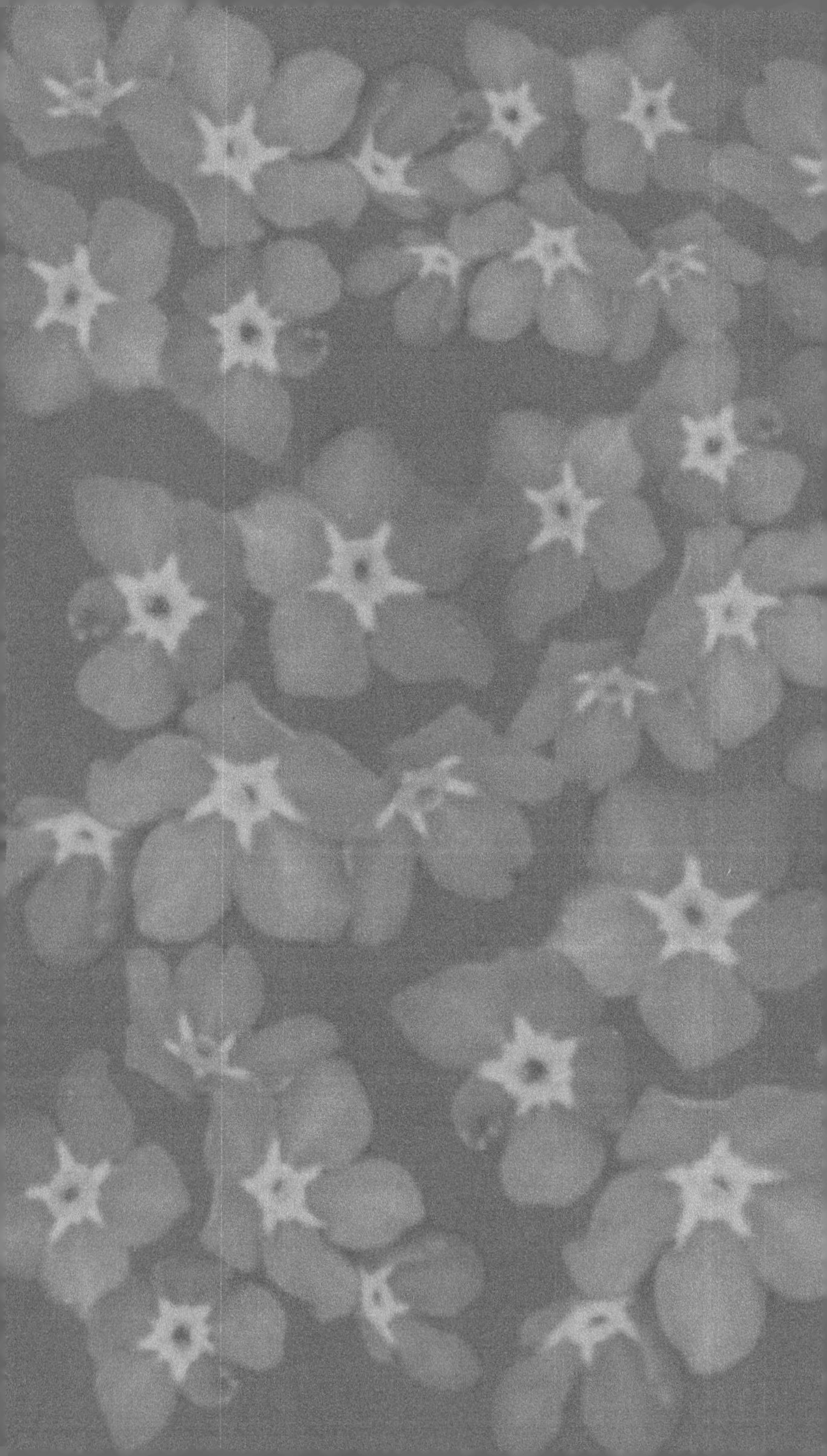

SEVEN

OVER THE WEEKEND, I decided to run off all this added tension that's in my life lately.

Saturday morning, I lace up my running shoes and braid my hair down the back of my neck. It's six thirty in the morning, so Dad and Sid are still asleep. I slip out the back door and decide to run more trail than asphalt. This town—*my town*—has a forest on the edge of the city limits, right behind my house.

I spend five minutes in my backyard stretching my muscles before taking off. I run through the trees, hesitant at first, slowly weaving through them, then more confidently. It's an amazing feeling to let myself go like this.

The wilderness is mostly silent except for the rustling of animals here and there, but I don't stop. There are no thoughts crowding my head out here. Nobody is watching my every move. I feel freer than I've felt in a long time, and I can't help but laugh a little as I run.

I push myself faster, becoming more sure-footed as I go. I've run a lot before, but now that I'm in the woods, I feel faster than ever. I take a sharp turn to the left and hurdle over a fallen tree in my path.

I don't see the drop-off, so I don't have time to scream, as I'm already tumbling down the hill. Small sticks and rocks scrape my skin as I continue to roll, unable to stop myself until my head collides with something hard and everything goes black.

I come to blinking my eyes to see light shining through the trees right across my face. I'm lying on my back, and my head's pounding. I reach up to feel my head where the pain is coming from. The last thing I remember is my face becoming best friends with the dirt. I try to sit up but can't. My body isn't responding, like it's paralyzed.

I'm struggling to stay calm and get up at the same time when I hear voices coming my way.

"She's over here!" A guy's voice rings out, sounding familiar, but I'm too disoriented to place it.

"What happened?" a man with a deeper voice asks.

"She rolled down the hill and then headfirst into a boulder." The guy with the familiar voice sounds upset.

A boulder? Are they talking about me? That would explain my headache.

"She would be a clumsy ass and do that," the other one says with a chuckle. "Well, did Drew heal her?"

"Yes."

"Then why are you bringing me here?"

"Because I can't help her. You know that." Someone sounds annoyed now. There's a pause. His voice softens, defeated. "Just do what I ask, please."

They're really close now. I can hear them perfectly—their voices, anyway. But I can't hear . . .

"You know I'll do anything you ask me after all you've done for us." The one with the deep voice is extremely close.

I hear a pair of footsteps fading away and another coming closer much more quickly than before. I look around for the person coming for me. It's obvious they are talking about me, and I'm getting a bad vibe.

I don't trust them.

They know what happened to me, and they're planning to do something. I struggle harder to move, praying to whatever higher power there is that I can get out of this in one piece. It's getting harder to breathe as my heart beats frantically in my anxious state. Then everything goes black *again*.

————

I wake up to my world swaying. I'm being bounced around when my eyes open. I look around and find myself looking up into wide dark green eyes.

I panic.

"Calm down! I found you in the woods. I'm just bringing you to your house." The man carrying me tries to hold my squirming body still without dropping me.

"How do you know where I live? Let me down!" I struggle harder to get out of his strong grip, but my body isn't responding as I'd like right now. He said I was in the woods, but I don't even remember getting out of bed this morning.

"Your Dad was calling when I spotted you, so I told him that I found you passed out in the woods, and he told me where to go." His voice sounds strained, probably from having to carry all my weight and fight with me.

As he says this, we come into view of my backyard. Dad's on the back porch peering our way with a hard look.

"Why were you in the woods so close to my house?" I ask.

"I don't see why that's any of your business," the man replies with a smirk.

"Kairi, are you okay?" Dad asks when we're less than ten feet from him, never once leaving his spot leaning near the back door.

"I'm fine," I say quietly, looking away from him.

"She seems fine, sir. Not a scratch on her." The man sets me down on my feet. "She lucky."

"Thank you so much." Dad's voice is anything but appreciative.

"Not a problem, but I'd stay out of the woods if I were you," he says, looking directly at me now.

I look back into his bright eyes and search for the truth. Something isn't right. It's hard to read him with Dad's scolding gaze locked on me.

I narrow my eyes as we look at each other before he turns to leave. There's nothing there. No thoughts running through his mind. I hear absolutely nothing.

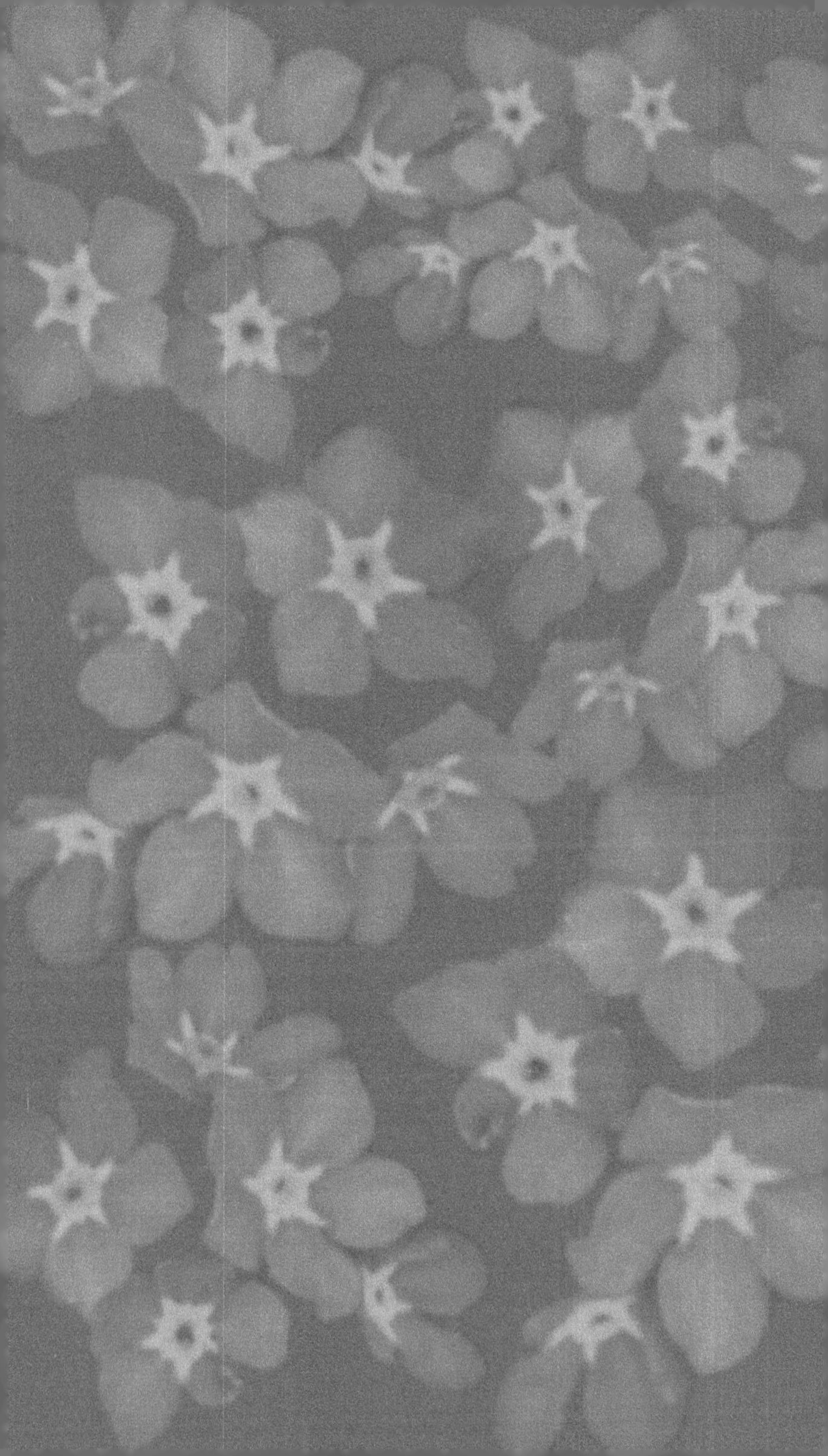

EIGHT

WHEN THE WEEKEND ends and I put most of my suspicion of that stoical face with the piercing green eyes aside, Monday is finally here. No one should be this excited to go to school. It's pretty pathetic, actually, because I know I shouldn't be. I finish my morning routine and wake Sidney up. We walk downstairs together and see that Dad's already left without any warning.

"Hey, Sidney, I need you to get dressed. You can eat on the way, okay? I have to take you to school."

She nods and heads back upstairs, still half-asleep.

"And try to hurry, please!"

In the truck, I ask her what time her school lets out, and she holds up three fingers. I nod. I'll have to hurry and get home so she won't be alone for long after she rides the bus today. I can almost guarantee Dad won't be home that early.

When I eventually get to campus, the parking lot is full. I grab my things and have to run to class. I get there just before the professor.

Chelsea passes me a note asking about Jaxon. I turn to her and shrug my shoulders. I can tell by the determination in her eyes that she is far from letting this go. Like many times before, her persistence grates on my nerves.

After class has officially started, Chelsea scoots her desk closer for partner work on the novel we're studying. When she's in place, she prompts, "Well?"

"Well what?" I feign confusion.

"You and Jaxon."

"I don't know what you mean." I tilt my head innocently.

"Oh, come on, Kairi."

"What?"

She scowls and points a finger at me. "What's going on between you two?"

"I really have no idea what you're talkin' about."

Chelsea rubs me the wrong way. Her constant need to be in my business is something I can tolerate for only so long before it pulls a reaction out of me. She has been crossing the line of friendly banter and curious questions to get to know me. I don't know what her goal is by acting as an interrogator, but all she's doing is making my walls higher.

"You two talk all the time," she says.

"So I can't have friends?"

An uncomfortable pulse of pain starts in my temple. I already took migraine medicine today hoping to prevent this, but the signs are there. It's going to be a long day.

"You know that's not what I meant. He's around all the time."

"He's in all of my classes on one of my days. I don't really think that qualifies as 'all the time.'"

She raises an eyebrow at me, keeping the scowl on her face.

"And I don't see him unless it's in those classes, and it's not like I can avoid him there." I say the last part more to myself.

"It's obvious he likes you." She keeps pressing, but there's a little bit more irritation in her tone now than before. Maybe she has a crush on him and wants his attention. I'm not sure; her mind is always either blocked off from me for some reason or too jumbled and blurry for me to understand her intentions.

"I guess it could seem that way from the outside."

"Outside, inside, and all around." She covers her mouth and lets out a giggle that sounds a bit forced. "You know it's true."

"I don't know anything anymore. Bein' here makes everything make no sense," I whisper.

She shakes her head but lets it drop for now.

The next couple of hours go by in a blur. I get to the cafeteria and sit at the end of the table. Travis tells me about something dangerous he did this weekend. I'm only half listening when I feel someone touch my back. I don't have to hear her thoughts or see Chelsea's reaction to know who it is. Feeling the electric current surge through me is enough. I look up at him in fabricated surprise anyway.

Jaxon smiles. "Do you mind if I sit with you today?"

I open my mouth to respond, but Chelsea answers before I can.

"Of course!" she says with a smile that may split her cheeks and giggles obnoxiously when Jaxon smiles back at her. She's trying too hard, and it's tough to stomach.

Jaxon doesn't say anything for a while; he just looks at me.

"So . . ." I wait until his eyes focus to continue.

Well, I was going to anyway, but Chelsea beats me to it —again.

"Are you going to be sitting with us now?" She seems excited by the thought.

"No, I just came to ask Kairi a question." He turns from her to me and smiles.

"Oh." Chelsea pouts, which Jaxon doesn't seem to notice, or he ignores it.

I look at him, raise an eyebrow, and wait. When he doesn't say anything, I say, "Well, you've been sittin' here for ten minutes. What's your question?" I don't mean to sound rude, but my headache is coming in full force, and Jaxon being so close always makes me feel unlike myself, which puts me on edge.

He blinks twice. "Oh, right. Well, I was curious if you were going to the mixer with anyone." A fox smile surfaces on his face.

I hear three gasps, but none come from me.

"Uh, is there one comin' up?" I ask.

"Yes. I wanted to see if you were free and wanted to go with me." He waits for me to answer, but all I can do is stare at him. "It's this Saturday."

More than anything I want to say *HELL FREAKING YES*, but Saturday, the movers are coming, and I have to unload everything on my own because Dad will be working all day, of course.

"I'm sorry, but I can't," I finally say.

I look away from Jaxon's dark eyes and see everyone is staring.

Geez, can't anyone have any privacy around here?

I look down at the table, feeling suddenly self-conscious. Images of the girls closest to us dancing and doing other things with Jaxon trickle from their minds to mine. Things I really wish I didn't have to see ever in my life.

When my eyes focus back on him, he's still smiling, but his eyes have a little less spark than they did moments before. I'd be lying if I said I didn't get a little bit of joy out of making Jaxon feel like he isn't as irresistible as I'm sure he thinks he is. Knocking his ego down a few notches feels like a true accomplishment.

"Can I ask why?" he asks, and his tone is much softer than before.

I open my mouth to answer, but then I see the time and give him a sad smile before getting up to leave. "I'll see you tomorrow in class." I pull my bag over my shoulder and turn to the exit before he can respond, but I stop. I look over my shoulder to see he's standing to leave as well. "Bye, Jax."

The strong pull I feel toward Jaxon is strange and a little scary since I barely know the guy. I get a weird vibe from him, and the fact that I can never get a read on him is unsettling. Until I can figure out my own life and feelings, I should steer clear of adding Jaxon to the mix and confusing myself more.

I head home with a small smile etched on my face that doesn't leave even when I lie down and dream of two deep pools of darkness staring back at me.

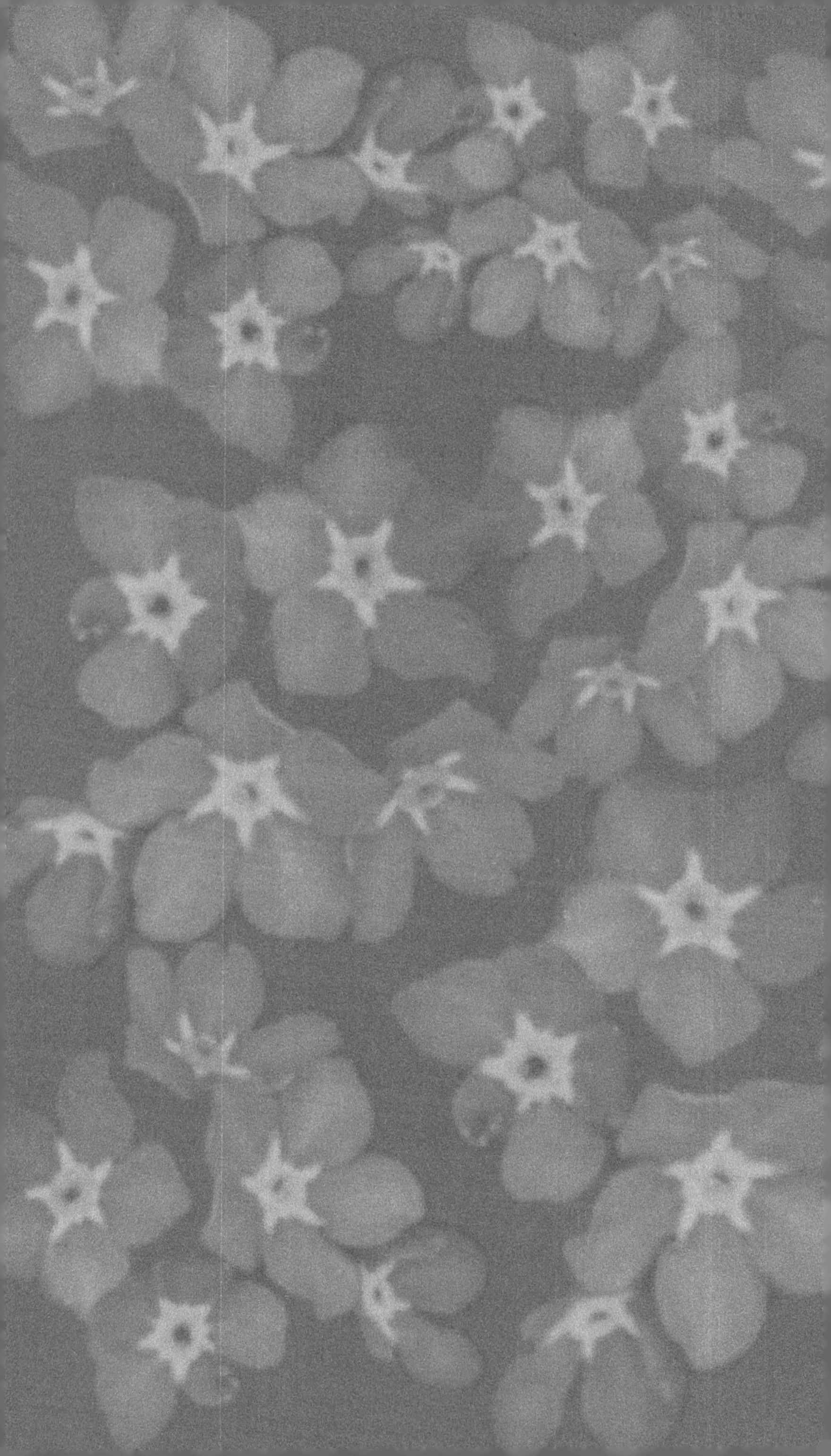

NINE

WHEN I WALK INTO GOVERNMENT, Jaxon is already in his seat beside mine, and he wastes no time asking about my refusal to go to this party with him.

"You don't take rejection well, do you?" I ask.

The deadpan look he gives is unamused but hilarious to me. I try to hide my mirth and decide to give him a break. "This weekend is when the movers are coming, so I have to be there to unload and watch my little sister."

Jaxon looks at me with an expression that seems to mean more than I'm willing to look into at the moment. "Will you need some help?"

I'm taken back. "Uh, possibly?"

"Then I'll be at your house around noon." He flashes his perfect teeth, probably at whatever look is now stuck on my face.

He doesn't give me a chance to comment, protest, or anything. The professor calls on me a million times during class, and as soon as class is dismissed, he vanishes before I can catch him.

I can't concentrate until I walk into my next class. I see Jaxon in his seat—waiting for me?

No, of course not. That's his seat.

I shake my head and sit down. I'm about to write down the assignment for the day when Allison comes and sits on my desk facing Jaxon. I look at her with disgust and barely concealed rage as her fat ass is quite literally in my face. My expression must seem funny to Jaxon, because he's trying really hard not to smile.

"So I hear you're still dateless for the mixer." She waits until he nods. "I came to offer to go with you."

I stifle a laugh, and she glares at me briefly. Jaxon smiles while she isn't looking but composes his face by the time she turns back to him.

"Actually, I have plans." He gives me a quick look and then focuses back on Allison.

"Oh? What are you going to do instead?" I can hear the annoyance in her tone now, and I have to choke down another laugh trying to escape me. You can tell she doesn't get turned down often; her mind is in an uproar.

"I'll be at a friend's house helping them out."

"Oh well. Next time, then," Allison says, already planning her next victim.

"Maybe," Jaxon says, immediately turning his eyes to me.

When Allison gets up, she knocks everything on my desk off onto the floor. I stare after her for a moment before turning to pick up my things, but Jaxon has already done it.

"How do you move so fast?" I ask.

"You were looking over there." He points to the front of the room. "So how could you have seen if I was moving fast or not?"

Point taken.

"Why didn't you tell her you were gonna be with me Saturday?" I ask.

Still looking into my eyes—or more like straight into my soul—he smiles like he always does. "She doesn't need to know everything I'm up to, does she? We don't need her getting jealous."

All I can do is laugh.

"What?" he asks.

"Why would anyone be jealous of me?" Shaking my head, I look toward the front of the class.

"How could they not? You're a very beautiful and confident girl. I'm even a little jealous." His smile widens, and I'm sure he's teasing me now.

"Allison doesn't strike me as the jealous type," I say.

"I guess it's just because I have eyes for someone other than her." His smile gets even bigger, if that's possible. It makes my heart race, and I hope my face isn't too red.

"Oh, really?" I keep my eyes ahead of me and away from him.

He reaches over and puts his hand on top of mine. I look up.

"Yeah," he says with a perfect country accent, teasing me again. I pout, looking away, but he continues, "Kairi."

Jaxon puts his finger under my chin to turn my face to him, only seriousness in his tone now. I notice how he touches me when he can get away with it, and I can't say I don't enjoy it.

When I finally meet his eyes, he says, "I only have eyes for you." His big smile fades to a softer, sweeter version.

"Why?" I breathe out when I see the look on his face. "You barely know me."

His touch makes me feel strange yet passionate things for him. They feel foreign but so familiar at the same time. His eyes that have haunted my mind for days seem like a memory.

His expression grows fond. "But I feel like I've known you my entire life, and even though I'm sure you don't agree"—

which I don't—"it doesn't change the fact that I'm drawn to you."

My heart races, a swarm of butterflies in my stomach, and I want to say that I feel the same, but I stay silent. I can't find my voice, so I smile shyly, and he lets my chin fall.

"You know that you don't make any sense, right?" I ask, still in a daze.

Now it's his turn to smile and avert his eyes back to the paper in front of him.

To be honest, Jaxon scares me sometimes. He makes me feel like he's several steps ahead of me and knows more than he's letting on. I can't shake the feeling that he's keeping something from me. He's being too friendly to have only known me for a couple weeks. I've searched my memory over and over, but his face isn't one I would've forgotten.

It's also Jaxon's imperfections that make him so attractive —the little hook in his nose that looks like he broke it a long time ago and never had it set properly, the faint scars on his face that suggest he's been in his fair share of fights. I'm sure there are more hidden under his clothes.

Not that I'm thinking of him without his clothes on . . .

Jaxon just looks . . . dangerous, like playing with fire. It's always fun to play around with until you get burned, and trust me, I learned that lesson firsthand.

Whatever direction this is going is a direction I want to go in. The logical side of my brain is telling me something isn't right, that he's coming on a little too strong, but I want to figure this out. I want to figure him out.

For the rest of class, I can't focus on anything with Jaxon's words racing through my mind, along with the thoughts of everyone else who had apparently been eavesdropping on us. When the day is done, I head straight to my car and pull out my phone to see I have a missed call and voicemail.

"Ms. Rush, I was unable to get a hold of your father to

pick Sidney up from school today. She's missed the bus, and you're the only other person listed as a contact. We'll be waiting for you in the front office. Thank you."

As I jump in and rev the engine, something moves outside my window, and I choke down a scream when I see Jaxon standing there, motioning for me to roll down my window.

"What's the rush?" He seems amused by my panic.

"Look, I'm sorry, but I can't talk right now. I gotta go." I move to put the truck in reverse and head toward Sid's school.

"Something wrong?" His brows push together.

"No, I just have to go pick up my sister from school."

"Do you want some company?"

His answer catches me off guard.

"I-I don't—"

"If you're too scared to be alone with me, I understand." A lopsided grin creeps onto his face.

This time, I can't deny—even to myself—that I want to be near him and maybe learn some of his secrets. "Hurry up and jump in," I finally say.

Jaxon flashes me a full smile now. He goes around, gets in, and we speed away.

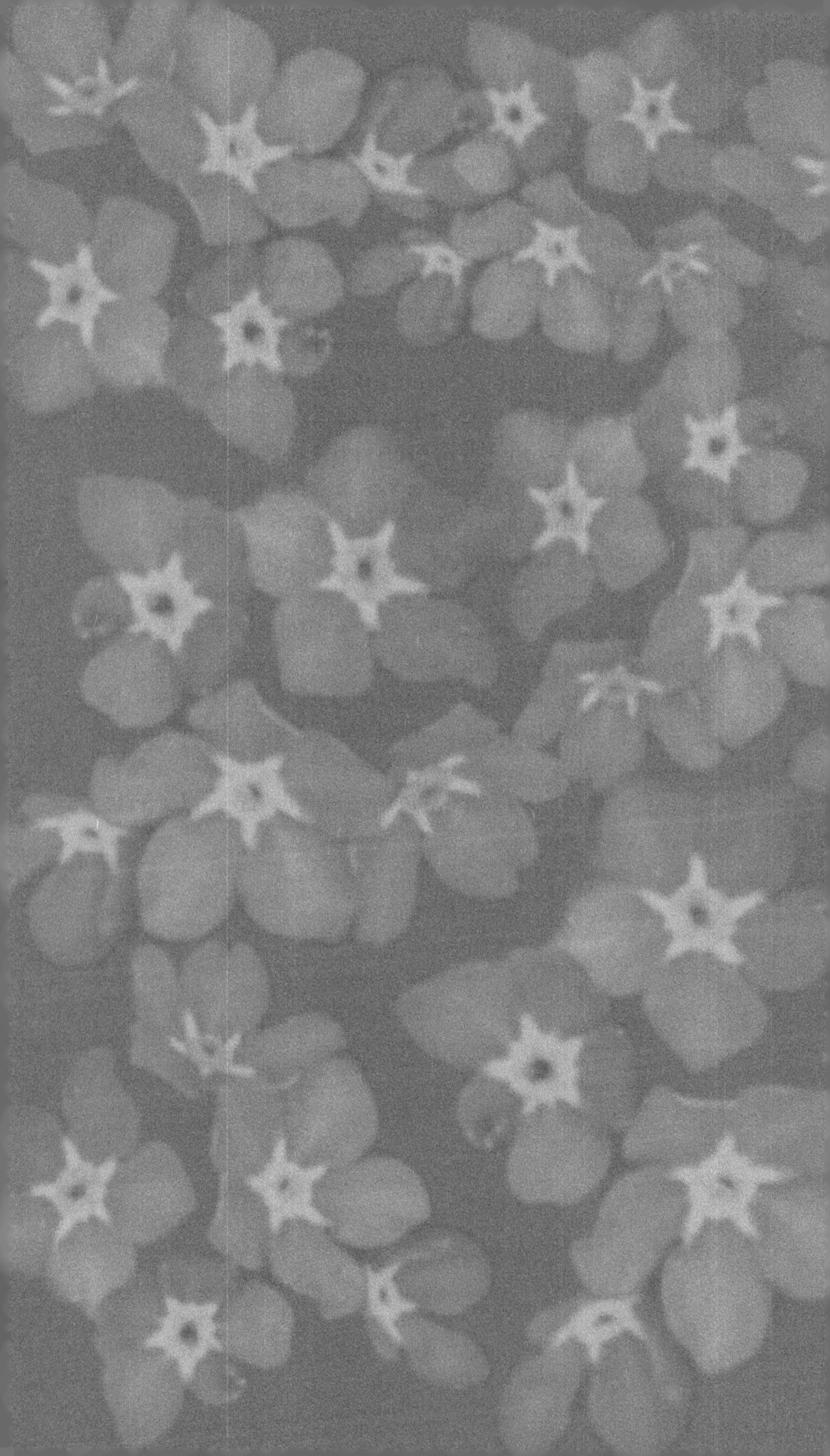

TEN

WHEN JAXON and I get to Sidney's school, I bolt for the door to sign her out.

"Sorry I'm late. I didn't know you were gonna need a ride." I look down at her with a sad smile.

Sidney pouts. "I couldn't find Brownie, so I missed the bus."

Brownie is Sidney's favorite stuffed horse that she carries around with her everywhere. I've hardly ever seen her without it.

"Who's that?" Sid's voice pulls me from my thoughts, and I look to the passenger seat of my truck as we make our way over.

"A friend," I say, not wanting to meet her eyes.

She smirks, not believing me, but there's nothing I can do about that. The kid is more perceptive than almost anyone I know.

No one talks on the ride to the house. As I pull up, I break the silence, telling Sidney to go ahead inside. She nods and goes without another word. I wait to make sure she makes it in, then I look to Jaxon. "Where to—"

He cuts me off with a shake of his head. "My brother will get me when he gets off work."

"Oh, okay." I turn off the ignition and head for the door. I'm halfway there before I realize Jaxon hasn't moved yet. "Uh, you comin'?"

"Don't you know I'd follow you anywhere?"

Rolling my eyes, I give him my back, which only makes him chuckle as we go inside. After making sure Sid has everything she needs, I go up to my room with Jaxon following behind. He sits on my bed and watches as I put all my things away. When I'm finished, I sit on the only other furniture in my room—a rocking chair—and look at him.

"You weren't kidding." Jaxon takes one more look around the room. "I thought you just didn't want to go with me."

The absence of furniture reassures him, I guess. I see now why he wanted to come along with me to get Sidney and see my house—to see if I was lying. I'm sure he gets turned down about as much as Allison does. He probably feels better now that his ego is no longer wounded by a nobody turning him down.

"I didn't wanna go anyway," I say. "I can't dance, and I embarrass myself enough without that humiliation tacked on."

Jaxon looks at me with clear amusement on his face. "I doubt that. It's all in the leading." His smile grows. "I could show you."

"That's okay," I reply quickly.

"Kai . . ." I turn to see Sidney at my door. "Can you make me some popcorn?" Her eyes dart between me and Jaxon suspiciously.

"Yeah, I'll be there in a sec." She leaves, and I look back at Jaxon with a sigh, then head back downstairs. Jaxon follows me down, and his eyes follow me without a word. I pour the popcorn in a bowl before taking it to Sid.

I turn to leave. "Uh, Kairi?" I face her, and she whispers, "Are you datin' that boy in there?" She points toward the kitchen.

Most of the time, I like that Sidney understands the things my parents can't, but right now, I wish she was clueless. I glance in the direction of the kitchen. Jaxon's smiling face lets me know he overheard her, much to my embarrassment.

"No, we're not datin'."

I walk past him to the refrigerator, then pour myself some orange juice and call over to Sidney: "If you need me, I'll be in my room!"

When we get back to my room, Jaxon sits in the rocking chair and gazes at me, never looking away.

"What?" I ask after minutes tick by.

Jaxon doesn't answer right away, then finally says, "It's nothing." I don't believe him, and I can tell he knows it. He smiles. "I was thinking about what your sister said." My heart starts to beat faster than I ever thought possible. "And I was wondering . . ."

I realize I'm holding my breath when I get slightly light-headed

". . . if you would go somewhere with me?"

It takes me a few moments before I can respond. "Where is this exactly?"

"Just a place I like to go, and I think you'll like it too."

"I don't know." I haven't decided how I feel about Jaxon. I'm attracted to him, sure, but what girl wouldn't be? He's so closed off though, and I don't know what to think about him more than half the time.

"Are you scared to be alone with me?" he teases with questioning eyes.

"Obviously not. I'm here with you now, aren't I?" I gesture to the space between us. "When would we go and where? 'Just someplace I like to go' is not a good enough explanation."

"Sunday."

"And?"

He just smiles.

"I don't know. I told Sidney we could spend some alone time together this weekend." Turning away, I glue my eyes to my bedroom window and hope he can't hear the lie in my voice. I'm scared he has some ulterior motive, and not knowing has me on edge. He's not really giving me a lot to work with here.

Excuses, excuses.

"One day, I'll convince you to take a chance on me." Jaxon says this without a doubt.

The way he's looking at me right now spurs an uncontrollable urge to do whatever I can to close this distance between us—physically and mentally. I resist . . . barely.

He reaches into his pocket and pulls out his phone, looking at it briefly, then at me. "My brother's here. I'll see you tomorrow." He rises to his feet and heads toward the door.

I follow him down the steps to the front door. "Actually, you won't." I try to keep a blank face.

My words make him stop mid-stride. "Why?" I can tell that he thinks I'm joking, then he gets lost in his own thoughts when he actually registers my expression.

"Well, Sid and I are gonna take the day off. Skipping is . . . a relief, takes our minds off . . . things. Besides, my Mom's comin' to visit for the day," I say in a rush, defending myself for no reason. My face is still like stone. I don't really want to spend the day with my mother. She's the one who left us. Sidney is so excited though, and I don't want her to go on her own.

"Oh, well, then there's no need for me to be at school now," Jaxon whispers to himself, clearly thinking I can't hear him before meeting my eyes. "I will see you on Saturday, then."

"Wait, won't you be there for the rest of the week?"

"Like you said," Jaxon says, pausing at the door. "Skipping is a relief and healthy every now and then." With that, he takes my hand and kisses the knuckles, and then he's gone.

I walk to the window and see him get in a sleek black Dodge Challenger. I can't see his brother, and as soon as the car door closes, I'm staring at taillights as they speed away. Turning from the window, I clench my hand that Jaxon kissed into a fist and hold it close to me. I glance at Sidney as she watches TV, then walk back up to my room.

I walk through my door and stop. On top of my pillow is a small bunch of flowers—small stems with dainty little blue petals. I brush my fingertips across the delicate petals, and suddenly, a scene flashes before my eyes.

"Forget-me-not," he says. "They're the beautiful color of your eyes and a reminder that you'll never forget me."
He smiles and touches my cheek.
"I don't need a flower as a reminder." I laugh and lean into his hand. "I'll never forget you."
***It's our flower now**, he says in my thoughts.*
I love you, Jax.

I drop the flowers I hadn't even realized I picked up as though they shocked me and back away.

What the hell was that?

I touch my cheek where Jaxon just caressed it in that . . . whatever that was. My cheek is still warm and tingling with sensation. I don't know what happened. All I know is every time Jaxon comes around, I get dizzy, become unsure, and experience a whole lot of other emotions I don't even want to admit.

I can't deny that something just happened when I touched the forget-me-nots. It was like a dream—a sweet dream—but it felt so familiar, like a memory. The déjà vu that threads through me is staggering. In the depths of my mind, I can feel the truth in the scene I saw. That thought alone is unnerving, and when it comes to Jaxon, nothing seems to make sense. I'm always led to a dead end and left with more questions than answers.

I wonder if that was a fluke, a hallucination, or something else entirely. I kneel down, crossing my arms on the edge of my mattress, and rest my chin on top of my arms, looking at the flowers, debating on what I want to do next.

"Hey."

I choke down a scream as I spring to my feet and try to hold my heart inside my chest as I turn to the door. Dad stands casually in the doorway.

"Good Lord, Dad. You scared me."

"What are you doin'?" he asks me, letting one quizzical brow raise.

"Nothin'."

"What's that on your pillow?" His gaze snakes around me to my bed.

"Just some flowers."

"They're beautiful, Darlin'. Where'd you get them from?" he asks in a surprisingly fatherly tone, walking over to my bed and picking up the little flowers in his hands. He stares at them intently.

I eye him cautiously, but it seems to have no effect on him. Maybe it was a one time thing, or maybe I'm just in desperate need of Jaxon-free thinking time and a shit ton of sleep.

"They were sellin' flowers at school for a fundraiser, and these spoke to me, so I bought some."

I couldn't explain that they just appeared in my room after a guy he doesn't know was here—a guy who didn't have the flowers on him while he was here. That would sound insane. I'm not sure where Dad's sudden interest in anything to do with me is coming from, but I need to play this off as casually as possible.

"What kind of flowers are these?" He runs his fingers across them.

"Forget-me-nots," I say with a smile as I remember the scene that appeared in my head, then frown. *No smiling, Kairi.* I should be extremely freaked out by the fact that touching a damn flower made me hallucinate.

Dad doesn't say anything, but his eyes go cold before he turns and leaves the room without a word, flowers still in hand. I stare after him, not sure what made his demeanor change so abruptly. I learned a long time ago not to question him.

It isn't until I'm lying down later that night that I remember what Jaxon said before he left. He said, more or less, that he was going to skip school tomorrow, but not until after he found out that I wasn't going to be there.

My heart hammers with the only two possibilities that came to mind. Either Jaxon already had plans for tomorrow that he forgot about until I said I wasn't going to be there, or his planned absence has something to do with me. My paranoia kicks up a few notches with the nagging feeling that it's the latter.

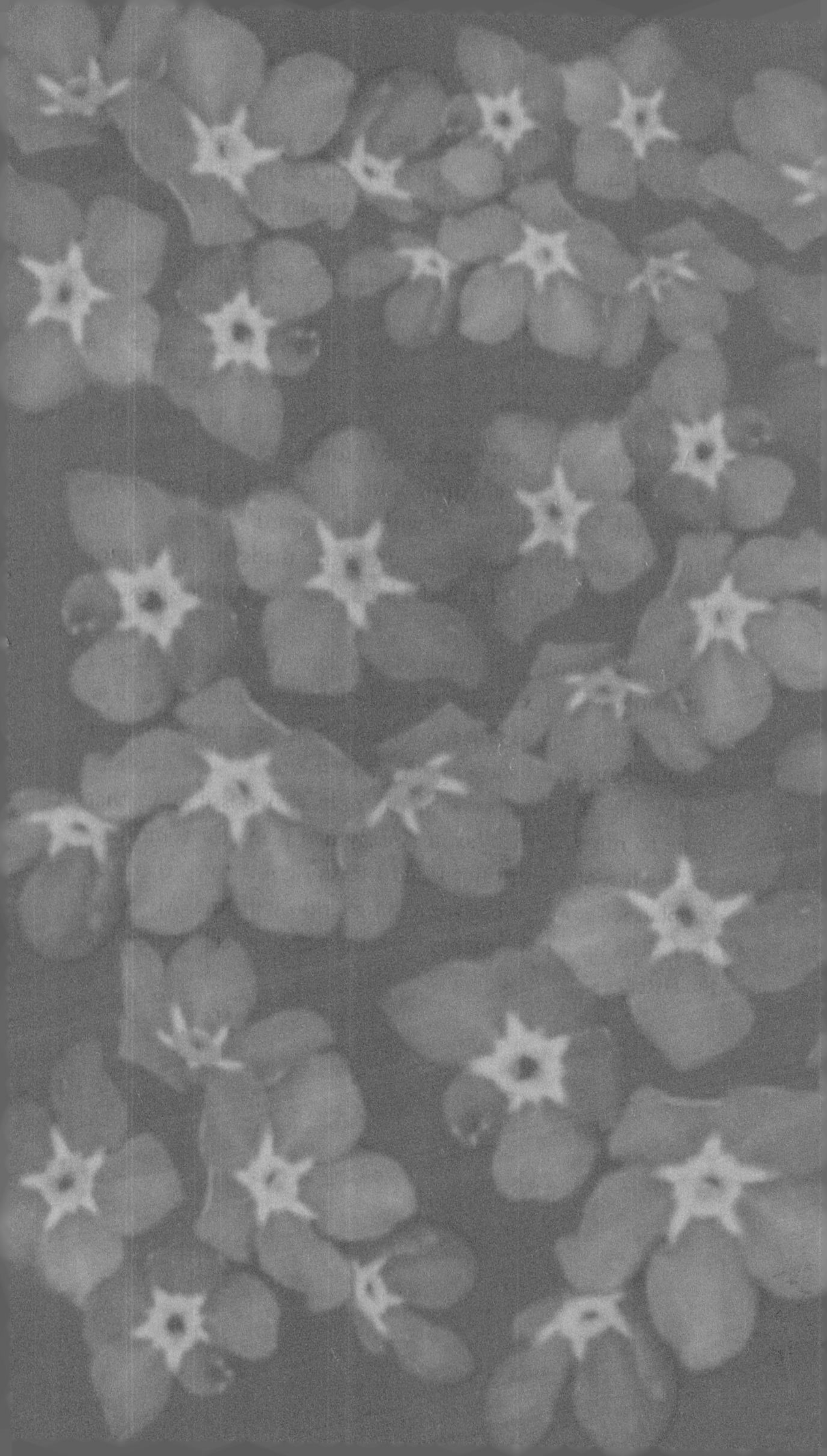

ELEVEN

THAT NIGHT, my dreams are pulled to Jaxon. They switch rapidly from one to another.

First, I dream of Jaxon holding my hands tenderly, sending shocks of electricity through my veins as he kisses the skin just below my ear, one of his strong hands on my waist holding my body close to his without any space to separate us.

Then I dream of Jaxon and I lying on a blanket in an open field of bright green grass with patches of beautiful wild-flowers across the plain around us. His arm winds around me while I lay my cheek on his chest. All I can see are his beautiful eyes staring into mine when I glance up at him.

Next comes more of a nightmare. I'm walking around town. My heart beats rapidly, and I walk past the same block over and over again. I try to speed up, but the world is moving in slow motion. I see Jaxon around every corner. His eyes have a sinister edge to them. His body language pulls me to him like a magnet without a choice, but his eyes are so empty and cold that all I want to do is run. I can sense the danger. I can't help but be torn between allure and panic.

I don't have a choice though. It's like another force is dragging me to him in slow motion against my will. His arms are outstretched like he's going to caress my cheek, but his hands move to my throat, and as soon as I feel the bruising pressure, the scene is gone.

I wake up in a cold sweat with wide eyes and a racing heart. I'm not sure how long I lie there before I drift off into a restless sleep until the sun shines in my window to pull me from my worries.

Mom's here to see me and Sidney for the day. I don't know where she's been, but she couldn't have been in Texas to come all the way to North Dakota for one day only. She must've moved somewhere closer to us. She's never made one attempt to see us though; she's made no attempt to contact us at all.

I can read in her thoughts that she's scared of something, but she keeps it well hidden. Something is apparently keeping her from us, but I don't care. If she really wanted to be a part of our lives, she would've been, no matter what. She's our mother, and we needed her. But I don't anymore. I don't care. I don't want someone who could so easily abandon me when I needed them the most.

We go around town shopping. She buys us some school clothes—clothes for a fresh start—like we do every year. I don't object to new clothes, especially since I'm not the one paying. Sidney's ecstatic, of course.

Shopping together is really me and Mom following Sidney around as she bounces happily from store to store. I can't help but smile at the energy she has today. There's a different spirit in her that hasn't been there since we moved here.

As Sid disappears into another dressing room carrying a mound of clothes, I stand awkwardly next to Mom.

"So . . ." she begins.

I sigh and direct my eyes to her. I know what's coming, but I act clueless, as if I'm not about to attempt small talk with her.

"How is school goin'? Are y'all adjusting to the change okay?" she finally asks, turning toward me fully.

"Yeah, it's fine," I mumble.

"Makin' any friends?"

"Yeah." I shift impatiently from foot to foot, wishing Sidney didn't have to try on every single thing in every single store.

"Kairi." My mother places her hand on my shoulder. I shrug her hand off but turn to face her. "Honey, please work with me here," she whispers. Her eyes are serious, but her tone is pleading.

"I don't know what you're talkin' about, Lacy." I shrug my shoulders, ignoring her hurt expression at my use of her first name.

I do know what she means. She feels guilty for making me feel abandoned, and she wants to make it up to me. I just don't see how she can. Maybe if she'd tell me the reason she left, I could try to understand. That's not going to happen though, and it's behind a wall I can't reach. It's something she wants to keep hidden so badly that she won't even let thoughts of it enter her mind. I stare at her with accusing eyes before turning away.

"I'm gonna go to look around." I walk away, not waiting for a response and disappearing into the outlet mall's crowd of shoppers.

When Mom is out of sight, I get a small twinge of guilt but only for a second before I drown it in anger. I don't know how long it will take me to forgive her without an explanation, if that day even comes.

I stroll through the outlet mall, in and out of stores, buying a shirt here and pants there. I walk aimlessly and don't really think about anything in particular. It's probably an hour before I notice something odd.

There are two to three people I can pick out that think differently than the rest of the crowd. These people think in similar patterns, and it throws me off. I can only describe them as being *highlighted*. They stand out in a specific way to me, just like the guy who *saved me* in the woods.

Thinking back to that day now that my mind isn't hazy from the fall I took, I know there's something familiar about the men in the woods. They talked as if they know me, but the man that carried me home is a stranger to me. There was a glint in his eyes that held humor and familiarity, but I can't say the same for myself. Someone healed me, but it wasn't one of the two men there. I still can't place the familiar voice of the two, but it makes me think of certain mysterious dark eyes that have been causing me more stress than peace lately. It couldn't have possibly been Jaxon though. If it was him there, why wouldn't he have taken me to my house himself?

These people around me now are all people that filtered their thoughts, just like the two from that day in the woods. Regular people can't control the thoughts that go through their head—not really. They have random thoughts floating around and decide on particular ones based on what's going on around them—which is why I usually have a constant headache when I try to sort it all out—but when they focus on specific thoughts, those come out louder and clearer, and the others disappear into the background, like they're physically speaking.

The thing about a couple of the people here is that they don't have all that background noise. They have one very specific train of thought or nothing at all, and then something I can only describe as a locked door.

I can't pinpoint where these people are either, just that they're here. I do a double take when I see a faintly familiar large man around my age. I lose sight of him but not before getting a glimpse at a pair of dark green eyes. He licks his lips before sticking his tongue out, taunting me, then disappears into the crowd. I want to chase after him and demand answers about what happened. I want to know who was with him in the woods, why they were near my house, why he helped me, and why the hell he just stuck his tongue out at me. *Asshole*.

But I don't have time to do any of that before Sidney and Mom find me.

"Hey, baby girl. Did you have fun?" From the doorway, Dad smiles down at Sidney, whose arms are full of the bags of things she got today.

"So much fun, Daddy! Look at all I got!" An enthusiastic Sidney jumps up and down before giving Mom a quick hug and thank you before rushing inside to go through all of her new things.

"Charles."

"Lacy."

I watch my parents as they eye each other silently before Dad shakes his head and heads inside without another word.

I turn to face Mom. She's looking down at her fidgeting fingers before she looks at me with a sad smile. "It was really good to see you girls. I hope I can see you both again soon."

With that, she turns to leave, and I stare after for a minute, not sure how I feel about seeing her car pull away from the curb and down the street out of view. I head inside, ready for some time alone. The stab of abandonment hits my heart even though I know she doesn't stay with us anymore.

This night is turning out to be the same as the last, with my mind swirling around Jaxon Benievere—the good and the bad. My thoughts always run right to Jaxon, usually when I least want them to.

I can't grasp why he leaves me questioning everything and with so many more questions than answers. It's like he knows exactly what he's doing. He knows how to make me squirm, and I feel like he enjoys it. I can tell that he's keeping things from me. And with his mysterious wall blocking his thoughts from me, it makes me that much more suspicious of him. He's hiding something.

Of course, it's not like I expect him to be open with me when I'm not being open with him. Why would I even want him to after such a short time? Or at all? I wish this ridiculous pull between us would go away for no other reason than my teetering sanity.

Then there were those people in town today. It's not until now that I'm away from it all and focus on my abilities rather than avoiding Mom that I can organize my thoughts. They seem like me and send off a different vibe than a *normal* person does. I decide to put Jaxon in this group. He's too closed off from my abilities, too perfectly controlled, and he sends shivers down my spine, which seems like reason enough regardless of the way he makes me feel. Chelsea and Travis have also been able to block some of their thoughts from me, so I add them to the group for that and their suspicious behavior since I got here.

Over the next few days, I try to look around me with more of an open mind. I see everything a little differently now that I know what to look for. Without Jaxon as a distraction, I can focus on the ones that stand out from the others—Chelsea, in particular. She puts on a good show, but she's like me; she has an ability. I'm blocked by a wall I can't break through when I try to read her, and I get a twist of pain in my head. This has never happened before, so she must know I'm onto her. Thinking back, all of my headaches at school always come on when Chelsea's around. I'm not sure if she's the cause or not, but that's the way it's starting to seem. She never hints at anything, so I don't either. We both act oblivious, but you know what they say about keeping enemies close. For now, I have to wait and see how this plays out.

Over these days, I make a list of the names and descriptions of people I notice. I try to make sense of it, but I can't put the pieces together. Once again, I'm at a dead end.

Jaxon, true to his word, misses the rest of the classes we have together. I still can't shake the feeling that he's missing classes because of me, and like everything else about him, it makes me even more cautious and suspicious. It doesn't help that he's going to be at my house tomorrow to help me move in. I kick myself for agreeing to let him into my house the first time and now agreeing to let him in again.

In Jaxon's absence, though, I have noticed a pair of green eyes in his dark ones' place. This linebacker of a man seems to pop up everywhere. He doesn't approach me and keeps his distance, and I do the same, but he always makes sure to make eye contact and make some sort of face at me like he did in town that day—sticking his tongue out, winking, smirking, crossing his eyes. But he never stays around long enough after class for me to confront him, which only furthers my irritation. From roll call, I discover his name is Bentley, and I've made it my mission to corner him one way or another to get some answers.

I think Jaxon being at my house tomorrow will be the perfect opportunity to dig a little deeper and fish out answers while I have him alone.

Answers that I don't know if I want to know or not.

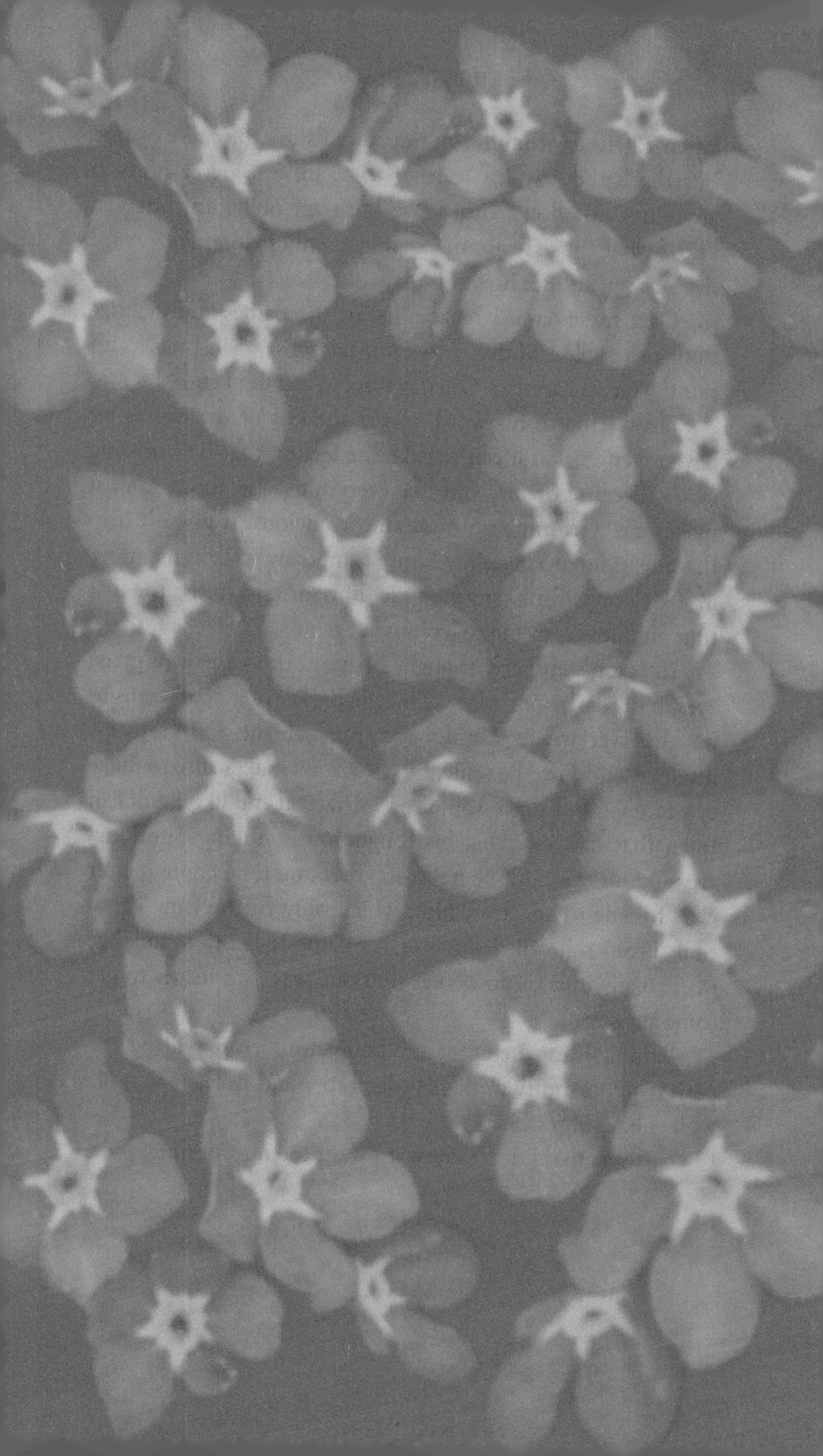

TWELVE

I WAKE up at ten and go downstairs to look out the window toward the driveway, and what little hope I had fades from my body. Dad said he had to work today, but I was hoping he'd show some mercy and not make me do all moving on my own. I pour myself some cereal and eat while waiting for either the movers or Jaxon to show up first. I shouldn't be surprised to see it's Jaxon, but I am.

"Why're you here so early?" I say, looking at him standing in the doorway.

Jaxon's dark denim jeans hang low on his hips, and his navy blue cotton T-shirt that clings to him in all the right places is sure to be a distraction I'll never admit to . . . ever.

"It's ten. How is that early?" He mirrors my look of confusion.

"You said you were comin' at noon"

"I didn't know what time the movers were going to get here, so I wanted to try to get here before they did." What he says makes perfect sense, but I don't like being taken by surprise, and with him, it seems to be a regular thing.

I nod and let him inside. He sits across from me and

watches as I eat my food but refuses when I offer some to him. It's beyond awkward. I'm sitting here stuffing my face with Lucky Charms, and he's just staring at me.

After I'm finished, we sit at the table and stare at each other some more before I can't take it anymore.

I huff. "Do you have to always stare at me?"

He doesn't respond right away with anything but the twitch of his lips as he tries to fight a smile. "You know," he finally says, "I'm rather disappointed you can't come with me tonight."

"And I'm rather baffled by that." I mimic his dated speech "How can you possibly be inclined to feel such a way?" As I lean back in my chair, he leans forward in his.

"I already told you I'm drawn to you."

"For reasons that we've yet to discover," I say, not quite done with my sarcasm yet.

His smiles drops slightly. "I really do feel like I've known you for a long time."

"But you haven't." I point a finger at him, seeing if he'll reveal any of the secrets I know he has that include me. He has to have some. There's no other explanation.

"I want to get to know you," is all he says, and the way he says it makes me want to add the word *again* at the end.

I don't respond, and he sits there thinking hard about something before he decides to speak again. "Tomorrow, I'm going to throw a party, and I'd like you to come."

"Uh . . ."

"You know, you say that a lot." He gives me a half smile, revealing a dimple in his left cheek.

I tilt my head. "Say what?"

"*Uhhh* . . ." He holds out the word for emphasis, and at first I'm confused, then I realize he's making fun of me.

I scowl.

"But seriously, it wouldn't be the same without you." He

bats his long eyelashes and flashes a seemingly innocent smile that doesn't fool me. I'm not sure if he's taunting me or if he's still poking fun at my expense.

"How many people could possibly come on such short notice?" I ask, trying to find an excuse not to go.

"Well, no one has ever been to my house, so they will all be there to see the mysterious Benievere home. Being somewhat popular and having never thrown a party before, I'm sure it'll bring a crowd."

Cocky ass.

He pulls out his phone, presses a series of buttons, then puts it away again. "Done. Now everyone's been invited."

I roll my eyes. "You do *not* have the number for everyone on campus."

He's smug when he hands his phone to me. I look through his phone and pause. My eyebrows pull together. There has to be at least five hundred different names and numbers in here. I shake my head. His arrogant side is showing, and I don't particularly like it.

As I push his phone back to him across the tabletop, he asks, "So, now that you're convinced I did actually invite everyone—"

"Why do you have everyone's number, anyway?"

He smiles. "For times like this."

I scoff.

He asks again, "So will you come?"

"I don't know." I look away.

Grabbing my left hand in both of his, he gently strokes my fingers. "Would you please come tomorrow?" He's speaking to our hands, but my mind still can't pull itself together. It's a good thing he isn't looking me in the eyes right now, because I don't know what I'd do if he did.

I keep my eyes away from him as I answer. "I'll have to see. I don't know if I'll have to watch Sidney or not."

"Mm-hmm," he hums deeply, and that's the end of our conversation.

The movers show up about forty-five minutes later. It's mostly a painless process, until I drop a box of Dad's books on my foot. If me jumping around on one foot for five minutes isn't enough embarrassment for one day, Jaxon collapsing on the ground, rolling with laughter definitely is. We'd just gotten everything moved in except for that damn box of books, so I carry them inside and lock him out to enjoy his amusement on his own while my foot throbs.

Two minutes later, I hear the doorknob rattle as he tries to turn the locked handle. I smile to myself and look through the peephole at him, but no one's there. I feel a pinch of guilt and open the door. I didn't want him to leave; I was just angry, more at myself for setting myself up to be the punch line of another joke.

I step onto the porch and look out in the yard, but he's gone. Out of nowhere, I'm grabbed from behind and swept up into strong arms and taken into the living room. I squeal as he throws me onto the couch and attacks me with his fingers, tickling me relentlessly.

"Trying to run me off?" he taunts above me.

Gasping for air, I struggle to respond. "S-Stop! I can't b-breathe!"

He finally stops his revenge. His hands rest on my tortured sides, and he looks down at me with humor shining in his eyes. Mine are filled with tears from laughing so hard. While my breathing returns to normal, we stare at each other, our faces only a foot apart with equally large smiles resting on our faces.

In this moment, I let myself go and feel everything I've been holding back. I like Jaxon—*a lot*. His deep dark eyes look at me knowingly and seem to know my every move. Those same eyes that hold secrets but are completely open at the same time. His touch surges through my body like electricity, and I feel it in every nerve. He sends shivers down my spine, and goose bumps follow the trail his fingers make on my skin. His mouth goes into that crooked smile that cripples me and causes my thoughts to go fuzzy. His lips . . .

He moves in closer. Before I can wonder if I should panic or not, I realize it's my hand fisted in the front of his shirt that's pulling him to me, and he doesn't resist. Our foreheads press together, and our noses just barely touch. I close my eyes, and he lets out a sigh. I move closer until I can feel his breath on my lips . . .

A scream comes from upstairs. The sound makes me jump, and I bump my head into Jaxon's, who is looking upstairs now.

Sidney.

"Sid?" I called up to her.

No reply.

I push Jaxon off me, roll off the couch, and bolt upstairs with him following close behind. "Sidney!"

I turn the doorknob and bust into the room. She's collapsed facedown on her bed, sobbing with her face in her pillow.

"Sidney, what's wrong?" I can see she isn't hurt as I sit beside her on the bed and rub soothing circles against her back.

"She . . . Her leg . . ." She's choked up and having trouble telling me the problem. Her shaky finger points at Brownie, her stuffed horse. The leg is ripped slightly—an easy fix.

I smile. "Sid, I can fix her leg no problem. I'll take Brownie downstairs and sew it back together, okay?"

She peeks out from her pillow and searches my face for the truth, then looks at Jaxon and back to me. Then she nods her head.

It's a simple fix and only takes two minutes. Once her best friend is out of surgery, she hugs her tightly to her chest and walks back up the stairs to her room and shuts the door without another word.

I sigh and mumble, "Sensitive and dramatic." I look at Jaxon now. He's looking out the kitchen window down the street. "Hey, you okay?" I touch his arm softly.

At my touch, he looks at me. So many emotions play across his face. More than I can name.

"Yes."

"So, how long are you stayin'?" I don't want Jaxon to leave, especially with how we were before the Brownie issue.

"Until you're ready to kick me out." He smiles, but it's forced. He's keeping something hidden away; I just don't know what it is.

I nod, not knowing what else to do or say. All I can think about is the couch. By the minute, the air between us is growing more and more awkward as I think about how close we were.

As if reading my thoughts, he smiles and grabs my hand, and I let him tow me along to the living room. He sits down, still holding my hand, and gives it a tug for me to join him, but I stand in front of him. I don't know what's stopping me. Inside, I'm kicking myself. I can't decide what I feel or what I want to feel. I don't know if I'm more nervous considering what almost happened last time we were on this couch or scared. The problem is, I don't know what I'm scared of—him or being with him.

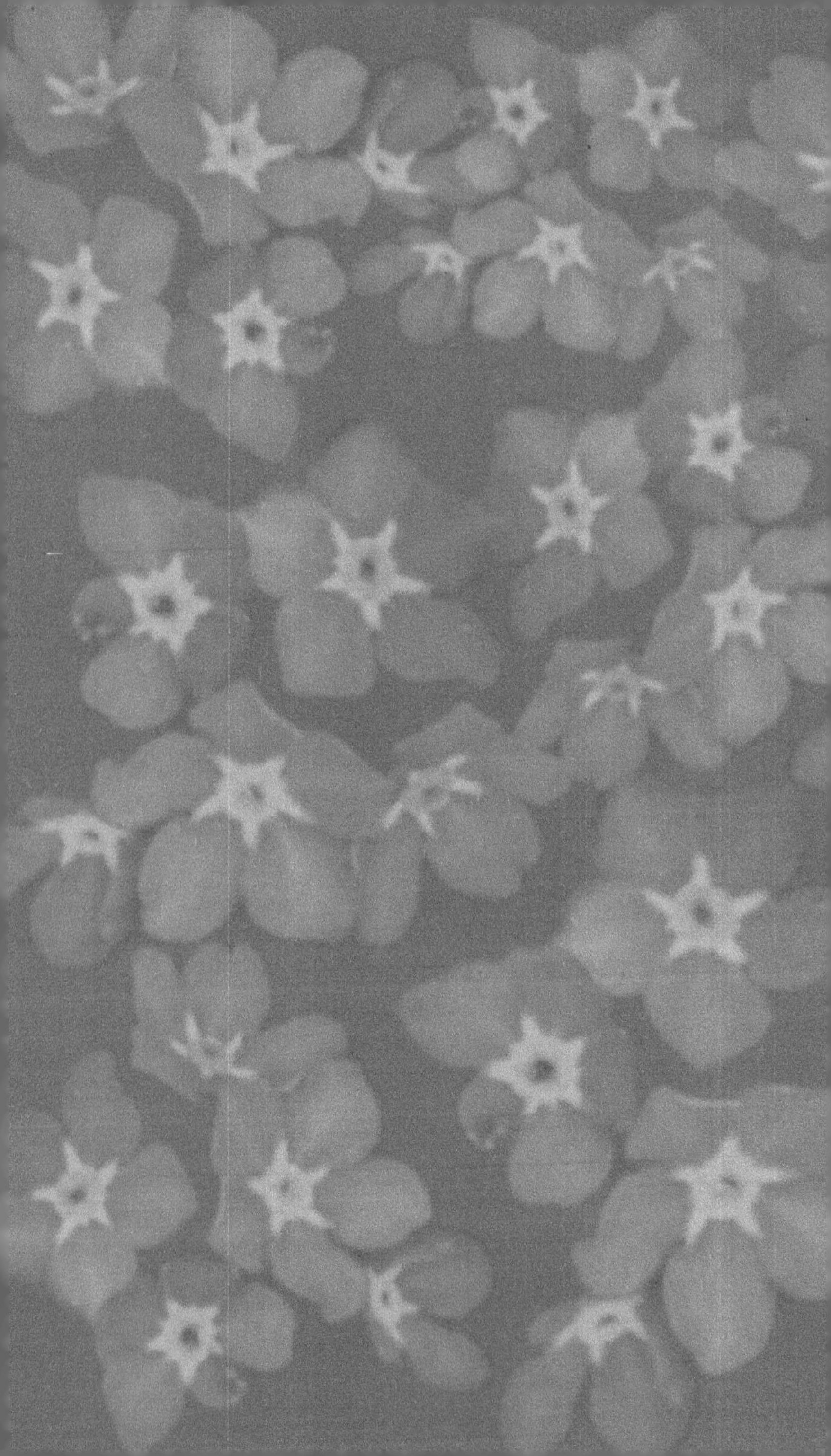

THIRTEEN

"WHAT'S WRONG?" His brow creases. He can clearly see the space between us as I stand in front of him now, and it's the same space I was eliminating before. He looks confused, and I can't blame him.

I want to say nothing's wrong, but what is that going to do? I sit down next to him, keeping a small space between us. It's more of an answer than any words can convey right now.

He drapes his arm over the couch with his hand touching my shoulder. I try to discreetly move out of his reach but not discreetly enough.

He turns his entire body to look at me. "Kairi?"

"What are we doin'?"

"What do you mean?" Jaxon's eyes pierce into me.

"This." I gesture a hand between us. "What are we doin'?"

"What do you think we're doing?"

He's got me there, because I don't know what I think we're doing. I mean, I think we were about to kiss before. I replay what happened in my mind, and I *know* we would have if Sidney hadn't screamed. Right? Instead of embarrassing myself more than I already have, I turn away and start to get up.

He grabs my arm, stopping my ascent. "Kairi, you can talk to me."

"I don't know what you're talkin' about," I say, still refusing to look at him.

"Come on." He sighs. "I just want to know what you think."

I don't want to say anything, mostly out of fear of being shot down. "We're just friends from class, and you helped me with some manual labor today 'cause you'd have felt guilty making me do it on my own once I said I needed help." I look into his eyes. I want to hear him challenge me. I want him to say I'm wrong and that there actually is something between us.

"Is that what you really think?" He turns it around on me again, his tone hard.

"Yes."

He smirks. "I know you don't really believe that." He sounds sure of himself.

"You don't know me."

"I know you write poetry as an escape from your pain. I know you take care of your sister like a parent. And I know you feel something for me. I can feel it. There's something between us, whether you want to admit it or not."

I know it's stupid to get angry, but I can't help it. It rises in me like a volcano about to explode. "Well, if you know everything, then tell me what's goin' on, because obviously, I'm too slow to keep up," I say as calmly as I can manage through gritted teeth.

"I know how I feel. It's *you* that I don't know about. You're so closed off and hard to read." Jaxon's jaw ticks in obvious effort to control his own temper.

I let out a loud laugh. He thinks *I'm* hard to read? I literally read people every day, and his mind is one of the only ones

I haven't been able to access until recently. As I think about it, it only makes me more frustrated, and the lava level keeps rising.

"Look I've been through a lot this past year, and I don't need some player making me another notch in his belt," I snap at him. "I'm not lookin' for a relationship anyway."

Jaxon leans closer to my face, and I freeze. I couldn't move away even if I wanted to. He keeps coming until our noses are about to touch and then stops. I use every ounce of willpower I have to keep myself where I am and not lean into him.

"You're lying," he whispers. I can hear the smile in his voice without having to see it as he plays with a strand of my hair, looking me dead in the eyes when I open mine.

My heart skips. I take a shaky breath, trying to regain my once boiling rage that's draining at a dangerous rate. Only seconds pass before I'm in the palm of his hand again.

"You don't know me," I whisper, defeated.

"I've got it bad for you, Kairi." His smile is so soft, honest, and mischievous at the same time.

My body stills again. I'm unsure of what to say. I know how I feel, but how far do these feelings go? How long have I known this guy? A few weeks? Seems like a short time to be exposing emotions like this. I know I'm avoiding the truth though. I've already admitted to myself that I like Jaxon more than I should. I just can't bring myself to tell him that.

"I see the wheels turning behind your beautiful eyes. You're thinking really hard about something." Jaxon pulls me out of my thoughts and back to him.

"I'm just a little shocked," is all I can say.

"Why? It couldn't have been that big of a surprise." His eyes search mine.

He's right. It isn't that I'm shocked by the way he's been acting; I'm shocked that he feels that way for *me*. "I just don't get why you feel that way."

"And I don't understand why?" Jaxon smiles, trying to steer me back to the thing I'm desperately trying to avoid.

"I don't want to be another notch in your belt," I say again.

"What makes you think I have notches?" He tilts his head.

"Uh, hello . . ." I gesture to him up and down.

He follows my hands, glancing over himself before looking back up at me. His eyes lock with mine. "There you go again with the *Uhhh* . . ." Jaxon mimics my accent.

I narrow my eyes. He's ignoring the point to either make fun of me or because he doesn't want to admit the truth. Right now, I'm leaning toward option C: all of the above.

"Oh, loosen up, Kairi." Jaxon touches my arm, causing my body to heat up. I can't contain the shiver of pleasure it gives me, which makes him smirk. "I'm not that kind of guy. You can even ask around. I don't date just anyone."

As I look into his eyes, I believe him. It's hard not to,. I'm sure any girl in the school would be bragging about being with Jaxon Benievere. I have to think back to confirm that I've never heard he's even talked to anyone.

"I know you're reserved, but I thought if I told you how I felt, you'd be able to open up too." He leans closer and puts his hand to my face so that my cheek is resting in his palm. I lean into it and close my eyes. The warmth of him feels so amazing, and his skin smells like a perfect mix of mint and spice.

I open my eyes and look at him. Jaxon's leaning back against the couch and staring at me in a way that makes my stomach flutter. I realize what I want. I want Jaxon. I don't care about my past. I don't care about Chelsea and all the others like her, just *Jax*.

Instead of answering, I lean in and press my lips to his.

Jaxon isn't my first kiss, but I've never experienced

anything like this. My lips burn with pleasure under his. After just a simple touch, I pull away.

He places his hands on the back of my neck and pulls me back to reconnect our lips. His tongue swipes my bottom lip, and I open my mouth obediently for him. With our mouths parted, I struggle to control myself. One touch burned my lips, and this full-on kiss contains passion I've never experienced. It consumes me as our tongues dance together. I want him closer —as close as physically possible. My hand flies to his hair and tugs on the strands, pulling a groan from him that sends a delicious shiver down my spine. I've never felt this kind of need in my entire life.

Being with Jaxon and feeling his touch feels like coming home. When I push all the negative thoughts and fears out of my mind, I feel safe with him. When I'm not at war with my mind and heart, I feel at peace for the first time in a long time. Jaxon makes me feel that way.

His hands move from my neck to my shoulders, down the length of my arms, gently brushing my skin as he moves to rest his hands on my lower back, pulling me flush against him as he dominates the kiss.

Oh God. I've missed you.

I freeze and pull away.

Jaxon's hooded eyes look confused. "What's wrong?" His husky voice has me pressing my thighs together.

Hearing him speak confirms the fact that I just heard him say he missed me. I pull back farther to ask him what he meant when it dawns on me that he wasn't speaking out loud when he said that. I put my fingers over my swollen lips and try to hide the panic in my eyes.

I heard his thoughts for the first time, which is why I was so confused at first. Everyone's thoughts sound a little different than their speaking voices. They sound similar enough that you know who it is with enough of a difference to tell the two apart.

"How'd you—" I stop myself. The last thing I need to do is admit I can read minds and expose myself to ridicule or worse. "I think you should go."

"Why?" Jaxon narrows his eyes, studying my face.

"I just think it's time for you to go." I get up and go to the front door. I place my hand on the knob and look back at Jaxon, who is still sitting on the couch staring at me. There's a flash of hurt in his eyes before they go blank. Before I can feel guilty, I tell myself that I can't ignore what happened, that I need to figure it out when he isn't distracting me.

Jaxon lets out a sigh and heaves himself up from the cushions, then walks toward me. "I hope I didn't overstep," he says evenly as he stands beside me next to the still-closed door.

I think for a moment on how to respond. "You didn't."

Jaxon smiles. "Then I'll pick you up tomorrow around six." He pries my hand off the handle, kisses it, and walks out without another word too quickly for me to object.

I watch him get into the same black Dodge Charger. After he leaves, I slide with my back against the door to the floor.

Why was I able to read his mind when we kissed?

Why did I kiss Jaxon?

Holy hell, I kissed Jax!

I smile to myself despite it all, because out of everyone, he chose me when he can have anyone. My smile drops. Maybe it's one of those guy things where they want what they can't have. Tell them no, and it makes them want it more. No matter the reason, kissing Jaxon was amazing. I'm still on a high. I'll worry about the mind reading later.

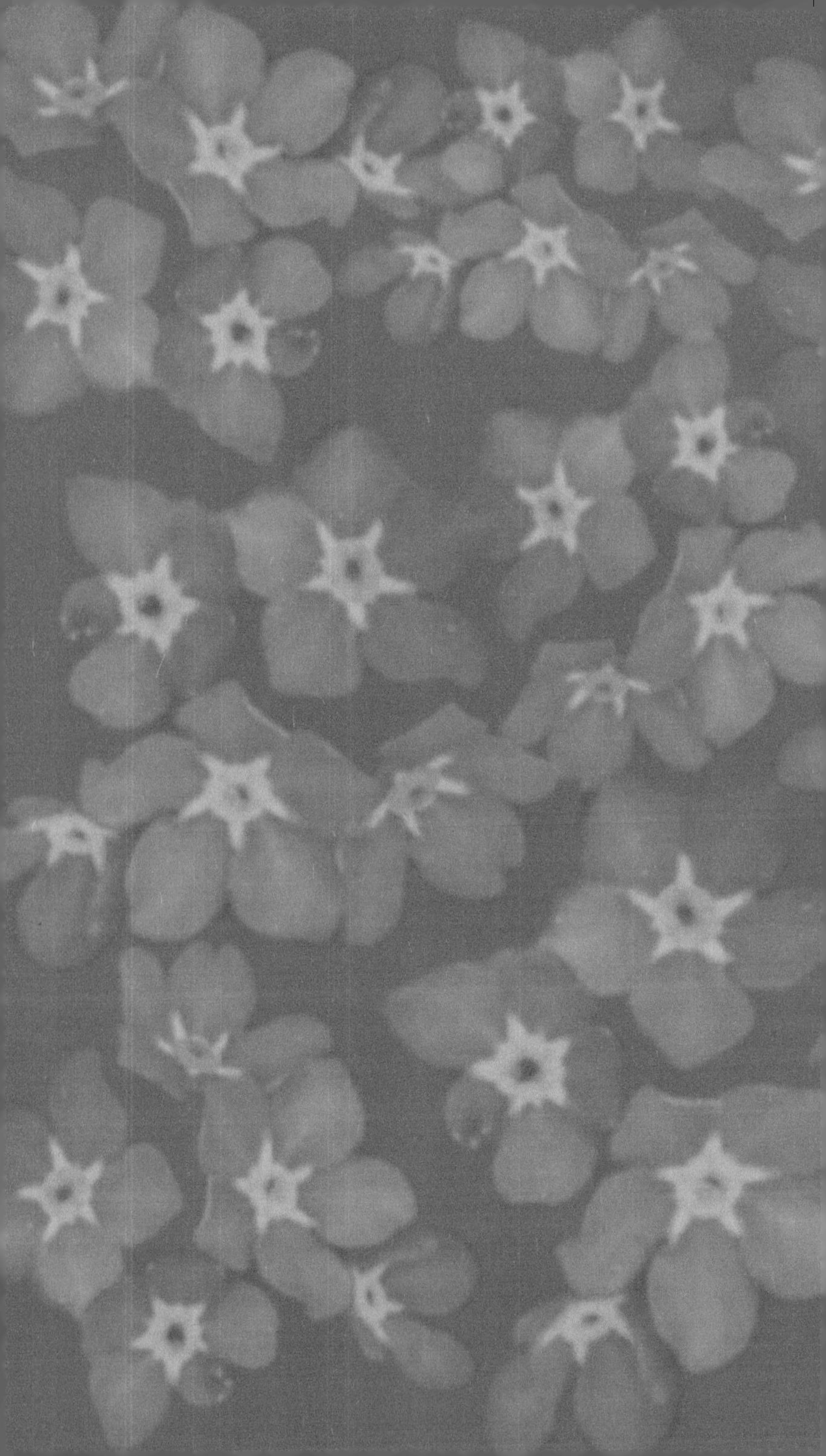

FOURTEEN

IT TAKES me at least fifteen minutes before I can pull myself to my feet and continue the day. I unpack all the boxes and make our house look somewhat like a home. I ordered Chinese for dinner because we still don't have groceries. I leave Dad voicemail and tell him about dinner so he won't bring anything home.

"Hey, girls," Dad says after walking in the door. He sets his bag down and takes a seat at the table with us to eat. He looks around the room. "The house looks good." He nods.

You're welcome?

"I got to sit in my room the whole time while Kai and her friend moved everything in," Sidney says right before she takes a huge bite of pizza.

I nearly choke. I can't believe she just said that and *on purpose*. Sidney and I have always been a united front against our parents, because when it comes down to it, it's usually just us because of Dad's work and Mom not being here. Her mind is a flurry of jealous thoughts because Jaxon was here and I didn't spend much time with her, but I didn't think she'd throw me under the bus like this. I take a few deep breaths and pray Dad doesn't make a big deal about this.

"A friend?" Dad asks. When Sid nods her head while staring at her food, his eyes move from her straight to me and harden once they reach me.

"A guy from my class offered to come help me move everything in since you were gonna be at work," I say.

"That better not be attitude I hear." He glares, his tone hard.

"No, sir," I say quietly, lowering my eyes and fisting the end of my shirt.

"Does this guy have a name?"

"He really was just tryin' to be nice . . ." I attempt to avoid his question.

He sits back in his seat and crosses his arms across his chest. "Kairi Rose . . ."

I fidget in place, not wanting to tell him about Jaxon. Dad's only controlled or blatantly ignored me for as long as I can remember. I don't want him to take whatever this is or could be away from me. I force myself to raise my eyes to meet his.

"He won't be back. I don't see how it matters," I mumble, unable to get the words out clearly.

At that, I stand up from the table with my food and rush to my room. I don't have to turn to see Dad's hard stare to know it's locked on me as Sidney starts chatting with him about her day. I make it to my room and lock the door behind me.

I'm angry at Dad for not being here for me—not only for the movers today, but ever since I got out of the hospital. He hasn't been the father I need or want in a long time. It may be childish, but I'm done acting like the perfect daughter for a man who acts like he can't be bothered with me.

I'm angry at myself too for not being able to stand up to

him. I can't do anything but let him walk all over me, even when I know he's in the wrong. When it comes to him, I act like a scared little girl.

When Sidney and Dad go to bed, I jump in the shower. I turn up the heat and let the water wash all my stress away. When I feel calm and my mind has dismissed enough of today that I can breathe normally, I get out. I look at myself in the mirror and see a smiling girl.

"I don't know why you look so happy. He's just playin' with your feelings," I say.

Yet I still have that stupid smile on my face. I want to slap myself until I believe it. I shake my head and walk out of the bathroom wrapped in a towel before I do anything else questionably unstable.

When I lie down under the covers, safe and sound, I bring the subject back into my mind.

I read Jaxon's thoughts today . . .

From the moment I met him, he's intrigued me, because for some reason, his mind was closed off from me. No matter how hard I tried, I could never break down the walls that blocked his thoughts from me. I still firmly believe that Jaxon's hiding more than he's letting on. There's no way I can feel this kind of connection with someone I just met. And I can't put my finger on it, but I think he's like me, with an *ability*. Of course, I can't prove it . . . *yet*.

The other thing is that he said he missed me. That just reinforces the fact that he *does* know me, and he knew me before I moved here. What I don't understand is why don't I remember him and why he hasn't told me. Why is it a secret? That'd explain why he's been so forward with me. There's a piece of the story that is missing, and I need to find out why. Whether I like the answer or not.

I wonder if I was able to read Jaxon's thoughts because he let me. But if that were the case, he wouldn't have left without understanding why I asked him to leave or saying anything else. Then again, it's not like he should know I can read minds. Maybe his emotions just took over and he let his guard down like I did. I know I was barely controlling myself. I don't know all the answers, but I sure as hell am going to find a time to ask sooner or later. For now, I'm going to call it a night.

Like every other night since I've been here, I dream of Jaxon Benievere.

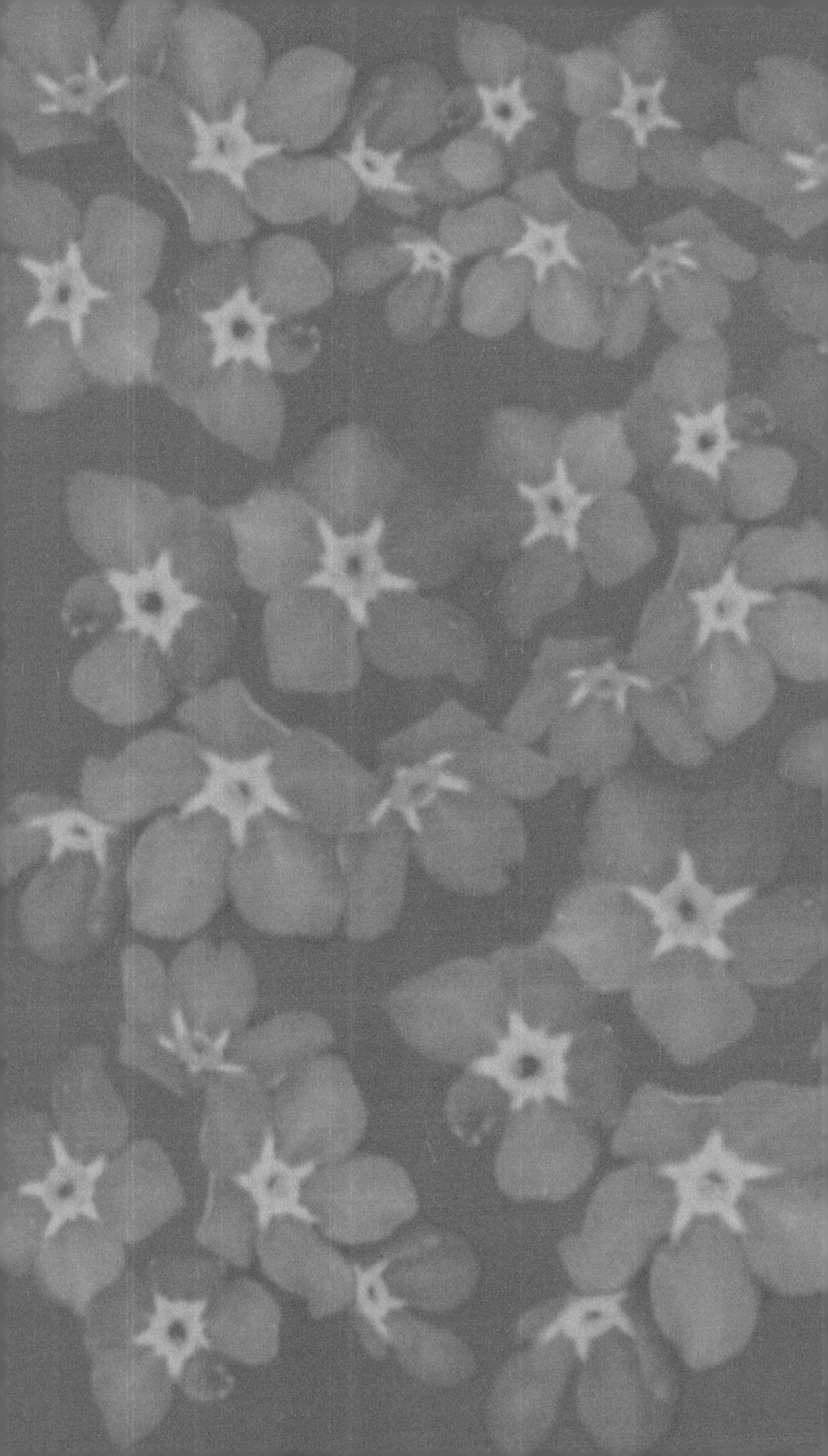

FIFTEEN

I WAKE UP, rolling over to see my clock's dim lights come into focus. Two o'clock. My phone starts ringing from under my pillow. Pulling it toward my face, I try to make out the number. It's not one that I've saved.

"Hello?"

I hear a familiar sexy chuckle on the other end, and my heart thunders in my chest.

I'm wide awake now.

"You're still sleeping?" The humor in Jaxon's voice is evident. "I bet I just woke you up."

"Uh." I look out my window and see it's not two in the morning but two in the afternoon. "No . . ." I lie. I can't believe I slept all day. "But I'm not at all surprised you're into gambling."

"Uhhh, *yes*," Jaxon says in a faux country accent. "And I'm not a gambler. I'm calling to say that I'll be there in ten minutes but if you're still sleeping . . ."

"I'll be ready," I say. I have to since I already said I wasn't sleeping.

"Great. See you soon, Darlin'." And the line goes dead.

The next ten minutes are the most stressful of my life. I rush through brushing my teeth, getting dressed, spritzing myself with strawberry body spray, and choking down a granola bar. I'm glad to see Dad's home for once watching TV.

"Hey, Dad. Are you gonna be here all day?"

"Yeah," he says, turning to look at me briefly. This is the first time in a while I've been able to get a good look at him. His short brown hair that's peppered with gray is cut to look professional, and his cold brown eyes are lined with permanent stress wrinkles from all the work he's been doing over the years.

"Okay, 'cause I'm goin' out with some friends for a while."

"All right." He directs his attention back to the game on the flat screen.

He used to be so uptight and overprotective. He's different now, working constantly and not caring what I do as long as it doesn't interfere with his rest time or his work schedule.

I go back upstairs and examine myself in the mirror. I'm smiling when I come back to my face after doing a once-over. I feel like myself again, which is hard to do considering. It feels nice.

There's a knock on the front door, and my bright smile returns as I run down the steps to answer it.

"Bye, Dad!" I yell and open the door, but no one is there. I walk out, closing the door behind me.

I heard the door, right?

I look around and still nothing. I walk to the edge of the porch and see nothing but a big black Jeep parked across the street in front of our neighbor's house. I turn to go back inside when I'm grabbed around the waist. I let out a surprised squeak.

"Gotcha," Jaxon's whispers in his mock southern accent.

He kisses me on the cheek, still standing behind me with his arms around my waist.

"You scared the crap out of me!" I turn around and slap his shoulder.

Jaxon laughs but doesn't move. I turn in his arms until we're standing face-to-face with my hands on his hard stomach and his arms still wrapped around me.

"I'm sorry." His eyes are filled with more humor than guilt.

"Mm-hmm." Shaking my head, I avert my eyes.

He backs away, letting go of my waist. He grabs my hand and gives it a soft squeeze. "You ready to go?"

I nod and follow him to the Jeep across the street. "I thought you drove a black car," I say.

"I have more than one." He shrugs.

Of course you do.

He doesn't say anything else, but he has a small smile on his face as he helps me into his Jeep.

We stay silent for the ride over, so I keep my eyes on the passing scenery, trying to avoid any more awkward moments. More than anything, I try not to think about the warmth on my cheek where he kissed me. Thinking about that will only make me think of the full make-out session we had on my couch that led to hearing Jaxon's thoughts. I know I need to address all of this with him, but I want one night that's stress free, especially since it seems like we're gonna pretend that it didn't happen. I want to feel normal and push this aside for one more night before I confront Jaxon about it.

"You're blushing."

I turn my face away from his eyes, trying to hide from further embarrassment as my cheeks burn deeper.

"Come on, tell me. What were you just thinking about?"

I respond before I can catch myself. "You kissed me on the porch." I keep my eyes on the trees passing by.

"I only got your cheek. I actually feel like I've been cheated now that I think about it." He teases. "You full-on kissed me yesterday." He chuckles as my face goes up in flames.

Apparently we aren't gonna completely ignore yesterday.

"Moment of weakness," I mumble, though apparently not quietly enough.

"Moment of weakness?" he repeats heavily dipped in sarcasm. I can tell I've struck a nerve. Jaxon pulls over and kills the engine but keeps his line of sight on the road and hands clenched on the steering wheel. "What's that supposed to mean?"

"You're so confusing," I say.

"How am I confusing? I've shown you how I feel. You're the one playing with my feelings!" he shouts. "Moment of weakness my ass. You knew what you were doing, and you know what you want, but you're too scared to own up to it, aren't you?"

"I don't want to get hurt. You don't know what I've been through." We're leaning toward each other now, glaring hard. Tears sting my eyes. I lean away from Jaxon and look back out my window, trying to regain control, willing my eyes to dry and not let the tears fall.

I don't know why I said that and started this argument to begin with. My emotions have been all over the place since moving here and now Jaxon's the one getting hurt unintentionally. I've tried to push them all down, grin and bear it, but now, more than anything, I just want to go back home and cry into my pillow. Looking into the trees now, all I can see is fire. The moment that made me this way. The turning point where my life went up in smoke. The fire that made it so I hear everyone's thoughts, an ability that makes me feel cut off from everyone around me. It's like I don't belong anywhere anymore.

"Why do you think I would hurt you?" Jaxon's tone is soft but strained.

"From experience, I expect it from everyone." Such as Mom leaving and Dad avoiding me like the plague unless it's to scold me.

"Kairi, how can I show that I'll never hurt you? How can I make you believe me?"

"Just stay around, I guess," is all I can say. The only way to show loyalty and commitment is by being there. It's as simple as that. "I don't see why you're rushin' this though," I add softly.

"When you know, you know." He shrugs when I look back into his eyes. I see sincerity there, and I wish I had his ability to brush off the tension that's around us. He never seems to let anything get to him.

My heart melts when I look into his eyes—his eyes that hold so much depth and familiarity. I've noticed before but keep telling myself that a lot of brown eyes probably look similar. I don't know what to think. Looking into his eyes now, I can see it clearly, like a memory. I'm surrounded by flames, and before I black-out, a pair of dark eyes are watching over me.

There's something inside telling me that the same eyes that were watching me then are watching me now. I didn't know Jaxon then though, so something isn't adding up. A lot of things aren't adding up.

"Kairi." Jaxon's voice brings me back to the present. I must have been staring at him like an idiot while all that ran through my mind.

"Sorry, I was just . . . thinking." I smile apologetically.

"Do I get to know?"

"Where are we?" I ask instead.

"My house," he says, letting talk of my thoughts drop.

Jaxon's house is a two-story red brick home with too many windows to count. There are four elegant pillars in the front that look out over a beautiful green lawn with what looks like wildflowers growing across the surface.

"Wow," is all I can say. I thought Jaxon had randomly pulled over but I hadn't realized he stopped in his driveway the whole time.

"What do you think?"

"It's beautiful, Jax," I answer in awe.

"I'm glad you like it." Seemingly pleased with my response, he gets out of the Jeep and walks around to my door. After opening it like a real gentleman, he takes my hand to help me down. Jaxon leans in and whispers in my ear, "I wanted you to be the first one to see it."

My stomach flutters. "I bet it was amazing growin' up here." I imagine Jaxon as a little kid running around with his brother. It makes me smile.

"I've only lived here for about a year, so I'm fairly new too." A hard but sad expression covers his face.

"Really?" I guess that explained why all the girls are still falling all over him. Although, I don't know if anyone could get used to a guy like Jaxon.

"Yeah, my brother and I move around a lot."

"Seems like an expensive house to have if you move around so much." I've always dreamed of living in a house like this. It's as if it came right out of my fantasy.

"Our move here was"—he pauses to look at me—"unexpected." A distant but sad look eclipses his features and pulls at my heartstrings. I wish I could comfort him some way. Being this close to Jaxon makes my thoughts fuzzy, so I decide to keep my arms at my sides instead, which is a feat all on its own. The other half of me is busy wondering what that unexpected thing was that made him move.

"I've always wanted to live in a house like this," I confess.

He smiles genuinely, which is what I really wanted. "I'm more than happy to let you stay if you'd want to."

"So, how many people are gonna be here?" I ask, changing the subject.

A thoughtful expression covers his face. "Well, I invited about five hundred people. I think I got around two hundred responses."

I blink up at him, waiting for him to continue. He doesn't, but when his smile starts to widen, and it clicks. "Two hundred people? Here? Tonight? Are you insane?"

Jaxon laughs now. "Yes. Come on. I'll show you around."

He takes my hand and walks me through his house, showing me the spacious living room with a large sectional to the left of two armchairs. On the wall hangs a large flat-screen TV surrounded by floor-to-ceiling shelves filled with various movies, music, and books. I follow him through to a fully decked-out kitchen that's unbelievable. Jaxon's house is designed with charcoal tile floors, light gray paint, and all the furniture is either white or black or a combination of the two.

It's modern and elegant, and I love it. I think I love the backyard the most though. French glass doors lead to a dark wood patio looking out on a beautiful garden. There are trees scattered about and patches of every different type of flower imaginable—all beautiful. There are little paths here and there that lead through what looks like an eight-foot maze. I've never seen anything like it in my entire life. I want to go out there, get lost, and never come out—kind of like my own *Alice in Wonderland* experience.

Jaxon comes up behind me, wrap his arms around me, and leans in close. "Do you want to go outside?"

I nod vigorously.

We walk through the doors hand in hand, and he leads me out to the edge of the patio.

"It's beyond beautiful, Jax." I can't tear my eyes away from the scenery in front of me.

"It's a nice quiet place to go be by yourself. I come out here a lot just to think," he says.

I'd love to go out there and explore, but I want to wait for the perfect moment.

Jaxon looks down at his watch. "Everyone should be getting here soon."

Just as he says this, the doorbell rings, and we turn to look at each other.

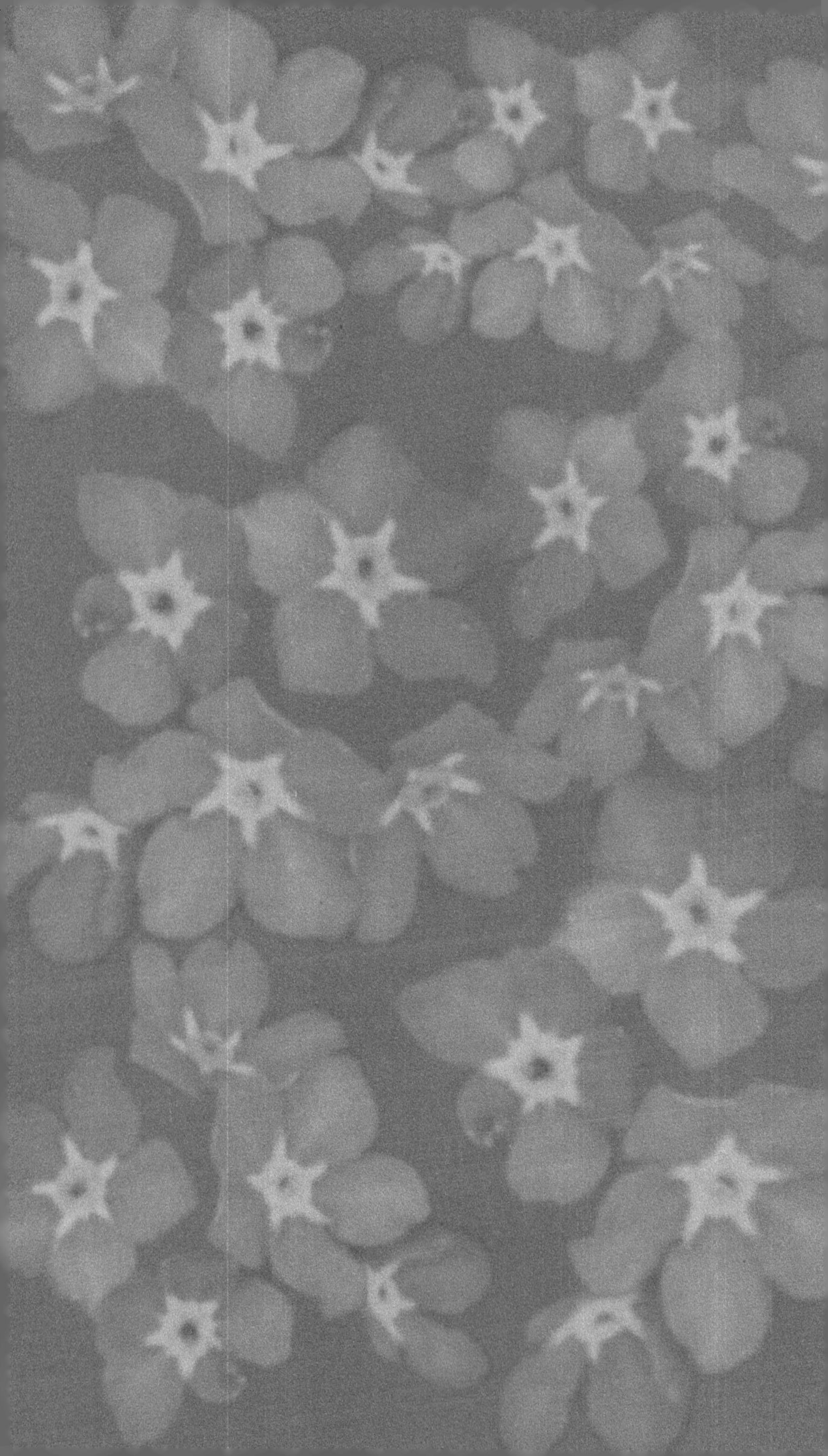

SIXTEEN

I HAVE my head inside Jaxon's fridge looking for another soda. Someone came and spiked all the drinks, which is why I'm looking for the only safe option left—an unopened can. I finally find one in the back of the bottom drawer underneath a mound of vegetables, oddly enough.

I'm not much of a drinker, and I don't have a taste for alcohol in general. Though maybe something strawberry . . . . Nope. I'm determined to stay sober tonight and stick to my previous sobriety.

There are people everywhere and barely any room to move an inch in any direction. It seems like almost everyone invited showed up. It's incredible and crowded.

I'm not having a horrible time per se, but I'm not really having any fun either. Most of the night, I've spent my time holding my head up with one hand while rubbing my temple with the other, trying to ease my monster of a headache. The combination of pulsing music, screaming voices, thoughts blaring, and blurred intoxicated images that eclipse my own eyes and slowly melt my brain are to blame for the headache.

Seeing the minds of drunken students is like watching a static-covered television screen.

I really need to try to block the voices out, but there's too much going on and too much noise right now for me to focus enough to put a barrier up around my mind.

I look out into the ridiculous crowd of people, searching for someone I know or would actually like to talk to. I see Chelsea talking to a big group of guys. When she catches my eye, she gives me a smirk and wink before turning back to them. With a twinge of pain behind my eyes, I turn to see Travis sitting on a couch looking down at his phone. I'm really looking for Jaxon. I haven't seen him much since people started showing up. Trying to be a good host, I'm sure.

I continue to scan the crowd, amused by their flippant behavior. My eyes land on a familiar bulky male. As soon as he turns, I see his eyes, and I'm positive. At this point, I'd know those green eyes that supposedly saved me anywhere. He catches my eyes for less than a second before he smirks and disappears from view. I have to suppress the urge to follow him. I don't want or need any drama right now. I have enough going on. I'll worry about the green-eyed hulk another day.

I keep my eyes peeled for Jaxon in the crowd. He brought me early to show me around, and I thought he wanted to spend time with me, but I can't find him anywhere. Maybe I was wrong. Maybe he's just being nice. But we did kind of make out on my couch, and he kissed me this morning, on the cheek but still. With Jaxon, I'm always left guessing, which is annoying and refreshing at the same time. We always seem to butt heads and argue so easily too. The need to be around him more is starting to cloud my judgement. I've never felt this kind of pull to one person, and it's making me overlook the red flags that have been popping up since I've met him.

I decide to go sit with Travis when I see her.

Allison.

I can see she's drunk and hanging all over the guy in front of her. She laughs with her arms coiled around the guy's neck like a snake, swaying to the music in a sloppy fashion. She thinks she's being sexy and seductive, grinding and rubbing on him. *Poor guy.* She looks hilarious, and I can't help but I stay to watch a little longer. I finally turn to continue my original trek to Travis, but then Allison falls over, and the guy has to turn toward me to catch her. His dark brown hair falls in his face and his muscular arms flex as he stands her back up.

Allison is out of control laughing, still in Jaxon's arms. Her thoughts are all over the place. When Jaxon has her standing up straight and somewhat balanced, he smiles and says something to her. What it is, I don't know. I'm still staring, completely frozen in place at the edge of the living room-turned-dance floor, when she leans forward and crashes her lips into his.

A sudden wave of rage, betrayal, and pain storm through my heart as the weight of it all makes me struggle to stay on my feet, especially when he doesn't push her away. I'm still staring in a daze when they part. He has his hands on her shoulders and a smile on his face. I want to smack the arrogant smirk off her face when she sees me, but of course I can't. I have a feeling the pain I feel inside is reflecting clearly on the outside too. When Jaxon follows her line of sight and his eyes meet mine, I know it is.

I stand there for only a second longer before disappearing into the crowd, frantically pushing my way through the dance floor full of sweaty people grinding and jumping around into each other. I don't stop when I get to the couch where Travis is still sitting. I go straight for the back door, onto the patio, through the grass, and into the garden maze, not once looking back.

I take off into a run as soon as I hit the grass, tears steadily streaming down my face. I swat them away, angry at myself for letting my stupidity take over. I let Jaxon in and believed what he said he felt for me.

I don't need him. I don't need anyone. I'm fine on my own.

I run and weave through the trees and vines, trying desperately to get lost both physically and mentally. It's the perfect place to separate myself from the rest of the world—from Jaxon and Allison. The only downside is its unfortunate location at his house.

I don't stop until I see an old two-seater bench swing covered in vines. The white paint is chipping, and the color is faded, but it still looks beautiful. I sit down on one side to pull my feet up on the other, taking up the entire seat. I let the wind push me back and forth slightly as I lean my body against the backrest and let myself cry. I don't wipe away the tears now. I let them pour out of me and allow the pain I've been feeling to swallow me whole.

I'm angry at Jaxon for stringing me along and making me feel hopeful for once. I should've listened to my gut. There was never a way for us to truly be together. It just didn't make sense with us being in entirely different leagues. The real damage is because I believed his promise. I believed it when he said that he'd never hurt me, and now that's exactly what he did. I let the way I feel when we touch erase all the fear and skepticism I felt, and now I'm paying for it.

And I'm mad at Dad for never being around anymore when I really need him. Always treating me like I don't matter nearly as much as my sister. Acting as if he can barely stand to look at me, let alone be in the same room with me.

I'm hurt that Mom left us. She chose not to be strong for me and Sidney and instead decided to be a coward and leave me to pick up the pieces. Now she wants to walk right back into our lives like nothing happened, and I'm supposed to act like that deep betrayal didn't happen. She left me with a man that is now more of a stranger than a father.

Deep down, I'm upset at Sidney too. If she hadn't been so reckless, I wouldn't have to worry about all of this noise in my head. She's the one who was playing with the matches that started that fire, and she's still put on a pedestal by Dad while I'm treated like an inconvenience.

I don't know how long I've been sitting here, and I don't know what time it is, but the sun's starting to set. If I can find my way out of here, I'll walk home. I'm not going to be crammed in a Jeep with Jaxon—not now.

I swing my feet off the bench and stand just as Jaxon jogs around the corner. He comes to an abrupt stop when he sees me. We hold each other's eyes for another moment before I look away and start walking.

"Kairi," he says.

"No."

You're such a fucking idiot!

I whirl around to face him now. "What'd you say?" I'm seriously debating punching his handsome face for lying, for hurting me, kissing Allison, everything. The confused look on his face slowly turns to recognition. He didn't say that out loud. I read his mind, and now he knows my secret.

Before he can respond, I turn on my heels and sprint away, hopefully to the house or a street. Anywhere but here.

"Kairi, wait!" Jaxon yells after me. I can hear his footsteps coming up behind me, but it only pushes me faster.

Please let me explain.

He's speaking to my mind now. I choke on my sobs as I run. I thought I'd be able to keep this secret for a little longer than this. I start feeling dizzy, and the vines seem to reach out to wrap around my arms. I have to take a lot of sharp turns to avoid walls of roses that seem to come out of nowhere. My anxiety and determination skyrocket as I try even harder to avoid the veins reaching out to stop me.

Finally, the house comes into view. I glance over my shoulder to see that Jaxon is still chasing me. While I'm looking back, I run into what feels like a brick wall that sends me on my ass. I look up and see a man in his midtwenties. He's muscular like a bodybuilder with short dark brown hair and eyes. I can feel a magnetic pull behind me and know Jaxon's standing there, making my heart jump all over the place despite my fear and simmering anger.

"What's going on?" The man in front of me looks at Jaxon now.

"Andrew, what are you doing here so early?" Jaxon asks, completely out of breath, ignoring Andrew's question.

Andrew. Drew. This can't be the person they said healed me in the woods, right?

He studies us for a second. I'm still panting from sprinting, and I still have tears that refuse to stop pouring over my eyelids. I probably look like a hot mess. I hear Jaxon breathing heavily too, but I refuse to look at him.

"You can't Jaxon," Andrew says, not answering Jaxon's question either.

Andrew smiles down at my confused eyes. I'm trying to get a read on him, but I can't. I'm too exhausted to control my powers. Or maybe he is the guy that healed me if I can't get a read on him. Maybe his ability is to heal.

"Now is as good a time as any." Jaxon walks forward and stands next to where I still sit on the ground.

"What have you been doing? You're going to ruin everything? You're going to throw all our hard work away over her?" Andrew asks.

"It was always for her. You know that."

"This has been going on long enough, and I—"

"I figured it out," Jaxon says. "Well, she pretty much showed me, but I know now."

I turn to Jaxon, who's smiling down at me. His eyes twinkle with mixed emotions—excitement, relief, affection, and even fear, I think.

I knew you were special.

Yeah, but what's bein' special gonna cost me?

His face turns bewildered, and his eyebrows are pushed together now. He's studying me. I don't know why, unless . . .

"You heard me, didn't you?" I ask him, but I'm already sure.

He nods his head. "Yes."

"What's going on with you guys? I swear you two are even weirder than before." Andrew shakes his head, smiling at us.

What?

"She doesn't know yet." Jaxon's voice sounds strained now. I can't see why because he's blocking me again.

"Well, go on, then." Andrew waves his hand at me with a glint of humor, then walks back into the house, leaving me and Jaxon alone in the yard.

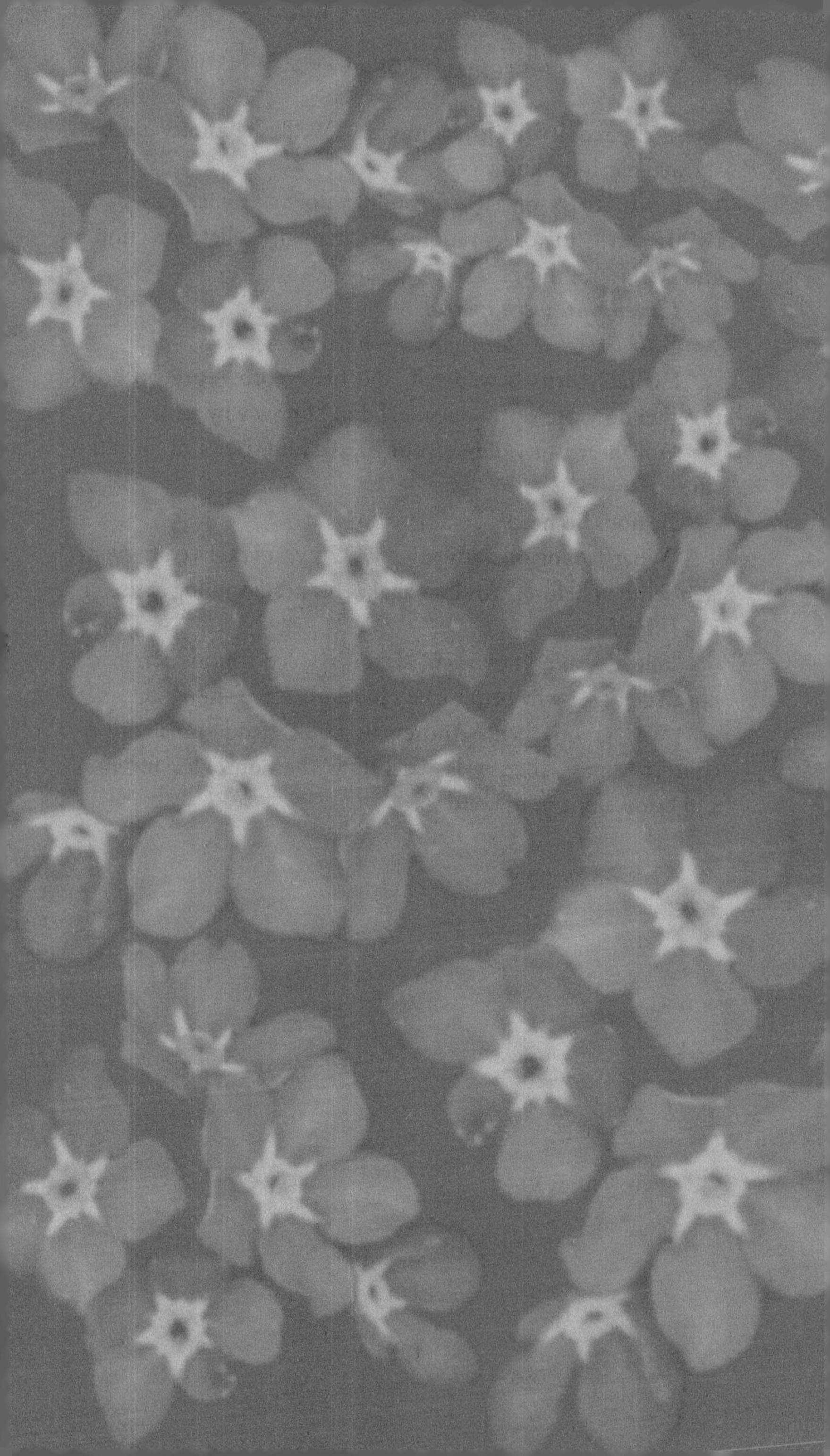

SEVENTEEN

I WATCH Andrew until he's out of sight before turning back to Jaxon, who's already looking at me.

"What did he mean when he said 'before'?" I ask.

Sighing, Jaxon sits on the grass next to me. I search his eyes for answers, but as usual, he is impossible for me to read. He looks into my eyes too, searching for something. The longer I look, the more I'm sure these are the eyes I saw the night of the fire—the night that changed everything.

I break the silence. "You knew me before I moved here." I state it as a fact, not a question.

I've never seen his face look so vulnerable and pleading. He's holding the truth back.

He sighs again. *Yes . . .*

I keep my face neutral. I have to stay calm and act like him speaking to my mind isn't freaking me the hell out; otherwise, he isn't going to tell me anything.

Tell me, please. Everything. I stare into his eyes, willing him to trust me with the truth.

"Look," Jaxon begins, "this is really hard for me to explain."

I wait.

"Not to mention that this is going to be extremely hard for you to hear." He looks away into the garden for a few seconds before turning back to me. "You deserve to know the truth though, even if you don't believe it."

I wait.

He sighs. "Yes, I knew you before you moved here. Long before you moved here, actually."

I stare at him for a second, and he stares at me too. He's going to see how I handle each little bit of news. I have to control my breathing, heart, and mind if I want to know the truth. "How long?"

"We were kids," he says.

"How long, Jax?"

"Since you were twelve."

"Twelve?" I narrow my eyes. "That was eight years ago."

"I know."

"So what? We met once?"

He runs his hand through his hair. "This is where things get complicated . . ."

Jax, please just tell me.

What part? There are so many strange and difficult things that I have to explain here, Kairi.

Start with how we met.

"It's more complicated than that."

"Then what can you tell me?" I let my own frustration leak into my voice.

"We met when we were around eleven or twelve, and we became friends. We could talk about anything and everything. It wasn't long before we spent all our free time together. Over the next few years, our feelings grew stronger . . ." He stares off into the garden again.

"Jaxon." I reach out and touch his arm.

He still refuses to look at me.

I fell in love with you. I send the statement into his mind.

He looks at me with surprise and hope in his eyes. It isn't that hard to imagine. I'm pretty sure I already am now too.

"Do you remember?" he asks, his voice hopeful.

I shake my head, which deflates his expression a little. "If this is true, how come I can't remember the past however many years of my life?"

He sighs. "This is the part of the story I'm worried about you not believing."

I quirk a brow. "Because what you just told me is the easy part to swallow?" He gives me an unimpressed look, and I relent. "Try me."

"We have a dark and horrible past," Jaxon says, a distant look on his face, not looking at me anymore. "There's a hidden secret agency that doesn't exist unless you're directly involved. They call themselves HUE—Human Underground Experimentation. They're scientists who think they're improving the human race. They make some improvements to the body—making it more durable and strong—but they mainly work with the brain and its functions. They're more or less trying to make a superhuman. HUE did experiments on animals. After years of work, they finally ironed out the kinks and were ready to proceed, but where do you go from there? Human trials . . ."

He meets my eyes now. I keep still and struggle to seem calm. I still don't understand where this is going.

"What exactly were they doin'?" I ask.

"I'm getting to that," Jaxon says with a sad smile.

I sit and wait for him to continue.

"You see, their main goal is to improve the human race, but when they were ready for their real project, they hit a wall. How were they going to find actual people to experiment on? Of course, confidentiality was a major priority, so they needed to get people who would volunteer to leave their lives behind and stay with HUE for basically the rest of their lives to keep their secret a secret. But who in their right mind would give up their life to be a lab rat?"

Jaxon shakes his head. "It's my understanding that it was the head scientist who got their experiment back on track. His idea was to adopt very young orphans. These were kids no one would miss or look for, kids that didn't have much chance for a future anyway." He pauses to study my face.

Orphans…

Who in their right mind would do human experiments, let alone on little kids? My heart races. It seems far-fetched, but his face is so open, honest, and *convincing*.

"How many kids were there?"

Jaxon shrugs. "I'm not really sure. For many years, we were kept separate while they monitored and made adjustments to their serum."

"We?" I stare wide-eyed at the man before me, who once again avoids my gaze. "You were one of those kids?"

He turns to me with sad eyes. "Yes."

"How old were you?"

"When was I orphaned, or when HUE picked me up?"

I hesitate. "Both, I guess."

He takes a deep breath. "I was in the orphanage for as long as I can remember with my older brother, Andrew. I think I was around five or six when a man came and 'adopted' us."

If he grew up in an orphanage, he probably has no idea who his parents are. "Do you want to find your parents?"

"No," he says immediately. "They left us, and that led us into a living hell. Even if they had a reason, whether they are dead or alive, I don't care. There's nothing they could say or do to reverse the damage that's been done."

I nod and let the information settle. "Your brother, Andrew, does he have a nickname?"

"Yeah—Drew. Why?" He raises a brow.

"Does he have an ability?"

"Yes."

"What is it?"

"Why the sudden interest in my brother?" His eyes narrow.

"It wouldn't have anything to do with healing would it?"

His eyes widen, and he stays stock-still while staring at me in question.

"I may have heard about a Drew that can heal while I was passed out in the woods once." From the look on his face, I know I'm on the right track. "I heard a voice that seemed familiar to me at the time. You wouldn't happen to know who that could've been, would you?" I ask, resting my chin on my fist.

Giving me a guilty smile, he says, "I just wanted to make sure you were okay."

"So you stalked me, followed me into the woods, had your brother heal me, then had someone else take me home. All because you wanted to make sure I was okay?"

He thinks for a moment. "Yes," he says, like the whole thing was normal and not weird at all.

"Right. So why couldn't you take me home instead of the green-eyed hulk?"

Jaxon leans forward as a deep belly laugh springs from him. With tears in his eyes, he finally calms down enough to speak. "Oh my God. Bentley is going to love that. *Green-eyed hulk.*" He chuckles.

"Yeah, Bentley. He and I need to exchange some words."

"I don't even want to know why," he says, still laughing.

"But why couldn't *you* take me home that day?" I ask again.

"It's more complicated than that. I wanted to; I just couldn't."

I don't understand, but I don't think I'm going to get any more of an explanation from him right now.

"Okay." I squeeze his arm. "I'm sorry for what you've been through, plus being on your own with only your brother. I have no idea what that must've been like." Although I'm not completely sold on his story, I can see in his eyes that he has been through something terrible. Hard to believe this stuff actually happens to people.

The sadness in his eyes thickens.

My eyes grow wide as I move away, separating myself from him.

Kairi . . .

"No. Are you tryin' to tell me I was there? That I was an *experiment*?" My volume rises with every word. I can't believe this. I pull further away from him. How could he say that *I* was an experiment? He's crazy. He's lost his damn mind.

"Kairi, please," Jaxon says, his voice begging me to hear him out.

"No. I had a life, friends, and a family. I was not an experiment. How dare you even suggest that?" I'm standing over him now, finger pointed, practically yelling in his face.

His eyes are solemn, but his face is stone-cold now. I can tell I've struck a nerve. He stands to face me. "You think I'm making this up? Do you think I *want* to hurt you like this? Bringing all this pain back up and tearing the life you thought you had apart?"

"I think you've been a little too friendly since I got here," I say switching this conversation back to him, as it should be. "You've come into my life like a bulldozer, destroyin' everythin' I know. You've done nothin' but keep things from me, hurt me, and make me question everythin' about my life. I knew somethin' wasn't right deep down, and now I know why. You're crazy!" I stand my ground, holding the tears back.

His face and body language shift—more confidence, more power rolling off of him. "You know me, Kairi."

"I don't know anything about you."

"You remember me from before you moved here. I could tell on the first day. Your mind hasn't lost all memory of me like he hoped it would." He lifts his hand and taps his index finger lightly on my temple. "Our connection is still in there. I know you can feel it."

"I didn't know you before, and there is no *connection*." I lie. From the first day, his eyes pulled me back to the fire and his touch has always felt like home. I know a part of me recognizes his touch. That doesn't mean anything he's said is true though. "Who's he?"

"The head scientist for HUE. They had to be the ones that did this to your memory. You know that you remember parts of me at least. I know you do. I can see it written on your face. I can see the wheels turning." He smirks.

"So what? You followed me here?"

"I got word that you were moving here, so yes, I did come here for you."

So he came here in hopes of me remembering him and picking up where we left off? I don't think that's the only reason. I'm not buying the story about experiments. No matter how much I want to deny it though, I'm curious about our connection. It's obvious, and I can't just brush it off.

"Prove it," I say, voice level now, challenging. "If you're like me, what can you do?"

He walks up to me, twists his wrist around, and a small stem of tiny flowers appears in his grasp. He holds it out for me.

"I don't think bein' an amateur magician counts."

"They called me an illusionist—able to make people think something's there or happening that's nothing more than a trick." His face is set, no emotion showing through, as he watches me carefully.

"Is this garden real?" I ask, remembering the plants springing out to slow my attempt at escaping Jaxon earlier.

"The garden's real, but I did add to it with my powers. It's almost exactly like the garden we always talked about wanting when we got free now."

I look back over to the endless rows of colorful plants and flowers, and fight a smile, because this *is* everything I would've wanted in a garden.

"So it's all a trick, like everything else you've been doin' to me this whole time?" I twist his words to prove my point, looking back at him.

Jaxon huffs, rolling his eyes. "Kairi."

"What, Jaxon?" My voice starts to rise again.

"I'm only trying to make you see the truth." His eyes turn dark for only a second before they go blank again. He extends the flower out to me. "It's a forget-me-not. It's the only flower I ever gave to you. In vain, it seems." He whispers the end more to himself than me. He waves his hand and the flower in my grasp is now only a twig.

"I've never gotten a flower from you," I say.

"I meant before . . ." His eyes are sad now when he looks at me.

"So if you're an *illusionist*, then what did they call me?"

"A mentalist, but we never really knew what it meant. Most of us didn't know each other's powers."

"Why didn't anyone ever ask?" I ask.

"The hold they had on us was more than being physically captive."

This was a mistake. I shouldn't have sprung this information on you like I did. I'm sorry, Rose.

Rose. That's my middle name. I have never told him my

middle name. I don't think I've told anyone my middle name ever.

"What did you call me?" I ask, thinking maybe I heard him wrong.

"Rose," Jaxon says.

"Why did you call me that?"

"That's always been my nickname for you."

"That is my middle name."

"I know it is."

"But how do you know that?'

"You told me a long time ago."

My hands start to shake. "I don't know how you know that, but I don't tell people that."

"Kairi, I don't know how to convince you or prove myself except to lay it all out there. That's what I've done. Now it's up to you to choose what you want to believe, but I have never lied to you."

The look in his eyes is sincere and honest. I know he believes he is telling me the truth. I just don't know if I agree with it. I don't know if I will ever *want* to believe this. I need to be alone. I need to get away.

"I need time to digest this," I say, looking away from him. In all honesty, I don't have the nerve to look at him. Not after the story he just told me. Not after the fact that before this evening, I knew I was falling for him. The pain and humiliation are too much to bear. Let's not even let the fact that Allison had her tongue down his throat come to the forefront of my mind on top of everything else, or I will lose my shit.

"I understand," Jaxon says low, as if sensing my distance. He steps back, and I watch him out of the corner of my eye. His body language radiates caution. He squats down next to where I've sat down to meet my eyes where I've found myself hugging my knees to my chest. "Kairi." He pauses to get my attention. I finally meet his gaze. "I can tell that you don't want to talk to me right now. But the only reason I told you all this is because something's changing. I never gave up looking for you after you were taken. Then I finally found you, only to have you almost taken from me all over again, just in a different way."

He hangs his head and sighs. I'm not able to hold the tears back anymore. I sniffle, and that makes Jaxon look up. His eyes are full of so much emotion: pain, despair, and . . . heartache. The look in his eyes make my tears flow harder.

He runs his fingers through his hair, as if pulling at it will somehow pull out the words he's searching for. He eventually lets out a long shaky breath. "I did it all for you. All that I've done, all that I've sacrificed, has been for you."

He finally rolls back onto his heels, and as he does, he leaves the forget-me-not right outside my fingertips' reach. I look at the pedals, so soft and blue—the same shade as my eyes when they decide to be blue instead of gray.

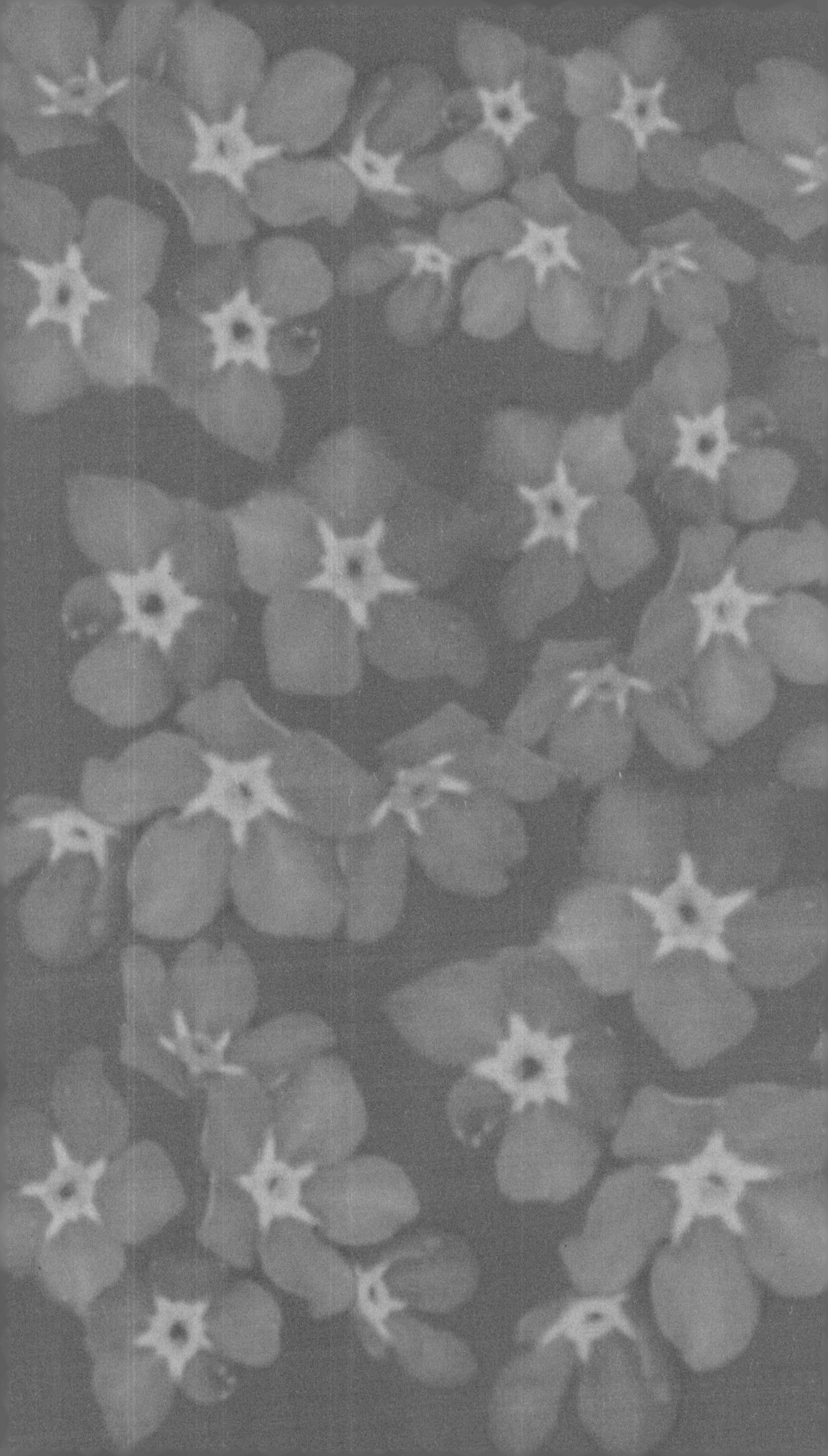

EIGHTEEN

I'M SORRY.

His words ring in my head as I watch his back as he walks away. I stare after him, unsure of how I'm supposed to feel. I'm angry at him for trying to convince me I was part of a human experiment and telling me everything I've known has been a lie.

I do feel bad for him, because it's obvious he has been through a lot, whether I believe his crazy story or not. No matter how much I deny it, a part of me wants to believe him. A part of me *does* believe him. It would explain a lot of things.

I think back now that I'm alone. I hate to admit it, but it makes sense that my life as I've known it hasn't been entirely true. I try to focus on certain memories, but they're all . . . fuzzy, not concrete. The only thing that sticks firmly in my mind is the fire, but I push that memory away.

Almost as much as I'm confused, I'm hurt. I trusted Jaxon. I was falling for him—hard—and now I feel betrayed and fooled.

He said something's changing. What's that supposed to

mean? That I've changed from the version of me he claims he knew before? That he's changed? Into a crazy person maybe, but truthfully, I wouldn't even know the difference. I could try harder to read his mind, but I'm not sure I'm ready for what I might find.

He also said he'd been looking for me and found me, only to almost lose me again. It's like he talks in circles just to give me a headache, leaving my mind chasing itself around and around in hope of finding the answer. I'm too drained in every way to even start to use my brain to decipher it all.

I think back to the moment I first felt drawn to Jaxon Benievere. It was immediate. I always felt there was something more between us that he wasn't telling me. Now that he finally tells me—tells me something, anyway—I push him away.

It's his eyes.

His eyes of darkness that have haunted my dreams from my first day I got lost in them. Those eyes that have drawn me in and consumed my every thought. The same eyes I'm sure I saw the night of the fire. Every inch of my body, heart, and soul believes it was Jaxon that night. Jaxon saved me from burning alive. He'd been there all along, watching over me, protecting me.

I feel a pang of guilt but push it away. Looking at the sky as the sun sets, I'm not sure if I really want to walk home in the dark. I look back at Jaxon's beautiful house and garden. I want to go home more than I want to stay.

I go to push myself off the ground, and that's when I see it —the flower he left for me lying just beyond my fingertips. Looking down at it, all I can think about is the last time my fingers touched a forget-me-not's delicate petals.

Thinking of the images that came flooding back to me last time strikes fear through me now. After the last time, my emotions were so torn. I can't shake the feeling that those flashes were memories. The rational side of my brain thinks I'm going insane, but how is reading minds is any less insane? The curiosity is eating away at me. Was the time before just a fluke or not?

I stand without taking my eyes off the flower. I want to leave. I want to leave and forget everything that's happened today. I want to go back to before Jaxon told me he's known me for longer than my time in this town, to before I started to fall for him, to before I even moved here, and before reading minds made my life so damn complicated.

But I can't.

I can't change what's happened to me or how I got to this point. I can only change how I decide to move forward on the road that's been laid in front of me. I'm just not sure which way is the right way right now.

I look back at those pale blue petals with a deep breath. If this flower could be a key to my real past, no matter how afraid it makes me, I think not knowing is worse. So I bend down and reach for it, closing my eyes right before my fingers brush the stem.

They're real, not like the illusion Jaxon made before.

We're standing hand in hand, and I can feel the static pulsing from his hand to mine. It has always been like this between us—electric.

He's brought me to one of the only places that's still beautiful at all to us now. It's hard for us to find time to be alone in the compound, but Jaxon always finds time for me. Today, he's brought me to the greenhouse, where we can actually be alone, unlike the recreation yard with everyone else.

"I wanna give you somethin'," he says, turning to face me.

"You don't have to give me anythin'."

"Has that ever stopped me before?" His smile grows, touching his eyes. He's right. He always gets his way.

I let out a sigh. "Fine." I close my eyes, already knowing the routine.

"Okay. Open!"

I open my eyes to find him on one knee with a flower in his hand. I laugh and bring my hands to cover my mouth. "It's beautiful!" I say, reaching for it.

He pulls it back and smiles at me. "This is a forget-me-not."

"I remember." I laugh and reach for the flower again. He pulls away and grabs my hand. "Rose, I know this life's not ideal, but we're together, and I don't wanna ever live a day without you."

"I love you, Jax." Tears form in my eyes.

"I love you, Kairi, which is why I have this for you too." He reaches into his pocket and pulls out a small silver metal band as he keeps his eyes on mine.

My heart pounds in my chest as I place my free hand back over my mouth. "Jax . . ."

"I'm not proposin'." He chuckles but slips the ring on the designated finger anyway. "But I am gonna marry you one day when we're out of here—when we're free—if you'll have me."

"Of course I will!" My eyes fill as I sink to his level and press my lips to his.

The vision shifts.

I spot him sitting on the one bench in the recreation yard, walk over to him, and plop down.

"Hey, you." I push my shoulder into his before leaning in to leave a chaste kiss on his cheek. He doesn't look at

me, just stares at everyone else around us. "Jax, what's wrong?"

Without looking at me, he says, "Somethin's happenin'."

"What do you mean?"

"I'm not really sure, but somethin's gonna happen soon, and I don't have a good feelin' about it." His worried eyes finally meet mine.

I lean in for a kiss, and he kisses me back without hesitation. "No matter what happens, we'll be together." I smile at him.

He smiles back at me and pulls me to him. "Despite all of the things they've made us do, I got you out of it, so I can't really complain."

"No, you can't." I kiss his neck.

Our little moment of peace, calm, and love is shattered in a matter of seconds as men come charging in. We jump to our feet, and every one of our friends scrambles. I turn and see Andrew and Dominic running to us with a group following them.

"We have to do this now!" Andrew yelled over the chaos.

Jaxon nods and grabs my hand. I squeeze back.

We all knew this day would come, and we're ready.

Jaxon and I make sure we get everyone moving in the right direction while Dominic, Bentley and Andrew try to hold off the guards.

I turn to Phoenix with worried eyes, and he gives me a side hug before letting his eyes glaze over as his power starts to rush through his veins, preparing to help Zayn, who struggles under four guards. I clear my mind to help my friends when arms grab me from behind. They rip me from Jaxon's grasp. Before I can scream for Jaxon, I feel a pinch in my neck, and I'm plunged into darkness. I can hear him calling to me before everything goes black.

I gasp and fall backward onto the grass.

"I never gave up looking for you after you were taken."

That's what Jaxon said. That must have been the time he was talking about. I run my fingers through my hair, pulling for the truth. These have to be memories. There's no way they can't be, but it still doesn't make any sense.

I feel like I'm going insane. I can't determine the truth from lies, fact from fiction, dream from reality. At this moment, I just want to know the truth; I want to know what happened to me—or what didn't. I'm being pulled in so many different directions and don't know which way to go.

I throw the flower away, wanting nothing more to do with it or the visions. I get up, shake my trembling hands, and pace while shaking my head. I feel so jittery that I can't sit still. I look to the sky. It's darker than I remember. I look toward the house.

I want to talk to Jaxon, but then again, I don't. I want a break from all the craziness, all the voices and visions . . . from Jaxon.

Decided, I turn away from the house and walk to the street.

I look to the stars for the answers. I can feel it. I can feel that Jaxon's right. I can feel that my life is even darker and more complicated than I ever imagined.

I still can't understand how it all happened, how my family fits into it. And where are all those other people I saw in the last vision? I know them. Dominic, Phoenix, Zayn, and Andrew, Jaxon's brother—their names sound so familiar to me. Everything I've seen is something I already know but don't remember.

Admitting to myself that I know the truth is completely

different from telling Jaxon that I believe him, even when I feel that what he's said has always been true. Saying it out loud just makes it feel too real for me right now—maybe ever.

Without allowing any time to convince myself to stay and search for more answers, I turn away from the house. I start down the road and don't look back.

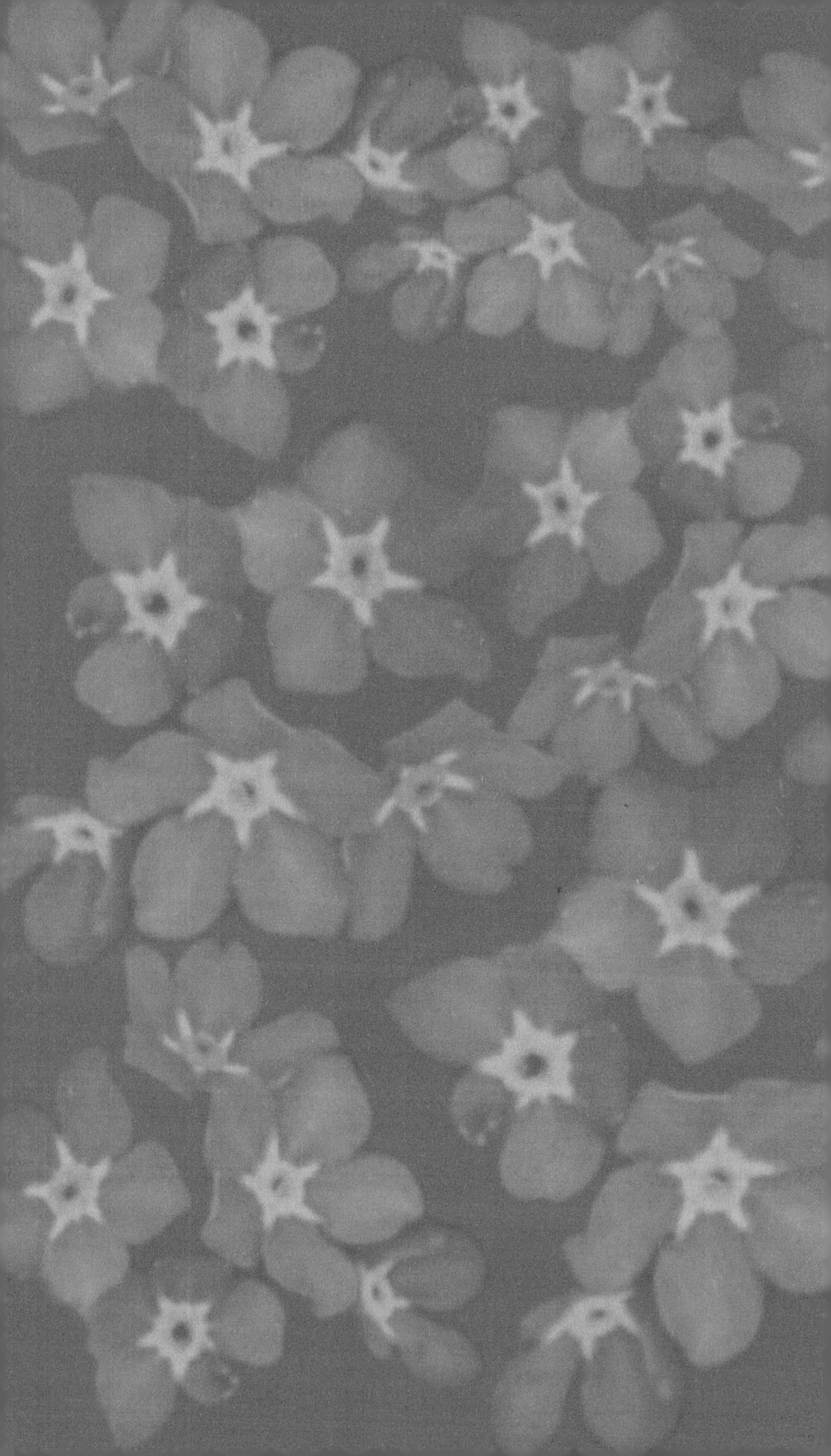

NINETEEN

WHEN I FEEL I've put enough distance between me and his house, I slow my pace. I don't want to think about Jaxon, but I can't stop my mind from wandering to him. I wonder if he went back inside to Allison and had a good time. I wonder if he met his brother back inside, and they laughed at the fact that I'm the butt of some colossal joke. Then there is the one scenario that would wound me the most: what if Jaxon came back outside to talk to me and I wasn't there, as if I'd just vanished? It hurts to see his face in my mind, the defeat I imagine would be written clearly on his face. I push the thought away. *I'm* the victim of whatever the hell is going on.

I'm the one with holes in the memories of my past, which completely blurs my future. I'm the one seeing everything I've ever known crumble around me. I'm the one that's questioning everything and everyone.

Not him. *Me*.

Has anything I've ever known been true at all?

Throwing my hands up into my hair, I let out a frustrated huff. I want answers, and patience has never been my strong suit.

I'm not exactly sure where I am, though I'm pretty sure I'm headed in the right direction. None of these houses look familiar, but in all honesty, I didn't pay that much attention on the way to Jaxon's house. But I didn't think I'd be walking home either.

Way to go, Kairi.

All I can do is keep moving forward and pray I make it home before tomorrow morning. I don't want to have that conversation with Dad ever.

That prickly feeling you get when someone is watching you surges through me. A nagging ache in the pit of my stomach brings on a wave of nausea, making the hairs on the back of my neck stand up, my heart race, and my breathing to become shallow.

I glance around, searching for something, anything that seems out of the ordinary.

I don't see anything, and that's more unnerving than if I did. I'm tired of the unknown that seems to be running my life. I can't shake the feeling that something isn't right.

My instincts are telling me to get the hell out of here, forcing me to pick up my pace. I wonder if I should just call Jaxon, let him come pick me up, and take me home. Then I'd have to explain why I left without any warning at all, and I don't really want to tackle that just yet. I'm not about to call Dad—not that he would even come. So, unable to come with a suitable solution, I keep moving forward on foot.

A car comes around the corner behind me, its headlights blinding me as I turn to look. It's too dark to see anything except that it's a small four-door vehicle. When the car closes the distance between us, it starts to slow.

Okay, no big deal. They must be about to turn in somewhere around here, I tell myself.

I look around, but the only places anywhere near me are closed businesses or shops that haven't been open for quite some time. I didn't realize until now what kind of neighborhood I'm in. There are only two streetlights in either direction that are just now starting to buzz to life. The houses and buildings on this street seem abandoned. I don't think most of the houses are even livable.

I'm not sure exactly how I got here. I was so lost in my own thoughts that I've been walking around aimlessly. I think I would've remembered passing by these sad and decrepit homes on the way to Jaxon's swanky house. I cross another intersection that has no street signs to even give a clue to my location.

I look back at the car. It keeps slowing the closer it comes. Trying to steady the growing panic inside of me, I pretend to be one the phone and start to jog. The car flashes its lights at me, but I refuse to look. It speeds up, passes by, and then comes to a stop about twenty feet in front of me. Three people exit the car.

I come to a stop, knowing immediately that something's wrong. Though it's hard to tell with all of them dressed head-to-toe in black and their faces concealed in shadows, their body structure and the way they hold themselves screams male. I can hear them whispering among themselves, though I can't understand what they're saying. Their backs face me for now, so I try to calm my nerves and command my feet to carry me forward.

I glue my eyes to the concrete sidewalk in front of me, looking straight ahead, trying to radiate a fearlessness that I clearly lack at this moment. I know that as soon as I let them see how shaken I am, this could get messy fast, and I'm not sure that I'd be able to defend myself. I mean, I'm not completely helpless. Perhaps being pushed into a corner with no other choice, I could surprise myself.

"Hey, sweetie," one man calls out to me. His voice is deep and masculine. "Looking for some fun?"

"No thanks," I say, trying to keep my voice as level as humanly possible. I shove my hands in my pockets to hide the fact that they're shaking. Keeping my eyes forward, I come to the end of the next block, look around, and decide to take a right down another long stretch of homes that look deserted.

Is there anyone that lives around here? Seriously?

"Oh, come on, baby. Don't be like that." It's the same man's voice. By the sound of their footsteps and his voice, they're closing the distance between us.

I think we can have some real fun with her.

My heart skips at that. Maybe if I can figure out what they're thinking before they do anything, I can get out of this and. The thought of what they consider "fun" makes my blood run cold.

"Not in the mood for any fun, thanks." I try to sound firm and dismiss any attempt they may try next.

"Sweet little southern thing like you sounds just like my kind of fun though."

I'm not sure what it is that makes me stop and whip around to face this man, but I do. I feel a fire burn within me that I never knew I had.

"Oh, a pretty thing too. Even better." He smirks. This man has about a foot on me. His hood is removed to reveal his dark complexion, clean-cut face, and an arrogant smile that creeps up to his forest-green eyes. The look on his face is as if he's won the lottery and I'm the prize. I want to smack the look right off his face.

He has no idea who he's dealing with.

In truth, I don't know who he's dealing with either. I don't know who I am or what I'm capable of anymore.

"Leave me alone." I glare.

He takes a confident step forward, and I take a step back. I inwardly curse myself for doing so because it only makes me look weak and scared.

What if Jaxon was telling the truth before? By some strange twist of fate, I can hear others' thoughts, but how far does that power extend? The human mind is complex. I wonder how far my ability can go.

I look deep into the large man's eyes as he stands before me. I already know his intentions. His thoughts are clear. This isn't the first time these men have stalked women like prey. They always follow a similar pattern of pulling their car along behind her as she walks down the road, then ambush her. They taunt her until she's paralyzed with fear, then take turns playing out their sexual fantasies with her.

I wonder what would happen if I dug a little deeper, pushed my power a little further . . .

I concentrate and project my thoughts toward him.

Step back.

He shows no reaction, so I try again, pushing my thoughts toward him with more force.

Step back!

He blinks his dark eyes repeatedly, and the confusion is clear on his face. Then, as if without his permission, he takes one step back away from me.

I take the opportunity to explore this new discovery further and take a step forward. The power surging through my veins feeds off the adrenaline and fear. It's overwhelming but calming at the same time; it's a familiar feeling. My mind is working overtime, and I let this power lead me. It's as if my body instinctively knows what to do.

Step back!

His body moves in a robotic motion as he steps away from me. I advance toward him. His friends look back and forth between us, confused as to why their friend is backing away from such a fragile-looking woman.

I see in my peripheral vision that one of the men is thinking of being brave and moving in on me. My power pushes in his direction to keep him where he is as I control the one that deemed himself the leader of this little sadistic group.

Stay where you are!

He looks around as if to see the person who just spoke to him. Confused and a little shaken, he doesn't move any farther.

Did you expect me to be an easy victim?

"Yes," he says, eyes as blank as a night sky, no stars, no moon, and no clouds—just an empty canvas waiting for an artist. The power pulses inside me proudly as it commands the men in front of me. They are helpless to fight against my control over them. My heart races as I revel in this power that allows me to take charge for once in my life, and it's coming to me naturally.

I take a step toward the leader, and he steps back not because I told him to, but because, unlike earlier, fear is radiating off him. I close my eyes and project my thoughts toward all three of them as loud as I can.

Get in your car and drive away!

I leave my eyes closed for a few more seconds until I hear car doors close. When I finally open my eyes, I am alone. In the distance, I can only see taillights.

I stand there for a moment and marvel at the unbelievable thing that just happened. I can really do it—everything Jaxon said. The next chilling thought is what else he could be right about. The past.

The adrenaline that was my driving force before leaves my body rapidly now. My head becomes hazy; my legs get weak and wobbly. Black spots dot my vision, and the world spins around me. I try to keep my balance, but just before everything goes dark, I see the earth rushing toward me.

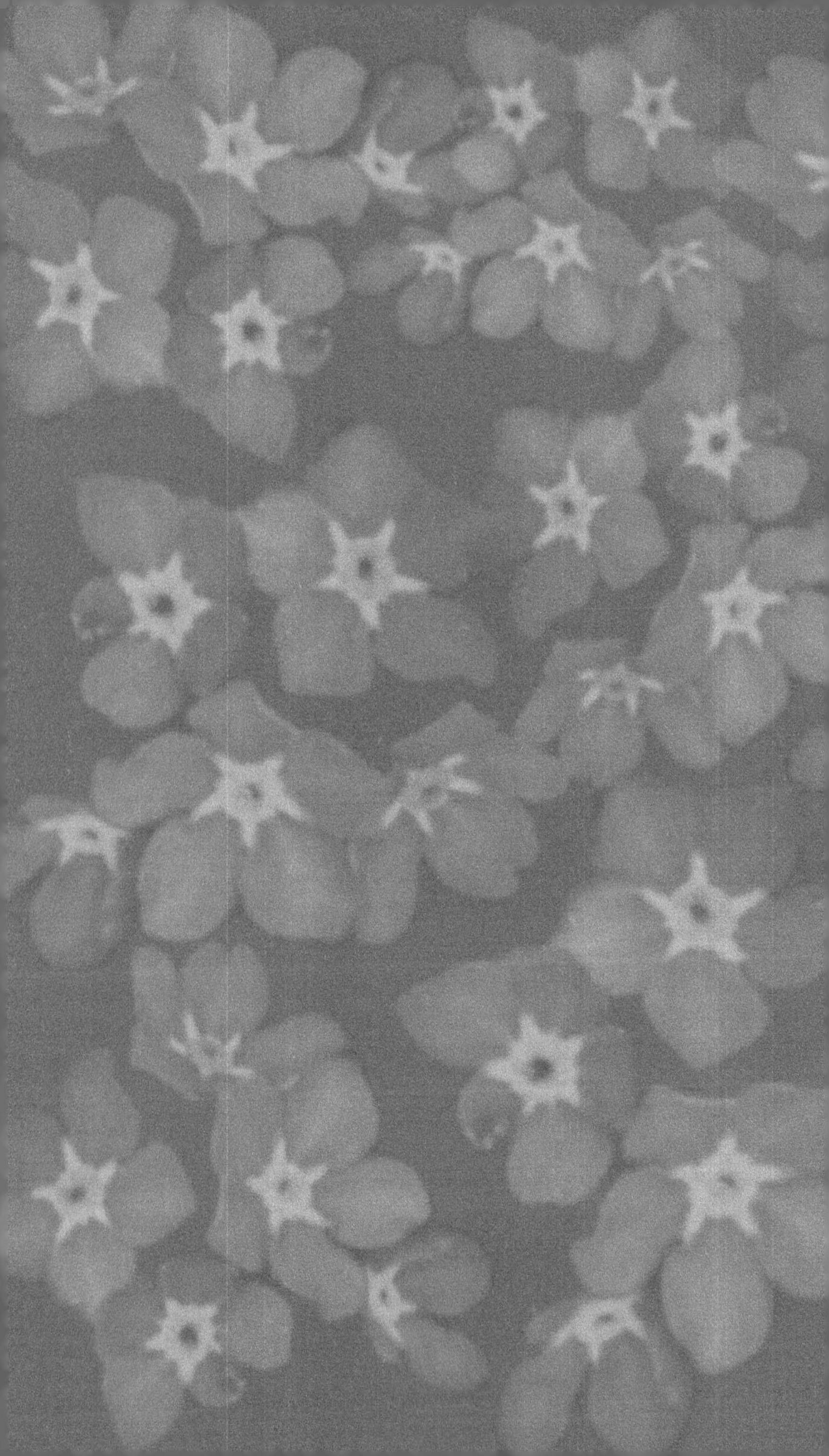

TWENTY

KAIRI.

I hear a voice whispering my name. I know that voice. It's the same voice that causes a flurry in my stomach and goose bumps on my arms.

My eyes flutter open to see Jaxon jumping out of his ostentatious Jeep and rushing toward me. Clearly, he was shouting, not whispering. Jaxon stops a few feet away. He seems unsure if I would want him to come to my aid. I guess with the way I treated him earlier, I wouldn't come running straight to my side either.

"Hey," I breathe out.

"Hey?" he repeats incredulously. "You just vanished from my house, and all you're going to say is 'Hey'?" He sounds like a father scolding a child.

"I found out I can handle myself on my own." Well, at least I thought I could, but being found unconscious on the sidewalk isn't really helping my argument.

"Yes, it clearly looks that way." He scoffs, gesturing to me still lying on the cold concrete.

I let out a frustrated breath. "Oh, never mind."

Jaxon sighs. "What do you mean, anyway?" He kneels by my side.

I try something new and play back what happened with the hooded men and push the images into Jaxon's mind. With my eyes closed, I see the whole event play like a movie in my mind as it does in Jaxon's. Being able to push thoughts came second nature to me, and pushing images instead isn't that much harder. These abilities are either developing more rapidly than I thought, or I'm already capable of so much more than I can even imagine.

I push myself into a sitting position, then eventually to my feet. I wait while Jaxon processes what happened only moments before he found me here. I wait for the worry about my safety and the anger that I tried something so dangerous on my own, but he surprises me, which is not very easy to do today.

He closes the space between us and scoops me up. "You're amazing!" he raves as he spins me around in the air. "I knew you were special."

Jaxon sets me down, and we're standing nose to nose, with barely any space between us at all.

"You were right"—I breathe against his lips—"about everything."

He smiles sadly and takes my face in his hands before leaning away from me to scan my face. "You've always known the truth, Kairi. You just needed someone to remind you."

I smile up at him. "Why'd I faint?"

He keeps his smile on his face, but it isn't quite as warm as it was before. His eyes harden. "You just aren't used to using that much of your brain's capacity."

I slap his arm, and his warm smile returns softer than before.

"Kairi, I'm serious. You need to take it easy with your powers until you're used to using them again. It takes a lot of energy to do what we do, and you can't burn yourself out like that. If I hadn't come along, who knows what could've happened to you."

My heart rate is steady now and I'm not feeling weak or faint. I'm smiling, because for some reason, I can only smile when I look at him.

"Come on." Jaxon motions for me to follow him back to his Jeep, but I don't move. "What's wrong?"

"I can walk home." I'm still standing a few feet away from him as I attempt to sound convincing.

He seems a little taken back. "Kairi, you probably don't even know where you are or how to get back to your house."

"I'm sure I can figure it out," I say, standing my ground. Do I really think I should be walking around after dark by myself? No. I did fairly well on my own about thirty minutes ago, but I don't really think I should push my luck either.

I know I'm being a little dramatic and difficult about letting Jaxon give me a ride. It's not that Jaxon has done anything to make me think he'd ever put me in harm's way. There's so many things that have come into the light today. Yes, Jaxon was right about the powers, but I'm still not sure what I think about what he's said about our personal past. I can't deny that there is a connection between us. Being around him makes my judgment waver.

"So you're telling me you're going to wander around in a dark abandoned neighborhood and just *hope* someone worse than the guys you already dealt with don't show up?" Jaxon raises an eyebrow, sounding infuriatingly confident.

I go through all the pros and cons in my head.

I'll get to be around him a little longer, even though I hate to admit I really like his company. I can also try to get more information out of him on the HUE experiment program and maybe try to find out more about the past us and how I was when we were together.

The other side of it all is that I feel like my brain is going to explode with all I've learned today bouncing around in there. I want some time alone to stew over it and make sense of my feelings on the situation.

"Fine, just take me home," I mutter.

He smiles triumphantly, takes my hand, and leads me to the passenger door. As we drive away, I look back and wonder if this power I have is really good or really bad.

As Jaxon drives, I tell myself I'm not going to bring anything up, that I really just want to get home and be alone. But that's not entirely true. I glance back at Jaxon one last time and sigh, curiosity winning over once again.

"Jax." I pause. "Can I ask you something?"

He shifts his gaze to me quickly, then back to the road. "Of course."

I take a deep breath, not sure how to begin now that I opened the door to the conversation. "You said you can make things appear, like the flower you left for me at the house?"

"Yes."

"Is that all you can do?"

He lets a quick smirk escape before hiding it away behind an emotionless face. "More or less."

I huff. "Well, what's the *more* part, then?"

"Kairi, what is this really about?"

He glances at me now, but I turn to look out the window. I watch the town pass by and still nothing looks familiar.

"Kairi," Jaxon prompts, pulling my attention back to him.

He's stopped in a gas station parking lot now. His brown eyes look so deep, like endless pits I could just fall into. He's turned in his seat to look at me directly.

"Can you enchant items too?" I finally whisper. The question sounded much less idiotic in my head.

Jaxon's face is still serious, but his eyes have a playful glint now. "What exactly do you mean when you say 'enchant'?"

I take a deep breath and look away. "When you fabricate these objects for people, can they make them see things that you want them to see?"

"Kairi." I feel his hand on my forearm, urging me to look at him. "I can make people see objects and make them real right in front of them, but that's all they are. Objects." He pauses, studying my face. "What is this about?"

"You've left me more than one forget-me-not since I moved here, haven't you?"

Jaxon seems taken back. I assume that isn't where he thought this conversation was going. "Yes, I have."

"What would you say if I told you that each time I touched the flower, it made me see things?"

"I would say it sounds a little crazy but also strangely gives me a sense of hope." He smiles. "What exactly did you see?"

I'm not sure I really want to tell him. What if it *does* give him a sense of hope? I don't know what those visions mean. What if they're wishful thinking on my end? Or memories from another life? I'm not sure I want to know the answer to any of these questions. Right now, there is so much uncertainty in my life, and I'm not sure who I can trust or believe.

I do know that the only one who can help me with the forget-me-not visions is Jaxon, because they're both tied to him directly.

I look at him, searching his eyes. I don't know what I'm looking for, but right now, at this moment, I trust him. "I saw us," I whisper.

I can tell he's trying very hard to hide his eagerness. "What do you mean?"

I take a deep breath. "Each time I touched the flower, I had a vision. Images of us talking about loving each other; you giving me a flower in some sort of greenhouse, then a ring; sitting on a bench, then being attacked; me being dragged away."

Jaxon's eyes widen as I finish. "And what do you think of these . . . visions?" His face is stone, voice indifferent.

"To be honest, I don't know. I don't remember any of it. But every time I think back to them, it feels real." I try to read the expression on his face he's cleverly hiding from me. "All I know is, things you've told me already are true. I just don't know anything anymore. I don't know what or who to believe. They feel like memories, Jax. I just don't have any proof, and it's difficult for me to believe in something that sounds so crazy to me."

Jaxon studies me quietly, which only irritates me.

"Would you please stop starin' at me like that?" With narrowed eyes and a huff, I look away from him.

"Like what?" He tries to sound innocent, but he isn't fooling me.

"Seriously?" I stare back at him. "Never mind." I sigh, completely done with this conversation. If he's going to beat around the bush and play dumb, then I want nothing more than to go home. "Just take me home, Jaxon."

"Oh, come on. I was just teasing." I don't have to look at him to know he has that smile on his face that makes me weak.

So I don't look.

"Please just take me home."

A sigh leaves his lips as he puts the Jeep in drive. For a while, he says nothing, and neither do I. We both keep our eyes on the road and passing homes.

"Just so you know, I didn't enchant the flowers I gave you. I don't know why they're making you see visions, but it does give me some hope."

Unable to hold it in, I groan. "That's what I was afraid of."

"Why?"

"Because *Jaxon Benievere* . . ." I emphasize his full name, unable to hold in my frustration any longer. I let it all out. "I didn't want to tell you about the visions in the first place because I didn't want you to get your hopes up. I don't want to have to live up to this girl you remember. I don't even know how to process everything you've told me, let alone *believe* it all."

More than that, I don't want to believe that my family has lied to me all this time. I'm not even sure how much time they've fabricated. I don't want to admit that I feel like I know absolutely *nothing* about *anything* anymore.

He doesn't respond right away. I look back out my window, and it's not long before he's pulling into my driveway.

Jaxon kills the engine. I look over to see the white in his knuckles from the stern grip he still has on his steering wheel. I want so badly to reach out and comfort him, to calm his mind that I know is at war right now, but I can't even do that for myself, let alone try to help him.

Jaxon.

At the sound of my voice ringing into his thoughts, he turns toward me, but his grip never loosens.

"I'm sorry," he says, his voice sounding defeated, his eyes empty.

I give him a sad smile. "You may have been the one to tell me all these things, but everything that's happened is not your fault. That much I do know." I reach out and grab his hand. He willingly lets go of the wheel and threads his fingers through mine.

He looks down at our hands, studying them, then looks back up to meet my gaze and attempts to smile. I know that deep down, he's still blaming himself.

"I just . . ." he starts but stops, then turns to look back at our hands. "I just want you to know that you can trust me."

I place my hand under his chin and pull his eyes back to mine.

"It's not that I don't trust you. I just need time to process all of this, okay?" I caress his cheek with my thumb. He closes his eyes and leans his cheek into my hand.

At this moment, in the safety of my own thoughts, I admit that I am, without a doubt, in love with Jaxon Benievere. The connection we have couldn't have been forged in the short time I've been here. What we have is something words cannot easily describe.

I want to tell him how I feel, but something's holding me back. Maybe it's the fear that since we were last together and I lost my memories, I may not be the same girl he remembers. What if this version of me isn't who he wants as much as the former? Maybe it's the fact that I've come to this realization, and telling him that I love him means I have to accept that the rest of what he's told me is true.

My past is a lie. I'm not even sure if my family is even my family. More than anything, I wish I could continue the rest of my life with the fuzzy memories I have of my past. I really wish I could, but I can't. Now that this has all come to light, I can't live a lie anymore.

I focus back on Jaxon, who's still breathing deeply with his cheek in my palm, eyes closed peacefully but still so very sad. I smile at him even though he can't see it. I lean in and gently kiss his lips.

"I have to go," is all I say before I turn away from him and use the hand that was touching his slightly stubbled face to open the door. I exit his Jeep and jog up to my front door, turn the knob, and enter the house without a backward glance and without a chance for him to say anything else to me.

I've had enough for one night.

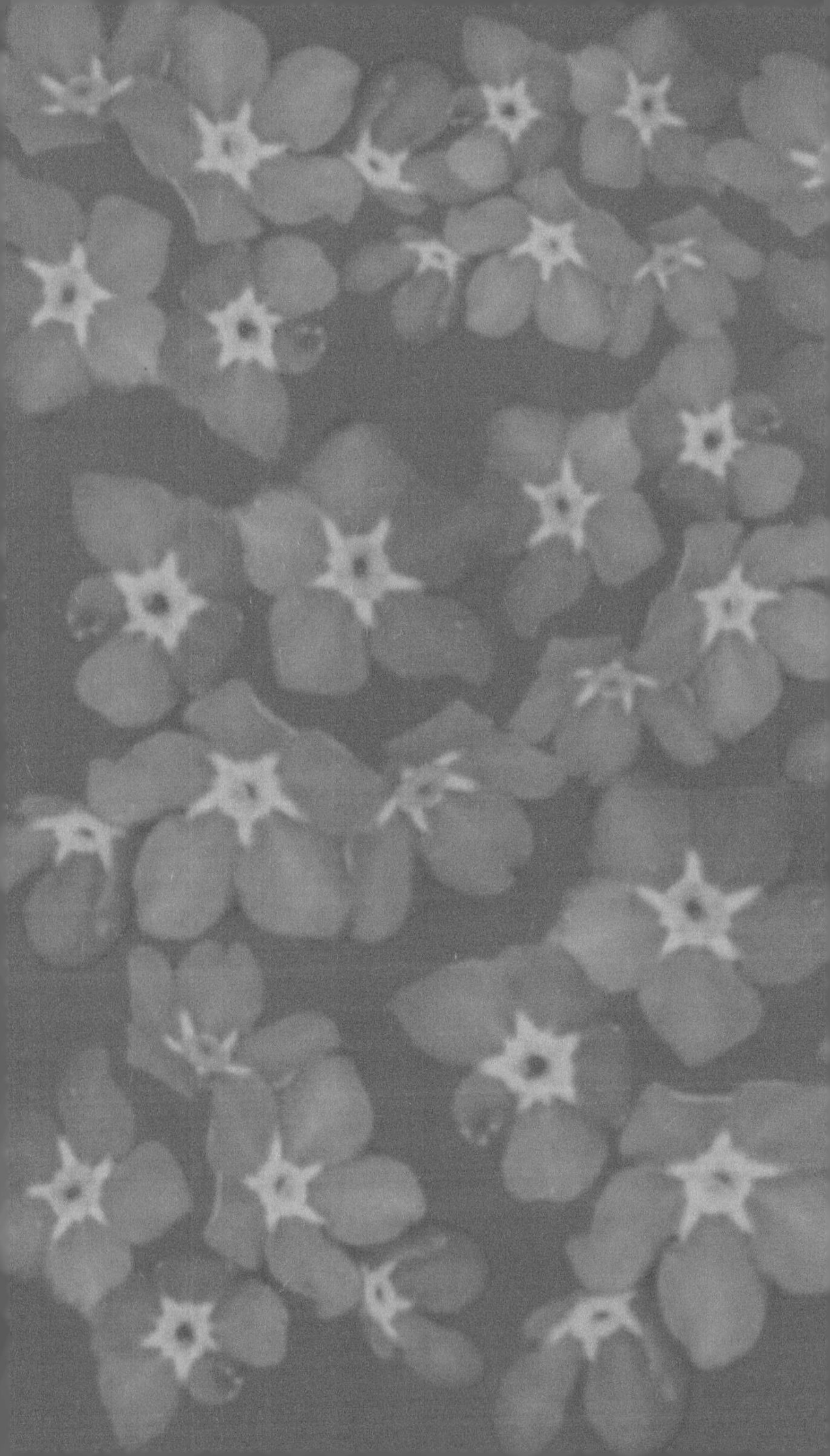

TWENTY-ONE

ONCE SAFELY INSIDE, I lean my back against the door and close my eyes. After several minutes of deep breaths, I hear the Jeep pull out of the driveway and disappear. I push myself off the door and toward the stairs, wanting nothing more than a shower and deep sleep before school tomorrow.

I walk past the living room. On the TV plays an old Clint Eastwood movie—not really sure which one.

"Kairi?"

I nearly jump out of my skin as I turn back with my hand over my racing heart. My father's head peeks over the top of the couch.

"Jesus! You scared the shit outta me!"

"Language, Kairi Rose," he grumbles, standing up and stretching out his back and arms before walking over me. "I must've fallen asleep waitin' for you."

"I didn't think you'd be waitin' for me."

"I still worry." He creases his eyebrows together, studying me.

"Of course. I'm sorry, Dad." I wonder if he's even my father. At this point, I'm not sure what could surprise me. I immediately wish that train of thought never entered my mind. It's like saying things can't get any worse, then that's exactly what happens.

"So, how was the party?" He's faking interest.

"It was just a party. Nothin' too interesting."

He doesn't seem convinced. "Didn't a boy come and pick you up earlier?"

"Yes . . ." I say hesitantly.

"Well, why didn't he come to the door and introduce himself properly?" His voice hints that he's upset, but I'm not sure if it's the fact that Jaxon didn't meet him before taking me to his party or something else.

"Dad, he knocked on the door, but you were too distracted by your work to notice, just like always." I don't want to have this debate with him. I want to go upstairs and be alone with my thoughts, because that's the only way to start sorting out this mess in my head.

With each passing moment, the pounding in my head gets louder and louder, and I want nothing more than to sleep this all off.

"My work's very important." He crosses his arms across his chest and a hard look takes over his features.

I mimic his stance. "To be completely honest, I have no idea what you even do, so I guess I'll just have to take your word for it." I stare at him. I have so many things I want to say to him right now, so many questions I want to ask.

Why does it always seem like his work's more important than his family? What kind of work does he even do? More than anything, I want to ask him about what Jaxon said. I want to know if he's my father, if this is even my family, if my entire past is a lie. I've always thought back on my younger myself as being daddy's little girl, but right now, looking at him, that's not the case anymore. I'm not sure it ever was.

As sad as it is to admit, I don't think I should bring any of my comments, questions, and definitely not my concerns to light right now. I don't trust the man I believe to be my father.

I sigh, letting my eyes soften. "Look, Dad"—I nearly choke on the word—"I'm not feelin' very well, and I really just wanna take a shower and go to sleep."

Without giving him a chance to say anything else, I hurry up the staircase, taking the steps two at a time, then lock myself in the bathroom. I turn the faucet and sit on the floor next to the tub with the back of my head against the wall, barely paying attention as the water slowly rises. I decide a calming soak would be better for the way I'm feeling right now. When I want to think, I play a single song on my phone on a constant loop and let the never-ending tune drift into the back of my subconscious, allowing my thoughts to organize themselves.

I find myself in the bathroom, my body submerged under the steamy hot water with my favorite strawberry aromatherapy bath salt, for longer than I even realize. I just lie there, looking up at the ceiling, thinking of everything but nothing at the same time.

I try to think back on my life and remember certain details, but I'm not surprised that I can't. Some images are clearer, like my family: Dad, Mom, and Sister. And the fire.

Then others I try to recall, like playing sports, having friends or boyfriends, my first kiss with a high school quarterback—those are *fuzzy*. Unclear, like a still picture in my mind instead of a smooth flowing memory. It wouldn't matter if I wanted to forget my past and start a new life here, memories don't just turn off like a light switch.

Then again, my mind is much more complex than I could've ever imagined. My thoughts shift back to the three men that approached me a few hours ago. I pushed my ability in a direction I had no idea was even possible. The scary part isn't the fact that I knew exactly what these men were planning to do or that I had some kind of control over them.

It's that I liked it.

No, I *loved* it.

I loved the rush of power that ran through my veins as I made those men do things against their will. I made feet take steps that their owner never commanded. I made grown men leave in fear. I got a high from the strength, and it made me want nothing more than to continue doing it.

That's what's scary. I enjoyed taking away their free will. Sure, I can tell myself that I did what I had to do to defend myself, but that doesn't make it right. I'm afraid to find out just how far my power goes. Invading someone's private thoughts is bad enough, let alone *this*. Jaxon told me earlier that once I practice and learn to control my power, it won't make me feel so drained every time I use it. But what if I don't want to learn to use it? What if I don't want a part in any of this?

I guess there's no point in what-ifs. This is my life now. I have mental abilities I can't even begin to comprehend, and if I don't learn to control them, I could hurt or even . . . kill someone.

With that, I let the water drain from the tub and step out. I walk to the mirror and turn to face myself.

I wish I could understand what Jaxon sees when he looks at me. There is so much emotion in him—in his eyes—that I'm not sure I can ever understand. I shake my head, wrap myself in a towel, and head to my room. After throwing on some shorts and tank top, I crawl into bed.

I think back on the evening and how it all took a turn for the worst.

Allison.

Anger and betrayal build inside me as I remember her kiss with Jaxon. I just want to . . . well, to do a lot of things actually. I want to slap her smug self-importance right off her high-dollar face. I want to tell her off for trying to take what's mine —though I guess he isn't technically *mine*. And I want to yell at Jaxon for putting himself in any situation that includes Allison.

How dare they?

I can't believe I completely forgot about that whole thing until now. In hindsight, it's the lesser of the things I'm digesting now. It seems being told that I'm an experiment of a secret organization that injects children to make a super-human race is a bigger pill to swallow than the mean girl kissing the guy I like.

I know the whole thing sounds crazy, insane, mental, batshit, and I don't think anyone would believe it. Even though I told Jaxon he's a lunatic for even thinking that I'd believe such a crazy story, there's something deep down gnawing at me. I can *feel* that everything Jaxon told me is true. I don't know if you'd call it intuition or what, but a tiny part of me believes him because I can remember it. What I don't understand is how what I know and what I believe to be true are completely different things.

Let's just say that I *am* an experiment and that Jaxon and I fell in love living in our own hell. I remembered being taken away from Jaxon when I touched the forget-me-not. Was I taken from the others because of a power I've only just begun to scratch the surface of? Was I the greater threat that had to be singled out? The petty, self-absorbed side of me wants to believe that, but I don't think that's the case. I can't shake the feeling that I was important to someone there other than Jaxon. I sense that I knew it then, and I can start to feel that truth now.

I groan and run my fingers through my hair, then massage my temples. All this thinking is giving me a headache. I hope it's just the thinking, anyway. I've been having more lately than I ever remember having before. I wonder if I can focus hard enough to prevent myself from getting headaches ever again. I close my eyes and concentrate on the pressure in my head fading. . .

Fading . . .

And fading . . .

Nope. It's definitely worse now. A whine slips from my lips as I reach over to my bedside table and shake out four pain reliever tablets. I swallow them down without a chaser. I turn out the light, roll over, and sandwich my pounding head between two pillows and pray for sleep.

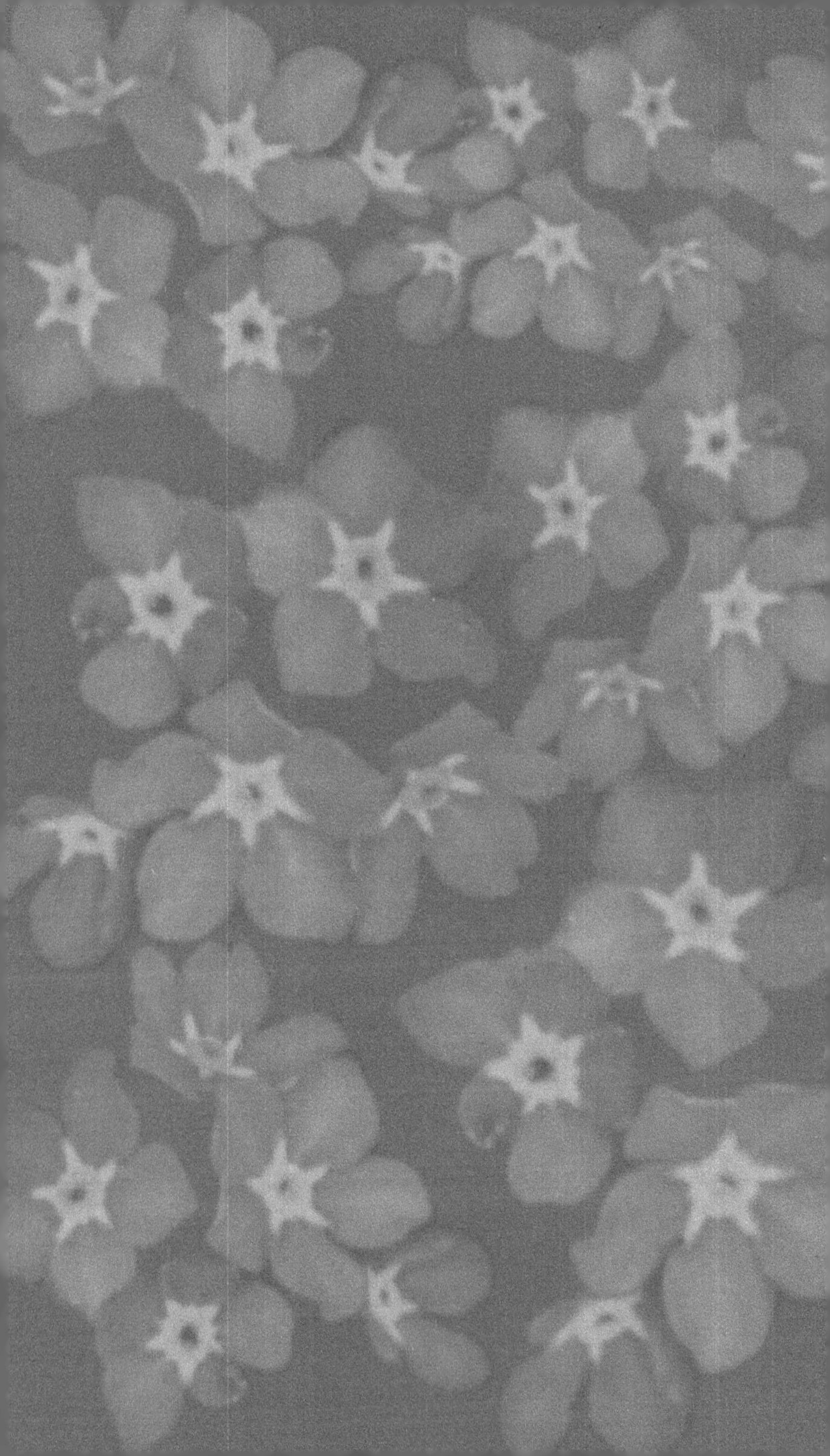

TWENTY-TWO

I CUT my eyes to the evil morning light shining through the curtains. I feel as if I've got a maximum of twenty minutes of sleep. My head is *still* throbbing, and I feel like complete shit. Groaning, I roll over and stare at the ceiling, letting my eyes adjust.

My mind wanders back to all the frustrating topics from last night that made me feel this way in the first place. I rub my fingertips over my temples, attempting to massage the pain away.

I turn my head toward the door when I hear three crisp knocks on my bedroom door.

"Kairi."

"Yes, Dad?" I grumble.

"Did you plan on going to school today?"

I reach for my phone and see it's past eight. I'm already really late. I slap my forehead and regret that stupid decision immediately.

"Are you feeling okay?"

That's it!

"No, I have a huge migraine and just feel like crap."

Fingers crossed.

"Maybe you should stay home today and rest up. I'm gonna take Sidney to school. We'll see you later."

With that, I hear his footsteps retreat down the hall, and I'm in the clear.

I know that I need to try to figure this all out, and it seems like I'm going to have to do it with the company of this headache. Something else I know: I can't face Jaxon again until I've come to some sort of conclusion.

I decide to do what I do best and write down everything I know so I can physically see what I'm working with and go from there. I go to my backpack and pull out a spiral notebook and a few different color pens, because color coordination is key. I plop down on the floor on the side of the bed facing my window nook.

"Okay, let's start at the beginning." I crack my knuckles and move my head from side to side to pop my neck.

I write down things from my past that I remember the most—memories that are concrete or branded in my mind—then the ones that feel more . . . fabricated. I separate the two different parts of my past with two different colors.

I start with the ones I know are true: my family, my mom, dad, and sister. I only remember them later in life though. It's as if my first memories with my family are only a few weeks before the fire. I remember us all eating dinner together. I remember Sidney coming home from dance and wanting nothing more than to show us everything she learned. I remember tension between my parents. They would argue a lot, and it always seemed to be about something Dad was doing.

Everything I recall about my family are memories like this —us being together, like a normal family. It's more and more of the same up until the fire, when everything changed forever, and we ended up here.

I look out the window and let my mind wander. Maybe I'm trying too hard to remember and the memories will come back to me if I relax. The weather outside is beautiful today—a nice baby blue sky with no clouds in sight. The leaves on the tree move back and forth in the breeze.

I imagine being out in a field on a day like today, stretched out in the grass. I feel the warm rays of the sun on my skin and the soft grass beneath my outstretched arms. I'm surrounded by wildflowers.

"There's my girl."

I snap back to reality and onto my feet.

I walk to the window and look toward the woods. This is what happens when I let my mind wander—I daydream about Jaxon.

The thoughts that come to mind the easiest revolve around him. Jaxon has a way about him that pulls my heart in every direction possible but still seems to make me feel grounded.

This is the first time I see a memory, a vision, a daydream of me and Jaxon without the forget-me-not. I'm not sure what it means, but I like it.

I shake my head. I can't let Jaxon distract me from my mission. I need to figure out what's going on, and I can't do that with him consuming my thoughts in both good and bad ways.

Forcing myself back on track, I try to think harder and focus on any details I can remember. The pieces that are hazy include anything that happened before those few weeks—any of my time spent at school, with my friends, or at extracurricular activities. It's as if the things that made me who I thought I was are all fabricated—the type of people I surrounded myself with, the friends I shared my secrets with, the guys I dated, and the things I did to express myself. Writing seems to be the only thing that's remained constant.

I let my eyes wander back toward the window and gaze into the thick brush of the forest that takes up the land behind my house. Maybe a little fresh air would do me some good. I can't help but remember the last time I was there, when I tried to run to clear my head. Let's hope history doesn't repeat itself. With my mind made up, I lace up my shoes and head downstairs, out the back door, and toward the woods.

As soon as I take my first steps outside, I'm hit with the scent of the woodlands so strongly I can almost taste the wind rolling out of it. I shield my eyes from the rays of sun beaming down between the clouds. It warms my skin. As I step across the invisible boundary line where my safe backyard ends and the uneasy dense trees begin, I can't help but feel like I'm entering an entirely different world. I carefully make my way deeper into the trees, watching my steps, and think back to the last time I was here. I don't think I can ever forget my very intimate encounter with that *very* large boulder.

Once I feel like I've walked a safe enough distance from my home, I stop. I look up to the sky. The trees go up so high, as if to kiss the clouds. It is so peaceful here. A soft breeze rustles the limbs, causing leaves to fall every now and then. Two squirrels chasing each other jump from limb to limb, tree to tree in an endless game of tag.

Walking through these woods is like walking into a world full of peace and calm with a deathlike silence that echoes on for what seems like eternity.

Thinking of the dangers I could come in contact with make me wonder if my abilities will work on an animal. I hope I don't have to find out. There's a difference between man and beast that I don't want to experience. The men I faced before made a choice that led me to my actions; animals, on the other hand, only act out of instinct, and it wouldn't feel right punishing them for it.

On the other hand, just because I've only used my power

to control those men doesn't mean the only use for it has to be malicious. I could try something easy, like getting an animal to approach me.

I pause, listening to the world around me, trying to find the faintest sound to work with. I close my eyes and focus. I hear something shuffling around to my left, and as I turn, I freeze.

Standing not even thirty feet away, emerging from the brush, is a female mountain lion. She pauses mid-step, eyeing me cautiously, taking each of her steps with ultimate precision. She's sizing me up. I instinctively take a step back and immediately realize my mistake as she bares her razor-sharp fangs and lets out a cross between a hiss and roar that sends shivers down my spine and goose bumps up and down my arms.

She takes a step toward me, lowering her head, as if daring me to run. Moments ago, I wanted to try to get an animal to approach me. Now I want nothing more than to be here all alone. What if I can't get this giant cat to do what I want and get mauled to death in the middle of the woods when no one even knows I'm here?

I have limited choices here. This giant cat can either attack me because my powers don't work on animals; they *could* work, and I could tell her to leave; or she could walk away on her own and lose interest in making me her next meal. There's only one of those options I can even try to rely on to get myself out of this.

I don't dare close my eyes, and I try my best to show no fear. I stare right into her soft caramel eyes and think.

Sit.

I don't know what else to do, and dog commands are the only things that come to mind. I don't know if I'm more shocked or relieved when she slowly moves into a sitting position, never breaking eye contact with me.

Still unsure if she sat on her own or really obeyed the command I directed at her, I try another one.

Lay down.

This time, she lies down without hesitation, yawning and running her tongue over her white fangs before cleaning off her paws. I try to push my heart back into my chest and let out a sigh of relief. On the plus side, I'm not gonna die from a mountain lion attack today and I can also control animal's minds.

This is kind of awesome.

Feeling much more confident than I was about five seconds ago, I decide to try something bold. While keeping eye contact with the enormous predator before me, I gradually sink down toward the earth until I'm in a sitting position with my legs crossed. I drum my fingers across my knees, take a deep breath, and attempt to summon her to me.

Walk toward me. Slowly.

Before I can have an internal debate on whether or not this is a horrible idea, she gracefully rises up on all fours and strolls toward me. Within seconds, she's no more than a foot from me, staring directly into my eyes. I can feel her hot breath on my face, but I feel no fear because I no longer see anything wild in her eyes.

We stay that way for what seems like eternity as I take it all in. I wonder how many people can come face-to-face with a mountain lion and walk away unscathed. I'm so in awe at the fact that, if I wanted to, I could reach out and pet this wild animal like she were my house cat. A newfound love for the wildlife that shares my backyard grows in my heart, but unfortunately, all good things must come to an end.

I can feel the temperature begin to drop as the sun starts to set. I should head back so I'm not walking back in the dark, but I wish I could stay here a little longer. At least I know I can come back and practice some more of my more harmless talents on the animals.

I look deep into this beautiful creature's eyes.

Go home to where you belong.

She pauses for a moment, and I start to worry that maybe I got lucky before and she's about to eat me, but then she turns and casually walks away, disappearing into the woods.

I sit there for only a second more before I rise to my feet and make my way back to the house.

That night my family eats in silence, which has become part of the normal routine—going through the motions of having a family dinner without feeling like a real family anymore.

What's even more sad is that it doesn't even bother me. Sidney's more or less a normal girl going to school, which I love for her. She deserves to be normal, even if I'll never get to be. My father is drowning himself more into his work than ever before, which only makes me more suspicious. Every time I look at him now, I can only think that maybe Jaxon was right and that he's hiding something.

After dinner, I sit by my window, looking out at the stars, letting my thoughts consume me while listening to music play in the background. I smile to myself.

I can't help but let the music take root in my mind. There's something about certain songs that just seem to fit a situation too perfectly. This is one of those times. I wish more than anything that I could remember the life I had with Jaxon. It'd make everything so much less complicated. If what we had was real . . .

Jaxon.

I've been trying so hard to push him from my mind. The only person who sends my body into a frenzy and makes me question everything I've ever believed. He can be obnoxious, arrogant, sweet, caring, mysterious, frustrating, patient, and sexy as hell at the same time.

In just a few months, he's completely captured me, body and soul, whether I'll admit to him or not. So many times, I *almost* jump into his arms, *almost* kiss him, *almost* tell him that I believe him, *almost* tell him how I really feel. *Almost*. But almost is never enough. Never enough to change anything. It's like looking back on your life and getting caught up on the what-ifs. It won't change anything.

Maybe I should leave the past in the past and focus on the now. Will I ever be able to truly move on without knowing who I was or what's happened to me? Our experiences shape who we are, and I'm afraid I don't really know who I am now. I don't know what I'm really capable of—or maybe I do and I'm afraid of what I'll do with this much power.

Hours pass and my eyes get heavy, so I make my way to bed. I lie still, drifting off to sleep.

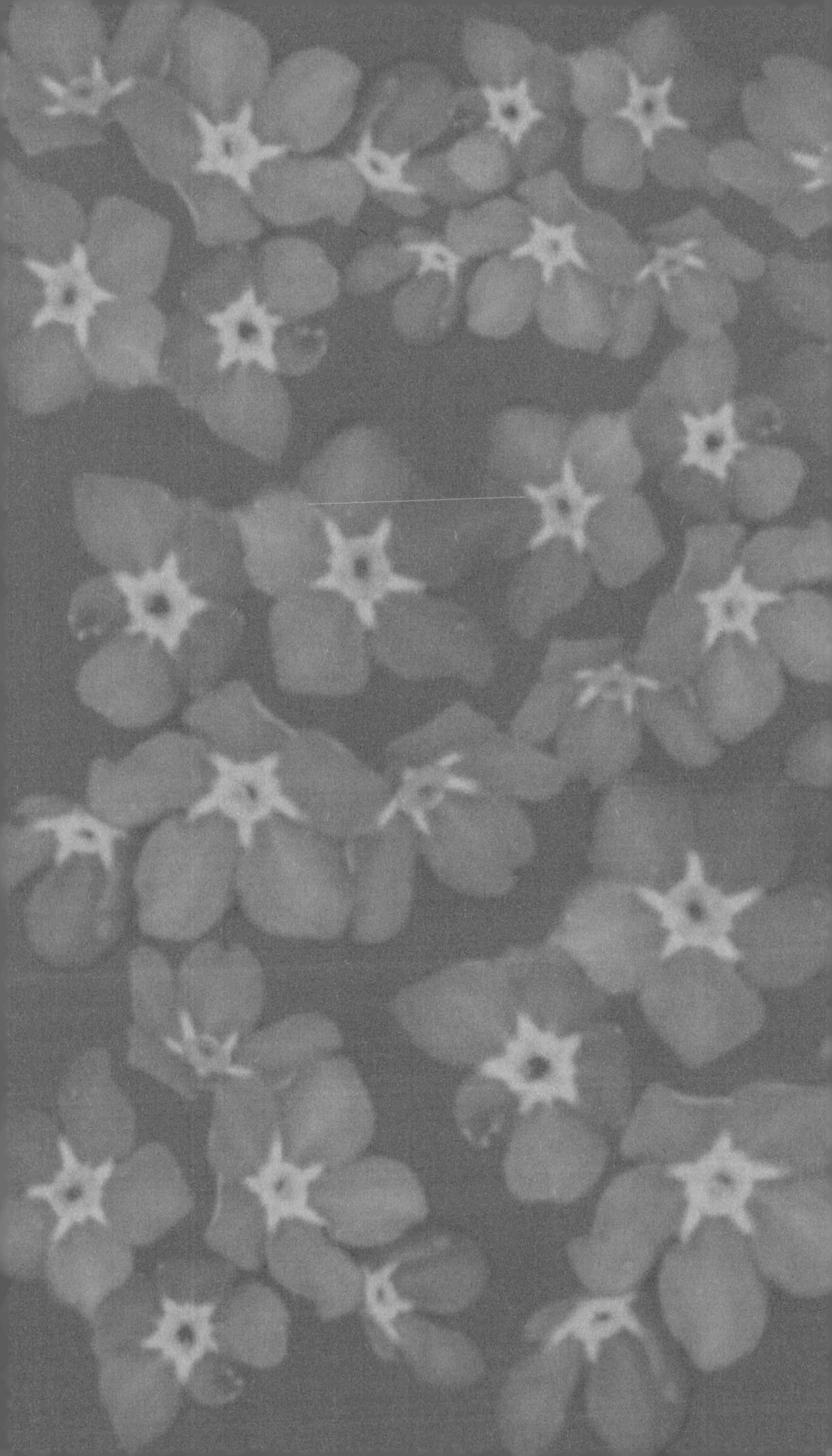

TWENTY-THREE

THE NEXT SEVERAL days consist of me going to the forest, working on my ability to control animals, writing down everything I can remember from my past that's true verses the memories that don't feel right, having not-so-real family dinners, and sitting at my window trying to decide where to go from here.

I roll over and check my phone. Friday morning, almost noon—I guess I should get up. Well, what's five more minutes? It's not like I have anything better to do. I've already done everything I can this week. But my mind is already going ninety miles an hour. I'm not gonna get any more sleep now.

I drag myself out of bed and make my way downstairs because my body's need for food overpowers its need for more sleep. Since it's just shy of noon, pizza rolls are calling my name. I guess since I've just woken up, it kind of feels like I'm having them for breakfast. No shame.

I pour some onto a plate and place them in the microwave. I stare out the kitchen window toward the woods while I wait. I wonder if I should go practice today.

There's a knock at the door. I'm not expecting anyone,

and I really don't want to see anyone, for that matter. Dad and Sidney shouldn't be home for hours, not that they would knock anyway, for obvious reasons. Maybe if I keep quiet and pretend that I'm not here, whoever it is will go away.

Another set of knocks comes louder and more aggressive than the first. I guess that's a no, then.

I sigh, walking toward the door. As soon as I turn the knob, I realize I can't hear anything and already know who it is.

"Jaxon." I stare into his dark eyes, completely composed, void of emotion. Jaxon, on the other hand, looks beyond pissed. Then like flipping a switch, his features go cold and detached, mirroring my own.

"Kairi," he says dryly.

Only when looking at him now do I realize how much I've truly missed him. Even though his demeanor is anything but the carefree man I've come to know, he's still as handsome as ever. I want nothing more than to jump into his arms and feel his lips on mine again, but I can't. With Jaxon, there are still too many questions and not enough answers. Besides that, I can't ever seem to control my hormones or form a coherent thought when he's near me.

"What're you doin' here?" I break the silent staring contest.

"What am I doing here?" Jaxon laughs, but there is definitely no humor in his voice. "It's like you fell off the face of the goddamn earth!" He's leaning forward now, bracing himself on the doorframe with one hand and pointing at me with the other. His face doesn't hide his anger now, and my own slowly rises.

"I've tried to call and text you all week. I was worried about you!" he says. "But here you are"—he gestures toward me—"perfectly fine. So you either broke your damn phone or you've been ignoring me all week. Now I'd like to know why."

Jaxon looks me in the eyes, clearly expecting me to answer his questions while he's practically screaming in my face.

That would be a negative, Ghost Rider.

"One," I say, holding up my index finger, "my phone ain't broke."

His eyes are now slits, hardly showing any of his dark irises to me. He furrows his brows, clearly irritated.

"Two." I bring up my middle finger to join my index finger, extending my arm and putting them right in his face. I decide to play this up a little, since he thinks he can just show up at my home and demand answers by yelling in my face, as if I'm gonna submit to him like a wounded animal with my tail between my legs. "I've been gone from school all week because I'm avoidin' you and ignorin' all your attempts to get a hold of me." I say with a grin.

As I say this, something flashes in his expression, and his eyes eclipse and darken, pupils blown, solid black now. For the first time since I've known Jaxon, he looks truly terrifying. I keep my composure, not giving away the fact that his demeanor is affecting me.

"And three." I bring up my ring finger to join the others, even though he sent a brief wave of fear through me. I have to work to keep my face composed. I'm still trying to get under his skin and have to resist the urge to smile through the fear at his reaction to my words. I never realized how easily I could affect him. "You have no right to come here and demand answers from me. It's not like we're datin' and I owe you an explanation." I stare into the black holes that were once his eyes, and I swear you can see the wheels turning and steam coming from his ears. I cave and smile at him now. "You're just a guy who sits next to me in some of my classes. So, if you'll excuse me . . ." I turn away from him, having every intention of slamming this door in his face.

Although I'm playing this up to mess with him, I'm serious. Ever since Jaxon came into my life, it's as if he feels like he's owed something or that he has the right to influence my thoughts and views. He must think because he's told me things about my past with him, I should hang on his every word and command.

It's true that he isn't my boyfriend, no matter how much I may want that deep down. Past, present, and future self.

I turn to close the door, opening my mouth to say good-bye, but he isn't there. I peek my head outside the door to confirm that he really did seem to vanish into thin air. His Jeep still parked on the street in front of my house.

Where the hell did he go?

Losing my resolve, I close the door and sigh. It's getting harder and harder for me to justify pushing Jaxon and my feelings for him away. The logical side of my mind can't trust a guy who's purposefully keeping things from me, and the things he *has* told me have made me question who I am as a person, my life, and my very existence. No big deal.

That being said, those things seem to matter to me less and less as time goes on.

I rest my forehead against the door. "Well, that could've gone better." I breathe out.

"I was thinking the same thing."

I scream, spinning around with my hand over my heart. There's Jaxon, standing there with a smirk on his lips, arms crossed, as if he didn't almost give me a heart attack.

Bastard.

"What the hell, Jax!" I shout at him.

As if my body has a mind of its own, I close the distance between us and raise my hand to slap that satisfied grin right off his smug face. Just as I'm about to make contact with his stupidly handsome mug, he closes the remaining distance, grabs my wrist, then the other, and pins me up against the door. His muscular body presses firmly against my own, and he pins my wrists above my head in his left hand, making it impossible for me to move even an inch from his grasp.

The curses I'm getting ready to spit in his face dissolve when I look into Jaxon's dark eyes. The almost black orbs have a playful yet mischievous glint to them now as he leans his head forward, cocking it to the side, his nose just barely touching mine.

He whispers, "You want to try that again, sweetheart?" His breath dances on my now parted lips as his right hand moves up to my cheek with a featherlight touch. Jaxon never breaks eye contact while his hand keeps up the soft touch that moves slowly down my neck.

My breath catches in my throat, and his fingers continue their descent. Jaxon's hand creeps down the curve of my breast, along my ribs, and finally stops to rest on my hip.

My eyes are still locked on him, unable to look away. My heart races in my chest. It's as if a fire is being lit inside me, spreading throughout my entire body and eventually making it to my cheeks. He smiles, but there's nothing sweet about it, because he knows he's got me, and there's not a thing I can do about it.

"J-Jax..."

"Shhh," he whispers, shaking his head only slightly, silently telling me not to speak, and my body, betraying me again, obeys. "Now." Jaxon leans back slightly, but his eyes never leave mine. "You've got quite the mouth on you."

My body unconsciously tries to follow him, and I swallow hard, then let out a held breath. I can think of a few things he can do to me, attitude or not.

Oh God. I'm glad I'm the one who can read minds right now. I need a cold shower . . . in holy water.

I break eye contact first, slouching down in defeat. Practically everything about Jaxon is unfair. He has the ability to get about anything he wants from me with a touch, a look, or his words. Here I am, obeying his every command, even after my firm mindset to do the opposite, and here he stands, completely unaffected by me whatsoever.

As much as I hate to admit it, Jaxon probably has this effect on everyone, male or female, straight or not. There's just something about him that makes him persuasive; it's part of his charm. I'm not entirely sure what it is he wants from me exactly. Does he actually want me? Is this just a game to him? Does he want the version of me he seems to remember but I don't? Or is he planning to use me to his advantage to help him take down this organization he keeps talking about? HUE?

I may never know the truth, but my heart betraying me isn't helping and will only get me hurt in the end.

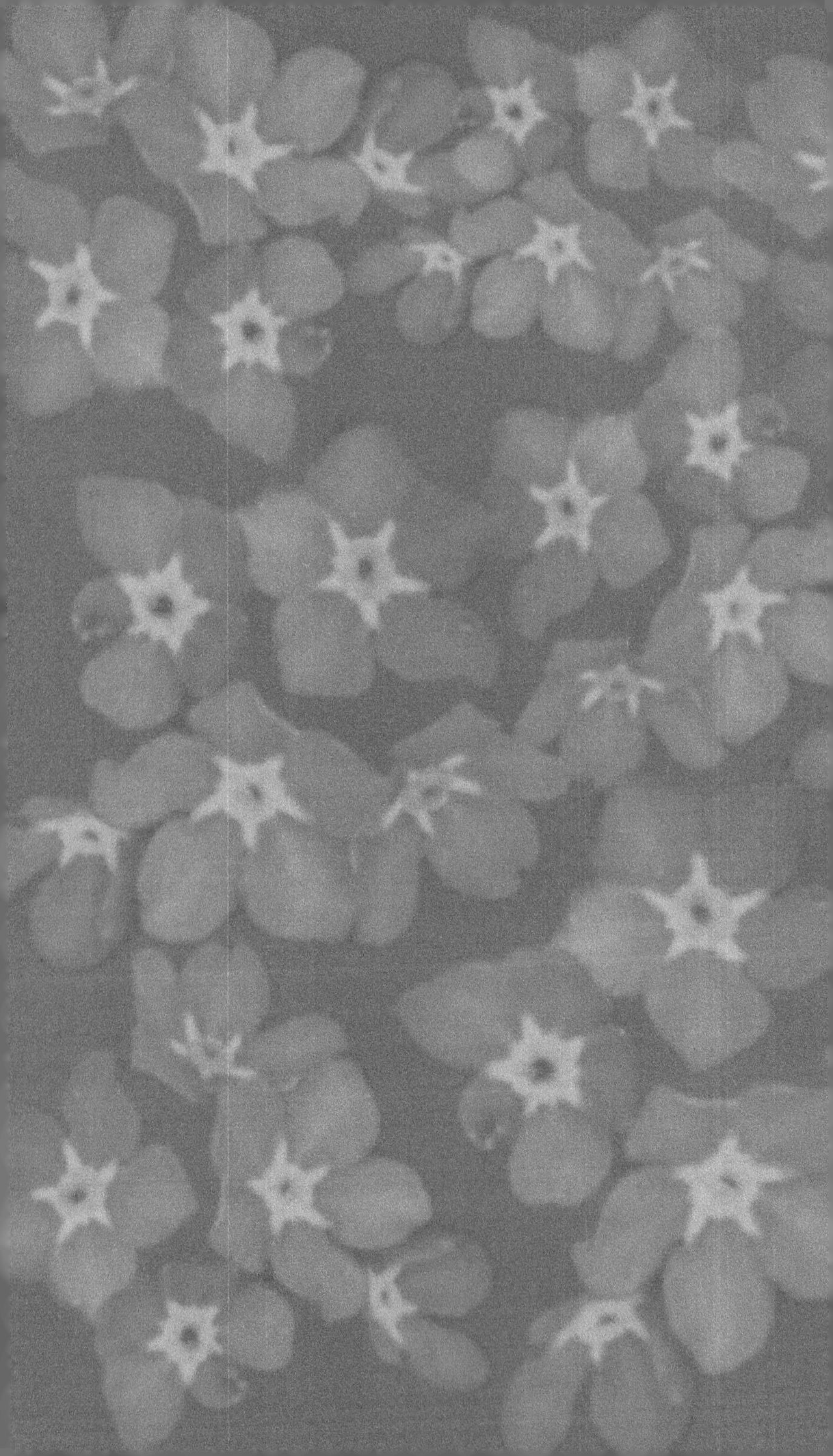

TWENTY-FOUR

"GIVING UP ALREADY, ROSE?" Jaxon places two fingers under my chin to bring my eyes back to meet his.

"Sure." I shrug and look away again, no longer having the energy to play this game.

"Hey, what's wrong?" He leans toward me to get me to make eye contact with him again.

"I'm fine, Jaxon." I remove myself from the cage his arms have made around me easily because his grip loosens at my use of his full name. I move far enough away to be out of his reach. "Why're you really here?" I ask, finally raising my gaze to meet his.

He pauses, clearly confused by my question and change of demeanor. "I came to see you." He takes a step toward me but stops when he sees me maintain the distance by stepping back away from him again. No matter how quickly he tries to hide it, I can tell my need for distance hurts him, and I'll never admit that it's making my body ache too. "Why is that so hard to believe?" He leans back against the door now, arms crossed over his chest, anchoring himself to the surface.

"Because you've always been so upfront and honest with

me, right?" I snort and find myself also crossing my arms, leaning back to sit on the arm of the couch.

"Seriously, Kairi?" His eyes narrow.

"What?" I hold my ground. "Are you tryin' to tell me you've always been transparent with me?"

Jaxon pushes off the door like he's losing his patience with me and begins to pace back and forth in the entryway. "I've never lied to you," he says, not looking up from the floor as he continues to pace. The look on his face suggests he's at war with himself.

"Have you ever purposefully not told me somethin'?"

Jaxon stops and glances my direction before looking out the window toward his Jeep, making me wonder if he is about to leave me here with more unanswered questions.

To my surprise, he doesn't. He simply lets out an exasperated sigh and turns to face me. The conflicting look he had in his eyes moments ago has disappeared. "Yes, I have."

Rage flares within me. "What gives you the right to decide what I should or shouldn't know about my life?" I point at him, not attempting to hide my emotions any longer.

"You couldn't handle it then, and I doubt you can now." He says this with no emotion in his tone, eyes, or posture— the complete opposite of me right now. I feel like I'm about to explode.

"You have no idea what I can handle, Jaxon! You don't get to make those decisions for me!" I spit the words at him, losing what little control over my rage I had left.

"Your behavior right now is why!" Jaxon gestures me up and down. "Have you already forgotten what you did the last time I tried to be honest with you?"

He had me there. I remember that night all too well—the night my life changed, the night I began questioning who I am and who my family is. And I can't ever forget my confrontation with those men. I don't like to think about what I could have done to them.

Instead of letting it be known that he's made his point, I walk off toward the kitchen to retrieve the pizza rolls I completely forgot about until now.

"Where are you going now?" I can hear Jaxon following me.

I touch my finger to my food to see if by some miracle they're still warm. Of course not. I close the door and restart the timer.

"Ignoring me again, I see."

I look over my shoulder to see Jaxon looking out the kitchen window at the forest, much like I was doing right before he knocked on my door demanding answers.

"I'm not ignoring you."

He finally looks at me and smirks. "Just don't want to admit I'm right, then?" he says, as if he thinks he's always right.

I shrug, not wanting to feed his already inflated ego, and get my food from the microwave, then make my way over to the table and sit down.

"If you've only come here to see that I am alive and well, you can see that I am. Good to see you. See ya later." My voice is monotone to hide the unwanted hurt I feel deep in my chest. My eyes remained glued to my plate and far away from Jaxon's penetrating gaze.

He scoffs and makes his way toward me. I keep my head down but hear him not so gently pull out the chair across from me, spin it around, and sit in it. He crosses his arms over the backrest and leans on them.

"Is that really how this conversation is going to end?" There's a bubbling frustration in his voice, but I don't feel like arguing anymore.

If I give in to Jaxon and talk about why I'm truly avoiding

him, I will have to face the reality of it all, and I don't think I'm ready to do that. The truth is, I may never be ready.

"Rose?" The pleading sound of his voice makes me look up to meet his dark eyes.

I don't wanna fight anymore.

He seems startled, clearly forgetting I can put my thoughts into his head—only for a moment though, then he's back to his calm and calculated self.

Why're you really here? What do you want from me, Jax?

He seems confused, but the look on his face is as if it were obvious. "I'm not sure what you mean. I told you I came to see if you were all right and to find out why you disappeared."

But why?

"Kairi." He sighs. "I thought I made it clear that I care about you, and can we please have this conversation out loud?"

I look out the window, fighting with myself on whether or not I should dive down this rabbit hole. I guess the curiosity is too much, and I'm tired of all this weighing me down. How can I be angry with him for not being honest or keeping things from me if I'm doing the same thing?

"You care about the girl you think I am, the girl I don't remember. The thing is, I don't know her. She's not here anymore," I whisper.

"Kairi, I . . ."

I think it's time you let me and her go. Out of fear my voice will crack under the heavy emotions I'm feeling, I only speak to his mind again while I try to get a handle on myself.

"I can't."

I look back at him to see he's hung his head with his fingers laced together on the back of his neck, looking the most defeated I've ever seen him. It's heartbreaking.

"Why?" I ask.

Jaxon doesn't move or make a sound, as if he's a beautiful statue of pain.

"It doesn't matter," he finally says. He pauses and looks around, asking, "Why are you here by yourself?"

I tilt my head to the side, confused by his sudden subject change. "Uh, because my sister's at school and Dad's at work, like a normal Friday?" I don't know why it came out as a question, but I'm not sure why he was asking me such a stupid question with an obvious answer.

"What does your dad do for work?" His eyes dart around the room, brows furrowed, like he's thinking hard.

"Some sort of research, I think." I realize I've never taken an interest in knowing what Dad does for a living. That fact is almost as strange as the way Jaxon is acting right now. "Are you alright?" I ask, trying to get him to look at me.

"Is that where he's always at—work?" he asks, completely ignoring the fact that I said anything, still acting weird.

"I guess, but why're you askin'? Why're you actin' so weird all of a sudden?"

Jaxon stands, places his hands in his back pockets, and paces around the kitchen. I follow him with my eyes as I pop another pizza roll in my mouth. His continued habit of pacing is making me uneasy.

"Do you know where he works?" Jaxon stops for a moment, looking out the window like he did earlier, lost in thought.

"Not specifically." I really don't know anything about Dad's work, but I never thought I needed to know. I was never curious until now, and that's only because Jaxon has a sudden inexplicable interest in him and is acting like a loon.

"That doesn't strike you as a little suspicious?" Jaxon's still looking out the window, talking more to himself than me.

I'm officially losing my patience. I stand up and walk over to Jaxon. Just as I am about to react out to touch his back, he turns on his heels and briskly walks toward the living room like a man on a mission.

I huff and follow after him, about to lose my shit.

"Jaxon!" I shout, making him stop and finally turn to face me. "What the hell's goin' on?" I demand. "Why'd you change the subject to ask me about my Dad?"

"I didn't."

That's it. I'm done.

"Okay, I think you should leave." I head toward the door.

"What? Why?" Jaxon asks in a whiny tone that just pisses me off even more.

I swear, everything about this man gives me whiplash. "I'm not stupid, and I guess it's true, then."

"What are you talking about?" Jaxon walks up behind me, placing his hand over the door as I reach for the doorknob to open it and kick him through.

"You don't really care about *me*. You come here thinkin' I owe you somethin', get all weird askin' about my Dad, then just ignore the fact that you're doin' it at all." I've had enough of the emotional roller coaster that is Jaxon Benievere for today.

"You honestly think I don't care about you?"

The irritation in his voice makes me look up. I'm unsurprised to find an expression that matches the tone.

"If you really care, then for once, will you just tell me the truth about what's goin' on?" I challenge him, praying that he won't keep hurting me and will be honest.

"Kairi . . ." he starts, but I cut him off, having reached the limit of bullshit I can stand in one day. The hesitation in his voice is clear as day and gives away the fact that he's still hiding things from me.

"You need to leave. I refuse to sit here and let you keep lying to me." I push his arm off the door, turn the knob, open the door, and gesture for him to make his way out of my house with his secrecy. "I can let go of the past and the fact that you kept all this from me because I had no memories of anything. I understand that now, but I won't let you continue to treat me like a glass doll."

"Do you think your dad could be working for them?" The words tumble out of his mouth so fast I'm not sure I hear him right. The look in his uneasy eyes, as if he's unsure of what he said but said it anyway.

"For who?" I press, still not sure where this conversation is going.

"For HUE. Who else?" The way he's looking at me suggests I should have come to that conclusion on my own.

"That company that did the experiments you were talkin' about?" I'm still a little confused. "You can't be serious." I scoff, studying Jaxon's dark eyes for that playful light I've grown accustomed to to tell me he's joking around, but it's not there. He's actually serious. "You think my dad experiments on children?" I can't help but let out a humorless laugh.

"You don't know what he does for a living, who he works for, or where he works, and he's always gone and secretive. He knows your fake past, but does anyone else in your family? He could've been the one to put them in there." He touches his index finger to the center of my forehead, his eyes still dark and serious as he lays out the "evidence" before me. "You can't tell me that it can't be possible."

"Of course it's not possible!" I scream at him. "And for the record, you don't know a damn thing about him to make those kinds of accusations! Just 'cause I don't know what he does for work doesn't automatically mean he's involved in somethin' like that." I shove my finger directly into the center of his chest. I have to push away the thought of how muscular his chest is. I bet he has muscles everywhere . . .

Nope. Pull your mind out of the gutter, Kairi.

"Come on, just think about it for a second." Jaxon takes a calculated step closer to me.

I narrow my eyes as I look up at him but don't dare move an inch. I'm determined to stand my ground and hide how being this close to him affects me.

"Think about it like this." He places a hand firmly on the wall behind me next to my ear, leaning in. "What if what I'm saying is true and you're living with the very man who did all of this to you? To us? What if you're in danger and you don't even know it."

I keep my face stagnant, but his words rock me to my core. I've been thinking similar things for the past few days. It's becoming sickeningly clear that I don't know who I can trust —if I can trust anyone at all. Out of everyone, I want to trust Jaxon, but I can't bring myself to do it blindly because he's the one that started all this self-doubt in the first place. If he'd never come into my life—or back into it, according to him—I wouldn't have been told about my phony past and this human experiment insanity. On the other hand, I'd never have felt what I've been feeling for him—a feeling that's once in a lifetime. Am I really willing to let what I could have with Jaxon go out of stubbornness and fear of the actual truth? Would I really be content living a lie forever? I don't know. I really don't know.

"Tell me that you don't feel this." With his hand that isn't propping him up on the wall behind me, he grazes the skin of my arm, dragging his fingertips up and down, leaving a trail of goose bumps and heat in their wake. I unwillingly close my eyes and sigh, reveling in the heaven only the slightest of touches gives me. I can only imagine what would happen if I got more than just the few tastes of him I've been given. I'm not sure I'd be able to handle what it would do to me.

I let out a heavy breath. "It doesn't matter what I feel."

"I know you feel the same way I do, Kairi. I don't want

you to run from me anymore," Jaxon whispers, mere inches from me now.

My eyes flutter open to meet his intense stare. I don't know what to tell him. I don't know what to do with everything I've learned. I don't know what to do with these feelings I have for him.

"I just need some time, Jax," I say. It's hardly even a whisper.

He scoffs. "I feel like I've given you more than enough time with the way you've dodged me all week, but if time is what you think you need, then fine. You'll get all the time in the world." Jaxon's tone is anything but gentle or understanding as he puts space between us by taking two steps out the front door. Hand still on the knob, he turns and looks me dead in the eyes one last time. "Just remember, Kairi, whatever you decide to do, the truth will remain the same. I've given up more for you than you'll ever know, but ultimately, this is much bigger than you and me. You have my number when you make your decision." With that Jaxon, turns his back to me, jumps off the porch, and reaches his Jeep in a few large strides. He revs the engine and speeds away down the street and out of view.

I stand there, mouth slightly agape, staring off after him with his voice still ringing in my head and touch scorching my skin.

You'll get all the time in the world.

With my heart aching painfully in my chest, I turn, shut the door behind me, and slide to the floor.

What have I done?

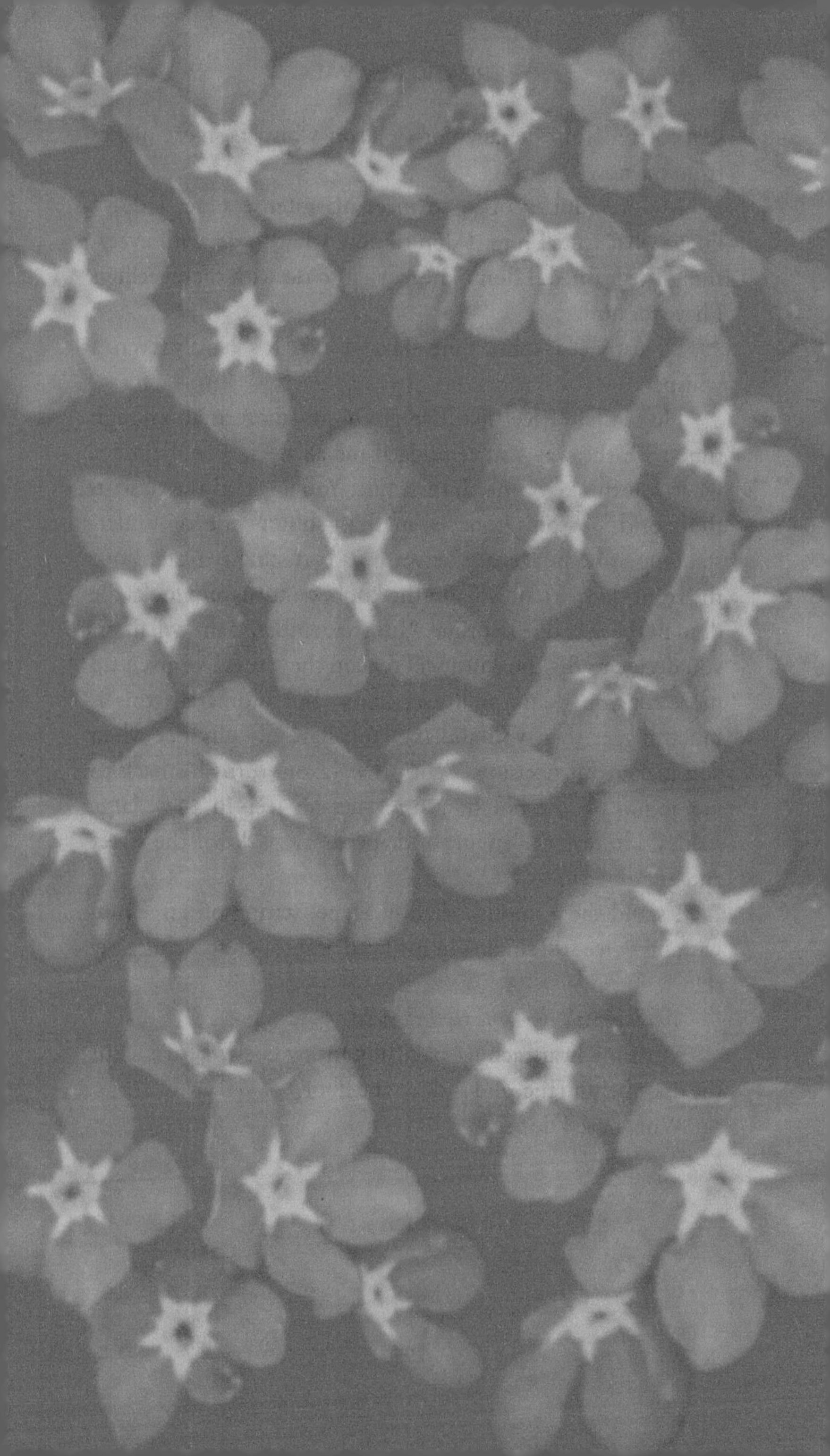

TWENTY-FIVE

TO SAY that the following days are depressing as hell would be an understatement. I go back to school, but Jaxon isn't there. Chelsea and Travis are more clingy than usual, stuck to me like glue. I'm not sure if they notice I never pay attention to their conversations or if they just don't care. More than once, I wonder why they attached to me so quickly, but considering the circumstances, I choose to let it drift to the back of my mind.

I'm cautious around them regardless. Besides the fact that my headaches have turned to migraines, and it seems that they're always at their worst around them, I know they aren't quite as normal as they want me to believe. Chelsea's starting to snap more and more at the littlest things. Travis is enjoying Jaxon's absence a bit too much. But for now, keeping up appearances feels like a better option than not, so I let it go. For now.

I didn't think too much about Jaxon's statement about giving me time until he all but vanished from my life. I've been tempted to text or call, but for some reason, I can't bring myself to do it. I'm not sure if it's everything I know

now, that I'm aware of the facade of my life, or my self-doubt, longing, love, and fear. Either way, it all comes from Jaxon.

Just this once, it seems I'm gonna have to do this on my own and figure out the answers to my own questions.

If I'm in class, the house is empty. Sidney decided to spend some time with Mom. Though I was confused with her decision because I thought she'd made some friends, with things spiraling out of control and having no idea what could happen at any moment, it's probably best she's safe and away from here.

Dad's been more absent than usual, working extra hours. I have too much alone time, and my thoughts are starting to wear me down. Being an over-thinker has always been my downfall.

Today's another day without a word from Jaxon, and I'm getting antsy.

"I wonder where Jaxon's been recently?" I think out loud.

"Who cares where that guy is, anyway?" Travis grumbles.

I turn to see a scowl on his face. I didn't realize he had such a distaste for him. He's taking this competition for my affection he's conjured up in his mind way too seriously.

"Um, because he's the sexy *Jaxon Benievere*?" Chelsea swoons.

"Seriously, Chelsea?" Travis points the same scowl at her now, clearly not in the mood for her fangirl mindset.

"Okay, okay. It *is* weird that he hasn't been here though," Chelsea adds as an afterthought, completely ignoring Travis's pointed look.

I push my food around my plate. I hope he hasn't gotten himself into any trouble. I don't think he'd rush into anything with these HUE people, but what do I really know about the guy?

"He probably got arrested or something."

"Why the hell would you think he got arrested?" Chelsea stares at Travis like he grew a second head.

"Have you seen the way the guy dresses and acts?"

Like that determines someone's arrest record, Travis. Nice. The urge to roll my eyes is too hard to suppress.

Chelsea does the same. "Travis, the only things I think about when it comes to his attire are letting him do dirty, dirty things to me, naked, in bed, all night, repeatedly." She smiles at him, and his face goes a little red, either from embarrassment or anger.

My eye twitches, and I have to bite my tongue at her attraction to Jaxon. I didn't think I'd become this possessive, but damn, I want to tell her not to talk about my man like that.

Can't really stake a claim on him when I'm the one who pushed him away . . . again. Why did I want to distance myself from that sexy man again? I can't remember.

"Look, the point is, the guy screams trouble. I don't know why everyone's so obsessed." Travis huffs and gets up, throws his food away, and walks out of the cafeteria.

"I wouldn't mind him making me scream." Chelsea smiles and wags her eyebrows at me.

"Could you not?" I mumble, rubbing my temples.

"What? I'm just saying."

"Yeah, well, I wish you wouldn't." I stand up and throw my own food away, then head to the parking lot. No way in hell am I finishing this day.

Once I'm seated in my truck, I pull out of the school parking lot and head toward town.

I'm not sure what to do now. I don't want to go home and drown in my thoughts. I could try to call Jaxon. It's been a week, and this time without him, no matter how small, has taken its toll.

I pull into a café parking lot and pull out my phone. I stare at the number for a few minutes before I take a deep breath and hit call. The phone rings a few times before it goes to voicemail. I guess I deserve that. What now?

"The person you were trying to reach is not available at this time. Please leave your name and short message, and they'll get back to you as soon as they can. Thank you," the automated recording says before I hear the beep signaling me to start my message.

"Uh, hi. It's Kairi. I wasn't sure if I was gonna call at all, really, but here I am." A nervous laugh escapes my lips without permission. I clear my throat. "I'm sorry for callin'. I just, uh, I just . . ." Sigh. "I just wanted to hear your voice, I guess. Sorry again. I think I'm just gonna go talk to my Dad about everythin'." I pause, not sure what else to say. "I miss you, Jax." With that, I hang up and decide to drive to the building Dad said he's working at. The most I know about his work is that it's some sort of research, when I looked through some of our mail I was able to find an address that was worth a shot looking into.

On the way there, I can't help but feel that I shouldn't have called Jaxon at all. God, why am I so stupid?

I groan as I pull into the parking lot of the research center. This has got to be the most boring building I've ever seen. It's a giant plain concrete building with no windows. There aren't even any signs except the one near the road that says *Research, Recruitment, and Training of North Dakota.*

I'm starting to worry if I should even be here. Dad and I hardly have a relationship, so I hesitate to pop up at his job where I know my unannounced visit will not be welcome. But I came all this way, and I've been wanting answers. I might as well try now.

With my mind set, I scoot myself out of the cab of my truck, close the door, and head for the front entrance. The dark feeling bubbling in me gets closer to the surface as the distance between me and those steel doors gets smaller.

Taking one last breath, I make my way inside.

The entryway is pretty much what you'd expect looking at the outside: plain gray concrete walls that give the room a gloomy and cold feeling; bright overhead fluorescent lights that give the feel of a hospital and make my stomach flip with nerves. I've never liked hospitals.

The lack of windows and stony foundation makes me feel like I'm walking into a prison. My anxiety builds with each step I take, like my freedom is being sucked out of me by just being in here.

What I don't see, however, is a front desk, waiting area, or a single person. I wonder if I have the wrong building. The lack of life in general is putting me on edge. I keep my eyes on the only other door in the room across from me and back my way toward the front entrance to get the hell out of here.

I don't know what it is, but I immediately feel like a cornered animal as soon as I take a good look around this barren entryway. My primal fight or flight instincts are trying to kick in as I take another quick glance around the room. In the top left corner above the door across from me, I see the red blinking light of a security camera and freeze. He's going to know I was here now, but why hasn't anyone come out already if they've seen me in here? I don't wait to find out. I turn on my heels and move as fast as I can without running and stride out the door of this ominous building.

Images flash through my mind: metal walls everywhere; rusty metal bars; chairs with restraints; neuroscans on giant screens; syringes; and faceless people covered in scrubs, masks, and goggles. The smells of dirt, sweat, blood, and feces burn my nose as the images keep revolving in my mind. I look out the window of my truck, and in the trees across the street, I see a shadowy outline. Squinting my eyes, I can only make out a bulky figure, but a sense of familiarity rockets through me as I hear the echo of screams in my ears. I let out a shaky breath as I turn the key over and leave this godawful place.

I try my best to stay as calm and collected as I can on the way home, but I still can't keep my hands from shaking. After pulling into the driveway, I kill the engine but don't move to get out. Too many thoughts are racing through my mind for me to process why I'm feeling the way I am. Walking into a basically empty room in a research center shouldn't have made me feel like I needed to run for my damn life. But it did.

There's something about that place that sets me on edge, and the fact that I can't figure out the reason is gonna drive me insane.

Taking one last deep breath, I head inside the house, up to my room, strip out of my jeans, crawl under the covers, and lay staring out the window until sleep finally overtakes me.

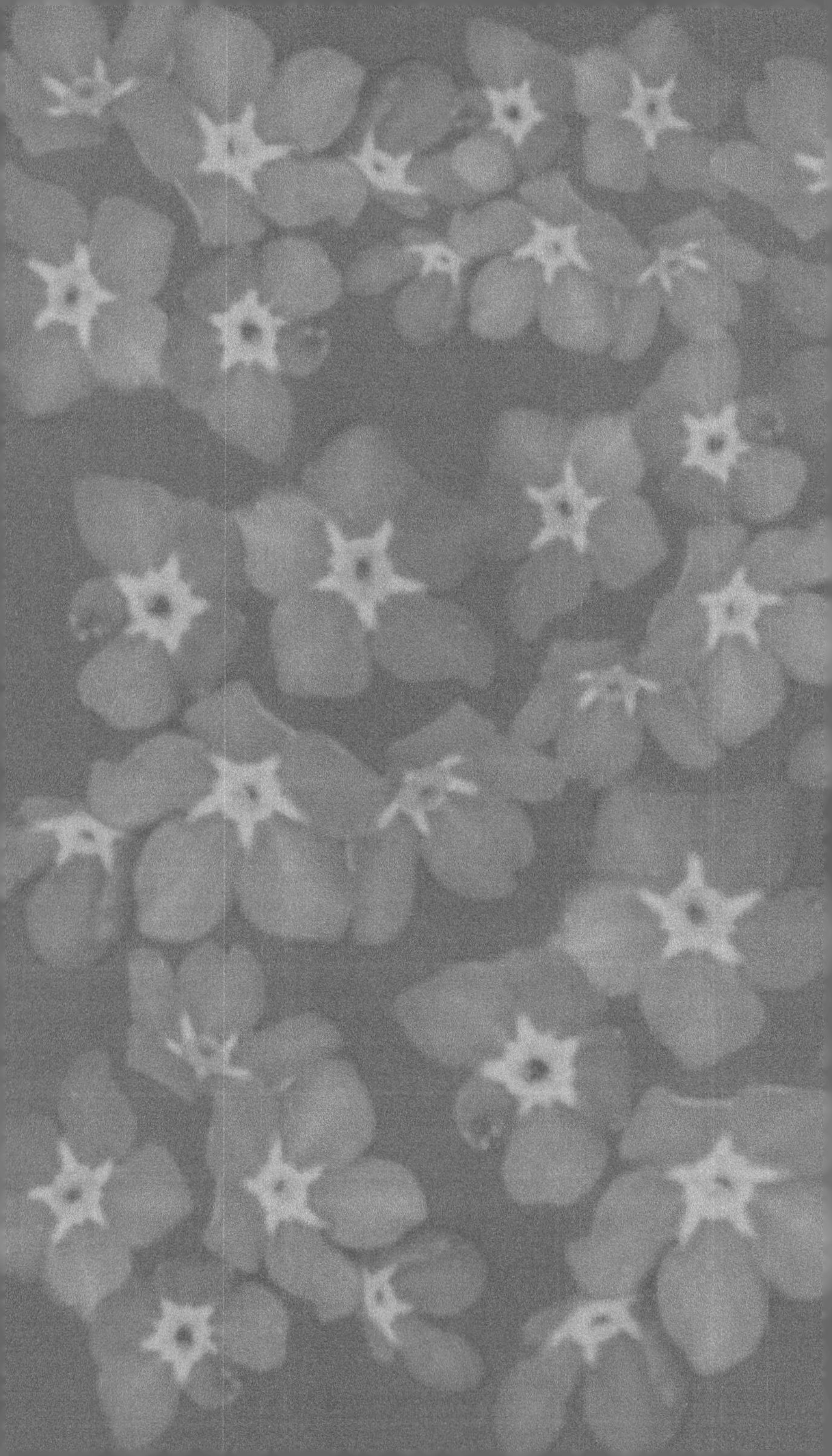

TWENTY-SIX

THE LAST FEW weeks since my trip to the research center have been complete shit. I still haven't heard from Jaxon. I don't know if he listened to my voicemail, but I sent a few more messages those first few days before deciding to give him space after never getting a reply.

It's hard not having him popping up out of nowhere. I didn't realize how much I loved and needed him around until he wasn't here anymore, bringing a whole new meaning to never really knowing what you've got until it's gone.

The first week, I was an anxious mess whenever Dad was around, waiting for him to bring up the fact that I showed up at his workplace, but he never did. He just carried on as if nothing had happened. That freaks me out more.

I've been trying to sneak in questions about his work, our family, life before North Dakota, but his answers are always extremely vague, or he dodges the question entirely. I always have to drop the subject so I don't risk him getting suspicious.

The thing that sets me on edge the most is that, out of nowhere, Sidney went to live with Mom. I just can't understand it. Sidney only talked about how much she liked it here and all the friends she'd made. Why would she want to move again? I didn't even get to talk to her or say goodbye. I came home from school one day, and Dad told me that she was with Mom and had decided to live with her and that he was mailing the rest of her stuff. Then he left to go to work. I haven't been able to get a hold of Mom to talk with her or Sidney about this either, which puts a knot in my stomach.

If it weren't for Jaxon being here that day, I would start thinking maybe they were figments of my imagination, because now it's like they never even existed.

So now, almost a month later, sitting on the forest floor, I'm feeling like a complete ass for not believing Jaxon sooner. Phone in my hands, I stare at Jaxon's contact information, trying to psych myself up to hit the call button.

He told me to call whenever I was ready and he'd be there for me, but I've tried to contact him, and he never responds. I don't know why he would now if he hasn't already. Like a dumbass, I probably blew whatever chances I had left.

Woman up, Kairi.

Taking a deep breath, I press the call button before I can talk myself out of it.

I put the phone on speaker so the only sound in the otherwise quiet woods is ringing of the phone and the audible sound of my racing heart. The longer the phone rings, the more my heart sinks. It finally goes to voicemail, and I end the call, not wanting to leave a message.

Instead, I send Jaxon a simple text that says I've made a decision and want to talk before turning my phone off and pushing myself back onto my feet.

Walking the half mile back toward my house, I clear my mind and listen to the life around me. I can hear the life of the forest going on as it should and can't help but wonder what my life would be like if it was happening as it should too.

No use wondering about what-ifs though.

After strolling for a few minutes, I catch the sound of something coming closer. I pause and try to see what it is. I don't have to wait long before a doe makes her way into my line of vision.

During my time without Jaxon, I've been trying to work more on this mind control thing. I've only had the courage to try small things on animals, because I still can't shake what happened with those men that night, how diving into their minds affected my own.

Clearing my mind and focusing on the doe, I get her to come within reach of me.

Don't be afraid.

I reach out and stroke her neck gently. I pet her for a short time before I send her back to wherever she was going and finish my trek to the house.

Dad's been gone more often than not lately. Now that Sidney isn't here, it's like he doesn't need to keep up the pretense and come home even some nights. The times he is home, he acts like I don't exist. I think I need to start looking for somewhere else to live before shit hits the fan.

I walk upstairs and take a quick shower. Then, wrapped in a towel, I head to the dresser to grab some clothes.

"Going to give me a show?"

I spin around fast, almost losing my balance, and squeak in surprise with my hand on my chest, trying to keep my racing heart inside my chest.

Two dark eyes are staring at my toweled body.

"Jax! What the hell!" With my heart still trying to jump out of my chest, I close my eyes and take a few deep breaths.

When I reopen my eyes, a gasp escapes me. Jaxon is now only a few inches from me. His pupils are blown, and I'm hyper aware that I'm standing in front of him practically naked. Getting a stronger grip on the towel, I rock my weight to take a step back and create some distance, but strong hands grip my waist.

"Jax, wh—"

He cuts me off: "You really like testing me, don't you?"

"Testin' you?"

"Mm-hmm . . ." Jax leans in. His nose brushes the skin at the corner of my mouth and travels up to my ear.

Letting out a shaky breath, I can't help but close my eyes and enjoy having him this close to me. "Jax, I don't—"

"Don't," he whispers in my ear. "Don't pretend your body isn't pulsing with electricity right now, Kairi." He runs his nose from my ear to my jaw and down the length of my neck. Jaxon takes his time leaving a trail of goose bumps in his wake, and I relish in the warmth that radiates within me from his touch. He stops, takes a deep breath, and places a featherlight kiss on my collarbone. "I know mine is."

Jaxon pulls his face up, making eye contact with me. I can't hold back anymore and reach my hand to his neck and pull him down as I push up on my toes to connect our lips.

Every nerve ending in my body instantly comes alight. Jaxon wraps one arm around my waist, securing me firmly against his body, while the other moves to cup my cheek as he tilts his head, deepening this kiss. I wrap both arms around his neck, trying to get even closer, leaving the space between us nonexistent.

Jax's tongue sweeping along the seam of my lips has me opening up to give him access without hesitation. A soft moan escapes me before I can try to hold it back as his tongue plunges into my mouth and explores every corner. I try to keep up with his fervor, but my consciousness disconnects from my body.

I wholeheartedly let Jaxon lead and dominate the kiss. Soon, he directs me toward the bed, and I can't help the bubbling excitement pulsing through me.

Jaxon breaks the kiss. We're both panting, attempting to catch our breaths.

"I think we should take this to my place," he whispers hotly in my ear.

I nod mutely and move to get dressed in the closet. The last thing I need right now is Dad showing up. I come out to find him in the exact same spot looking out the window.

"How did you get in here, anyway?" I ask.

He shrugs. "The door wasn't locked."

I give him a droll stare—like that made it okay to just walk in someone's house.

Outside, I say, "You know, I don't know if this is really a good idea." But I still climb up into his Jeep anyway.

"Why's that?" he asks, pulling out of my driveway and heading toward his own house.

I bite my bottom lip. "I saw you and Allison at the party."

Tense silence thickens around us as the seconds tick by. I'm not sure what I want him to say or if what he says will really change anything. I still want him, and I doubt his answer will make me forget my feelings for him.

"I hate that you saw that, Kairi." He sighs. "But she threw herself at me. I didn't know what to do, honestly. Despite how I may come off, I don't handle situations with women very well."

I smile at that. The image of this sexy man not actually knowing his way around women is hilarious. "I know, but it didn't make it hurt any less."

"I never meant to hurt you, Rose."

"I know."

"Think you can forgive me?"

"I'm sure you can make it up to me somehow." I smirk.

He chuckles. "I have a few things in mind already."

We laugh as the tense atmosphere between us lightens. Not long after, we reach his house and make our way to his room. The nerves creep up on me. All my previous bravado is nowhere to be found.

Warm hands snake around my waist from behind, giving me a gentle squeeze, before Jaxon turns me around until we're standing face-to-face. All my nerves and worries vanish as I'm locked into his eyes like black holes.

I let hands move from his neck and run over his hard chest. Feeling his muscular stomach through his shirt makes my own flip. I keep my gaze locked on his, which is filled with desire. I'm sure mine reflects the same intensity. When I reach the bottom of his shirt, I let my finger slip underneath to feel the smooth toned skin underneath. I brush my fingertips over his defined abs, making my ascent back up, bringing his shirt with me.

Jaxon holds my gaze and stays unmoving, letting me explore at my pace. I let my eyes fall from his face to his delicious body as he lets his T-shirt fall to our feet. I can't help but swallow to keep the building saliva in my mouth and not drool over the man in front of me.

As my eyes sweep over the well-defined muscles of his abs and chest, I let my hands brush over his burning flesh unabashedly. I'm not sure where my confidence is coming from, but I try not to think about it.

"Someone is quite forward today." Jax's voice rumbles much deeper as his hunger for more grows, much like my own.

I flick my eyes back to his for a moment as I feel heat build in my cheeks.

When I don't say anything, he places a finger under my chin, tilting my face, getting me to meet his burning stare. "Kairi." A soft smile spreads on his lips. "You have no idea what you do to me." Jax's fingers move to stroke my cheek, and I feel a small smile of my own grow at his words and touch. "I've waited so long to be with you like this again."

That's a reminder that I've had some kind of intimacy with Jaxon before; I just can't remember. Though that fact is incredibly frustrating, it's also comforting to know I once trusted him with my heart and body.

It's this moment when all previous doubt leaves me, and I know I'm ready to finally move forward with this man that has completely captured my body and soul once again. Taking a deep breath, I hold his gaze, brush my fingertips across his cheek, and take the leap and open up to him.

"I trust you," I whisper.

Jax softly smiles back at me.

I love you, Jaxon Benievere.

An amused giggle escapes me when his eyes go wide, no doubt surprised at my confession.

Suddenly, he takes a firm grip on my face and slams our lips together with so much passion, my legs wobble and he has to hold me up with one arm around my waist, gluing us together.

"And I love you. More than life itself."

At that, our clothes fly from our bodies. We collide and fall on top of the mattress and get lost in one another at last. A fire races through my veins, and I let it consume all of me.

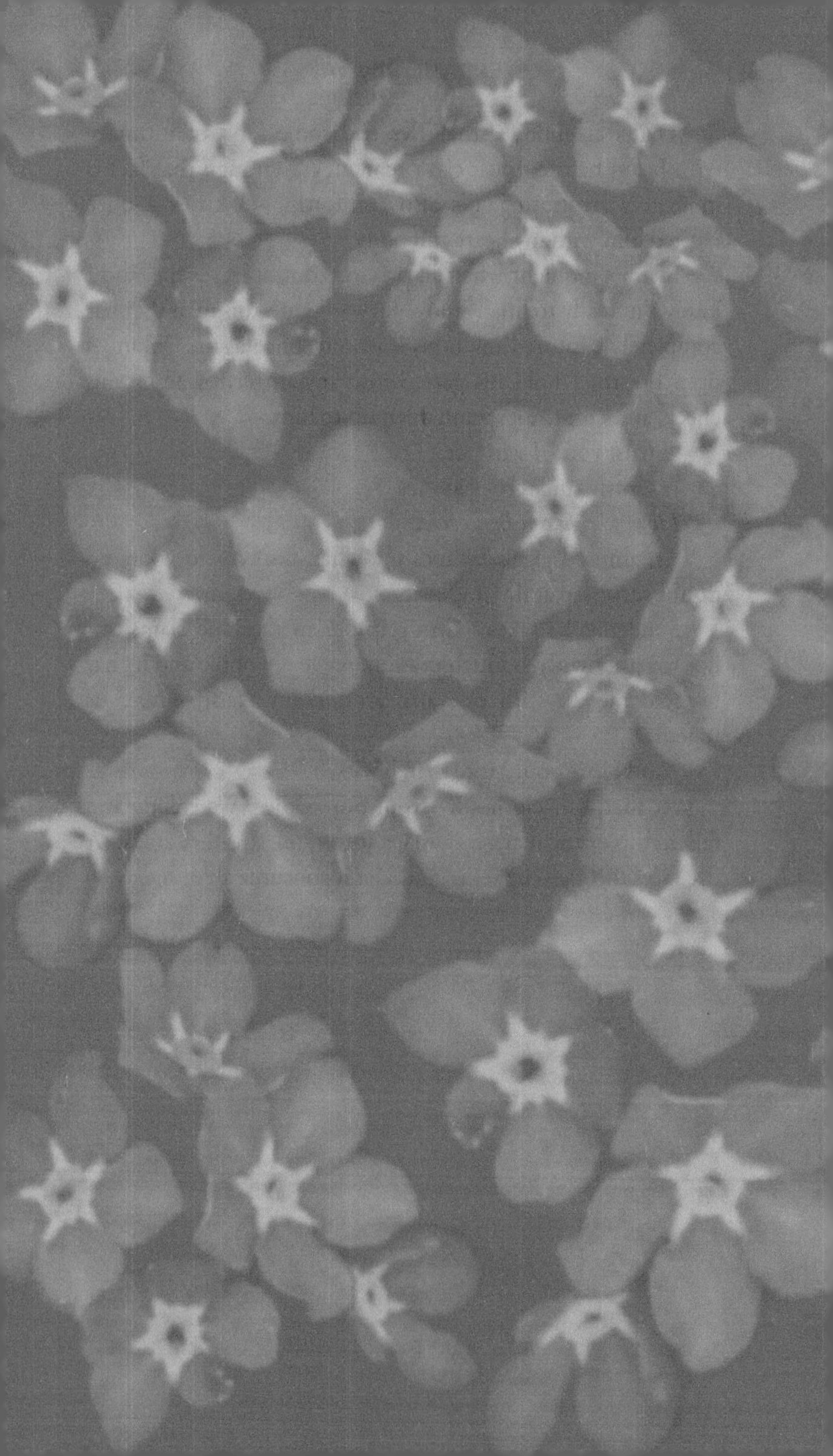

TWENTY-SEVEN

OUR LIMBS TANGLE together as our hands trail over each other's skin in only our underwear now. Feeling Jaxon's body against mine is everything I thought it'd be. Discovering each other's bodies like this is something that's a once in a life-time opportunity to have a second chance and to fall in love all over again. Feeling what I'm feeling for Jaxon and finally being able to express it in the purest, most carnal, raw way that I can is indescribable.

"You don't know how long I've been waiting for this." He says as he runs his nose up the column of my neck to my ear. "Are you sure this is what you want?"

There's no doubt in my mind that this is exactly what I want.

"You. I want all of you Jax." I breathe out and lock my gaze with his so that he can see how serious I am.

He nibbles on my ear and I can feel his smile against my skin. He trails kisses down my neck to my chest and rubs his nose along the swell of my breasts. He reaches behind me and unclips my bra before he tosses the fabric on the floor with the rest of our clothes and takes my nipple in his mouth. My back arches trying to give him more of me.

"So responsive." He growls out before taking my nipple between his teeth. Jaxon gives me a sharp bite before soothing the pain with his tongue and repeating the process over and over between both of my breasts, driving me to the brink of insanity.

My hands tangle in his hair tugging at the strands while pulling him closer at the same time. He finally shows mercy on my nipples and trails his lips down my stomach, nipping at the skin as he goes. I can't stop the moans from leaving my mouth at the feeling of his mouth on me.

"When I reach your pussy is it going to be dripping wet for me?"

Oh god, his dirty talk sends a shot of desire straight to my core and I may combust before he even touches me there.

"Why don't you find out." I find the words to sass him though my mind is a muddled mess of desire and anticipation.

"Don't mind if I do."

No other warning is given before he grips the straps of my panties and *rips* them from my body and dives in. My fingers tighten in his hair to the point that I'm sure it's painful now but he only moans into me. The vibrations off his mouth on my clit sends shivers down my spine.

"Jax." I moan out as he slides his tongue up my slit before circling the tip of his wet muscle around my bundle of nerves, teasing me. "Please..."

I feel him pull away slightly and I look down, meeting his mischievous eyes. "You know, I didn't think I'd like hearing you beg, but the sound of you begging me to let you come is making me hard as hell." He moans out before giving me one long lick along the length of my slit. "Say please, Love." He whispers as I drown in his eyes.

Right now he has me so worked up that I'd do anything he said if he'll let me come.

"Please, Jaxo-"

He cuts me off by diving back down and sucking my clit into his mouth and sucking hard. My back shoots off the bed and a scream tears through my throat as my orgasm slams into me out of nowhere. The force of it steals my breath and black spots rim my vision. I've never felt anything like it before, even when I've pleasured myself. Jaxon stays down there lapping up my juices before meeting my gaze.

"You're so gorgeous when you come." Jaxon says as he places soft kisses on my inner thigh. "Now I want you to come on my fingers."

I barely have time to catch my breath before I feel his mouth on my swollen clit and his finger runs along my slit, collecting the leftover juices from my orgasm. Once his finger's coated he presses the tip to my opening.

"Are you ready?" He asks sweet as sugar, always looking out for me.

"I've never been more ready."

He smiles at me and watches my reaction as he presses his finger into my pussy. He groans as I grip him, "You're so warm and tight." He says and he starts to pump his finger in and out of me. I'm a quivering mess as he adds a second and third finger, preparing me so I'm ready for him and the thought is enough to have a new wave of arousal gush around his fingers.

Jaxon curls his fingers and hits a spot inside that has me seeing stars as another orgasm rockets through me.

"That's my good girl. Are you ready for me? You want me to fill you with my cock?" He rasps out as he palms himself through his boxers as he sits back on his heels.

"Please, take me, Jaxon."

He grunts as he rushes out of his remaining clothing and I'm staring at him in all of his naked glory. I'm practically salivating at his long and thick member that's standing at attention for me. My breaths turn to pants as he starts to stroke himself under my stare.

"Like what you see?" He asks with a smirk.

"Can't say I'm disappointed." I smirk right back. "Right now I want to feel you inside me though." I say and spread my legs wider for him. I don't know where the confidence is coming from but seeing the heat in his eyes intensify makes it all worth it. "All of you."

I don't want anything between us.

Jaxon wastes no time settling between my legs, tossing the condom on the floor after I push the words into his mind. He grips himself and rubs his tip along my folds. He holds my stare for a moment before pushing inside of me.

We moan together at the feeling of us being connected in this way. When he meets resistance he looks to me and I nod before he pushes the rest of the way in and breaks the barrier of my innocence forever and I couldn't be happier that he's the one that I give it to.

He stills for a moment letting me adjust before he slowly pulls out and presses back in.

"God, you feel so damn good." He groans as he picks up his speed. His hands grip my waist firmly and he pistons in and out of me, picking up speed and force with each thrust.

"Yes, yes, yes. Ugh, Jaxon, more please." I dig my nails into his back and pull him into me as moans flow out of me continuously.

Jaxon only grunts and slams into me harder as he pushes my next orgasm to the surface while chasing his own release.

"That's it, Love. Come for me." He reaches down and rubs my clit in fast circles and a tidal wave of pleasure consumes me.

Jaxon moans at the grip my pulsating pussy has on his dick

that pushes him over the edge. He throws his head back as his hips stutter as he releases his come deep inside of me.

We collapse on the bed side by side and let our breathing return to normal while looking at each other. No words are needed. Jaxon pulls me into his arms and as I snuggle into his chest I know that there's nowhere in the world that I'd rather be. As he places a kiss on the crown of my head I know that I'll do whatever it takes to keep him by my side forever.

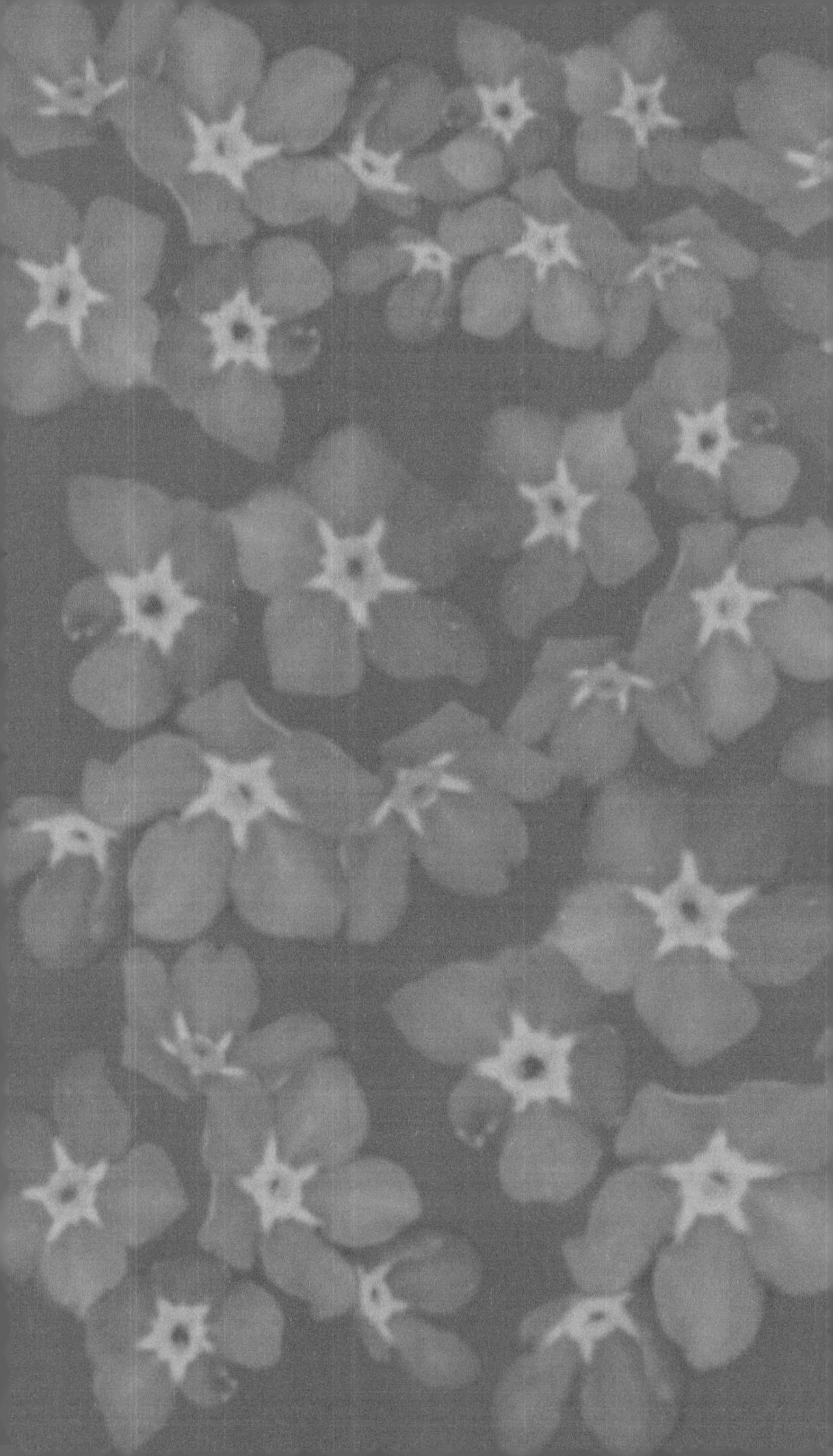

TWENTY-EIGHT

WEIGHTLESSNESS.

Floating within the clouds.

The sun is shining brighter than ever at this moment.

Complete bliss and peace of mind.

I've never felt as . . . whole as I do now. Eyes closed with a soft smile that nothing can wipe from my face, I savor the warmth that follows Jaxon's fingertips as they brush over my skin while he traces randomly over me. Involuntary hums leave my lips.

"You're so beautiful," Jaxon whispers when our noses touch, and my smile grows.

My eyes flutter lazily as I meet his gaze, and in his eyes, I see nothing but love that buzzes throughout my entire body. In turn, my own love and adoration pulses, hoping he can see the same in my eyes.

That was nothing short of amazing and everything I could've wanted. Jaxon was sweet and gentle, giving and attentive, but also firm and passionate. There isn't a thing I'd change. One thought keeps infiltrating my thoughts though: *was this even our first time?*

You always hear people say you never forget your first, but I can't remember almost anything about my *real* life, so that's out the window for me.

"Jax?"

"Hmm?"

I don't want to ruin the moment; I really don't, but . . . "Was this our first time?" Keeping my voice soft and lowering my eyes, I almost hope he doesn't hear me.

The few moments of quiet make me look at him again. Expecting to see guilt or maybe even sadness, I'm surprised when I see the same soft smile and twinkling eyes that have been looking at me since we made love.

"Yes." Jaxon presses a soft kiss to my lips, and I can't keep my eyes from closing as I relish in the moment. Pulling back, he cups my face tenderly. "And I couldn't be happier."

Smiling again, I smash my lips to his and wrap one hand around his neck and rest the other on his firm chest. "I love you," I mutter against his lips, then move to connect our lips again.

"As I love you."

"We still have more to talk about."

"Yeah, I guess we do." His chuckle sends a shiver down my spine.

The eye roll is inevitable as I roll away from him and head to the dresser for some clothes.

"I hate to see you go, but I love to watch you leave."

"That was so cringy." I can't help but laugh as I slip on my clothes. I turn just in time to see him stand and have no shame in staring at what just gave me so much pleasure.

"Want a picture?" A teasing smirk settles on his face.

"Maybe." Mirroring his expression, I close the distance between us and wrap my arms around his waist. "I won't need one if you always take this long to get dressed though."

Jax stares at me for a moment and says nothing. He eventually clicks his tongue and moves out of my hold to slip his jeans back on. "You're no fun," is all I hear before he turns around while pulling his shirt over his head. "Well, come on, then. Since you're rushing me . . ."

Amused, I smile and intertwine our fingers, letting him pull me down the stairs to the kitchen. We get some coffee before going to the living room. I take a quick look around, remembering that the last time I was here was beyond eventful.

"After not hearin' from you, I'm surprised at what happened earlier." In the living room, I get comfortable on the love seat and turn my attention to Jaxon.

"I wasn't expecting your message. Not so soon, anyway. But that didn't stop me from wanting to get to you as soon as possible." That dazzling smile brightens his face as he takes his place next to me. "Seeing you in that towel destroyed my final shred of control." He turns to face me fully and takes my hand. "I'm sorry I didn't respond to your messages, but I knew if I even read them, I wouldn't be able to give you the time you needed."

Guilt shoots through me. "I regretted our fight as soon as you left."

"Kairi, it's—"

"No. I need to get this out."

He sits back and waits patiently while I take a deep breath.

"I know you've noticed I've been pretty much against everythin' to do with you and this human experimentation stuff. I just didn't wanna let go of the little normalcy I thought I had. I've been thinkin' I was a normal girl that happened to have her life turned upside down because of a freak fire, but it turns out my life's been fucked up since the beginning, huh?" I scoff. "I was just tryin' to save my sister. I don't know how the fire got started. All I could think of was getting Sidney out. I don't even know why I went back for a phone. It still doesn't make sense to me why I would do that or crawl under the bed. Then the flames ate away at the bed frame and it collapsed on me, and the smoke got so thick. I couldn't breathe . . ." My breathing becomes labored as my mind takes me back to that day all over again.

"Hey, shhh. You're okay. You're here with me. It's okay." Jaxon's arms circle around me, pulling me into a warm embrace. He rocks me back and forth, whispering soothing words in my ear until my breathing's back to normal.

I give him a sad smile. "I'm sorry. I don't know where that rant came from."

Jax mirrors my sad smile. "I know I haven't exactly made this whole thing easy on you."

"I know I'm not the girl you remember."

Jaxon shakes his head. "Kairi." He runs his knuckles across my cheekbones. "You're too worried about trying to be who you think I want. The fact is that you *are* the same headstrong, argumentative, tender, and sexy little flirt you've always been—memories or not. You'll always be my Rose, no matter what."

Melting at his words, I try to blink the tears away. I really don't want to cry, but if he keeps being so damn sweet, they're gonna flow.

"You tryin' to sweet-talk me?" I say, leaning into his hand.

"Depends." He smiles, wiggling his eyebrows up and down. "Is it working?"

"You're a dork. How I ever thought you were some mysterious bad boy, I'll never know." I giggle and press a soft peck to his lips. "But yes. It's workin'."

Jaxon reconnects our lips, and I melt into him. He pushes until my back hits the cushions with him hovering over me, never separating our lips. Before I can completely lose myself in his delicious lips, I push on his chest to separate us and catch my breath.

"You're awfully touchy today." I pant.

He moves to suck the column of my throat, and my mind gets hazy. "Making up for lost time?"

"Is that a question?"

"Only if the answer is, 'Yes, Jaxon, make love to me.'" He nibbles on my sweet spot.

I moan and feel his smirk on my skin. Taking whatever remaining restraint I have left, I push on his chest again and smile at his pouting face. "We really do need to finish talkin'."

With a huff, he sits up straight. "Fine."

"Long story short from before we got distracted . . ." I send him a pointed look that has no effect on the shit-eating grin on his face. He's proud of himself. I roll my eyes at his antics. "I decided to trust my gut and follow my heart, which leads me straight back to you."

"You have no idea how happy I am to hear that, Rose."

"Anyway, what have you been doing all this time, besides ignoring me?" I smile, not the least bit upset now that I have him.

"Research," he says simply.

"What kind of research?" I dig.

"The kind involving the Human Underground Experimentation Project."

"Are you purposely being vague just to piss me off?" I glare at him.

He smiles sweetly. "I have no idea what you mean."

"I am about to punch you in the face. I swear," I promise with a smile.

What does he say to that? Nothing. He laughs.

Asshole.

"I love you—I really do—but you make it so easy."

I huff.

"Come on, I'm just picking. I was looking up what I could

about how the organization got started and what happened after a few of us got out that night."

"Did you find anythin'?" The anticipation has me leaning closer.

"I have an idea where some of the guys may have gone. It would probably be a good idea to try to reach out to them soon. Who knows what's going to happen, but having some more friends in our corner can't hurt, especially if this turns into some sort of fight like I think it will."

"That makes sense," I say. "But what about the start up?"

Jax sighs and looks away from me. That's when I get uneasy.

"Is it bad?" I ask.

"Yes."

"How bad is it?"

Sighing again, still staring at the far wall, he says, "Bad."

I look down at my hands in my lap and rub them together. "It has to do with me, doesn't it?" I say this as a question, but I can feel in my soul that it's about me. There isn't another reason Jaxon would be so reluctant other than that it has to do with me. From what I can tell, he always tries to protect me— physically and emotionally, whether I want it or not. "Just say it."

"I found out more about how the program was started," is all he says.

Rubbing my hands over my face in frustration, I glare at him again and will him to come clean. The longer he takes to spit it out, the angrier I'm gonna get. "Just be honest with me," I beg. "Please."

This time, when he sighs, it's in defeat. I like to imagine he's realizing the continued lies and withheld information is only gonna keep a rift between us. "I have a few leads on who could've funded this whole thing. They're from some weird little country I've never heard of. I'm still trying to get more information on them if I can." Jaxon takes a deep breath. "It's starting to look like everything started there, and I mean *everything*. I also found a company in Texas; that's the one they contracted to do what they did to us."

The veins in his neck start to bulge as a hard look overtakes his features. I rest a hand on top of his clenched fist, trying to calm and comfort him as best I can. I know this has been traumatic for all involved in different ways, but I need to know, and he needs to let it off his chest. He needs me to show him that he doesn't have to carry all the weight alone anymore. I send him a small smile of encouragement, which he returns meekly.

"That's where the top scientists got hired on to start what I'm assuming were basic ideas for the serum to eventually get this guy his own superhuman army."

"So my dad is one of those scientists?" I ask.

"I think so." He runs his hand through his hair and sighs again. "I've only actually seen the two main scientists a few times. They were always present for evaluations."

"Okay, so this little country paid a company to hire scientists to make them their own genetically-enhanced army?" I summarize to make sure we're on the same page.

"Pretty much, yeah. I'm still trying to see if I can find anything else out, but it's not surprising that they cover their tracks expertly. The only reason Andrew and I got this much information was because we've been in the program and know more or less where to look and what to look for."

I nod my head. Everything he's saying makes sense, but I thought this kind of shit only happened in books and movies. I mean, who in their right mind would think it's a good idea to experiment on kids to make an army?

"They aren't in their right minds obviously, or they wouldn't do this messed-up shit." Jaxon fumes next to me.

Sending him a sad smile, I climb onto his lap, wrapping

my arms around his neck. "I think you need to get your mind off all this for a while."

"Oh, is that so?" He smirks up at me, leaning back to rest against the back of the couch, pulling me with him while moving to rest his hands on my hips.

"We can worry about HUE later—or tomorrow or the next day. Right now, I want to focus on us and maybe try somethin' with you if I can." I brush my nose against his, a smile still firm on my face.

"I think I like where this is going." With a mischievous glint in his eyes, he bumps his hips up to mine while wiggling his eyebrows suggestively.

"Down tiger." I giggle at his antics. "Get your mind out of the gutter. I was talkin' about my memories. I think I have an idea to get some of them back," I say, biting my bottom lip.

Jaxon freezes and searches my face intently. I hold eye contact and let him see that I'm serious and finally ready to know everything.

"What do you have in mind?" He breathes out. I can see the hope in his eyes, but he's trying so hard to hide it.

"I wanna see if I can look into *your* mind, *your* memories. I think that seein' the past from your point of view may trigger my own," I whisper. "I haven't tried to do this yet obviously, so I'm not sure it will work. You'll also have to tell me if I hurt you because—"

"What do you need me to do?"

"Hold on a sec—"

"I want to do this. I don't need to think about it. If I can help you, then I'm going to," he says with a determined look on his face like I've never seen before.

While his enthusiasm is heartwarming, it's also stupid.

"I appreciate that, but I could really hurt you," I explain. "I didn't mean we had to do the whole thing right now. I'm still not sure if I can even extract memories yet."

"Don't know until you try." Jax smiles the smile that turns me into a puddle of contentment. "How does this work?"

"Well, I think if I focus enough and you open your mind to me, I may be able to see your memories as you guide me through them," I say. "Like any other time I've read thoughts, but this time, I want you to basically daydream our times together. I think we should do them one at a time and see if they pull my own memories back to the surface." I pause, making sure he understands. "Does that make sense?"

Jaxon doesn't even take a moment to think about it. "Yes. When do we start?"

Fearless as ever, I see.

"I was thinking we can after we eat somethin'. I have a feeling this is gonna take a lot of energy out of me." I laugh.

"Well"—he leans up to brush our noses against each other —"I could always tire you out first, *then* we could replenish our strength for memory sessions afterward," Jax suggests while moving his hand to rub against the skin under my shirt near my hips.

I hum but make no move to confirm or deny him.

Jaxon moves his lips to my jaw, then works his way slowly down the column of my neck to the soft spot where my neck meets my shoulder. He grazes his teeth on the flesh. I can't stop the breathy moan that leaves my lips as he grips my hips.

I take a hold of his face and stare into his dark lustful eyes, then give him a soft peck on the lips. "No. I need food." I detangle myself from his grasp, hop up from the couch, and head to the kitchen, leaving him groaning behind me as I laugh.

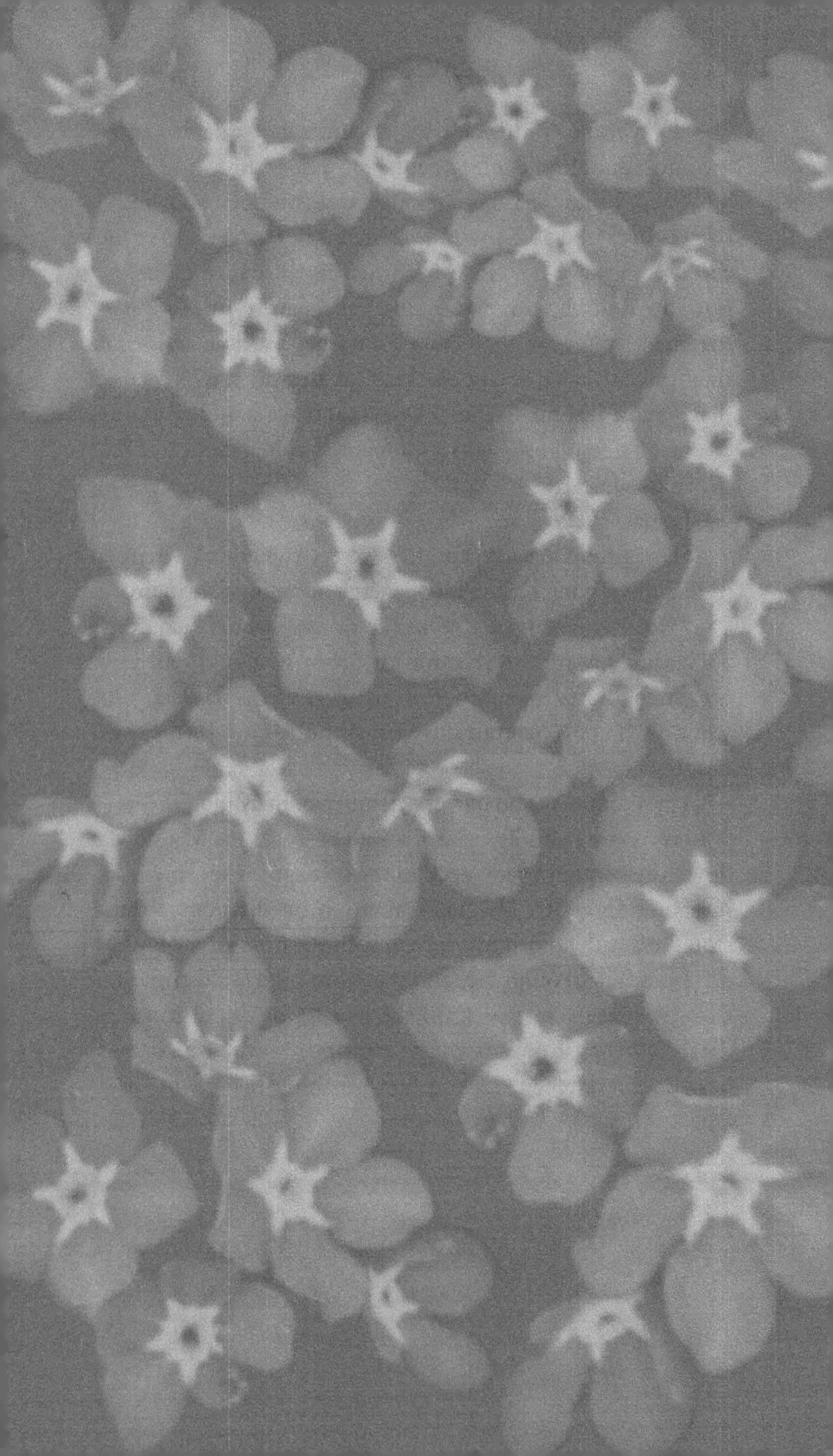

TWENTY-NINE

SITTING ON THE FLOOR, legs crossed and facing each other, we get ready to test out this theory to get my memories back. After a forty-five-minute mental preparation, I'm semi-confident I can do this as safely as possible. Jaxon's been so amazingly supportive and optimistic that it's hard not to soak in the same feelings.

For him, I think I'd do anything.

For us.

We're sitting close, knees touching, so that I can easily reach out and hold his head in my hands to help ground me to the task. And this way, he can break the physical connection if it gets to be too much for him.

"Are you sure about this?" I ask him for what seems like the one hundredth time.

"Completely."

"I think we should go over what's gonna happen again. Just to be safe." I huff at his eager attitude.

"If it'll make you feel better."

Rolling my eyes, I take a deep breath, trying to calm my nerves—and we haven't even started yet. "Okay, so first, I'm gonna to put my hands on the sides of your head to create a physical connection for the mental one I'm gonna try to make, okay?"

He nods.

"Next is really just a stab in the dark, but I think you should be able to feel my presence in your mind once you clear all the walls you may have up to block me out. Once that connection is there, I think you'll be able to start off with simple memories you want to share with me to see if this is possible before we try the more important ones that could trigger something in me. I don't wanna overload either of us from the get-go."

"Kairi." Jaxon takes my hands in his and sends me a small smile. "Everything is gonna be okay." He keeps our eyes locked and rubs softly across my knuckles with the pads of his thumbs, calming my nerves.

"I just don't wanna hurt you. We don't know how far my powers go, and I'm really not sure how to control most of it."

"Baby steps, Rose."

My heart warms at his use of my middle name, and I can't help but feel the love surging between our hands through my whole body. "Okay."

Jaxon gives my hands one last reassuring squeeze before he sits back, closes his eyes, and takes a deep breath, waiting for me to make a connection.

I take a moment to collect myself and admire him. Jaxon really is a sight to behold—and he's mine. I'm hoping this works so I can remember everything for myself.

Here goes nothing.

I raise my hands to cradle his head in my palms and close my eyes. It takes a few moments, but I push my consciousness toward Jaxon's mind. It's less of a physical thing and more like imaging myself entering his mind. I feel a wall-like block once I'm deep enough in his subconscious. The wall isn't dropping for me, so I try to coax it down. I rub my thumbs soothingly back and forth across his temples. I feel his body relax, but the wall's still there.

Jaxon's hands find their way to my knees, and he copies my movement and rubs his thumbs along my skin, as if reminding himself that I'm still here. I smile as the wall seems to evaporate, for lack of a better word.

As if in a dream, the first memory starts.

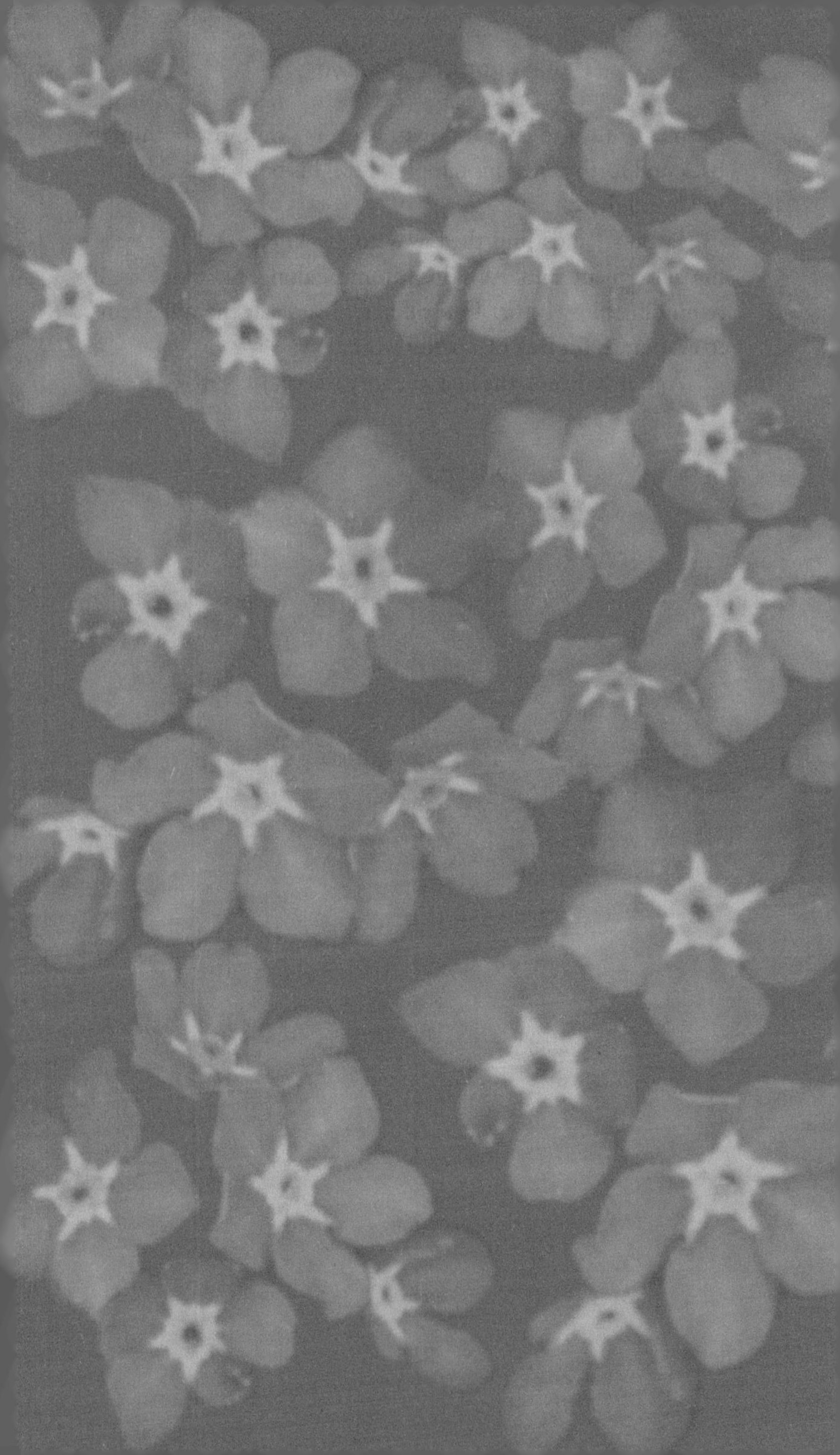

THIRTY

WHEN MY MIND REFOCUSES, I'm not in
Jaxon's living room anymore, and the Jaxon in front of me
looks around twelve years old. I see four other boys laughing
and shoving shoulders with each other. The tallest boy points,
and I follow his line of sight to see a girl on a bench with her
back to them. Her dirty blond hair is in a high ponytail. She
focuses on something in front of her, oblivious to her
surroundings.

I wonder where this memory is going.

Walking toward the boys, I wave my hand to find that I'm
invisible to them. I get close enough to hear their conversation.

"Come on! You gotta do it, Jax!" The tallest boy has dark
blond hair falling in his eyes and hazel eyes. He whispers excitedly to young Jaxon.

Jaxon seems hesitant, but there's humor in his eyes.

Mischievous little boy, I see not much has changed.

"Yeah, it's gonna be hilarious, dude," the lankiest—a boy
with brown hair and heterochromia with one blue eye and one
green—chimes in.

The other boys nod their heads in agreement.

"I don't know, Zayn. She's gonna be so mad," Jaxon says.

"That's the point! Plus, it's only a spider," the third boy with brown hair and deep blue eyes says.

Ugh, I hate spiders.

"Dom is right. What's the worst that can happen?" the tall boy says and the boy with piercing green eyes nods along. I know those eyes and I scowl at little Bentley.

Jaxon sighs. "Phoenix, you've heard about the powers she's got, right?"

"Dude, I've known her since she was like three. I know her powers better than you think and have a couple scars to prove it." Phoenix chuckles.

Zayn and Jaxon give him a worried glance, though he seems unfazed by his statement. I find this amusing, smiling at their debate on what I'm guessing is a prank they're trying to get Jaxon to play on the girl. I bet one of them has a crush on her.

"Wait." Bentley narrows his eyes at Jaxon, which pulls my eyes back and forth between them. "You don't like her, do you?"

I turn and see Jaxon's eyes bulge. "No, I don't!" he whispers heatedly, but the flush in his cheeks gives him away.

I knew it. I giggle, watching the other boys eye him knowingly.

"Man, you *would* have a crush on Crazy Kairi," Phoenix says.

Crazy Kairi . . .

I whip my head back to the little girl that's—well, me. They're trying to get Jaxon to play a prank on me.

Little punks.

"Don't chicken out, dude. Crush or not," Zayn adds.

"I'm not chickening out, and I don't have a crush on her."

"Then prove it." Bentley's smug little face leans in close to Jaxon's.

Jaxon huffs and looks toward the other boy, Dominic, whose face is as emotionless as it's been for most of their little conversation. Jaxon takes a deep breath and walks a few steps away from the other boys, who are all nudging each other in anticipation.

It seems I'm able to move around as long as I keep within Jaxon's line of vision.

Jaxon stops about halfway between the younger me and his friends. I move to get a better view of what's going on. After walking around the bench, where I can see both me and Jaxon, I take a closer look at my young face.

It's undeniable that this is me. Same hair, eye, and skin colors. Her hair's shorter; her eyes look larger on my face; and her skin has a youthful glow to it. Young me has a small chain necklace in her hands. She's lost in thought and unaware of the boy coming up behind her.

I cut my eyes to Jaxon, seeing him take a deep breath and close his eyes. He raises his hands and furrows his brows in concentration.

I watch him in a trance. I've never actually seen him use his powers. I've only seen the aftermath. To say it's interesting would be an understatement. I'm sure when he was younger, it took much more concentration too.

I'm not sure how long I watch him before his eyes flutter open and his stare glues onto the back of little Kairi's head. When I turn my head to follow his gaze, I see a huge tarantula on her shoulder.

Hell to the no.

It's not even on me, yet I feel my anxiety spike the same moment little Kairi's head turns to see it. Her eyes bulge from her skull as she sputters and trips over herself in her haste to get away from the beady-eyed creature. Then an ear-piercing scream fills the room, followed by the boys' laughter.

She hears it too and whips her head to them before locking

her eyes on Jaxon. He's still in the same spot, staring back at her with humor in his eyes.

"I'm gonna kill you," is all my mini me whispers as she stands up to chase after them.

Jaxon's eyes widen, and he turns on his heels and takes off toward the other boys. Once they see the chase start, they take off as well.

I stand there and watch them all run away from the fuming little girl. I guess looking at it from an outside point of view, it is kind of funny—sort of.

I was more embarrassed than angry at the time though.

The scene starts to fade away just as mini me pounces on top of Jaxon, and they tumble to the ground.

My eyes blink the blurred images away and focus on the concerned look on present Jaxon's face. I take in his living room we're still currently in while my mind reels from the information from the memory I just experienced.

"Still the same mischievous mindset." I smirk.

Jaxon lets out a breathless chuckle, while his eyes sparkle with an emotion I can't quite place.

He pouts. "They made me."

"Uh-huh. Sure they did."

He just smiles back at me, looking happier than ever. "I take it that it worked, then?"

I smile. "Yes. I'm ready to see more."

Jaxon softly grasps my hands again and closes his eyes. I follow suit.

Almost as a fade-to-black-and-back-again sequence, I look around and now see a teenage me about thirty feet away in a slightly lit area.

It looks like we're still in the same area of the compound, but I don't see anyone else around. I look to my left as I remember these are Jaxon's memories and see him crouched down with a soft smile on his face, staring at the other me in the distance.

I swear, if all these memories are of him pranking me, I'm gonna punch him when we're back in reality.

I turn back to face her. She's looking down with a smile on her face too. On the floor is a little trail of flowers leading right to where me and teen Jaxon are.

Her smile widens as she bends down to pick the little flower up and brings it to her nose to smell it. An even brighter smile takes over her face as she looks around.

"Jax?" she calls out softly, looking around some more before looking down again.

I watch her follow the trail while picking up all the flowers she can carry on her way. I look down at the flower trail closer to us and see why her smile's so bright.

Forget-me-nots. Our flower.

I glance up in time to see her reach us. Jaxon stands from his spot to catch her as she flings herself into his waiting arms.

"What's all this?" she asks, pulling back from the embrace but not out of his arms.

"A date, silly." Jaxon smirks as if it should've been obvious.

"Okay, then. Woo me." She smirks too, pushing up onto her toes to brush their noses together.

"Don't tease me." Jaxon warns with an indescribable look overcoming his face.

She bats her eyelashes innocently at him. "What do you mean?"

Well, I see that part of our relationship hasn't changed that much. Cheeky and teasing as ever—the both of us.

I watch with a warm smile as he places each of his palms on her cheeks and rubs his thumbs across her cheekbones. As if the feeling is too much, her eyes become hooded.

"You have no idea what you do to me, do you?" Jaxon asks

in a hushed voice, staring into her eyes, brushing their noses together again.

"Show me," she breathes out.

Show her he does as he leans in, connecting their lips together in a slow dance.

Our first kiss.

Warmth floods my body watching the cute moment. Being here watching our love grow is amazing. I get to say I got to experience us falling in love all over again, to see where it started.

I started to fall in love with him at this moment. From the way his hands held me like I was something breakable to the way his lips softly moved against mine, but mostly the way he looked at me. From then on, I could always feel the love he had for me radiating out of his dark eyes.

The smile on my face only grows as I see Jaxon give her a beautiful chain necklace strung through a delicate ring. I rub my bare neck as an empty feeling overcomes me. My most sacred possession—the dainty ring that holds a small forget-me-not in the center.

I keep watching as they fade and the next memory comes into focus.

When the scene becomes clear, I'm right behind teenage Jaxon and Kairi as they crouch in the corner of a long hallway.

"Be quiet or we're gonna get caught," Jaxon whispers while trying to keep his face composed and serious, but I can tell it's crumbling.

I look at my mini me. Her hands are over her mouth, trying her best to muffle her giggles. I find myself wanting to laugh at how they're trying not to.

"Okay. I'll be right back," Jaxon says, peeking around the corner before turning back to give the younger me a quick peck on the cheek before disappearing.

I follow behind him as he creeps along the wall like a spy

would in a movie. I snort and cover my mouth at the same time teen Kairi does behind me. Jaxon whips his head to shush her. I turn and see her head disappearing back around the corner.

Jaxon laughs silently before continuing forward in a more normal manner. He comes up to a door with a small window and gets up on his toes to look inside briefly before pushing his way inside.

Wait . . . Is he . . .

I hurry to look in the window. He swipes a box of strawberries from the refrigerator before speed-walking back to the door. I move out of the way as he flies through the door and heads back toward younger me.

Jaxon got these strawberries for me, and this is the night they became my obsession.

A lot of who I am revolves around Jaxon. Not in a way that I'm nothing without him, but he holds such a significant place in my history that I'm not sure if I ever *want* to be anything without him. Everything's always better with Jaxon Benievere.

I walk to the indoor garden, straight to the back left section. There is a small gap between two little trees that I squeeze through to get to our secret hideaway. When I get through, in the brush, I see the teen lovers lying side by side like I knew they'd be, staring into each other's eyes. Jaxon feeds teenage me a bite of the delicious fruit.

A small smile comes to my face as the scene fades and moisture fills my eyes. I close my eyes and blink, letting my arms fall from present-day Jaxon's temples and resting them in my lap.

It's silent for a few minutes before I feel a finger under my chin guiding my face up. I blink some more and lock onto deep brown eyes laced with confusion and concern.

"Rose, what's wrong?" Jax asks gently, moving his fingers

to brush my cheekbones like he always did when he used to comfort me.

"How could I have forgotten so much of us?" I ask, and the tears spill down my cheeks.

Jaxon pulls me into his arms and rocks us back and forth. "We're together now. That's all that matters."

I pull back to meet his gentle eyes with determination. "I'll never forget again. I promise," I vow, and I plan to make sure of it.

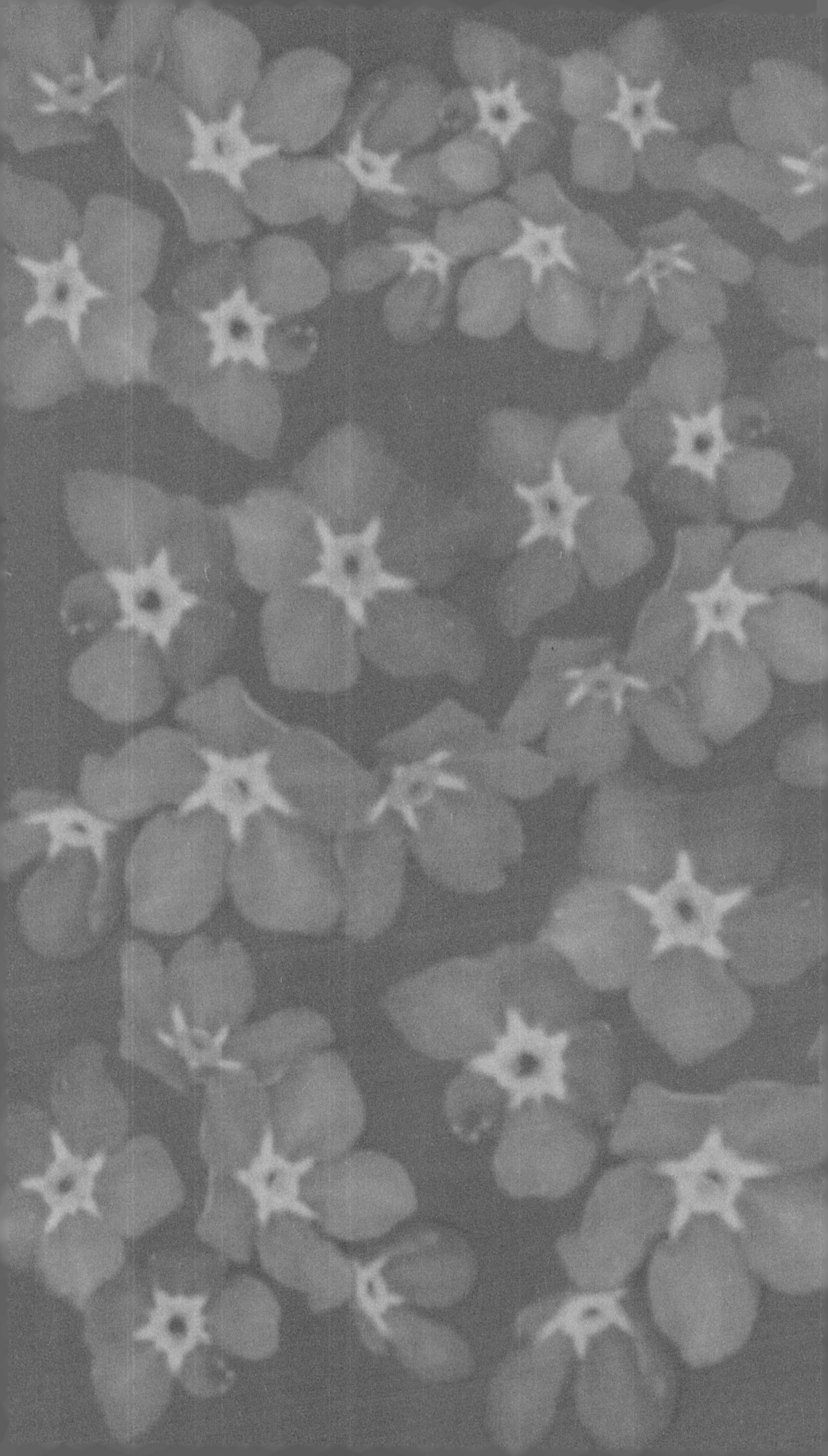

THIRTY-ONE

I SMILE with my eyes closed as I hold only to the front of Jaxon's shirt, our noses brushing, and bask in the feeling of having him here close to me. We've stayed like this for a while now since our memory trial. Though I didn't get all my memories back, I feel more like myself than I have in a long time.

Now we're enjoying being this close again. I can't imagine what it was like to feel as helpless as he must've felt all this time. I know he doesn't want me to feel guilty because none of this was technically my fault, but I can't help but wish I could've been strong enough to fight them off before this happened.

His fingertips move up and down my back, soothing my worries and starting to lull me to sleep. Jaxon moves and presses a soft peck on my lips before pulling away, making me open my eyes.

"Don't do that," he says.

"Do what?"

"Don't have such a guilty look on your face. I know you're drowning in unnecessary guilt right now."

I sigh. "I just wish I could've done more. More for you."

"Kairi, we're here now. Just be here with me and enjoy it."

I smile and reconnect our lips as my answer.

"What ever happened to that ring?" I ask after a few moments.

Jaxon smiles down at me, then rubs our noses together. "I have it. Hold on."

"How did you end up with it anyway?"

"When they pulled you from the room the chain was broken and it fell. It was lucky that I even saw it at all and I've been keeping it close ever since."

He stands and runs out of the room. Only moments later, he comes back with a sweet smile on his face. Wordlessly, he opens up his fist to reveal the same necklace and ring I saw in our memory. I smile at him and turn my back, pulling my hair to the side. Once it's settled on my neck, I turn and lean closer to him so our lips can meet.

Andrew chooses that moment to come storming into Jaxon's bedroom like a bat out of hell. We jump apart, and my heart tries to jump out of my chest.

"What the fuck!" Jaxon yells.

"Sweet baby Jesus, you 'bout gave me a heart attack." I gasp, holding my chest, still trying to calm my heart.

"I just got a letter from Hank," Andrew says.

"Who's Hank?" I ask Jaxon.

On his face is a mix of shock, excitement, and dread. A strange combination. "Did you read it yet?" Jaxon asks hesitantly.

Andrew rubs his lips together, taking a moment to answer. "Yes."

"And?"

"Um . . ." Andrew pauses, looking toward me like he's unsure if he should say it in front of me.

"You've never been one to tiptoe around me, Drew," I say.

His eyes widen as he looks to Jaxon.

"She remembers more now but not everything yet. Just a few holes left to fill. It's fine, Drew. Just tell us what it says."

"I think you should read it for yourself."

Jaxon gives him a questioning glance before taking the letter from his hands and opening it up.

"Just read it out loud to save time," I suggest.

Jaxon gives a small nod before turning back to the letter. I look at Andrew and the solemn look on his face as he leans against the opposite wall from us. His body language is putting me on edge.

"So who is Hank?" I ask again.

"Hank's someone we have undercover inside HUE as a medical assistant to give us as much information as he can when he can," Andrew says.

"You were able to get someone on the inside?" I sit up and look at them excitedly, to which they nod. "How'd y'all manage that?"

"It's a long story," is all Jaxon says as he meets my eyes.

"Okay and?"

"Basically, we ran into Hank not long after we broke out of the compound the day we were separated. The facility ended up being in the middle of nowhere. We felt like we'd run for miles through the woods before he spotted us. Hank grew sympathetic to our situation after a few weeks of staying with him once we explained what had happened. He said he'd do what he could to help us get on our feet and on our own way once we felt ready. He really was a godsend right when we needed it—almost too good to be true.

"Anyway, he agreed to help us in any way he could, and because he was a retired EMT with some medical background, it helped him get into the HUE assistant program. Finding the program was difficult but because we knew where we ran from all he had to do was follow the trail and bullshit his way in. He used Phoenix's name to get him in the door, saying he saw a group of boys in town raving like lunatics, claiming to be experiments, and heading toward Oklahoma, though we were still at his house. It got him a meeting with one of the head scientists and eventually a job with them too."

"Oh wow."

"Yeah, it was the first thing to ever go in our favor," Andrew chimes in.

"So he's the one who sent the letter? I guess that means he found somethin' worth mentionin', right?" I ask.

"That's what we're hoping for. We haven't heard from him in a few months. I was starting to worry he got found out." Jaxon looks back toward the letter, then to Andrew. "How bad is it?"

Andrew doesn't say anything, but the grimace on his face says enough, and when his eyes flick to me, the hairs on my neck stand up.

Jaxon's face hardens. "All right. Here we go, then."

He clears his throats as he focuses back on the piece of paper in his hands, then starts to read aloud:

"Hey. First, I want to say it's been crazy busy here. They're running this old man into the ground. The lack of respect is suffocating. Anyway, I'll cut to the chase. I got my hands on some files while helping Patricia, which led me to some paperwork left behind in an old office. I know, this old man is awesome. I picked the lock to get in—no big deal.

"So what I found in these files is why it's taken so long to get back to you guys. For the longest time, I didn't know what to say or how to say it. It's not good. I won't lie; it made me sick to my stomach and still does when I think about it. I finally decided it was better to just rip the Band-Aid off and tell it to y'all straight, but I'm just going to summarize it and send the copies I made of what I could so you can see for yourselves."

Jaxon stops and looks at Andrew for a moment before turning to me. I don't know what he sees in my eyes, but I can feel my hands shaking. As much as I wanna know, I'm scared of what this letter's gonna say next.

"Kairi, breathe for me," Jax coaxes softly.

I release a breath I didn't know I was holding and try to give him a reassuring smile. "Please just read the rest," I whisper. "I just wanna get it over with and deal with the rest after."

Jaxon nods and gets back to Hank's letter.

"I found a couple official records of the experiments at the very beginning of the human trials. Kairi and Phoenix were the first humans to be experimented on—Kairi at age three and Phoenix at six. Why Kairi and Phoenix were chosen wasn't in these files, but I'll get to that later. When the time came for them to start human trials for the 722 serum, they put their work and scientific advancement over the safety of these kids, obviously. The children are only tools to reach their end goal, which is why other kids were brought in later to expand their research.

"That's the gist of what the official reports say. Now to the more horrific news—like experimenting on kids wasn't bad enough.

"So Phoenix is the only child to his mom, Patricia, who is still the head scientist in charge here alongside a man named Charles, who is no longer at this facility. They're the two in charge of Human Underground Experimentation or HUE. I found a journal of sorts in his office, which is where the rest of this information is gathered from."

Jaxon turns to me. "Kairi—"

"Just keep goin'," I choke out.

"Charles writes about his family first. That's how I found out about his connection to Kairi as her father. Not long into this journal, his feelings are expressed rather brutally. I'm not able to

send this, but I'll tell you what I can. Charles's love for her faded rather quickly after her birth, unfortunately. Turns out his wife cheated on him with his brother, and that's who Kairi's real father is. Though he's always let Kairi believe he was her real father, he had no real love for her, which is why she was chosen to be in HUE.

"The journal has some gaps in time, so I don't think he wrote in it often, but when he—along with the other top scientists at HUE—heard talk of rebellion and that Kairi was one of the main leaders of this group, he planned a way to stop it. He knew that if she was separated from the group, Jaxon wouldn't be able to think straight until she was back with him, and because he was the other leader of this group of rebels, Kairi was the key component to stopping it before it started.

"It doesn't go into much more detail than that, and I don't know what a lot of this scientific gibberish means anyway, but I hope this helps with whatever you two are up to there. I'll keep looking for what I can and try to do what I can from inside. You boys stay safe. Hank."

I stare blankly at my shaking hands that lie lifeless in my lap. There's a ringing in my ears as my mind tries to work overtime to process what I just heard, but my thoughts are blank. Nothing comes to mind. Nothing makes sense.

Nothing.

I jump to my feet when I feel a hand touch my shoulder and turn to meet the darkest brown eyes I've ever seen. They swim with worry and make my pulse thump wildly.

I open my mouth, but no words come out, and I can feel the tears building in my eyes that are moments from spilling over. I shake my head furiously at his concern, at the sudden news that my da—that *Charles*—did this to me and I have no real father.

Jaxon pulls me into a tight embrace as I start to crumble to the floor. He lowers us down and holds me tightly to him. He rubs my back, rocking back and forth while whispering reassuring words into my ears, but I hear nothing. I keep hearing that deafening ringing as I try to make sense of this.

"Kairi," Jax whispers. "Just focus on me. Listen to the sound of my voice. Feel my heartbeat and breathe with me. You're safe. We're together. I'll do everything I can to never let anyone hurt you again. You and I are family. You're not alone." He chants this to me, and I try to do as he says and breathe with him. "That's it, Rose. I love you."

I just nod my head, not trusting my voice, and bury my face farther into his chest to hide from it all.

I have Jax, and that's all I'll ever need.

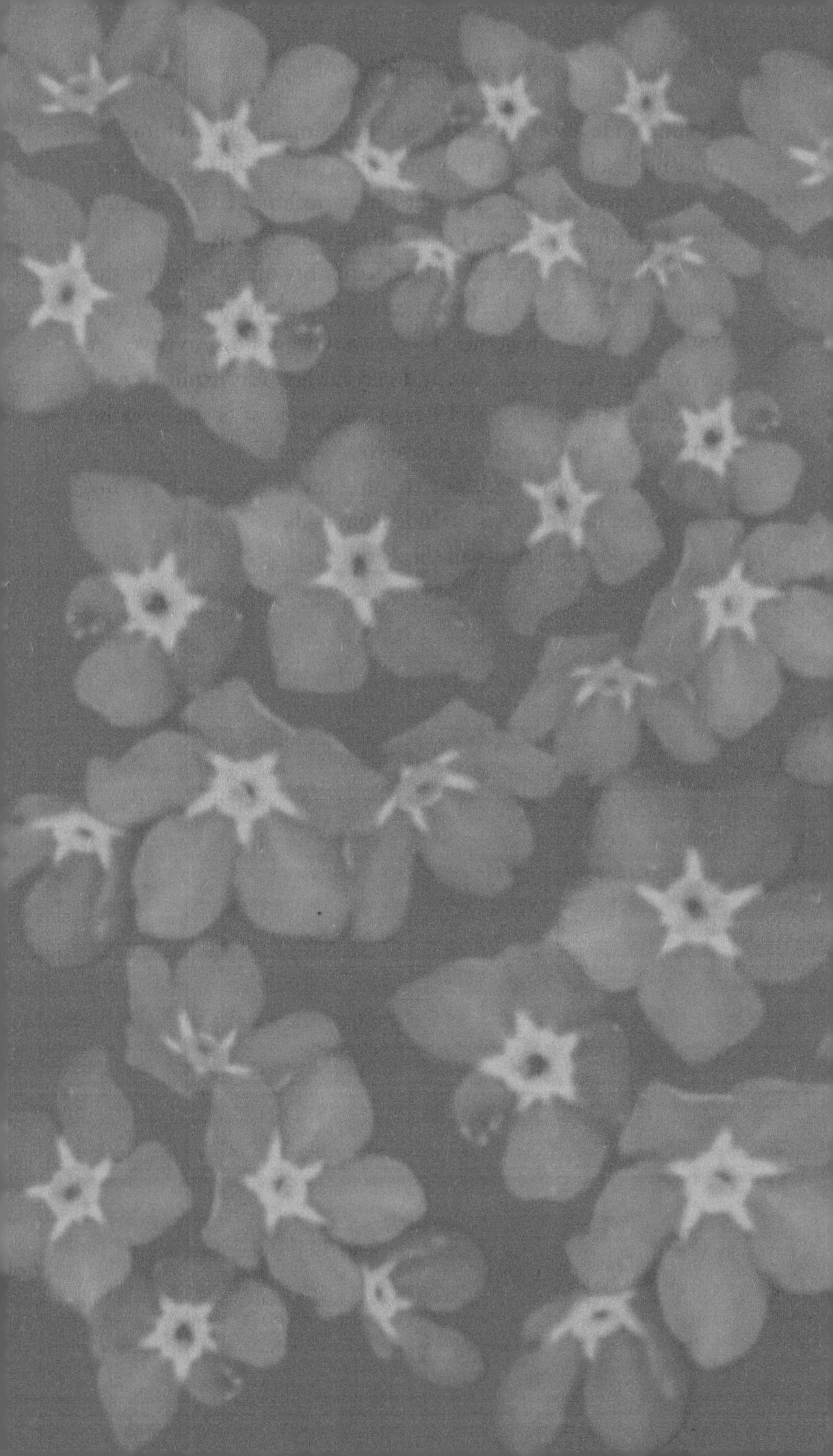

THIRTY-TWO

WE SPEND the rest of the afternoon talking about anything but Charles.

"I want to focus on what I can control now, not what I can't," I say to the boys as we sit around the table eating some cut-up fruit. They leave the strawberries for me.

"Okay. What do you have in mind?" Jaxon places a hand reassuringly on my knee.

"Self-defense wouldn't hurt," Andrew chimes in, dipping his fruit in sugar.

I perk up. "Like hand-to-hand stuff?"

"Yeah. No matter what we're all capable of now, it's still always a good to have. It saved my ass and Jax's on a number of occasions."

My eyes widen slightly as I turn my head to Jaxon, who is looking at his brother with an unimpressed look on his face. "What kind of trouble did y'all get into?"

"Nothing too serious," Jaxon says.

I turn when Andrew snorts in response, confirming my suspicions that it's more than Jaxon's letting on. "I'll get it out of you eventually." I smirk suggestively.

Jaxon looks at me with a smirk of his own, and Andrew dry heaves.

"Y'all need to quit that shit when I'm around."

I stick my tongue out at him and smile, then lean over to give Jaxon a quick kiss on the cheek. "I like the idea of learning to defend myself physically," I say, bringing us back to the subject.

"Yeah, especially since your powers take so much out of you," Jaxon adds.

Andrew nods. "There's no point in using your crazy mental powers if you're just gonna pass out right after."

"I'm still working on finding my limits. It all still feels so new to me."

"Well, to be fair, you never really knew where that line was that overloaded your system. You just focused on the simpler things you could handle."

"I guess that makes sense."

"So what have you been able to do in this second version of your life?" Andrew asks.

I laugh. "Not too much, really. I can read thoughts and put certain thoughts into someone's mind. I have actually controlled a few things before but was really tired after."

"Controlled things? What does that mean?" he asks.

"Well, Jax showed up after I controlled those guys and made them back away from me while I was walkin' home." Looking at Jaxon, I explain, "That was the first time I ever controlled someone that I can remember, but I passed out that time too."

"That was probably because you tried to control so many people at once," Jaxon points out.

"What else?" Andrew asks.

"I was in the woods behind my house clearing my head and saw a mountain lion and was able to control its movements. Kind of like how you tell a dog to come and sit—that's pretty much what I did. I've practiced on a few other animals too. They're easier and don't take as much energy out of me. I think it has to do with the fact that their minds have less resistance to manipulation."

The boys give me dumbfounded looks, and after they stare at me in silence for several moments, I decided to break it.

"What?" I ask.

"That's gonna be useful," is all Andrew says.

Jaxon has a look of awe in his eyes, and I smile at him, feeling a little self-conscious at the attention.

"So hand-to-hand combat's now on the list of to-dos, as well as continuing to harness these powers we have," Andrew says, drawing my attention back to him.

"What's your power, Drew?" I rest my chin in the palm of my hand.

"Rapid healing of myself and others." He smirks. "Who do you think healed you after you face-planted into that boulder?"

I send him a flat glare that has him letting out a deep belly laugh.

"We need to work on a plan to get Kairi away from Charles," Jaxon says, jaw clenched.

Andrew nods his head in agreement, finally simmering down.

"How?" I ask.

"I'm not sure yet. Maybe we can tell him there's something to do with school where you'll be gone for a while so we can work on something more permanent. The last thing we want to do is tip him off that we know who he is."

"I know." I grab his hand and rub my thumb across his knuckles with a sad smile.

Everything we do from here on out is gonna be risky. We

have no way to know what could happen if we get caught. I wanna be as careful as we can. Coming to North Dakota has done nothing but turn my life upside down from the moment I got here. After everything, I want nothing more than to keep what I've gained. I wanna keep Jaxon.

I haven't said anything yet, but after our little memory experiment, I've been having little bits and pieces come back to me on their own at random times. I don't want to say anything until they've all come back, but if they do, I'd like to do something special for Jaxon after all he's done for me.

When Jaxon drops me off at my house later that night, Charles isn't home, thankfully. I go to my room to get everything packed that I'll need for the next week with Jaxon and Andrew. I spend a few hours on the phone with Jaxon before finally falling asleep.

The next morning, Charles is eating breakfast at the table with a coffee and paper in hand.

"Good morning, Dad." I smile and hope my slight panic isn't present on my face.

He grunts in response without looking up from whatever article he's reading.

We sit in silence for a while, having our breakfast as I plan how I'm gonna pull this off. I go with the easiest option. Since he's never really home, it's not like he should have any idea what's actually going on in my life.

"Oh," I start, directing his attention to me, "don't forget to go grocery shopin' while I'm gone. I'd hate for you to starve without me." I laugh and take another bite of my cereal.

He's silent for a minute as his brows pull together in confusion. "Are you goin' somewhere?" he asks, looking up at me finally.

"I told you last month—the trip the school's taking to Devils Lake for a week?" I pray he can't hear the tremble in my voice giving away my lie. It was Jaxon's idea to use a field trip to the lake as a cover, because it's unlikely Charles would be able to cover the whole lake looking for us, and it also means he won't be looking for me in town either.

He hums before nodding. "Right, sorry. Work's been crazy, and you know I don't have the best memory to begin with." Charles chuckles humorlessly, then takes a sip of his coffee.

I let out an inward sigh of relief. I unlock my phone to check the time. "Well, I gotta get goin'. Everyone is meeting up in about twenty minutes before headin' out. Love you." I walk around the table and hold back the bile rising in my throat as I kiss his cheek like I always do when he's home in the mornings.

I all but sprint to my truck and head in the direction of the school to wait for Jaxon to pick me up. We thought it'd be best to leave my truck in the school's parking lot in case Charles gets the idea to check if I'm still gone. Just as I cut the engine, Jaxon's Jeep pulls up behind me. I jump in, and we head to his house. Being next to him is making me feel so much more relaxed already.

"How'd it go?" Jaxon asks cautiously.

"It went about as I thought it would. Even without all this human experimentation and superhuman power stuff, it's not like he was the best dad anyway. He was never home and didn't know about anythin' goin' on in my life." I shrug my shoulders and look out the window.

His reply is his hand on my knee closest to him, but he says nothing, which I appreciate. Words weren't what I need right now, and like always, Jaxon knows that.

The week goes by quicker than I would've liked.

I really enjoy spending so much time with Jaxon. This is the first time, past or present, that we've been together practically twenty-four seven. Waking up next to him with his arms around me, having breakfast and coffee, watching movies, laughing and talking together, getting reacquainted, the mind blowing sex—it's been great.

The training was killer though. I didn't know I had so many muscles that could be sore. It's crippling, and Andrew's relentless.

He's a hard-ass. Constant agility and strength drills in the mornings led up to the hand-to-hand combat training in the evenings. We spent our mornings on strength training, which included running for miles, squats, sit-ups, push-ups—the works. Then Andrew and Jaxon demonstrated some close combat techniques and stances. We spent hours working in repetition on a punching bag, then Andrew donned boxing mitts, and we took turns sparing between the three of us. At the beginning of the week, my limbs felt like Jell-O, but now, by the end, I've never felt stronger.

Today is the last day, and tomorrow, Jaxon will take me back to my truck where we'll put into action the steps needed to get me out of Charles's house for good without leading him to think we're on to him.

"Your brother's a demon," I say as I collapse, panting on the grass in their backyard at the end of the morning drills.

Jaxon's chuckles have me looking over to him. He's sitting down next to me. His breathings slightly labored, but he doesn't look winded. "He takes it very seriously," he agrees.

"I think it's a little more than that."

"Maybe, but it pays off in the end. You'll never have to worry about being able to defend yourself."

"I guess."

"Come on, you baby." He laughs as he stands up, offering me his hands, then pulls me to my feet.

We walk hand in hand up to his room to shower off the sweat from our bodies before heading down to the kitchen for some food. No matter how tiring the training is, we always have extra energy we use to devour each other. Roaming hands, exploring touches and sweet kisses.

I jump into his arms once he has his hands on my ass holding me up against the shower wall and he wastes no time filling me to the brim with his cock. I throw my head back in a silent scream as he rams into me like it's the last time he'll be able to be inside of me. It isn't long before we both find our release and rinse our naughty time off.

We smile and laugh as we make lunch for the two of us; Andrew always goes MIA after training. Jaxon says he's always planning and getting ready for whatever HUE could throw at us.

Like every other day, we sit side by side and eat in silence besides making casual conversation between bites. It's so peaceful like this. It feels like home. Everything with Jaxon feels like home.

"What are you thinking about?" he asks.

I turn and smile. "Just how happy I am right now."

A soft smile takes over his face as leans forward to peck my lips with a kiss. "Me too, Rose."

After lunch, we take a nap before our last training of the day. I have to say, falling asleep in his arms is a luxury I don't think I can get used to, and I'm gonna miss it the most when I'm back in that house with Charles.

When we make our way back to the backyard, Andrew's waiting for us, looking over the yard with a far-away look. He turns at the sound of our approach but remains emotionless. "Let's get started."

For today, we put what I've learned to the test, and it's two against one. I end up on my ass more than once, but after a few more rounds, I'm able to hold my own and eventually get Jaxon off his feet. Then I turn to Andrew, only to find he isn't there before I'm flipped over and land with my back on the ground and the wind knocked out of me.

"You've improved tremendously," Andrew says with a smirk. "Still not close to gettin' one over on me though."

I huff and stick my tongue out at him, which makes him laugh before he walks away.

I close my eyes and focus on my breathing. A shadow falls on my face, and I blink my eyes to meet dark ones. Jaxon smiles at me and leans in for a kiss. I place my hand on the back of his neck to keep him in place and turn my head to deepen our kiss. We stay like that for a few more minutes before breaking away for air. He shakes his head, leaning down for one more quick kiss before standing up and pulling me to my feet too.

"I think we need another shower," I say, leaning closer to rub our noses together.

Jaxon hums and takes a deep breath. "You *do* smell."

"Asshole." I huff and push away from him and make my way inside, leaving a laughing Jaxon behind me.

I make it all the way to the bathroom and try to hurry and close the door, but he blocks it with his foot and pushes his way in.

"Where do you think you're running off to?" he asks.

"To shower. *Alone.*" I turn away from him to turn on the water.

"I don't think so." Arms wrap around my waist and pull me back against his chest. He runs his nose along my neck. I can't help but tilt my head to give him better access and bite my lip to keep a moan in as he starts to nibble and suck at my skin.

"Jax," I breathe out, melting into his embrace.

"Let me take care of you, Kairi," Jaxon whispers in my ear before taking the lobe in his mouth.

"Please . . ." I whisper.

He smirks against my skin before our clothes fall to the floor. He leads me into the stream of steaming water, and take care of me he does and I can never get tired of him.

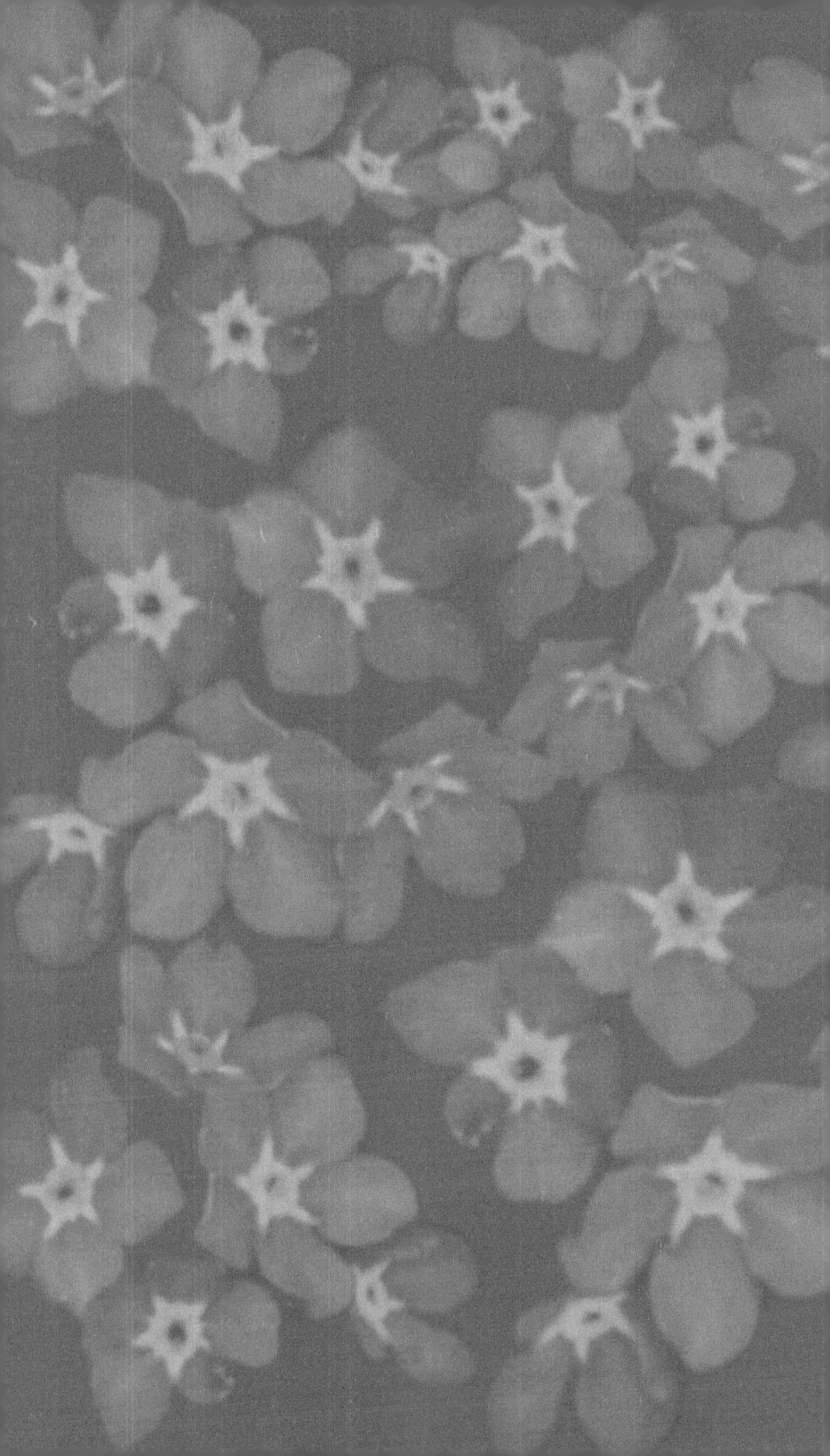

THIRTY-THREE

THE NEXT MORNING, Andrew, Jaxon, and I all sit around the table and talk about the best options we have moving forward since I'm going back to the *danger zone*.

"I think I should just say I wanna live in the dorms." I take a sip of my coffee. It seems like the obvious choice. Most college students would be staying away from home anyway. The semester is gonna be ending soon, so it'd be the perfect time to bring it up to him.

"You think it will work? I mean, that seems almost *too* easy," Andrew says.

"Well, anything else would seem suspicious aside from a twenty-year-old wanting to live on her own while she's at college," Jaxon chimes in.

"Why haven't you moved out already? It would've made this whole thing easier." Andrew grunts.

"New town, still mentally recovering from the fire, and seemingly new supernatural powers. I just wanted to be around what was familiar to me at the time. I couldn't have known all of this would happen." I look down into my mug.

I feel a hand on my knee and look up to meet Jaxon's eyes as he smiles at me.

"It's fine, Kairi. It'll all work out in the end, I'm sure."

Andrew hums around his drink but says nothing.

Not long after, Jaxon and I find ourselves in his Jeep. He drives me back to the school to get my truck. We don't say anything, just listen to the music play over the radio.

I look out the window and watch the houses disperse as trees take over my view. The route to the school takes us through a stretch of land where there aren't any houses. It's peaceful.

Though I enjoy the silence in the car, it's unusual when I'm with Jaxon. I look over to him and note his hard stare out the windshield as he drives with a death grip on the steering wheel. I reach over and place my hand gently on his forearm.

"Jax?"

He physically relaxes but doesn't respond or take his eyes off the road.

"Are you all right?"

"I'm fine," he says gruffly.

"Are you sure? You seem . . . upset."

Jaxon sighs, letting his shoulders slump. "I'm just worried."

"That he's gonna figure it out?" I ask.

He shakes his head. "That he already has." He looks into the rearview mirror.

I pull my eyebrows together, but before I can ask what he means, the car lurches forward. My heart beats wildly in my chest, and Jaxon curses, trying to correct the car while speeding up.

I take a glance behind us to see a black SUV racing back toward us. "What the hell?"

The Jeep lurches again, more violently this time, as the SUV rams us again. A strangled scream bubbles in my throat, that I fail to keep in as I try to hold on to anything I can. I don't have time to scream again before the Jeep is hit from the side and off the road. My voice leaves me as I reach for Jaxon. The vehicle rolls side over side several times before coming to a stop.

Dazed, I look around, trying to see Jaxon, but my visions blurred. I try to lift my hand to my left where he'd still be in the driver's seat, but my limbs don't want to move. Panicking, I try to force my body to reach for him but can only feel my fingers twitch before my car door is ripped open.

I can barely get my head to turn toward the open door before I'm pulled from the car by at least two sets of hands. I try to call out for Jaxon, for help, to find out who has their hands on me, for anything, but I can't get my vocal cords to work.

As I'm dragged from my seat, my awareness becomes clearer. I see Jaxon facedown on the ground with someone on top of him, their knee in his back, keeping him on the ground. At that sight, something in me snaps.

Hands off.

An overwhelming surge of power flows through my veins, and I move forward with tunnel vision set on getting to Jaxon. The hands once on me disappear, and I stalk toward the guy on top of Jaxon.

"What the fuck?" the man—who still has his knee on my lover's back—yells at the ones who were just restraining me.

Jaxon's face is in my direction, but his eyes are closed. At the man's exclamation, his eyes flutter open, connecting with mine. Jaxon gasps, and his eyes open wide as I make my way toward him. My gaze stays on him for a moment longer before hardening when I cut my eyes to the man still holding Jaxon down.

"Get off of him," I say, "before I make you."

The man laughs and digs his knee deeper into the center of Jaxon's back, making him grunt.

Anger flares through me. "Last warning. Get off of him."

A smirk makes its way onto his face. "I was told he'd put up much more of a fight. Little bump on the head, and he's under my control. Pathetic. Travis must've exaggerated."

As he shifts his weight to apply more pressure, my blood starts to boil. *Travis.* I should've listened to my instincts when they told me something was off about him. The possibility of working for HUE wasn't something I could've known until recently, but I still should've kept my distance. If Travis is involved, then Chelsea probably is too.

Stand up.

As if under a trance, he stands up and off of Jaxon.

Step back and stay still.

He does as instructed, and I move to Jaxon's side on the ground. I let my eyes and hands roam his body, looking for injuries. He seems to only have a cut along his hairline and some bruises that I can see, but he'll need to let Andrew look him over to be sure. My eyes soften when they meet his wide ones.

"Are you alright?" I ask.

"Me? I'm fine, Kairi. Are you alright? We need to get out of here." Jaxon tries to push himself up on wobbly arms.

"Stay still. We don't know how hurt you are." I gently push him back to the ground.

He goes to protest when I hear a snicker from my left. I cut my eyes to the man rooted to his spot. I'm fuming that he finds any of this the slightest bit amusing.

"Somethin' funny?" I spit out.

He continues to chuckle. "I just don't see what the big deal is with you two, honestly."

"Can't say I know the answer to that, but you and your men need to leave now while you still can," Jaxon says, which only makes the man laugh harder, considering the state Jaxon is in when he says this.

I let out a heavy breath through my nose and stand up. I see Jaxon's worried glance in my peripheral vision, but no matter how much I know he wants to do this with me or protect me, he's in no state to do so. Jaxon is my number one priority right now, and first thing's first—I need to get rid of this trash.

I turn to face the man still chuckling like an idiot.

I close my eyes, take a deep breath, and focus my thoughts on all three men before opening my eyes again.

He stops laughing when his eyes meet mine. I watch him for a moment before looking to the other two men.

"Come over here and stand together facing me," I say. My voice takes on an otherworldly tone, both deeper and higher than my usual pitch at the same time.

Obediently, they walk mechanically until they are side by side, facing me. I can see their lips moving, surely cursing me and the situation at this point. I turn to see Jaxon's lips moving as well, along with the worried look in his eyes, but I can't hear him. I feel disconnected from my body as my powers surge through me like a tidal wave.

The power is addictive; it's like I can't get enough. I send Jaxon what I hope is a reassuring smile, then turn back to the men.

"Take out your weapons." I stay unblinking.

They sputter a moment as their limbs do as I say. With widened eyes and shaky limbs, they try to resist my command. I smile at them.

"Now, you." I look to the man on the far left—one of the two that pulled me from the Jeep. "Why are you three after us?" I take a step closer to them.

His eyes glaze over. "We were sent to bring the two targeted experiments back to headquarters." His voice is monotone, and my senses clear to the other sounds around me.

"Do you believe you're doin' the right thing by kidnappin' people who were tortured and experimented on as children?" I ask, taking another step forward.

"Ye—"

I don't let him finish before I have him turn his gun to his head and pull the trigger.

"Disgusting," I spit. No remorse.

I turn to the next man, who's shaking, then turn my gaze to the man who couldn't stop laughing before but now looks like he's torn between rage and pissing his pants.

"You—Sir Laughs-a-lot." I smile. "Who sent you and your little friends to abduct us?"

I stare at him, amused as he tries to resist my powers and keep his mouth shut. I push more of my power onto him, causing him to fall to his knees.

"Chelsea," he grounds out. At this point, I'm not surprised to hear her name.

He continues to struggle against my influence. I almost admire his spirit. Almost.

His hand holding his gun starts to shake more violently. Out of curiosity, I loosen my hold on him. He looks up and glares in fury before he spits in my direction, then takes the barrel in his mouth and pulls the trigger.

"Pity. I wanted more time with him," I say and move my eyes to the last of the three, who is shaking like a leaf and has most definitely wet his pants. "Anythin' you wanna say?"

His mouth opens and closes like a gaping fish with wild eyes. I sigh and release most of my hold on him, and tears spring to his eyes. Bringing my hand up toward his face, I focus on his eyes drooping and becoming heavy.

"Jesus, just go to sleep," I say, and he collapses on the ground with a thud.

I turn back to Jaxon. The fog over my head starts to clear, and the sounds around me start to come back louder. I look into his dark eyes, but black spots take over my vision as my body sags in exhaustion.

My eyes get heavy as I smile at Jaxon and caress his cheek. "I'm glad you're okay. I love you."

Then everything goes black. The last thing I hear is Jaxon's panicked voice yelling my name.

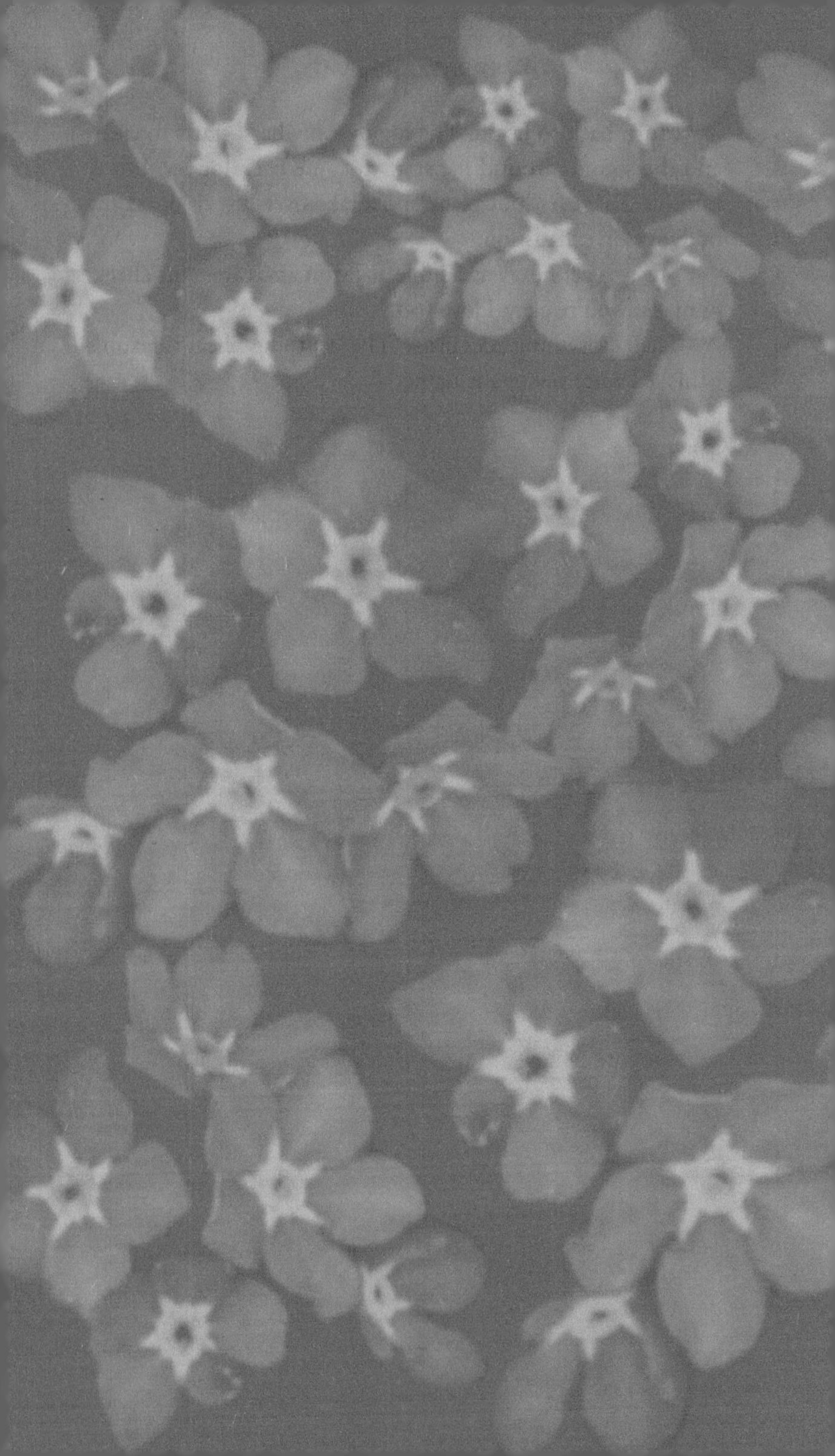

THIRTY-FOUR

A LIGHT SHINING in my eyes causes me to squint even with my eyes closed. A few minutes later, I try to open my eyes again, blinking rapidly from the brightness of the room before they adjust. I'm in a small plain white room with only the bed I'm lying on and a window that's currently trying to blind me.

I turn my head when I hear the door open to see a disheveled Jaxon walk in. He doesn't look up or seem to notice that I'm staring at him. He keeps his eyes down and shoulders slumped as he makes his way into the room.

I lick my lips, moistening them. "Jax . . ." I croak, my throat feeling like sandpaper.

Jaxon's head snaps up with wide eyes for only a moment before he rushes to my side and places his palms on each of my cheeks. He leans in and connects our lips briefly.

"I was scared shitless." He lets out a breathy laugh, but I can feel his hands shaking, so I raise my own hands to cover his still on my cheeks.

"Hey, I'm okay," I whisper with a smile when his eyes meet mine. "I love you."

Jaxon lets out a shaky breath. "I love you too. So much."

"Can I have some water?" I ask.

"Of course!" He reaches over to the bedside table and pours me a glass of water from the pitcher and hands it back to me.

After drinking the entire glass, I take a deep breath and look back into those dark eyes I love so much. "So what happened?"

"What do you remember?" Jaxon asks me.

"I remember makin' the man with the bladder of an infant go to sleep before he got the same fate as the other two bastards." I huff and look out the window.

I hear him sigh behind me, but I honestly don't care. Those bastards deserved it. The more and more I find out about myself, my past only makes me angrier. How could all of these people support this? I mean, those men were gonna kidnap people who were experimented on as children! I try to root myself in this moment and stare out at the peaceful setting of Jaxon's garden to calm myself down. Continuing to think about things I cannot change is only gonna lead to my insanity.

"We think the overexertion made you pass out. You went past your body's limits. You were already tired and recovering from all the training we've been doing, so when you used that much of your power, you overloaded your system," Jaxon says while rubbing up and down my arm.

"Makes sense." I yawn.

"You're still recovering, so why don't you go ahead and sleep okay?"

My eyes are already closing when I feel his lips on my forehead, and sleep takes over.

***

The tension in the car on the way to my truck because of the previous day is suffocating, but we make it there in one piece. Neither of us can bring ourselves to break the silence after what's happened and the turn our lives are likely to take from here on out.

There's only a silent kiss goodbye and tight squeeze before I'm seated in my truck and headed back to the house I've been living in since moving here. The closer I get to the place I called home, the more intensely my nerves seem to take hold of me. By the time I'm in the driveway, my hands are shaking on the steering wheel while I take deep breaths to calm down.

After a few minutes of not being able to move, I send a distressed mental message to Jaxon that I need him here. I need him to pull me close and tell me everything's gonna be okay when I feel like everything's gonna close in and crush us. I need him to palm my cheeks while he kisses my lips and pulls the anxiety right out of me to where I can focus on nothing but his lips moving with mine. I need him to support me and hold my hand while I take those final steps to the front door to face the man I've called my father for as long as I can remember.

I just need him.

I'm not sure how much time passes before Jaxon's Jeep pulls up behind my truck and he's opening my door.

"Hey, I'm here. You're okay," he whispers in my ear as he pulls me to his chest and, like always, is everything I need and more.

Once I've calmed down, we walk hand in hand to the door. I pull my keys out of my pocket to unlock the door, but it swings open first.

I look up at Charles and smile as best I can despite the turmoil going on in my head. I should've thought this through. It wasn't part of the plan to have Jaxon here with me. If Charles recognizes him, I'm not sure what he'll do.

"Hey, Dad. Sorry I'm late. We had a bit of car trouble yesterday." I laugh, looking down to put my keys back in my pocket. Jaxon tightens his grip on my upper arm to the point that it almost hurts. I furrow my brows, unsure what's wrong, and he has his mental block up, not letting me know what's going on. I school my features and pull us both into the house. I feel Jaxon hesitate when the door closes, and I turn to face Charles.

I suck in a breath when I come face-to-face with a gun.

My eyes go wide. "Dad," I croak when I see that the gun isn't actually pointed at me. "Please . . ." I hear my own voice waver.

"I figured you weren't alone when only one of those idiots came back without you in custody. I should've known it'd be *you*," Charles spits in disgust, eyes locked on Jaxon before returning to me. "I'm surprised that it took so long though."

He knew. He knew the whole time that I was with Jaxon, though he didn't know it was *him* specifically. I sneak a glance at Jaxon to see the hard look on his face before putting my attention back on the armed man before me.

"It wasn't time for this yet, but I guess I'll have to improvise." He smirks. "I got those two into the school to keep an eye on you and report back, but they couldn't even do that properly."

I was already pretty confident that Travis and Chelsea were working for HUE, but hearing it be confirmed is a whole other thing. "What—"

BANG.

My words cut off at the sound of the gun being fired, and I wait a moment for the pain to register. When it doesn't, I look to my right, and my heart drops.

Jaxon has a stricken look on his face and glances at me before falling to the floor. I watch him collapse, and all I can hear is screaming as I rush to his side.

Constant streams of "No!" and "You'll be okay!" fall from my lips, and tears flow from my eyes as I put pressure on the wound. As more blood pours from his chest, my heart fractures more and more.

I feel a prick in my neck, and sobs wrack my body.

"Please don't leave me. Jaxon, please. I love you. I love you... I love... I..."

I blink furiously before falling to the side as darkness takes over my vision. The last thing I see is Jaxon's hand reaching for me before falling limp at his side. As I feel my body being dragged away, I try to send a message to Andrew, but my mind's so muddled I can't form a coherent thought, and I'm not sure I was able to connect with him.

No...

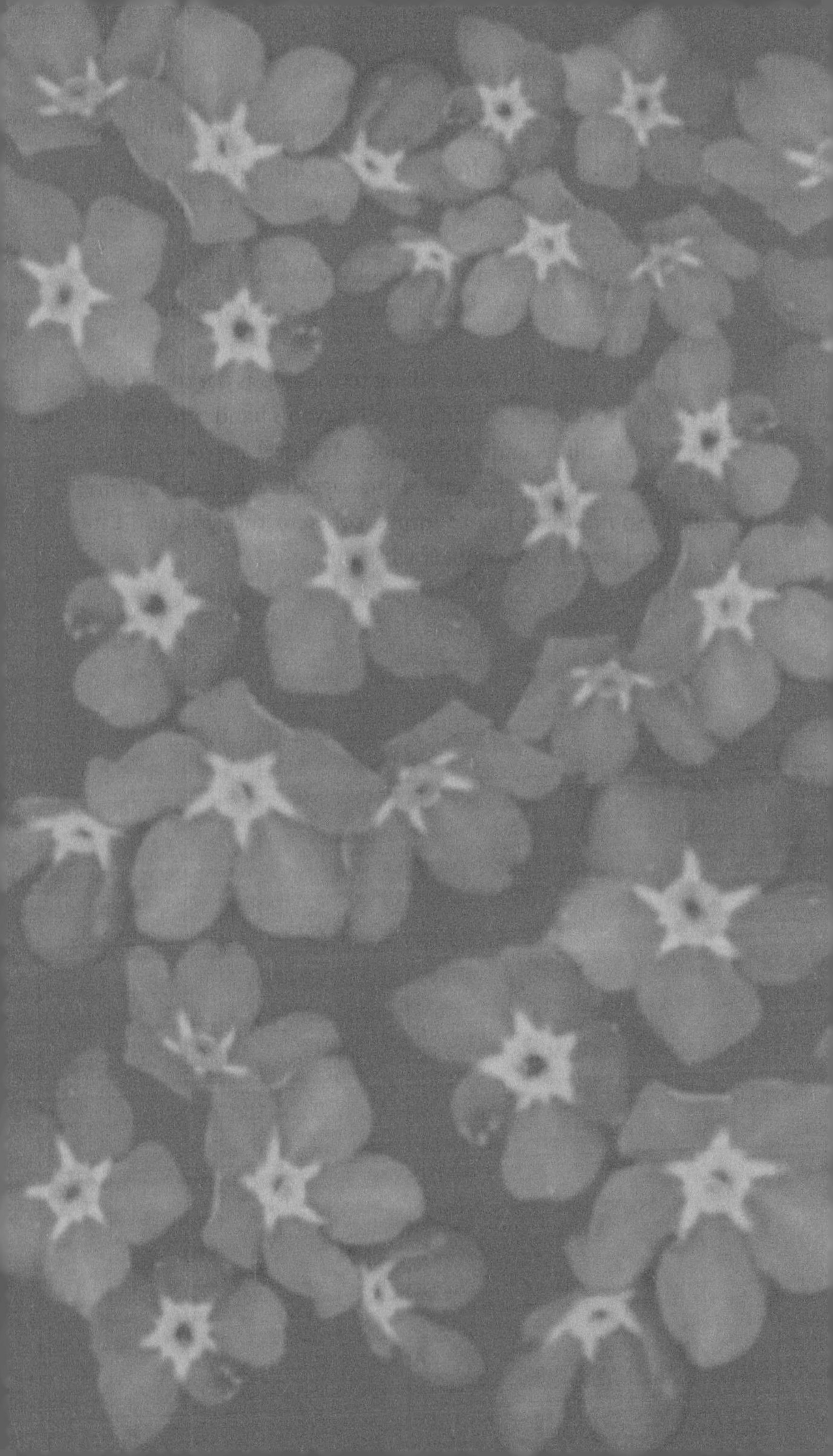

THIRTY-FIVE

THE PRESSURE in my head brings me to consciousness. As I become more aware, the pounding in my head gets stronger, pulling a groan from my lips as I blink my eyes at the fluorescent lights above my head. It feels like forever before my vision clears and I'm met with four plain steel walls. I look around and see no windows, not even in the only door of this small room. There's a small slot in the door that I assume is opened from the outside because I can't see any latches or even hinges.

I push myself up to a sitting position from the cold hard ground. No bed in here either . . . or toilet. I don't have time to dwell on the lack of basic necessities before the small slot in the door opens.

I waste no time shouting, "Where am I? Why am I here?"

There is no response, just a small paper wrapping and a bottle of water tossed through the opening before it's slapped shut again.

I huff and crawl to the items, still weak and groggy from whatever sedative I'm assuming that I was injected with. I pick up the water and uncap the lid, then take a couple big gulps of water before turning to the paper bundle. I unwrap it to find a simple ham and cheese sandwich, which I practically inhale. The fact that I'm so damn thirsty and hungry makes me wonder how long I've been unconscious.

Sitting back against the far wall across from the door, I try to remember what happened before I got here.

I remember Jaxon at my house and Charles opening the door. Charles had a gun—

My eyes bulge, and I jump to my feet, approach the door, and bang my fist against the cool metal as hard as I can as adrenaline courses through me.

"Where's Jaxon?" I scream as loud as I can and pray for an answer, but it never comes.

My heart starts to beat erratically, and tears sting my eyes.

God, please no. Please let him be okay.

I collapse on the floor as images of Jaxon bleeding out and reaching for me pull sobs from my throat, and I lose myself to the pain and uncertainty.

I try to reach out to him mentally with no response.

How could I let this happen? I didn't act fast enough. I could've helped him, but I froze. I just stood there and watched him collapse and fight for his life right in front of me and did nothing. I shouldn't have called for him to come with me. He was safe, and my weakness put his life at risk. He'd be at home with Andrew right now. Charles would've never shot him.

Charles did this. The man I believed was my father that loved me did this to the man I love more than life itself. As more memories come back, I see that he's continuously taken everything I've held dear. My childhood was taken from me in exchange for being his little lab rat, my freedom while I was locked in that facility, my only friends I made while in HUE, any chances of me ever having a normal life, and my memories —whether they were good or bad, they were still *mine*.

I don't understand how my own mother could let him do this to me. How could she let him experiment on me before I could even understand what was going on? Did she not think about the consequences of how their actions would affect me once I did remember? Did they think I would be ignorant for the rest of my life?

What did they plan to do with me—without memories but still holding all this power inside me? I may not have remembered everything, but I found my powers on my own. Jaxon didn't tell me I had powers; I already knew. And I took it upon myself to learn how to control them. There're still so many questions I doubt will ever be answered.

I spent all this time pushing Jaxon away, being angry with him, blaming him for ruining my life when I should've blamed my *parents*.

My *parents* lied to me, and Jaxon only ever told me the truth, whether I wanted to hear it or not. My *parents* took advantage of my vulnerability for their own gain; Jaxon took me in when I was vulnerable and helped build me back up stronger than ever. My *parents* never truly cared for me; I see that now. Jaxon always put his love for me before all else. He always put me first.

I may not have known better at the time, but I still let them manipulate me.

My mother may not have personally put the needle in my arm to inject the HUE serum, but she's just as guilty. It's almost worse. She knew what was going on, what Charles was doing to me, and she did *nothing*. Even when my memories were lost, and I was able to be normal for once, she still let him take me, and she never said or did anything to stop him. Now she's gone, and she's taken Sidney with her too.

I guess blood isn't always thicker than water.

Then there's Jaxon Ray Benievere.

I let out a shaky breath as my sobs slow to silent tears

streaming down my face. I lie on my side with my head resting on my arm, eyes closed and occasionally sniffling.

That man deserves so much better than what I gave him. I wish I could go back and be with him the way I was at the end. There's nothing good about dwelling on the what-ifs, but I can't seem to stop them from running through my mind. I wish I could've seen his smile, heard his laugh, felt his touch, kissed his lips, and smelled his woodsy smell more. I wish I could've had more of everything that's Jaxon Benievere.

Now I'm scared I'll never get to have more moments with him. I don't know whether he's still alive or if I'll get out of this alive.

I don't know how long I've been here, but I find out rather quickly that my ability to communicate through thoughts doesn't work here. That doesn't stop me from trying whenever I'm not drowning in my emotions. I never get a response, but I still wait for Jaxon's calming tenor to sweep through my mind.

I try to distract myself with our new memories together while holding tightly to the ring that's still dangling from the chain on my neck. At least they didn't take this from me.

A small smile stays on my face as I relive our moments as an escape from my dreary reality. Jaxon wouldn't want me to wallow in my self-pity—I know that. He'd want me to fight and live and bring them down.

As I lie here on the cold hard floor, I think back to what Jaxon's taught me and what we've worked on together. I just pray that the level my powers are at right now is enough.

Time moves so slowly here. I don't know if it's the silence, the lack of regularity, or the fact that there's no way for me to know how much time has passed that makes it so difficult.

Finally, I hear the sound of the slot in the door being unlocked, and I crawl my way toward the opening. I take deep breaths with my eyes closed while waiting for it to open. Once it does, I use all my focus, projecting my thoughts to the person on the other side of the door and pray for it to work.

You will place the tray on the floor by your feet, unlock this cell, open the door, and then step back against the far wall with your hands by your sides, and you will not make a sound.

I pause, hoping the small space was enough for my powers to leak through and my command to take hold of the person on the other side of the door. I don't feel tired, but with my lack of food and sleep, it won't take much for me to overexert myself, and passing out in this place is *not* an option.

My eyes snap open when I hear the click of the door being unlocked, then the creak of the hinges as the door opens just enough. Then there's only silence.

I get to my feet and take hesitant steps to the door. I push it open to see a man in his early thirties with his back against the far wall and his hands at his sides. His slim but athletic body's tense, and his mouth's shut, but when I look into his light brown eyes, I see multiple emotions—mostly fear.

A smile grows on my face, and adrenaline seeps into my veins as hope and determination radiate from within me.

I'm coming for you, Daddy Dearest.

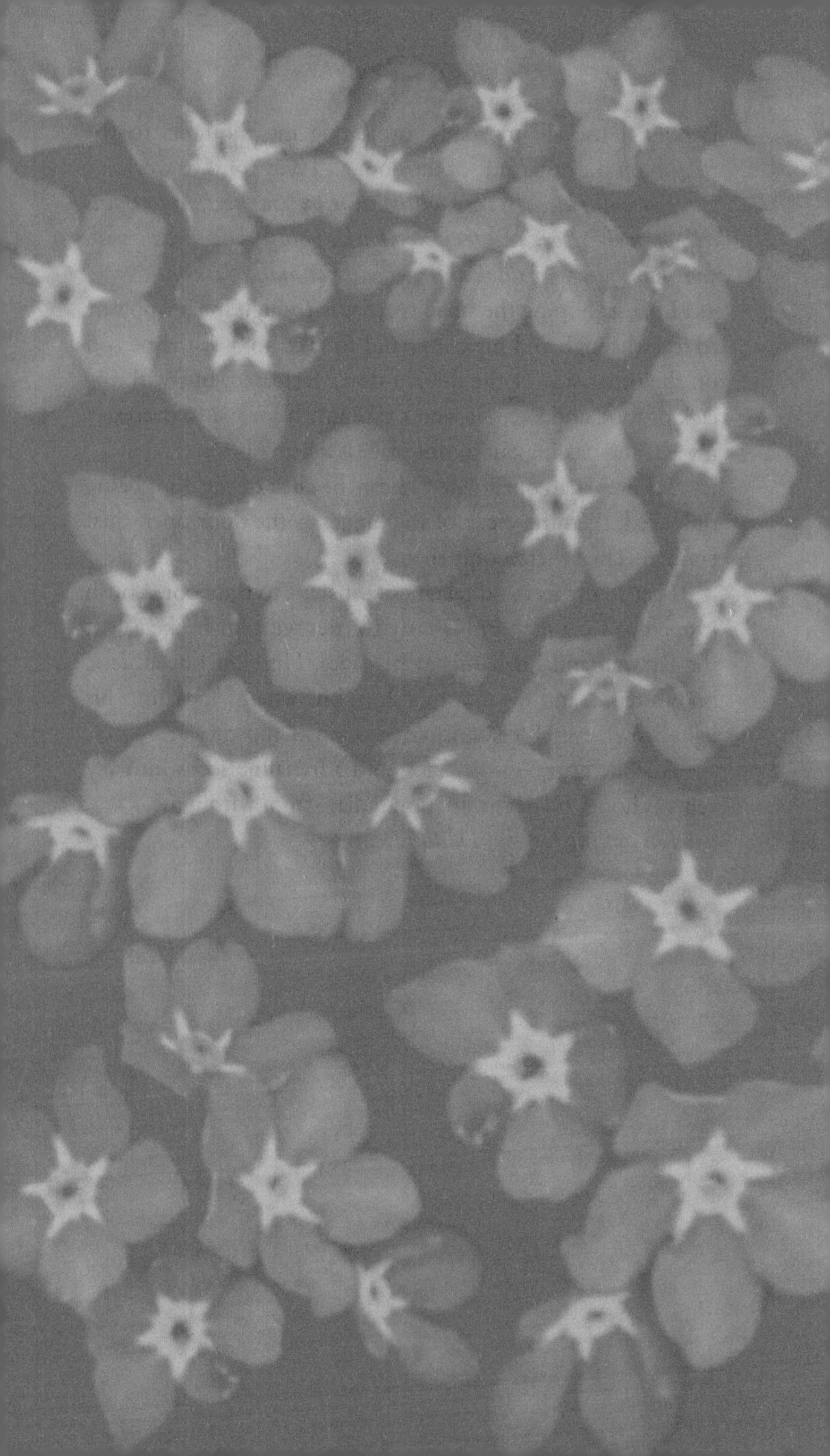

THIRTY-SIX

MAKING my way down the hallway is almost too easy. There's no one around. Besides the man I locked in my cell, I haven't seen anyone. I would've thought an underground science facility like this would have people all over the place, especially considering this is supposed to be the recruitment and training center. I keep my body close to the wall as I move through the compound, hoping to find an exit. I try to sense any other thoughts near, but because of the slight fuzziness in my mind.

I come to a corner, peek around, and see a door about ten feet away. I look around and decide that it's my best and only real option. I drag my feet as quickly and quietly as I can down the hall. With every step, my body feels like the weight of gravity is pulling me down, making me use extra effort with each step I take despite the adrenaline pushing me forward. As I reach the door, I can only pray I'm going the right direction.

"How did you get in here?" someone shouts.

I whip my head around at the voice and distant steps coming closer in a hurry. A middle-aged woman with short blond hair and a stern face marches in my direction. I scramble to think of what to do as she closes the distance between us.

"Oh . . . I was just leavin'." I turn to push through the door, then hear the click of a gun being cocked.

"I don't think so. Turn around with your hands where I can see them," she spits out.

I turn slowly with my arms raised. I can't get a read on her. I take a deep breath. Looking at the barrel of a gun again makes Jaxon flash through my mind, sending a sharp pain through my heart.

Her blue eyes roam my body, my dirty and worn clothing and unkempt appearance. I probably look like exactly what I am: an escaped prisoner. A look of recognition flashes on her face before she reaches for the radio on her belt.

Don't move.

Her body freezes mid-reach with wide eyes full of fear. I take a deep breath but keep eye contact with her. My head's swimming, but I have to stay strong and get out of here. I need to know what happened to Jaxon. I need to see him.

You're going to turn around and lock yourself in the nearest room without making a sound or alerting anyone about my presence.

She pauses for only a moment before swiftly turning on her heels and walking in the opposite direction of me. I let out a shaky breath as my vision blurs momentarily, causing me to stagger into the wall for support.

I'm gonna have to be careful. I'm not sure how much energy I have left, and I can't pass out in this damn building. I don't know how much more energy I can afford to use before I collapse.

I turn back to the door and push it open. I step through and let out a sigh of relief that it leads to a large empty room with a door on the far wall. I make it a third of the way across before I feel a hand on my shoulder.

"Hey! What are you doing out of your cell?" The deep voice booms behind me, and I turn to see a large burly man with crew-cut black hair, bulging muscles, and a glare on his face.

I take barely a moment to think of my next actions before I summon what physical strength I have left, turn my body, and grab a hold of the wrist of the hand that's gripping my shoulder. I use my body weight and momentum to twist his arm toward his back and pull with all my strength, breaking his elbow and popping his shoulder out of the socket. He screams out in pain, but I send a quick punch to his throat, cutting off his scream before sending a calculated punch to his face.

I stagger back a few steps and heave heavy breaths in and out as my tired limbs tremble. The burly man moans in pain on the ground, cradling his arm. His eyes zero in on me with pure hatred radiating from them.

Yeah, well, the feeling's mutual, buddy.

I turn to the exit and try to get to it as quickly as my exhausted body will get me there, but I can hardly move even a few steps.

"You bitch!" he spits as he faces me at his full height with the injured arm hanging limply at his side. Though he's still breathing heavily, his stance is strong as he takes slow calculated steps toward me.

I stand my ground and try to remember everything Andrew drilled into my head during our training. Luckily, our sessions triggered the training we'd received previously in HUE, and most of the hand-to-hand combat came back to me naturally. Now I just need to keep my mind clear and make the right decisions that won't get me killed or back in the damn cell.

I decide to go on the offensive, take two quick steps toward him, and send a quick punch to his injured shoulder before ducking under his good arm as it swings around to hit me. His foot comes out and causes me to stumble before he rears the same arm back. He gets me with his elbow to my cheek, and I fall to the floor.

Damn, that hurt.

He sends a series of kicks to my ribs that has me curling my body in to protect itself. He grabs a handful of my hair and hauls me up to his level. I struggle to get his grip to loosen as he rips my hair from my scalp.

With no other option coming to mind, I grit my teeth and reach both hands out, letting him continue to hold me up only by my hair. Through the searing pain in my scalp, I grab his face and headbutt him with everything I have.

He lets go of me, and we stagger away from each other. While he seems dazed, I push through my pain and exhaustion and send a punch into his jaw with as much power as I can manage. He falls to the floor, and I bend over with hands on my knees, trying to catch my breath.

I start to turn, but I'm tackled to the ground from the side. As we slam to the ground, the breath leaves my lungs and my ears ring on impact.

"You're going to regret doing that." Another man tries to pin my arms behind my back.

I struggle as best I can before I push my mind into his.

Get off!

His weight immediately leaves me, and I pant, dark spots covering my vision for a moment while I roll over to see him on his knees, shaking in place while glaring at me. My head starts to swim before we both climb to our feet. He keeps his distance, eyeing me cautiously.

"Why are you here workin' for these people?" I can't help but ask.

He studies me but keeps his mouth sealed shut. I sigh and will my body to not give out on me yet. I push myself forward as quick as I can and send a jab to his ribs. I duck under his arm that swings around to hit my jaw and send another jab to his ribs on the opposite side.

He grunts before grabbing my neck, squeezing while lifting me off my feet. I claw at his hand as it becomes harder to breath. Gasping, I take a chance and send a hard kick to his family jewels.

A girlish squeal leaves his lips before he throws me to the side and crumbles to the floor, cupping himself. I suck as much air as I can into my lungs before crawling toward him and placing my hand on his temple.

Sleep.

After what seems like an eternity, I get my breathing under control and pull myself to my feet. I stagger for a moment, huffing as turn back toward the door and freeze. Fear, hurt, and anger keep my feet glued in place. I can't help the bile rising in my throat. My body suddenly feels a thousand times heavier.

"Well, what do we have here?"

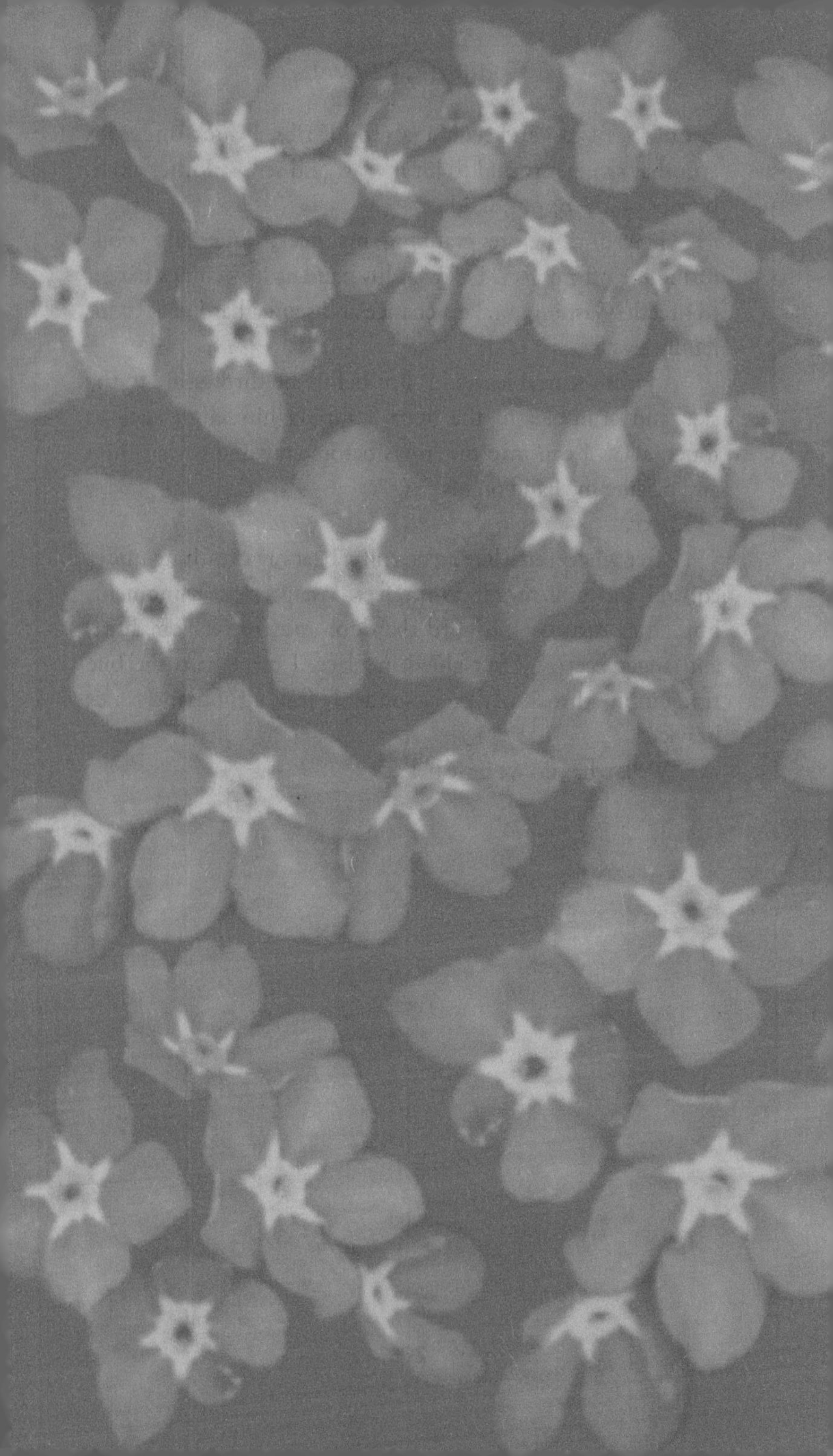

THIRTY-SEVEN

"CHARLES," I say as firmly as I can, hoping he can't hear the waver in my voice.

Charles gasps and puts his hand on his chest. He fakes a hurt look. "Is that any way to greet your father?"

"Maybe not," I start, "but you're not my father, are you?"

A sinister smile takes over his face. "Whatever do you mean?"

I scoff and roll my eyes. "Memory loss isn't permanent."

His gaze hardens as he observes me for a moment "My, my, have you grown a backbone recently. Where's my compliant little girl?" He sneers.

"I'm sure she's in the past where you left her before usin' her as a lab rat," I spit at him. How can he stand there so proud of his actions?

Disgusting.

"I'd ask how you found out, but I know it was that Jaxon boy. How is he, by the way?" His smile's anything but sincere.

My heartbeat quickens as the image of him lying there bleeding out in front of me flashes before my eyes. Jaxon is and probably has always been my greatest weakness for Charles and HUE to use against me.

"Why?" I find myself whispering. He raises a brow but says nothing. "Why'd you do this to me? I don't understand what I did to deserve this."

He scoffs. "You were born."

No matter what this man's done, I've considered him my father for all of my life that I can remember. That's what he was to me. Hearing him say that cracks something within me, even though I know I shouldn't care about his opinion, affection, or lack thereof for me. Why should I care what a psychopath thinks? He's made my life a living hell, so why the hell do I care?

Charles smiles. "So, now you know that I'm not your father." He pauses as I stand numbly and nod my head in response. "Your whore of a mother decided that my twin brother was a better partner for her, and here you are—the child she thought I'd accept, the child that ruined my marriage and happiness, the child that should've never been born. So why not get rid of the problem and have some use for you at the same time?"

"I had nothing to do with any of that!" I scream. "Why should I be punished for the sins of others?"

"Because you represent that sin and betrayal!" he bellows.

I flinch and curse myself for it. I see nothing by rage and resentment in his blue eyes, like fiery blue flames. He physically shakes in anger. He takes a few steps toward me, and I stumble back to maintain distance between us. I'm still trying to regain some strength to fight, because I know there's no way I'm getting out of here without one. By the look he's giving me now, I'm scared of how far he's willing to go. I hope I'm strong enough to defend myself and bear the burden of the result if I am.

"How were you able to do it?" I ask as I move around him

and keep the current distance between us. Charles's face is now emotionless as he counters my movements.

"You'll have to be more specific," he says.

"My memories. How were you able to wipe my memory and give me fake ones?"

"Simple really. You all received daily injections to suppress your abilities to prevent an uprising. With what I am capable of, it was almost too easy, really. With the added factor that a loyal experiment has the ability to alter memories it was perfect." He smirks. "Over time, it replaced the truth with what I wanted."

"You seem awfully proud of yourself and surprisingly chatty."

"I'm not an idiot, Kairi. I know that only one of us is going to get out of here alive. You may be the last one to hear of my accomplishments and to carry the information forward, or you'll die here, and I find your reactions to the truth amusing."

So he really is gonna try to kill me over something I had no control over . . .

I want to ask why he found my pain amusing but stop myself as I remember all the things he's done not only to me, but to the other experiments in this program—to Jaxon. Of course this sadistic bastard finds humor in this.

"So you did all of this to me because your wife preferred your brother?"

He sneers. "Why should I care for the bastard child of my cheating wife and treacherous brother? They really thought I wasn't gonna figure it out. Like I'm some sort of *idiot*!"

I knew it was probably a mistake getting him worked up again, but I can only hope that getting him worked up might cause him to make a mistake. A mistake big enough to give me the advantage I need to survive all this.

He continues to rant and curse my mother and uncle to

hell for what they did. It seems this is his trigger. While he's distracted, I can feel some of my power returning, as well as some of my strength. I see the flashes of flames and dark eyes like I have since I woke in the hospital. The only difference between now and then is that I recognize those eyes. I fell in love with the man behind those dark eyes.

"The fire . . ." I whisper to myself, but it seems to get Charles's attention. There's a sadistic sparkle in the blue eyes I share with him that sends a shiver down my spine.

"Unfortunate accident, don't you think?" He tilts his head and smiles.

My eyes narrow. Something inside this man I called my father seems to be unraveling right before my eyes—and fast. The wild look in his eyes; that wide smile; the constant movement of limbs, head, and body—he isn't at all the man I remember.

"What do you mean?"

"Well, I couldn't just let you go, but I certainly didn't wanna keep you either by that point. That stupid boy just had to play the hero and save the day, but I finally gave him what he deserved for always gettin' in the way."

He . . . he was gonna burn me alive? He was gonna kill me over pettiness, just like he plans to do now. Jaxon's the one that pulled me out of the flames and gave me another chance at a life that was so close to being snuffed out. Jaxon, like always, was there when I needed him the most.

"The fire was never in the house."

He just smirks.

"What the hell was the point of wipin' my memories if you were just gonna let me burn?" I yell.

"Well, it's always good to have a backup plan, and I'm so glad I did." He keeps that creepy smile on his face and takes several steps forward, closing some of the distance between us before I move as well to keep him out of reach.

"At least Mom finally left you, you crazy bastard."

His jaw ticks before he schools his features once again and reaches into his pocket. I feel my body tense.

"Now, let's get this show on the road." Charles pulls a syringe into view, and I stare, confused, before it clicks in my mind.

"Is that . . . ?"

"The new and improved serum 723." He smiles brightly. "I must say, it does make one feel . . . invincible."

He's been injecting himself with the latest version of the serum. That has to be why he seems to have lost quite a few screws he obviously needs.

I stare wide-eyed and slack-jawed as he jams the needle into his thigh and injects it right in front of me. He lets out a relieved sigh, like a drug addict who got his fix. His eyes roll behind his eyelids before he looks at me again. I can see the determination in his gaze as he stalks toward me, but I'm frozen in place.

I've been trying to mentally prepare myself for this moment, but nothing can actually prepare you for a real life-and-death scenario. I try not to think about the happy memories I have with this man, because I know they were more than likely a lie. Even if they did hold some truth and affection, that man in my memories of us laughing and spending time together is gone. The predator approaching me now is nothing but the shell of the man I once looked up to.

I defended him. I pushed Jaxon away for him. I put my supposed family before everything when they'd done nothing but stomp me into the ground. He's robbed me of every good thing I should've had and deserved to have in my life. He stole my childhood, my innocence, my memories, my self-confidence, my sense of belonging, and Jaxon. He took Jaxon from me.

I can feel the steely resolution settle within me as I meet his gaze with a burning glare of my own.

"You tried to take the only person who ever truly cared and loved me away," I say as I take up the stance Andrew taught me—a defensive stance to wait for Charles's first move before I counter with my own, a stance from which I can look for any weaknesses in my enemy. I can feel my power buzzing in my veins, but I'm still not sure I have enough energy to take Charles down without collapsing myself.

"How do you know I didn't succeed in killing that bastard?"

As though a cord snaps inside me, I struggle to hold myself in place and not blindly run to him and take him down. That's what he wants though. I can see in his smug face that he's trying to bait me into making a mistake. That doesn't stop my body from shaking in rage trying to keep myself rooted in place.

Suddenly, Charles rushes forward and takes a swing at me, but I duck under his arm, spinning behind him, and kick the backs of his knees, making him stumble and go down momentarily. I jump back out of his reach as he swings behind him and spins to face me again.

"I see you've learned a few things." He chuckles, tilting his neck in each direction to pop it.

I smirk. "You have no idea."

After a few more tries to get his hands on me, with me dodging just out of reach, I can practically feel the frustration rolling off him.

Good. The more he loses control, the more mistakes he'll make. I just hope I can knock him out and get out of here soon. My body's starting to tire out. I continue dancing around him, dodging every attempt to get me within arm's reach.

"ENOUGH!" he screams, red in the face, panting like he's

just finished a marathon. If looks could kill, I'd be six feet under. My eyes widen as he reaches behind him and pulls out a gun, then points it directly at my head. "No more dancing around. This ends here and now."

My breath gets caught in my throat. I'm not sure what to do now. I stare into the eyes of a stranger, who's willing to kill for greed, pettiness, and self-preservation. My hands start to shake as my powers seem to take on a mind of their own, trying to make me use them. I hear whispers in my ears, but there's no one else here. My vision shifts like it did before when I felt like I was taking a back seat to my powers. My bodily instincts take over, and I fight for control over my powers as they slowly try to consume me.

The crazed man in front of me steps forward with the gun still raised, and everything seems to move in slow motion. I hear the voice in my head whispering again.

You are stronger than him.
He can't control you anymore.
You can take your life back now.
Be brave.
Fight, Kairi Rose.

Tears build in my eyes, and I almost sob as I recognize the voice. I wish he were really speaking to me. I wish he were here. I find comfort and strength in the sound of his voice regardless.

I'm scared, Jax.

I know you are, Rose, but you're strong enough to do this. For you. For us.

I won't let him get away with takin' you from me.

I cut the voices out of my thoughts. My breathing's choppy as I take a deep breath to calm myself before fixing my gaze on Charles. I raise my hands.

STOP.

I force the word toward him, and he slows to a stop. I can

feel him resisting my command. I grit my teeth and concentrate as the full force of my power surges through every nerve ending.

"You had a lovin' family and a good life, but you ruined it with your pride and greed." My voice is emotionless, but tears slowly trickle down my cheeks.

His eyes widen while he brings the gun up to place the end of the barrel against his own temple. He's shaking with the effort to break my control. Deep inside, I know he won't be able to. I can still feel Jaxon in my mind, lending me his strength and support.

"You've brought this all on yourself. I never asked for any of this. I don't wanna be like this, but like an animal pushed into a corner, you've given me no other choice but to fight for my life, and I won't let you win anymore."

His eyes widen with fear now as he sees there's no out for him. I keep my hold on him and close my eyes. I think of all the good memories I've had with him—whether they're real or not—and project them into his mind before I open my eyes again. There's no regret in his eyes, just self-preservation. He opens his mouth, but no words come out.

I can let him go now.

"Goodbye, Daddy." My voice croaks as the tears now pour down my face. I squeeze my eyes shut and quickly pull my hand into a fist.

A gunshot.

A lifeless thud against the concrete floor.

The sound of cries.

Black dots take over my blurred vision as I open my eyes and see him in a pool of his own blood. A sob wracks my body. I shouldn't care about him, but all I can do is look down at my shaking hands and repeat the fact over and over in my mind: I just killed my dad.

"Kairi!" someone yells, but I can barely hear over the roaring in my ears.

My weak body sways as the power leaves it. Strong arms wrap around me as I tilt toward the floor and the world spins. I turn to the darkest eyes I've ever seen staring at me with concern, relief, love, and sorrow. I smile and try to reach for his cheek, but I can't find the strength to reach his skin.

"You're alive . . ." I whisper.

"You can't get rid of me that easily." Jaxon leans down to kiss my forehead before he lifts me into his arms and carries me from the room.

"She okay?" I hear a familiar voice.

"She seems okay, but I need to get her home and have Drew look her over," Jaxon says.

I turn my head slightly to see intense green eyes. "Bentley?"

"Hey there, Crazy." He smirks down at me. "You did a number on the folks here, don't you think?"

I give a small smile in return. "Did I have to remember you?" I joke.

"You wound me." He clutches his chest before he pets my head, then turns to walk deeper into the building.

My head lulls, and I look behind Jaxon to see Andrew pour something over the body of Charles. He stares for a moment before turning in our direction and connecting his eyes with mine, then he turns back to the body. He and Bentley talk briefly before Bentley disappears through the other door.

"Don't look, Kairi. You don't need to see it," Jaxon whispers as he pulls my head into his chest and walks through the door. As we reach the front entrance, I peek over his shoulder anyway. Andrew walks through the door behind us, and I see the flicker of flames behind him.

He's gonna burn like he tried to burn me.

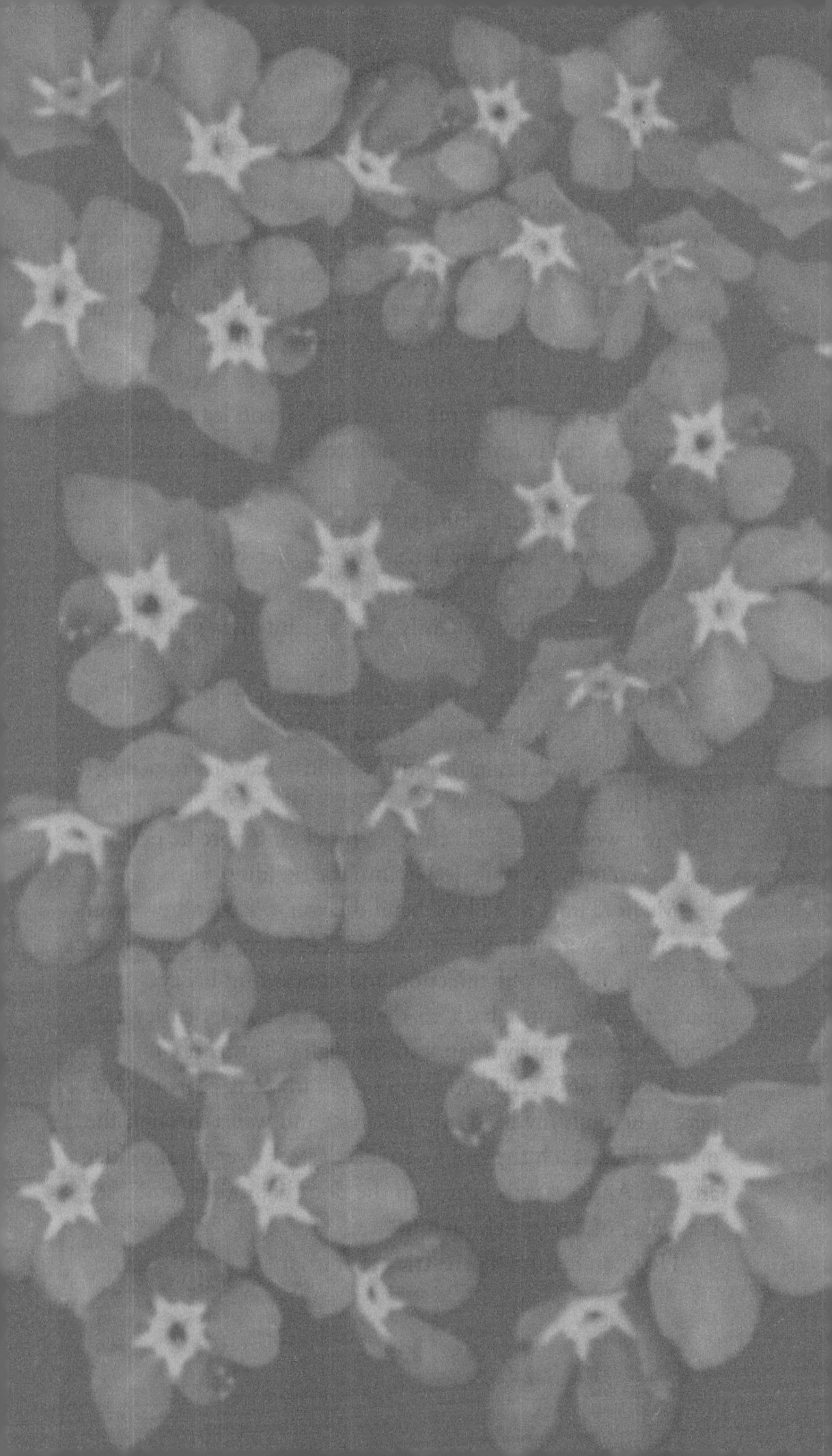

THIRTY-EIGHT

THE FOLLOWING weeks pass in a blur. The reality of it all is slow to set in. I'm still feeling a numbing denial of the events of that day. I've stayed with Jaxon and Andrew in their home, but I can't say I've been pleasant company to be around. Everything keeps spinning around and around in my head, and I can hardly focus on one thing at a time. My emotions aren't doing much better.

Jaxon's been nothing but patient and understanding with me, knowing just when to push me and when to back off, when to give me space and when to smother me with affection. Like the many times the thought has crossed my mind before, when I look at him like I am now, I can't help but think, *What would I do without him?*

"What are you starin' at?" I smile up at him as he lies propped on one elbow looking down at me.

Returning my smile, he leans close. "True beauty."

I snort out a laugh. "Why are you always so cringy?" I poke his chest, pulling a chuckle from him.

"Come on. Let's go get something to eat." He pulls

himself into a sitting position with a grunt before rolling off the bed and turning to pull me right up onto my feet.

We head down the stairs to the kitchen. Andrew sits at the breakfast bar with a sandwich and soda. He turns to us when he hears our approach.

"Hey," he says before going back to his meal.

We all sit in silence for a while before I break it.

"What really happened that day?" I ask them but keep my eyes trained on my plate.

They're both silent for a few minutes, and I keep my head down while they figure out either how or what to tell me. I just need to know.

"Well, after I hadn't heard from you two in almost five hours, I decided to go look for y'all. Then I got your distress message in my head. I rushed your house and saw the door wide open with Jaxon lying unconscious on the floor," Andrew says.

I flinch at the memory, and my throat's closing up, making it hard to swallow the lump formed there. I'm not sure I'll ever get the image of him that's burned into my mind to fade. The thought that he was so close to being taken away from me causes my chest to ache and eyes to burn. I'm glad Andrew was able to get my message.

I feel a warm hand rest on my knee and give me a comforting squeeze.

It's okay. We're both here. I'm still here.

Andrew continues, "I got to him in time to heal the bullet wound, and he recovered in a couple of days. You were still missing though."

My eyes widen. "How long was I gone? It felt more like hours . . ."

"Four days," Jaxon whispers. "It was four days before I felt your presence in my mind again."

"Once Jax felt that you were okay, we called Bentley to

meet up with us to look for you again. As we were driving around, Jax swore he could feel the space you were taking up in his mind getting more prominent, so we followed it like an intense game of Marco Polo." He huffs. "When we came to the compound you were at, we didn't waste time running inside."

"As soon as we opened the doors, we heard the gunshot . . ." Jaxon pulls my hands up to his lips, leaves a lingering kiss on my knuckles, and waits for my eyes to meet his before continuing. "I'd never been so scared in my life. I came through that door to see you standing there, and I couldn't get to you fast enough."

"I killed him." My voice shakes.

"He deserved to die for all that he's done to us," Bentley growls as he enters the room.

Jaxon's eyes study me for a moment before a soft look takes over his features. "You'll overcome this, just like you've overcome everything that's been thrown your way, and you'll be stronger than ever."

I move forward to lean our foreheads together as a tear slips from my eye. "Now what do we do?"

"Well, I'm gonna go back home and leave this damn state for good." Andrew grunts. "And I'm gonna try to get everything we'll need ready."

"What do you mean?"

"We can't let them keep getting away with this, Kairi." He looks me in the eyes. "It's time to take the fight to them and take our lives and our freedom back so we don't have to live in fear. It's time to take the Human Underground Experimentation down—for good."

I find myself nodding.

"I'll probably stick around here for a while to make sure this facility's shut down for good. I have some explosives I've been dying to play with. I'll just appear when summoned."

Bentley smiles to himself as he takes a bite of the sandwich he made.

Not for the first time, I worry about his mental state, but he's always kind of been off-kilter. Have to love him though. He's for sure the one to call when shit gets crazy.

"Why do I feel like you abuse your teleportation abilities?" Andrew says.

"I have no idea what you're referring to." He raises his brows innocently.

I change the subject before they get into it: "What are we gonna do about Travis and Chelsea?"

"Well, when I went to pay them a surprise visit"—Bentley winks—"I couldn't find them anywhere."

"What do you mean you couldn't find them?" Andrew asks.

Bentley huffs. "I meant what I said, Drew. Clean your ears out."

I wonder where they could've gone . . . "Well, what are we gonna do, then?" I turn back to Jaxon, ignoring the other two as they continue to bicker back and forth.

"What do *you* wanna do now?" he asks instead.

I think for a moment, but I've known since we got that letter from Hank. "I wanna try to find my real father."

Jaxon smiles at me and nods, and I smile in return. "Looks like we're all going back to Texas!"

A mock cheer comes from Andrew, and we all laugh— except Bentley, who pouts about having to stay in North Dakota a bit longer.

Later that night, while lying in bed, I pull back from Jaxon's chest to look in his eyes. "You're not goin' with me, are you?"

A solemn look comes over his face, and I let my shoulders sag. I feel his finger under my chin, raising my head back up so I meet his eyes.

"I'll be there with you while you find out where your father lives and get settled in."

"But you aren't gonna stay."

A sigh leaves his lips. "I need to find the others and anyone that can help us win this fight."

"Where are you gonna go?"

"Last I heard, I think Dominic's near Galveston. He always talked about goin' there as soon as we got out. It's as good a place to start as any." He shrugs. "Drew, Bentley, and I've talked about where some of the other guys may have ended up, and there have been some reports of people doin' weird things, so I'll just have to play it by ear and check out all the possibilities I can.

"Why can't I go with you?" I ask.

He smiles. "I want nothin' more than to have you by my side every moment of the day, but I think you need this time to come to terms with what's happened. You've had to deal with so much so quickly. I worry about leavin' you because I don't want the weight of it all to crush you, then I remember who I'm talkin' about. Kairi Rose Rush is anythin' but weak. You've been strong against all odds, and what you really need now is time to reflect on everythin'." He leans in and kisses me for a moment. "We'll talk all the time, and I'll be back before you know it. I know you understand that this is so much bigger than us. If we found each other again after so many things tried to keep us apart, we can conquer anything."

I love the sound of his southern accent coming back out now that he doesn't have to hide where he's from.

"I love you," I say.

"And I love you." He leans in to connect our lips again.

The hard times are hardly over, but I know that together, we can do anything.

ACKNOWLEDGMENTS

If someone told me that one day I'd have a book published I would have never believed them.

I started this story when I was a freshman in high school and over the years of struggles it's finally here for the world to read. It's a surreal feeling and I couldn't be happier.

I couldn't have done this without the ones closest to me being my biggest fans and supporters.

My best friend for always *trying* to understand how my mind works when I run ideas by her and being my critique partner.

My family has gone above and beyond to help make this happen when I thought I'd never be able to do it.

And thank you to the man that was my rock through the process, you know who you are.

ABOUT THE AUTHOR

Rebel Gallo's debut novel, Erratic Revival, is her first of the Human Underground Experimentation Duet Saga that is a collection of science fiction contemporary romance duet novels.. As an author she doesn't like labels but all of her stories are based around deep and true love.

Rebel has always had love for the written word. When she isn't working on her own novels she's spending time with her kids, friends and family or with her nose in a good book.

www.ingramcontent.com/pod-product-compliance
Lightning Source LLC
Chambersburg PA
CBHW010737310726
48971CB00010B/2860